THE DEVIL'S DUST

First published in 2010

This book is copyright under the Berne Convention. All rights are reserved. Apart from any fair dealing for the purpose of private study, research, criticism or review, as permitted under the Copyright Act, 1956, no part of this publication may be reproduced, stored in a retrieval system, or transmitted, in any form or by any means, electronic, electrical, chemical, mechanical, optical, photocopying, recording or otherwise, without the prior permission of the copyright owner. Enquiries should be sent to the publishers at the undermentioned address:

EMPIRE PUBLICATIONS
1 Newton Street, Manchester M1 1HW
© 2010 Brendan Yates

1901746 64X - 9781901746648

Cover images courtesy
Cover design: Ashley Shaw
Printed in Great Britain by 4edge Ltd, Hockley.

THE DEVIL'S DUST

BRENDAN YATES

EMPIRE PUBLICATIONS

PROLOGUE

AT TWENTY-SIX Conrad was getting restless. Although still a young man little was turning out the way he'd planned. He knew he was waiting too long for his breaks that he was starting to suspect may literally never arrive. Elsewhere the people he'd grown up with were fragmenting; growing apart, being what appeared to him to be so much more mobile and, above all, responsible. Times had to change; he knew he couldn't be a footloose young man forever. Privately, painfully, Conrad ached for more responsibility. He'd seen every film, read every book and heard every record. Popular culture – in the not too distant past his reason for living – he realised simply blew over and what was hot one week was virtually ancient history the next. Now that adulthood had arrived there seemed to be little excitement and, from what he could foresee, little to look forward to. He seemed to do little but get older.

He was single, had no children and no mortgage hanging round his neck. He was short-sighted and often felt drowning in a sea of student debt that the British government had saddled him with for a degree which, try as he might, seemed to provide no professional benefit. He had, quite accidentally, found himself employed with regularity by a variety of magazines and newspapers as a reporter and could afford to turn work down for sometimes weeks at a time since he'd learned how to manage his money. For work the stories he wrote, mostly local news, just came and went with no strings attached. He'd pitch his story, if commissioned write it and send it through. That was it. He'd see his byline, get his payslip and head off to the casino where he would still be playing long after his articles had turned into fish and chip paper.

In the beginning poker was just a sport – something to learn and, if liked, get better at and to a large degree that's what happened. He started playing online as a teenager in the early days of Internet gambling; first it was play money, then the odd pound here and there and then, after an infamous loss, prudent folding in home matches with old college mates. With great discipline he divided his monies precisely; living expenses and poker stakes, and however tempting never ever used his expenses to fund his stakes. He knew when to cut his losses. With rarely an alarm to wake him or a supervisor to overrule him, Conrad would naturally be awake long into the night either working on some story or other or be in one of Manchester's casinos where like most he believed that poker was indeed part luck but more skill than anything, especially once he found his feet reading his opponents; it could be a drink, a blink of the eye, a cough, anything at all could hint at the strategy of those sitting opposite.

In the summer when work was traditionally slower, at least three nights a week he'd be happy profiting just fifty pounds a night playing Texas Hold 'Em – a variant of the game that was fast, easy to learn and, with suddenly lots of vulnerable amateurs getting involved thanks to its incredibly successful exposure on late night TV, potentially very lucrative.

His opponents in more than one of the gambling houses he frequented were often not English. Many regulars were from Asia and though he was ultimately trying to take their money he enjoyed the banter around the table as they were interested in him as an English native. Recently arrived students from Japan and Korea were thirsts for knowledge about British politics, football, lager and girls, all over a fun game of Hold 'Em. And he was particularly curious to learn that be they working, studying or in many cases both, they still believed that they were going places. For working class Conrad, anyone still with ambition in their late twenties was a pariah, which was exactly the reason why he felt so welcome in such company. He had never been abroad, could speak only his native tongue and was professionally just floating along as a freelance journalist where there was never any sense of progression. Before getting into poker he was starting to believe that professionally and socially he might have peaked already, but, since these guys were all of a similar age and still full of ambition he realised that he too could yet have his eyes opened by an experience or two that would provide something both defining and truly memorable. But what could that be?

Paul, on the other hand, had by now accepted his ageing and was comfortable with it. He was thirty and an agency lorry driver, another example of how unstable the jobs market had become in early twenty first-century Britain. After dropping out of school he joined the army and spent seven happy years in the King's Royal Hussars who provided him with a belated education and disciplined but fun visits to Europe and South America. Once discharged he wanted his experiences to count for something when applying for jobs and was bewildered when he was often politely told that he was 'overqualified' when hoping for a position. The army might have given him the best years of his life up to a point but back in the real world it didn't appear to count for much and that was hard to take. In his time international conflicts were only cold; there were threats but no fighting, just training for the call that never came and while his life was never in danger, he did resent all the appreciation that his successors were getting in the war that was currently raging in the Middle East.

Not too different to Conrad he was ticking over and part of him also liked it; he was single and still lived with his father and younger brother north of Manchester in Rochdale. There was enough money to buy plenty of beer and the tools of Paul's vanity, and lots of them. Every week he'd be out spending on shirts, jeans, shoes, hats, sunglasses, necklaces; whatever caught his forever wandering eye. Living at home he had relatively few overheads meaning that he could afford what he knew was mostly materialistic crap but there appeared to be little else to spend on and nothing at all to save up for. If not his appearance (despite his thinning hair), then it was his appetite that he splashed out on; at times it seemed he was on a personal crusade to sample every type of cuisine in town – he figured that if you're going to spend on something it may as well be necessities like clothes and food and soon all the local restaurants had become familiar with his custom. Indian and Thai were his favourites.

With Rob it was a little more complicated. After a stint away from home down in Somerset where he worked in an abattoir, upon his return rather than face a long spell in the dole queue, like Paul he'd served three years in the army but unlike Paul he never stayed on since it was never a passion. His time in the services was, if not reluctant, then certainly never more than competent. He'd done his stint and got out, eager to experience other things though little went to plan.

He appeared simply not capable of holding down a job for longer than a month, two if he was really determined. All he could get around Rochdale and Manchester was menial labour that he naturally considered boring, not well paid enough or usually both. But he still had bills to pay. After belatedly following his school friend Will into further education with a stint at Sheffield University which proved too expensive, he dropped out and was yet again at a loose end. It was only nepotism from his mother that saved him from the jobcentre when she provided him with a near full time job in her pub, a position that he was soon able to balance with some work as an overnight security guard at a local chemical factory.

While Rob had been away Will studied Media at college where he met Conrad. It was on one of the many blurry nights in student nightclubs when Will brought Rob along during one of his leaves and introduced him. It was a fun time for Will but upon graduating and seeing Conrad initially struggle to become someone's employee he decided to bite the bullet and go self employed. Since he'd majored with great success in video production the thought of taking out a little loan to start his own business was the only thing that would give him the respect he craved – to him nothing was worse than working for someone else. He invested in all the equipment; the car, the office and, most importantly, the set of beautifully printed business cards that he just loved handing out at networking soirées to any bigwig that might believe he was a pro. But he wasn't, he was just another young man trying to break into the business and he found it tough going. Gradually over the next few years when he, Rob and Paul would head into Manchester they'd give Conrad a ring and make a night of it - the pub, the club, the take away and a shared taxi home. No one expected anything to change when Conrad casually mentioned one night that his poker hobby had been really developing of late: 'I won another hundred quid last night…' he said.

'You play poker?' wondered Rob as they sat there drinking during another black November Saturday. 'You never told me…?'

'I've been a member of a couple of casinos in town for a while and I'm doing good….'

'How much did you put down?'

'Not much more than twenty.'

Rob was intrigued: 'I wouldn't mind having a go actually. I sometimes watch it at night…'

'And what do you know?'

'That nothing beats a royal flush. When you going next?'
'Probably Wednesday. You coming?'
'Sure.'
'Well bring your money; I could do with more winnings...'

That night Rob stayed at Conrad's flat and sat at the computer as the rules were explained: 'You got the hand rankings?'

'Sure,' replied Rob.

'Betting rounds?'

'Got them.'

'I'm going to sit you at one of the easier tables, here. Alright then, I'm going to bed - I'll see you in the morning. If you lose me more than ten quid there's gonna be trouble. Have fun.'

Rob played all night with Conrad's money. By morning, especially since he'd took it upon himself to move up the tables Rob had made a nearly four hundred percent profit. Conrad was amazed when he woke but was far too proud to admit that he'd never done as well in years of playing as Rob had in a single night. He put it down to beginner's luck.

'My gift to you,' said Rob as he was leaving to get his day's sleep before another overnight shift at the factory. 'When are we going to the casino then...?'

In a few short months in both casinos and local home games, getting ever greedier, the pair of them had devised a series of signals to communicate across the table. They would arrive at games separately, pretending not to know each other and quickly proceed to rape the opposition out of its every last penny. Thumb flicking, teeth chatting, chip tapping, the lot. Sure it was illegal and downright immoral but in the end the money always talked, and when Rob learned of the advantages of being the dealer it was no coincidence that with his speed of hand he and Conrad were often provided with more than their fair share of sparkling aces. They were more than just good, they were soon virtually untouchable and ached to test themselves against tougher opposition. The extra winnings wouldn't exactly be unwelcome either.

Will meanwhile had recently secured a rolling job filming a choir while Paul had also just landed a big contract driving for a new logistics firm. Neither of them usually looked forward to Christmas and New Year but this year they'd both be happily working away and would even have some money left over for any lull period for a while thereafter.

One night Rob sat down with an announcement to make.
'What is it? That you're gay?' predicted Paul.
'Sorry mate – you'll have to find someone else…'
'Well what then?'
'We should go on a road trip across America?'
'*What?*'

No one answered once they realised he was serious. None of the four of them had ever been to America, they'd all certainly thought about it as kids but until now a lads' holiday had always meant nothing more than a week in Magaluf or some equally packaged European resort already overflowing with pissed-up Brits.

'Well, why not?' Rob continued, rubbing his hands together. 'What the hell else is there to look forward to?'

'Who can afford that?' asked Will.

'Look we can't afford not to go. Look around; people are getting married, getting stuck in crap jobs, having kids and growing apart. Imagine being an old man and thinking back that you had the chance to see America with your mates and didn't go?'

'For how long?'

'I don't know, a month?'

'A month? Do you think we're made of money?'

'Well three weeks then!'

'And what do you mean across America?' Paul joined in.

'We should see the whole country…'

'I'd have to save up for ages!'

'So…?'

'You know, you're right,' said Conrad, likewise feeling Rob's painful impatience. 'My eyes are getting a bit bored.'

Rob and Conrad's minds were made up; all they had to do was work around the cost: 'If four of us go then everything will be split and it won't be that expensive…?'

'What if we have to work?' wondered Paul.

'Well book your time off tomorrow and save up everything you can! Next summer we're going to the US of A…?'

'I'll think about it,' said Will. Rob persisted: 'Let's just buy flights as soon as possible and that'll get rid of any indecision…? All we need to do is go without spending on crap for a couple of weeks and we're going. Youth hostels, trains, buses, motels, you know, let's do the whole thing? We'll start in New York and get to Los Angeles?'

'Aren't they like on opposite sides of the country?'

'Too ambitious for you...? Look I'll go to some travel agents tomorrow and get a couple of quotes...'

'Anyway,' announced Will, 'I've just finished a big job filming a local council meeting and I got them to pay for my tapes and petrol that I already had. That's pure profit. Excellent!'

'Is it important then for you to make as much as you can get?' asked Rob. Will was not ashamed to admit that it was: 'Hey I'm self-employed – I don't work all the time and need to be able to finance the times when I'm not busy. So I might take home a bit more than you - but at least you have a continuous income so there's no need to be too jealous.'

'But you have to sort out your own tax and all that shit?'

'What's the point in declaring everything you earn man? Then you end up paying for other lazy people who claim to be not able to work and they're not my concern. This country's becoming a socialist prison and I want to be free.'

'You were never like this at school..?'

'That was ten years ago, everything was so much easier then.'

'Hey I'm also self employed' said Conrad, 'and let me tell you it's kill or be killed, though there's no excuse for not paying your taxes. I say we report him...?'

Rob nodded.

Back from the bar Paul was fiddling with his phone: 'Our boys are now in Basra...'

'What?'

'Troops have just took Basra...'

'Do you wish you were over there then?' said Will.

'Not really but this is pretty boring isn't it?'

'What is?'

'You know getting up, going to work, going home, watching TV and repeating it all until weekend, after which the same old crap starts again.'

'Yeah but what about the danger the soldiers are in?'

'Once you're dead, you're dead - and nothing matters then. I bet those lads are feeling more important than we are just sat here getting old. In the army you have a status that counts for something that you can build on and work your way up. Having to earn a living outside the chances are you're never going to do much more than kiss Mr.

Capitalism's ass.'

'That's why you should start your own business!'

'Oh don't start this again' said Rob. 'I'm going for a piss.'

With Rob gone Will wondered whether he was serious: 'Do you think he's right about America?'

'It's only a couple of weeks out of your life. Why not?'

Once Paul agreed Will began to sway.

SITTING AT THE SAME table at the same time next week there they were and true to his word Rob had indeed been round all the travel agents and discovered that flights into Chicago and out of Los Angeles would best suit their needs. 'There's one going out on the first of August and one coming back on the twenty third…The best I could get was five hundred and ninety quid…?'

'Five hundred and ninety just for flights?' asked Will.

'Including insurance…'

'That would be flights, insurance *and* spending money all round Europe..?'

'To hell with Europe man – that's crap, we're going to America. I say we should buy those flights as soon as possible then we have to go – none of us can write that off. We'll have six months to save up – plenty of time…?'

Since Rob and Conrad had again done rather well in midweek with the cards the cost of the flights was well within their grasp. Paul meanwhile was interested to know exactly what was between Chicago and Los Angeles, the parts that you rarely saw on TV. He was curious about the pleasurable thought of being lost somewhere where there might finally be no McDonalds, Subway or Starbucks: 'It's not just me who fancies spending the odd night or two in the tiny border town of Nowhereville is it?'

'Now you're talking.' Rob was psychologically dragging them to the agent's desk. 'We'll see all that and perhaps even some sunshine! Come on Will, what do you say…?'

PART ONE: THE CITY

ONE

IT WAS NEARLY a full hour after touching down at O'Hare before they finally stepped out from the likewise air conditioned CTA carriage at the LaSalle stop. Lugging their backpacks up the steps and seeing with their own eyes the intensity and sparkle of downtown Chicago was nearly as overwhelming as the heat. It was the first day of August and typically the height of summer everywhere in the northern hemisphere but during that particular week the Windy City was experiencing a heatwave unlike anything it had seen in years. The three of them stood amazed by the sight of yellow taxis whizzing by and the deafening screech of street trains above and below. The sun was blinding them, their exposed skin was instantly burning and all traffic moving across the East Congress Parkway seemed strobed by gaudy colour.

'Well which way is it?' shouted Rob above the din whilst rushing for his shades, 'left or right?'

Conrad threw his pack to the concrete giving him access to the top flap where he stored all the paperwork.

'It's right according to this,' Conrad replied, referring to the hand drawn map he'd copied from the hostel's website. 'It says "three blocks from LaSalle".'

'What's a block?' asked Will.

'I don't know. What could it mean? Before the next three junctions I suppose. Let's go.'

They walked right with Rob leading the way. He took a step onto the road only to instantly jump back to the kerb in terror at the sound of a honking car rapidly approaching from the left. The car flew past as Rob shook with both relief and embarrassment.

'Jesus Christ! You look left remember – they drive on the right here. Open your eyes man!' Will lectured in schoolteacher fashion. They then tiptoed along the street, strolling slowly, just having to absorb the expansive design of the cars and buildings along the way.

'There it is,' Conrad soon announced, pointing across the Parkway to a huge warehouse-like building wearing the famous Hostelling International logo. They carefully crossed the road and entered the building to see a security desk that more resembled a bank than a youth hostel.

'Hello, where do we check in?' said Conrad to the guy at the desk.

'The hostel reception is on the first floor, you can take the stairs or the elevator, both are by the store round there to your right.'

'Okay thank you.'

'Thank God for the air conditioning in here' said Will as they marched round the desk. 'At home we come in from the cold. Over here you come in from the warm.'

Rob and Conrad agreed, appreciating the new temperature immediately. They looked up and saw a sign:

4: *rooms 150 - 200, laundrette, female showers*
3: *rooms 100 – 149, TV room, kitchen, dining area*
2: *rooms 51 – 99, male showers, library, internet, bar*
1: *check-in desk, rooms 1 – 50, games room, tour starting point*

'It's only the first floor. Shall we take the stairs?' asked Conrad.

'No. My shoulder's killing me,' replied Rob.

Whilst waiting for the lift they noticed the hostel store manned by an older man of Asian descent. On his shelves were leaflets, guide books, international phone cards, padlocks, plug-converters, internet credit cards and an assortment of Chicago postcards.

'Can I interest you in anything?' the man said.

'Not just yet. We're just going up to check in,' answered Rob.

'Where are you young men from?'

'We're from England.'

The old man's face lit up.

'Ah, England!' he said. 'I'm from India. Our countries of course have a special relationship. India was once a great part of the British Empire. It's good to meet you. Hope you enjoy your stay.'

'Thanks,' they all said stepping into the lift.

When the doors opened they saw that the check-in desk was

total chaos, heaving with all kinds of travellers. There were tattooed surfer types in knee length shorts, young Oriental girls fiddling with maps, dreadlocked African Americans covered in what appeared to be genuine gold jewellery and amongst many others a likely touring rock band using their instrument cases as furniture. Commercial radio was blasting and there appeared to be no air conditioning.

'Look at this. It's going to take forever,' sighed Conrad in mild horror.

'What can we do?' said Will. 'It's too late to cancel our booking here and I bet we'd have trouble finding somewhere else this cheap for tonight.'

'Please wait at the back of the line' shouted a member of the hostel staff, ushering the newcomers into line and preventing them from obstructing the lift. 'Please have your booking confirmation forms ready.'

Conrad got out theirs and took off his jacket.

'Late afternoon. Wonder what time it is in England?' said Rob.

'I think it's about six hours behind' Will replied. 'We flew back in time. Yeah see, that's about right look up there' he continued, pointing up to the time of the London clock in amongst all the global city clocks high on the wall behind the desk.

After nearly half an hour leaning against the winding reception desk and inch by inch creeping their way round to service they were next up. A young man with Dylan written on his nametag shouted: 'Who's next?'

'Hello, we have a reservation for three nights...' said Conrad.

'Okay, can I see your booking form and photo IDs please?'

Conrad placed his email receipt on the desk while all three of them put down their passports. Dylan typed the code into the computer.

'Right you have a booking for three beds that we will allocate you in a dorm that has space for six. You are booked for tonight, Wednesday and Thursday. For non-members that will be a total cost of two hundred twenty-five dollars.'

They all reached into their pockets and looked at their American cash for the first time and didn't know what was what. Not only were the American notes all the same size but they were also the same colour, but at least they were clearly labelled – unlike the coins which they would never familiarise themselves with.

'Now I know what was taking so long,' giggled Will, almost

panicked by his obvious lack of suss regarding the local currency. 'It'll take us the three weeks just to get used to the money.'

Dylan was patiently waiting for payment.

'It's just seventy-five dollars each' said Rob winning the race to get his cash down.

'Alright then,' Dylan began, 'now I need all three of you to fill out one of these forms. I need your name, address, nationality and a contact telephone number in case of emergency and finally details of how you found out about us.'

They were given forms and pencils whilst Dylan photocopied their passports. Conrad then remembered Paul: 'We have someone else who we would like to stay with but he's not arrived yet as he's on a later flight. Could we reserve one of the remaining three beds in the room for him?'

'Unfortunately not,' replied Dylan. 'It's first come first serve. I know but it's a management decision.'

Once they were done Dylan stapled their receipts together and handed over their key cards. 'You're in room fifty four which is all male and on the second floor. Breakfast between seven and eleven is included and checkout time is midday. Enjoy your stay. Next please.'

They picked up their luggage and decided to take the stairs up to the second floor. Once they had found the room Rob got to the lock first with his key card. He slipped it into the slot and turned the handle on the green light to reveal their home for the next three nights. It was quite a large room with three made double bunks. There was a shower cubical, sink and mirror area and six metal storage cupboards that required padlocks to secure their doors. It was clean and empty which indicated that there was no current tenant. Will and Conrad collapsed onto their allocated beds.

'Not bad for the money,' said Rob opening the window and throwing down his bags. 'Though if it's first come first served and an expected full house there's a chance that Paul won't get in this room or even in this hostel at all. Should we just wait for him?'

'What time does he get into O'Hare?' asked Will.

'He should be landing soon.'

'Does he know where to come? Conrad?'

'Well the other night on the phone I read out to him all the directions we had and he took his time writing them down.'

'I'm sure he'll be okay,' said Rob. 'Remember he was the best soldier in his regiment for seven years so finding his way three hundred yards from the CTA stop to here shouldn't be a problem. We should go for something to eat, I'm hank marvin.'

'Alright.'

Conrad was first into the shower as Rob and Will began unpacking. Looking across the room Rob stared in amazement as Will unzipped his suitcase releasing an incredible spaghetti of cables, plugs and video recording equipment.

'Christ! What the hell do you need all that for?' asked Rob, completely stunned. 'Not exactly travelling light are you?'

'This is the adventure of a lifetime and I want to document as much as I can. I need all this stuff since I'm not just a traveller you know, I'm also a tourist.'

'You know if you look like a tourist you're much more likely to be the victim of crime.'

'You've seen too many films mate. America's one of the safest countries in the world. I'll be alright.'

Suitably refreshed, Conrad came out of the shower and saw the mountain.

'What the hell's all that?' he too asked a now half-embarrassed Will. 'They took my cold sore cream off me at the airport but they let you through with all that! Incredible! You should have at least got an anal search.'

Rob burst out laughing as Will grabbed his soap bag, towel and underwear and stomped into the shower.

'You know if he wants to spend three weeks lugging all that around in weather like this then that's up to him,' laughed Rob, 'what's he going to do? Make a feature film?'

Conrad put his faded black jeans back on and slipped into a plain white cotton T-shirt. For him this was the classic look with which it was impossible to go wrong. Whatever the temperature there would be no sightseer shorts or sandals for him; it was traditional wear that looked as good in Chicago as it did in Manchester.

'I can see you're travelling light then, unlike some,' Rob said.

'No flash-packing for me. How much do I really need?'

'Not much I suppose. Anyway I need a shave. Can I borrow a razor? I haven't got a two pin adaptor for my electric yet.'

'Sure, here.'

As Will was in the shower and Rob shaving, Conrad lay on his bed and pulled out his USA guidebook and began searching for the Chicago chapter. As he read about the city the more he gathered that apparently the architecture was one of the reasons why the place was a great American metropolis. 'Let's see for ourselves,' he thought as Will and Rob changed places.

'You'll never get that case closed again,' teased Conrad flicking through pages as Will put on his flip flops. 'Everything but the kitchen sink you've got in there.'

'Equipment and technology are important you know, you'll want a souvenir too I expect? Anyway what about Paul?'

'Try and phone him. I mean if you can get a signal that is.'

Will threw his comb down, searched for his phone and much to his surprise discovered that he could indeed get a signal. He skimmed through the contacts, hit dial on Paul and waited with the receiver to his ear. Suddenly Paul answered. Conrad looked up from his book. It had worked, regardless of any possible trouble with signals or simcards.

'Where are you, at the Airport?' Will excitedly said.

'That's right, it's almost right across the road but we'll meet you at the CTA stop then. Say in half an hour. Okay, in a bit.'

'Well is he coming here then?' asked Conrad.

'No. He's just got on the train and we have to meet him at LaSalle in half an hour.'

'Great!'

Wrapped in a towel Rob then emerged from the longest of all showers and stepped across to the sink and began drying his hair.

'We just phoned Paul, he's on the blue line and we're meeting him at LaSalle in half an hour,' Conrad announced.

'Alright! That does still give us time to get some food though, I tell you, that airline meal left a lot to be desired.'

'We can't fit all our bags in the lockers, look!' said Will, demonstrating the trouble they would have trying to secure their luggage in the metal cupboards. 'What shall we do? Just leave our stuff around on the beds?'

'We're going to have to aren't we?' answered Rob.

'What if a stranger gets put in here? Any swinging dick could just nick what they like while we're out!'

'It'll be alright. I'm keeping my passport, cards and cash on me at all times. If anything does go missing they'll be able to find anyone they put in here.'

'If you say so,' conceded Will, who was naturally the most worried since his equipment was more valuable than what the other two had combined.

Conrad and Will tidied up their beds and filled their pockets with cash and plastic. Rob hurriedly put on a T-shirt and shorts and announced that he would have to try his new card at one of the hostel's cash machines. All ready they locked up and headed down to reception.

'Can you tell me where the cash machines are?' asked Rob.

'Oh you mean the ATMs – they're just on the outside of the building near the store.'

'Please Swipe Card' said the digital display. Rob obliged, made his withdrawal and led the way into a sandwich bar next door to a barber's they had earlier walked past about half way between the hostel and train stop. It looked just as they do in England; the company logo was exactly the same, as was the menu and even the furniture. They may have been thousands of miles across the world but this place was as familiar as anything they'd seen since touching down.

'These franchise companies, they're everywhere,' said Conrad. 'Soon one company like this is going to completely dominate the entire world industry and there will be no little guys left at all. Everyone's going to be slaves to big shiny businesses. I tell you, they're taking over the planet.'

'If they serve food then I'm happy,' said Rob considering his options, before going for the meatball marinara while Conrad had the chicken tikka express and Will the turkey breast with sweet onion sauce. As they sat down they wondered how much the people who worked there earned per hour. Their servers were young black girls no older than twenty. They had been fast, efficient and friendly – everything a customer could want and, unlike at home, they could understand English perfectly.

'Do you think these girls are earning minimum wage?' asked Conrad.

'I don't know. How much do you think the minimum wage is over here anyway?' replied Will.

'I'm not sure, it may differ from State to State but apparently service people may well expect a tip remember..?'

'A tip? How much do you think is expected, or suitable?'

'Don't look at me.'

Rob too looked puzzled.

This presented a problem. No one wanted to appear scrooges but they didn't know how much to leave, they hadn't got used to the cash, didn't know if a gratuity charge had been added to their bills or even if the tipping etiquette applied to their only over-counter service.

'Let's just walk out, to hell with it' said Rob with no apparent shame. 'We're never going to be here again so who cares if they think we're stingy English bastards.'

'Man that's cold,' said Conrad who himself was not quite freezing but didn't understand why people should get a bonus as well as their regulation wages: 'But what if you can't afford to tip, like you just haven't got the money?'

'Paul's train will be getting in anytime now so we should finish up,' interrupted Will before visually making a point of putting three dollar bills down at the edge of the table. Conrad managed to do the same and Rob reluctantly appeared to leave a number of coins. Whether he actually knew how much was there or not was certainly a matter of conjecture.

Walking down the steps of LaSalle and hearing the thunder of departing trains Will was drawn to a wall map of the different coloured lines. 'It's obviously like the Tube in London but rather than being totally underground a lot of it's above the street,' he said.

'Not this part obviously' quipped Rob.

Will continued to read the map: 'It says that here, downtown Chicago is unofficially named "The Loop" after this two mile part of the circuit...'

Having no reason to go through, all they could do was stand and wait on the exit side of the turnstiles and look intently at the upcoming escalator.

'You made sure LaSalle on the blue line with him didn't you?' Conrad said to Will.

'Yep.'

Then, like the cavalry arriving on the horizon, up came Paul's familiar shorn head followed by the rest of him and two big bags.

'Christ, it's hot' he announced as he emerged up at street level and was led the short distance to the hostel reception.

'Can he be put in the same room as us? There are still three spare beds,' Rob said to Gina, Dylan's successor behind the desk. The check-in area was now nowhere near as busy had it had been earlier so there was a good chance that Paul would indeed be allocated one of the remaining spaces in the dorm.

'What room are you guys in?' Gina replied.

'Fifty four.'

She looked on the computer before looking back with a happy smile. 'Sure, we can do that, would you also like to stay until Friday?' she asked Paul.

'I would.'

'OK then I need your ID and I need you to fill out one of these and seventy-five dollars if you would.'

As Paul was processing his check-in Conrad nipped down to the old Indian to buy the postcard he promised he'd send his mother when he arrived. Will and Rob began messing around at a pool table across the room; violently throwing the balls into the pockets whilst talking about how they would spend their first night in America.

'Got any ideas?' asked Will.

'I'm not bothered really, we could just go for a walk and I'd be satisfied. Nothing too energetic since I'm starting to feel a bit jet-lagged actually.'

'Well I want to paint the town red.'

At that moment they were approached by two girls of Oriental descent with clipboards who were residents at the hostel and had been given employment there promoting its link-up with the city's tourist board. The girls were eager to get as many people booked onto that night's bus tour of Chicago's top attractions.

'You know I usually associate bus tours with football teams who've won trophies,' nonchalantly remarked Rob as he flicked the balls around the table.

'Sorry?' said one of the girls. 'Football trophy?'

She looked puzzled.

'What happens in our country is that young men only go round on open-top busses to show off their achievements in sport,' Will confirmed for her.

'Are you guys English?'

'Is it that obvious?' countered Rob, barely paying them attention.

'My father works for the English Soccer Association,' said the girl. 'He's a managing director in Public Relations and deals with corporate hospitality for the sponsors of Manchester, Arsenal, Chelsea and Newcastle. I know what you mean about open-top buses. My father tells me that amongst the marketing brass it's now considered an old-fashioned embarrassment and no matter how much there might be to celebrate, as a PR exercise the bus tour won't have a future in what's now an industry mainly operating for commercial gain.'

Having had the smug smile thoroughly wiped right off his face the girls now had Rob's full attention whilst Will couldn't help but smirk.

'Right I'm sorry,' Rob grovelled. 'Could you please remind me of what's happening here with you guys tonight then?'

'It's okay we don't mind,' the young woman assured him. 'Unlike English soccer suits we love the idea of riding around on open top buses. That's why we do this tour every week!'

'What do you do then for the hostel exactly?' asked Will.

'Well not always of course but often young people stay here not knowing a thing about Chicago and they're sometimes travelling alone and would like some company, so management started these activities to help them mix and settle in. They've also done deals with museums, amusements and nightclubs whereby residents get a discount and they've got us to basically tell people about it and where we can organise certain things. Would you like a leaflet about what's happening this week?'

'Sure.'

'Hope to see you sometime. Remember all tours depart from here and cut-rate tickets for the attractions on the leaflet are available from reception, to get them all you need to do is show your key cards and ID.'

The girl handed Will a leaflet and walked back across the room talking to her partner in what he assumed was Chinese. Conrad then reappeared holding his postcard and Paul also approached having completed his check-in.

'Well where's the room then?' asked Paul.

'This way,' responded Will, leading them to the lift up to the second floor.

Paul was not quite treated like a long-lost friend because they had all seen him less than a week before but he was still the only person the three of them knew in this strange country. They all sat on their beds as he took the bunk under Rob's and began unpacking.

'How was your flight, alight?' asked Rob who like Will was now changing into something more formal for the evening.

'Okay,' Paul replied, 'though the changeover in Philly was well boring, having to wait for my connecting flight for four hours. What have you lot done since you arrived, anything?'

'Nothing, we just came here straight from the airport, got changed, had something to eat and went to get you. Are you hungry?'

'No, I ate in Philly. What have you planned for tonight then, a big night?'

'Nothing actually. Will noticed an ad on the train for a short film festival that's happening nearby tonight, Conrad would like to go to a concert and this hostel have organised an open top bus tour of what are supposedly Chicago's top attractions – but we haven't decided anything.'

'What concert is it?'

'Conrad, who's the concert?' asked Rob.

'Grant-Lee Phillips. I would like us to go but he's also playing tomorrow so we don't have to go tonight.'

By the looks of things Paul had also not left much behind when packing his bags but his luggage seemed altogether more sensible than Will's video equipment or Rob and Conrad's scruffy collection of bare essentials. Paul had thought to pack things like sunblock, a padlock, a small pair of binoculars and even a torch.

'You should see what Will's brought,' said Conrad looking for a pen to write his postcard.

'Don't start that again,' predictably replied Will.

'When I was thinking what to pack I suddenly got some withdrawal symptoms from the army,' explained Paul. 'Remember they always told you that organisation and planning was essential to any successful exercise. If you fail to prepare then you're preparing to fail.'

'I just brought what I thought I'd need,' commented Rob, 'but I'll probably have to pick up a few things on the road.'

As they were all ready they picked up their cameras and headed out with Conrad collecting a city map from reception.

★

THE SUN WAS beginning to set as the four of them strolled east along the Parkway with no particular destination. The trains were screeching on the overhead loop held up by grimy metal stanchions that disappeared far up neighbouring South Wabash Avenue. They walked by what appeared to be a collection of Irish bars towards the next junction and an elegant stretch of greenery, identified on steel gates and Conrad's map as Grant Park. They stared at the surrounding skyscrapers, the families in the park and fellow tourists all laughing, playing frisbee and taking photos.

'Let's get some pictures,' said Will unzipping the handbag containing his new digital camera. 'All stand next to each other, hold that pose, hold it...'

Satisfied with his framing Will put his finger on the shutter and, just about managing to hold a pose the other three watched a nearby sprinkler suddenly erupt and instantly soak him to the drip. It was a classic moment.

'How's the picture Will?' Paul asked sarcastically, just about able to hold back the hilarity, 'do I look good?'

Will laughed too at his own misfortune and his snap was far from what he intended. 'I'm half drenched,' he barked.

'Don't worry, better luck next time,' laughed Rob. 'You'll soon dry off in this heat.'

Will hopped off the wet grass and ran to catch up with them along the pathway. It was annoying for him sure, but not the end of the world. The four of them slowly wandered around the immaculately tidy park that was prettily dotted with pedestrian lights, outlining all routes to Buckingham Fountain in the centre that was an incredible sight at dusk; lit up from the inside spraying white gallons round from all its levels and accompanying stone mermaids. Looking beyond across the vast Lake Michigan in front was almost as breath-taking as the city skyline behind.

'Do you think Americans are quite lucky?' asked Will to anyone who might answer.

'Lucky, why?' said Conrad.

'To have this scenery, this weather?'

'Of course, but remember we don't live here; this is only our first glimpse and we're in a glitzy city on a hot night. Wait 'till we see more of the country, I'm sure there are poorer parts to see - and remember that's the whole point.'

'What's the whole point?'

'To stay off the traditional tourist routes – it will be harder and less glamorous but more of an experience in the end. This is just the introduction – we're going to be travelling all the way to LA and we'll mostly remember the interior of the country.'

'The tourist people always tell foreigners not to hate Britain for the weather because it's no one's fault,' said Rob, 'there's nothing anyone can ever do about it so let's not flatter anyone because of a lucky force of nature, and anyway, I bet it's not always this hot.'

They headed out of the park, taking pictures along the way and into the Irish bar that they had passed earlier. The place was brightly lit and fairly busy with people mostly in their thirties. There were loud fiddles and drums crushing anyone's attempt at conversation and small TVs mounted high on the walls showing silent Baseball games. As they arrived at the bar the drinks menu was disappointing, especially for Conrad whose preference for bottled beer meant that his choice was limited to Budweiser, Miller or Coors. The tap choice was only slightly better but Rob could get a Guinness while Will and Paul were happy to go for the house lager. They found a table and sat down.

'This is just a Wetherspoons really,' said Rob.

'Don't tell me that's a bad thing right? This being like Wetherspoons?' replied Paul.

'No, of course not – it means I can get a decent pint of Guinness. Cheers.'

'God that music's loud,' complained Conrad.

'Enjoy yourself will you, it's the first night of your holiday – you've saved up all year for this,' replied Will, already halfway down his glass.

'You know I'm not saying we should go straight back to the hostel but a relatively early night wouldn't be too bad for us – remember we've been up over a full day for England and almost the same now for America. Not feeling tired?'

'Yes,' said Rob to a slight frown from Will. 'Well, I'm too tired to go mad anyway.'

'I'm going to look for the toilets,' mimed Paul as he got up.

'What did you get, Budweiser?' Rob asked Conrad whilst spying the label on his bottle.

'Well it says on the sticker that it's the 'King of Beers?''

'You mean it was all they had! Does it taste the same?'

'Yeah. As sugary as ever.'

'It's actually a live band playing you know,' shouted Paul on his return from the restroom. 'Round the corner there's a concert, shall we go and have a look?'

They followed the noise round to another room and saw a middle-aged five piece blasting through what underneath all the distortion just about sounded like traditional Irish folk. The singer, well into his fifties, was bald and wearing a green hat, he wore a beard; dungarees with braces, knee length shorts and buckle shoes. He was skipping up and down during instrumental breaks and forcefully blowing into a flute.

'Woodstock was never in Chicago was it?' Will shouted into Paul's ear.

Paul laughed and shook his head, though not knowing whether he was right or not.

The song finished to enthusiastic applause from the watching drinkers. Everyone's ears were ringing but Will could just about hear the singer's offer for the audience to make requests. He put down his empty glass and started bellowing.

'Oh no! He's pissed' muttered Rob in humorous disgust, 'and he's only had one drink!'

'Gloria!' Will called out. 'Gloria!'

'And you sir,' said the singer in a convincing Irish accent, 'Gloria by Van Morrison?'

'Yes please,' Will confirmed at the top of his voice.

'Alrighty then.'

The guitarist started the song and that was all the sign Will needed to make an example to everyone present that it was his request. He began dancing around like the singer.

'Control yourself, Paul,' Conrad joked, 'remember you're drinking the same as him; that mysterious house beer.'

'No danger with me mate. He's just a man who can't handle his liquor.'

Coincidently as this interpretation of the famous old song was spreading round the building, the room began to swell with what must have been most of the bar's customers. Four young English men were suddenly surrounded by an audience singing and clapping along and noticing this victory Will was full of adrenaline; he snatched the remains of Paul's pint before joining the singer at the mic for a duet. His fellow countrymen watched in horror.

'And her name is G. L. O. R. I. I. I. I. A. g.l.o.r.i.a. Gloria!'

It was the only part of the song that Will could sing but it didn't matter to him since he was now officially a king, if only for a few choruses on one song after twenty six years as an average schmuck.

'Shall we tell him that we're obviously going to use these memories as blackmail material, I mean they could be quite useful don't you think?' Rob joked to Paul, who was happy to see Will enjoying himself:

'It's funny though I couldn't get up there and do that no matter how much I've had. What's come over him?'

Will leapt back down to earth when the song had finished to a considerable ovation. He landed in the arms of his three mates who had to prevent him from crashing into the bar.

'Was I top or what?' shouted Will, not wanting to hear anything less. 'Entertainment you know?'

'I think we better take him home before he does something embarrassing' sarcastically suggested Paul.

'Don't be stupid man, I'm fine – I want another drink.'

They returned to their seat in the other room and collected their thoughts. Rob had the giggles, Conrad was tired, Will was hyper and Paul was sent to the bar for another round.

'So where are we off to after Chicago?' Rob asked Conrad, whose knowledge of American geography was by far the greatest of them all.

'Well I would like to go to Memphis since you ask. We don't have to but it's my nomination, if it's a democracy.'

'Why Memphis?'

'Well we've got three weeks, which is plenty of time to see places and Memphis I think would have its own Southern charms – have you got any suggestions?'

'Not really.'

'Yeah but is Memphis in the direction of LA?' wondered Will, surprisingly making sense.

'Well LA's down and all the way over and Memphis is just about as far down as LA so we wouldn't be going out of our way at all, but it's not directly on the straight line between here and there if that's what you mean.'

Paul came back from the bar with another round of drinks, prudently warning Will to drink slower.

'We're going to Memphis on Friday,' Rob informed Paul, who also appeared fine with a decision he didn't make.

'I'm tired now, this will be my last drink out tonight,' said Paul, by now fully feeling the effects of his two flights and laborious changeover. 'Before we set off for Memphis then what about tomorrow and Thursday, any plans?'

'Well I still would like to go to that concert tomorrow night, and at some time we could do with finding out the details of the trains down to Tennessee' sensibly recommended Conrad.

THE DEVIL'S DUST

'Anyone fancy going for a swim?' Rob suggested.

'A swim? Where?' wondered Will.

'There must be somewhere around the lake for swimmers, if the weather's this good I'd love to have a splash about.'

They all agreed, drank up and headed back to the hostel.

★

'HOLD ON WHERE'S my key card?' said Rob at the main entrance, worriedly searching his pockets. He eventually found it and repeatedly sliced it through the lock which didn't open. Conrad, Will and Paul all tried theirs and likewise failed to gain access to the building. Inside there was a light illuminating the security desk and CCTV monitors but the guards were nowhere to be seen. Will began banging on the door.

'For God's sake,' muttered Paul in frustration. 'What the hell's going on when all four keys won't work? Why can't they just give us old fashioned keys that turn the locks?'

At that moment two elderly African Americans lurked towards them from along the darkened Parkway. They were heavily dressed for the weather, one male and one female pushing a shopping trolley containing what appeared to be a duvet and a tatty wooden guitar.

'Spare a few cents please,' the woman called out rattling a tin in Rob's face, presumably for donations. 'Help the homeless...'

'Sorry' said Rob 'I have no change.'

The beggars didn't go away. Will was by now banging on the door faster and louder as the woman went round them all violently shaking her tin while her man peacefully attempted to roll a cigarette.

'Help the homeless! Come on!' she snapped.

'Look we have no money for you – go away!' shouted Paul.

A security guard with a torch appeared on the inside of the door and opened the slot to investigate the commotion.

'Are you residents here?' he asked.

'Yes, of course, we checked in today,' answered Will.

'Well why don't you use your key?'

'We've been trying all our keys for the last ten minutes but none of them seem to work!'

Will showed the guard his key card to which he examined with his torch. After a moment the guard got out his metal keys and opened the lock to let them in.

'These new plastic keys,' said the guard, 'some of them haven't been working too good recently. This has been happening a bit - sorry about that.'

'It's no problem,' replied Will as they all entered the foyer, 'though those homeless people were getting annoying. Are there lots of homeless around this part of town?'

'Not that I've noticed but I'm new here,' was his reply as they looked back through the glass to see the old couple spreading their blanket under the doorway and no doubt realise that America wasn't perfect after all.

As they were walking tiredly up the stairs Conrad quietly suggested to Rob that they stay on the first floor for a soothing orange juice and maybe a couple of games of Streetfighter in the games room.

'*Streetfighter 2!* – have they got it?' said Rob, as if finding a second wind after such a long day.

'Yes, it's in there, I saw it earlier this afternoon. Do you remember it?'

'Oh yes – it takes me right back to 1992. Let's go.'

They left Will and Paul to find their way back to the dorm as they strutted into the empty recreation room which contained around a dozen arcade games, a table tennis set-up, three vending machines and a couple of beanbags.

'I wonder if they've got a poker video game in here?' speculated Rob. 'Imagine that - you could consider probability all night?'

'Yeah, but you can't read the faces of computers and the cards dealt would be automated and unnatural like on the Internet. I'm not going rusty on you don't worry; you're still my wingman but I need a break from poker. I need a game of Streetfigher – retro style.'

Rob walked over to a quarters vendor in which he deposited a five dollar bill. 'Prepare to die man,' he asserted dropping the coins in Streetfighter 2: The World Warrior; 'I was the champion of this at school, in fact I spent my last two years playing truant all the time just so I could practise.'

Conrad chose to be Ryu and Rob was Dhalsim. 'Round One Fight!' said the machine as the action began.

Seizing an early advantage Conrad leapt at Rob with one of Ryu's flying kicks. Rob could not block and instantly protested that at least two of his six buttons were not functioning. He began to slam the controls and wrestle the joystick in an obvious panic.

'I've got you here mate,' gloated Conrad.

'I don't think so,' was his reply.

Desperately trying to defend himself Rob somehow executed Dhalsim's yoga flame which fried Ryu in an instant. Their character's energy bars were now about even and the tension was mounting.

'Oh yes, it's all coming back to me now,' Rob made it clear but Conrad wasn't to be outdone; subjecting Dhalsim's rubber limbs to an onslaught of fireballs and forceful dragon punches that was in the end too much for Rob's defence as he was knocked out having taken maybe only half Conrad's energy.

'Best of three remember, that's only the first round,' Rob announced as if to salvage some pride. By the opening of the second round he adopted more offensive tactics and was shrewd enough to exploit Conrad's recklessness when some of his high flying hurricane kicks left him vulnerable.

'I can just keep you at a distance,' explained Rob, as if he had a plan that was running like clockwork. He was clearly not as skilled as Conrad but was now consistently draining his energy with effective slide kicks and head butts.

'Where's the skill in what you're doing?' asked Conrad in frustration.

Rob didn't reply, preferring to just whack the buttons in his usual way.

'I don't believe that,' spat Conrad as the inevitable happened.

'And it's a near perfect knock out, ha!' Rob crowed.

'Best of three remember. Now it's the decider, enough messing already.'

It was a deserted games room in a youth hostel in the early hours of a weekday morning but it could have been Madison Square Garden on pay-per-view considering the tension. It was a cagey first few seconds but Conrad soon moved up a gear; smashing Rob with a one two punch combination that he was unable to defend. Dhalsim was stunned and Ryu wasn't slow to exploit the situation; Conrad leapt in to cause maximum damage as Rob hammered the joystick in an attempt to regain control of his man.

'Excuse me, does anyone know where I can find the laundrette?' said a young female voice from over their shoulder.

Conrad turned his attention from the game but Rob, perhaps unsportingly, did not.

'Is it this way do you know, the laundrette?' said a girl, a slim Caucasian brunette in her twenties carrying a bag of lingerie.

'I think the laundrette is right up on the fourth floor,' replied Conrad, who was stopped in his tracks by her elegant British accent.

'You're better off taking the lift which is just through in the next hallway.'

'Okay thank you – I'll try not to get lost,' smiled the girl.

Conrad returned his attentions to the game only to discover in horror that his Ryu character was all but knocked out.

'Sorry mate but you know I'm not getting distracted from this game no matter how hot the girls,' said Rob without remorse, before he proceeded to finish the job using Dhalsim's yoga fire as the *coup de grâce*.

'You might have won but where's your sportsmanship?' asked Conrad.

'Dude, you got distracted – it's your own fault.'

'Did you hear that that girl was English?'

'I did. So what?'

'Notice how after a whole day of listening to and overhearing Americans the first English accent you hear cuts you like a knife?'

'Do you think you're in with her then – is that what you're saying?' continued Rob, now beginning to play the computer in one player mode.

'Not like that but I think our nationality will help us bond with fellow Brits while we're over here. I just felt it then; a bit of unity I mean, that's all.'

'Believe me,' replied Rob, 'British people are spread very thickly all around the world. The stars and stripes is really just another extension of Blighty. I tell you us lot must get through more passports than just about any other nationality on Earth.'

As Rob was getting bashed up into Canada and back by the computer Conrad ordered an orange juice out of one of the vending machines. Collapsing on a nearby beanbag and seeing his reflection in a window he wasn't best impressed. His hair was dry and split and upon taking off his glasses suspected a ring of freckly sunburn round his forehead. His sweaty T-shirt was stuck to his torso and a familiar cluster of itchy red spots had appeared round his lower lip that signalled the arrival of a cold sore. All he could hear was the sounds of Rob on the machine – he was soon defeated.

Back in room fifty four they found Will and Paul still up with the light on. They were sitting on the floor playing cards. Will had a lot of his video equipment spread over the floor charging from the mains.

'Where have you two been?' asked Will.

'We just had a game in the arcade,' said Rob, 'Have you sobered up yet?'

'Don't be cheeky. I've got my bag ready for swimming tomorrow.'

'Well I'm just going to bed. Are you two dying to keep the light on for a long time?' asked Rob, just about mustering the energy to haul himself up onto his bunk.

'I'm going to bed,' announced Paul throwing his cards down.

'Me too,' agreed Conrad similarly dropping his jeans on the floor.

'I suppose I'd better retire as well then,' said Will, beginning to turn off all the switches on his gear. It was nearly 3am when they all hit the pillow to the continuous sound of a fan piercing the air.

TWO

SEVEN HOURS LATER the four of them were queuing for breakfast in the dining room. It was busy with dozens of guests lining up with their bowls at the cereal machines and toasters. Staff were working flat out trying to keep milk, coffee and jam pots filled and table tops wiped clean. The clatter of cutlery was omnipresent as they found a table they could all sit at.

'I've gone for the old tried and tested cornflakes,' said Rob unpeeling the wrapper off his small block of marmalade for his side order of toast. 'Cereal is probably not poisonous but I'm sticking to what I know.'

'It's a safe bet,' agreed Will, 'you should try one of these croissants – though this one's a bit soggy.'

'You know we should buy a phone, like an American mobile,' said Conrad, 'between the four of us it won't cost that much…?'

'Mine and Paul's phones already work remember,' replied Will, 'I phoned him at the airport yesterday.'

'Just between us then, me and Rob, we could still afford it?'

'What?' said Rob looking up from his cereal.

'Buy a cheap mobile, the two of us..?'

'Yeah alright.'

'Okay good. Look I'm going to the Grant-Lee Phillips concert tonight or rather I'm going to make an effort to, are you all coming?'

'Where's it at?'

'It's at a club called Schubas Tavern. I'll just have to get the exact details today. Anyone fancy coming out for a morning walk though, to see the river maybe?'

'I'll come out for a look,' said Will as he scraped up every last spoonful of flaky pastry.

'I've actually got a few things to sort out at the moment' announced Rob. 'I've got to give my mum a ring and do some washing believe it or not. I'll leave you lot to it. I have to run down and buy a phone card from the shop. I'll see you back at the room – excuse.' Rob picked up his plates and put them in the dishwasher before squeezing past queuing diners on his way downstairs.

'I've got a bit of unpacking to do myself,' said Paul, 'sorting my clothes out, and I'm dying for a shower.'

When the remaining three were all fully satisfied they cleared up and returned to the dorm. Will zipped his camera into one of the thigh pockets on his shorts and Conrad picked up the postcard he'd written for mailing at reception. Walking out the door they saw Rob slamming down the receiver to one of the telephones on the landing. 'Do any of you two know how this phone card crap works?'

'Never tried it,' said Conrad, 'remember though after all the codes for the phone and card you press 011 to dial outside America and then 44 for the UK and then remember to knock off the first 0 of your local number. See you in a bit.'

★

OUTSIDE ONCE AGAIN the sun was incredible though unlike yesterday there was a pleasant breeze travelling up the Parkway. Looking at the crunched up map that had been stuck in his pocket from the night before Conrad deemed it wise to just follow the CTA stanchion north up South Wabash Avenue. This part of downtown was bursting with morning life. People sat outside cafes reading magazines and small supermarkets were receiving deliveries of all kinds of stock. Convertibles and hardtops were jostling along and store employees stood outside loudly urging people in for a look. And that was just at ground level. Tilting their necks upwards Conrad and Will were amazed at the design and ambition of the tower buildings that they thought could easily have contained Manchester's entire workforce.

'These buildings are amazing,' said Will fiddling with his camera bag, 'there must be some big business in these places.'

They walked past record stores, newsagents, electronic shops, banks and Internet cafes whilst being continuously reminded of the overhead transit screeching past. After nearly half an hour walking straight they came to a huge crossroads, over which it seemed that the enormous buildings had suddenly shrunk to about a third of their relative size. Conrad and Will carefully wandered over a nearby footbridge to look down and finally see the Chicago River horizontally cut across the street.

'Look at this in the middle of a city,' Conrad said, though quietly, perhaps not wanting to sound too much like an awe inspired sightseer, which he now most definitely was. 'You'd never even guess a river like this could be in the middle of a big metropolis.'

On the river two tour boats were leisurely gliding the waves and even a few swans were paddling away not unlike how they would in a Lancashire pond. Caged off less than a hundred yards over the northern bank was the construction of yet another skyscraper about halfway complete; it was surrounded by moving cranes, cement stacks and dozens of hard hat workers calling out to each other across the site. The ambition of the city's enterprise was incredibly still a work in progress. Conrad stood looking over the chiselled stone wall as Will snapped away.

'This must be the financial area of town,' said Conrad. 'Fancy another coffee?'

'If you want.'

★

ROB AND PAUL were preparing themselves for the day ahead. None of them were sure what that was exactly but Rob's suggestion the previous night that they go for a swim was certainly on the agenda. They were sitting on the floor reviewing and organising their belongings. Rob was measuring up what he could squeeze into his locker.

'So where do you want to swim then?' asked Paul, 'do you know where?'

'There must be somewhere round the lake. If we find somewhere are you swimming?'

'No.'

'Why not? Have you forgot your armbands or something?'

'Because I've grown out of it man,' replied Paul, who was maybe none too keen to show off his none too impressive torso. 'I'm in my thirties now you know!'

'Yeah so what? Don't be so boring. It'll be great - you should make every effort to enjoy yourself.'

Rob was ready in his polo shirt, shorts, sandals and wraparound shades that were for the moment pushed above his fringe. He'd packed a towel, spare underwear, socks and trainers. He wandered over to Conrad's pack and began searching for his guide book. Upon finding it he climbed onto his own bed and began flipping through the pages. Paul was still kneeling on the floor deciding what to wear.

'Where do you think those two have got to?' he asked.

'God knows, lost probably. Anyway do you fancy getting a train at least someway to LA?' asked Rob reading about the Amtrak Service losing customers – opening the possibility of cheap fares. 'It says here that rail travel can be a beautiful way to see the country. Also Chicago, it says, is the country's central hub for public transport.'

'I've heard that the rail network here is not as extensive as Europe? Does it say anything about where we can get off the train along the way?'

'No. Let's look on his laptop.'

Rob proceeded to remove the computer from Will's case that was now fully charged and immediately googled Amtrak. Paul busily packed away his belongings that he felt were redundant for the day having settled for a cotton shirt, trainers and tracksuit bottoms.

'It looks from this like we can get two trains,' said Rob, 'remember Conrad wants to visit Memphis and a train goes from here to there and there's another line that's more direct to California, through the Rocky Mountains.'

'Does it say anything about prices?'

'Not as far as I can see hold on...'

At that moment Conrad and Will arrived back at the room, Will immediately wondering why his laptop was in use and likewise Conrad his almost as useful guidebook.

'What kept you two?' asked Paul.

'We just went to see the river and had a coffee,' responded Will. 'Are you two ready to go?'

'Yes. What's it like outside? Do you not need to get anything before we go?'

'Not really,' said Conrad, 'we're okay as we are. Well I am anyway.'

'Me too,' confirmed Will picking up his bag that he'd prepared the night before. Rob shut down the computer and with the rest of them headed for the door. In the lift the four of them found themselves sharing with their countryman; the laundry girl from the night before who recognised Conrad.

THE DEVIL'S DUST

'Hello again,' she said in her gorgeous upper-crust accent. 'Are you guys in town for the big festival that's happening in the park this weekend?'

'Er no, we didn't know about that,' said Conrad, 'is that why you're here?'

'Yes of course, it starts on Friday, haven't you noticed that the hostel is filling up?' she smiled with some fine English sarcasm that they could all instantly understand. 'I'm really looking forward to it. Whereabouts are you from?'

'We're all from Manchester.'

'I'm from a village in Kent. Okay be nice to see you again, this is my floor see you later' she said departing for reception, leaving some to ponder staying for possible rock festival attendance.

'Do you know her?' asked Will.

'I saw her in the arcade last night,' answered Conrad.

'We should well stay at least another night to see some of this festival' announced Rob, though his motivation for wanting that probably wasn't entirely down to a passion for past it heavy metal groups.

'You've no chance with her mate,' said Conrad, ever on hand to dash dreams. 'Remember what your mother should have told you: "You can marry outside your nationality, you can marry outside your religion but under no circumstances should you ever marry outside your social class," because the British aristocracy of course have trouble understanding our stuff like, you know, cloth caps.'

'When did I ever say I was looking for a wife? Just an evening's entertainment perhaps...'

NOT THAT ANYONE was very familiar with the city but the first port of call was obviously Grant Park since no one was opposed to seeing if it was as stunning during the day as it had been at night. The temperature had become unbearably hot again with the blazing sun reducing everyone's mobility to mere strolls. They managed to gather the energy to get themselves down to the lawnland at the park's limit north along the coastline and into what appeared to be a private marina. Shoulders aching and feet starting to blister, everyone needed to recuperate. They noticed the luxurious speed boats that were evenly spread round the L-shaped harbour. The boats were decorated with sunbeds and flags and were all safely tied to several wooden jetties which ran alongside the pathway where they again paused to ponder. The city skyline had crept slightly out of sight and suddenly downtown Chicago looked like the Mediterranean.

'Well I can't swim in there,' announced Rob pointing out several signs illustrating just that. I wonder if we could get on a boat round here like a water taxi…?'

Following their ears they soon emerged from the boating yard to a minor slip road barely off an Interstate that just about gave them chance of hailing a cab. Rob stuck out his arm and a suitable vehicle duly pulled up.

'Can you take us to a beach?' he asked the driver as they drove off.

'This is Ohio Street Beach' said the driver, 'it's nine dollars.' They each handed him three one dollar bills, grabbed their bags and exited the car to see the most beautiful and modern looking beach any of them had ever seen. It was maybe only a hundred yards across from a grassy embankment and fifty yards long with golden sand quickly disappearing under the most perfect blue stretch of lake that couldn't reflect a single cloud. It was mid-afternoon and in the mid-nineties; weather indeed for a couple of hundred bathers to already be soaking up rays. As they walked across the road and down onto the grass seeing a row of now familiar skyscrapers emerge from across the delta was a sight to behold.

'I've seen nice beaches before and I've seen cityscapes before but never as close to each other as this. It's like Ibiza across the road from Wall Street,' said Paul.

Throwing their bags down at the end of the grass Rob was first to drop his combat shorts revealing his Union Jack swimmers, followed by Will. Conrad however would just strip to his boxers and leave his money, keys and glasses in his shoes. As he was taking off his T-shirt some serious looking sunburn caught Will's attention.

'Christ – you're like beetroot!' he said.

'Where?'

'On the back of your neck. Is it sore?'

'My neck is getting quite sore now you mention it but I hadn't realised. Paul, can I have some of your sunblock?'

Paul opened his bag and pulled out a tube of sunblock which Conrad took and began rubbing onto his hands. After he'd pressed his hand onto his chest and thighs Will and Rob did the same. Feeling safe Conrad leapt onto the sand only to start dancing around like Will in the Irish bar the night before, though with evidently less pleasure.

'What is it? What is it?' shouted Paul.

'Hot! Hot! The sand's burning my feet!'

Conrad moonwalked back onto the grass.

'It's not that hot is it?' asked Will.

'I dare you to put your full foot down on the sand for five seconds.'

Having had his pride called into question Will stepped off the grass and stood down full onto the sand only to flinch in pain and skip back to sanctuary.

'How are we supposed to get to the lake?' wondered Rob, himself poking down a big toe, 'it's half a football field away!'

'You're just going to have to make a run for it,' said Paul, rather smugly since he'd always made it clear that he wouldn't be stripping or swimming. Though the prospect was daunting, Paul was right - they'd been searching for hours for this place and it would be nothing but a waste of a day to not have a splash now. All that stood between them and their first swim since getting their length certificates twenty years earlier was a fifteen second run on white hot sand.

'Let's go,' laughed Conrad before departing as fast as he could. Rob and Will were hot on his heels. Hobbling on the outsides of his feet Conrad winced as he scampered forward. It was both funny and painful for him to see Rob and Will overtake him in the dash. Were they faster than him? Did they have a more efficient method of managing the sand? Either way having seen them come past his shoulder he expected to witness them each execute a beautiful Olympic style swan-dive into the water. A yard before the waves they tripped and fell in head first.

'We need to get some pictures,' half laughed Rob as he splashed around.

'What?' shouted Will.

'Pictures of us in here' he confirmed.

'We can't get cameras wet.'

'We don't have to get them wet. I'm going back for mine,' Rob made clear, implying that he intended to again take on the sizzling sand. Conrad too splashed around none too worried that being without his glasses would cause him many problems since eyesight was not required when floating in what was gorgeously cool water.

Will meanwhile kept disappearing under and re-emerging elsewhere as if his anchor had been dragged; on one occasion hilariously popping up and banging into the dingy of the passing lifeguard. On his return Rob approached a fellow bather to do the honours with his eight quid disposable. Arms wrapped around each other with the Chicago skyline in the background the photo would probably be a little overly sentimental but no one was bothered.

After an hour or so the return to Paul back on the grass saw everyone in good spirits.

'Man you should have been in there, the water is so nice' said Will.

'I enjoyed myself here,' responded Paul, who had taken fine care of their belongings, astutely covered himself in sunblock and had his sandals off allowing his feet to breathe.

Though it had only been a few moments since they left the water with just one scrub of their towels Rob, Will and Conrad were practically bone dry.

'This weather makes all the difference in the world — I love it,' confirmed Rob. 'Let's come back tomorrow..?'

Everyone else was already yards in front, walking back to the concrete and over the street onto a huge pier of amusements where they would thoroughly dry off before taking a taxi home.

★

BEFORE HEADING FOR the concert Rob and Conrad nipped out to get their hair cut at the barbershop they had seen the day before near the sandwich bar. They arranged to be back within the hour leaving Will and Paul to relax by themselves. With the two of them gone Will led Paul round to the hostel library.

'This is a massive place,' said Will swinging his laptop, camera and connecting lead as Paul lagged behind. 'We need to see if we can look at some maps and at least get a paper idea of our route, and I need to free up some space on my camera.'

The library was adjacent to the Internet room. Empty, it had two tables and walls covered by bookshelves. With Will on his computer Paul wandered into the Internet room, slipped a five dollar bill into the only available terminal and logged on himself. Anxious to know what was happening back home his first visit was to the BBC homepage that was, as ever, dominated by coverage of the Iraq war. Paul began reading

THE DEVIL'S DUST

as the rooms were becoming busier.

'Excuse me, can you get free coverage here?' said a redheaded girl to Will, understandably curious as to whether he'd paid for a password to a local wireless network that would have given him web access only feet away from where it was definitely costing Paul money.

'Yes, there is no code needed for the connection, well not so far anyway!'

'I wish I'd thought to bring my laptop, you know not just because it would be free but of course the ones in there are often all being used. Where you from?'

'England,' Will answered plugging his camera into his PC.

'England! Wow, whereabouts?'

'Have you heard of Manchester?'

'Just the name. My sister's currently living in Newcastle. She say's it's lovely. Have you been there?

'Er no,' responded Will, turning his attentions to her full time. 'Newcastle is quite far from Manchester.'

'Quite far? Your country is so tiny!'

'I have nothing to compare it to since I haven't really travelled before. Are you not from Chicago?'

'I'm from Australia.'

'Ah well yes then compared to your country England is very small!'

As they were chatting away Paul was still reading the news about the war. '*More troops killed this week in the Middle East. Record number of casualties but Blair stands defiant*' he read; initially assuming it was more exaggerated drama that the journalists had spun to stay in work; it was only after he read the name of a Regiment involved that his heart sank: The King's Royal Hussars – where he had spent seven happy years. As Paul read on with concern he became ever more distressed. A photo showed a soldier clearly wearing the uniform he once wore engulfed in flames whilst leaping out of a tank. Paul got up and left the building in a dazed panic, aching for some time alone.

'Oh looks like a computer's free,' the Australian girl said to Will on Paul's brisk exit, 'have to go.'

'Wait,' said Will to both Paul running in one direction and the girl another.

Noticing that Paul didn't give him any attention he followed the girl who sat where Paul had been and told her to take full advantage of his remaining credit.

'We're leaving on Friday, heading down south,' Will announced. 'Can I give you my email address? I want to know how you get on here…'

'Sure,' she replied, giving Will a beloved opportunity to hand her one of his sophisticated business cards.

Outside Paul was alone leaning against the railings watching the traffic go by. It could very well have been his former closest friends killed in Iraq; had he still been serving he himself could have been dead. Though he'd been out some years and not kept in touch with anyone, the realisation that life was so very precious had never been more sharply in focus than it was now. He was beginning to wish he'd never read the article and tried as best he could to put it to the back of his mind.

'All right there,' said a familiar voice.

Paul turned to see Rob and Conrad had returned from the barbers with Conrad especially sporting a smart new trim.

'What you doing out here?' asked Conrad.

'Nothing, just getting some fresh air.'

'Is Will in the dorm?'

'No. He's in the Internet library with some girl.'

'You coming up? I need a shower to get the sand out of my toes.'

The three of them returned to their room and found Will relaxing on his bed. Fatigued by all the miles they had walked the race for the shower started. Conrad was the first to feel the stinging pain of the water on his sunburned body but once fully rinsed, he saw a strange white blotch on his chest that did not hurt, though the crimson all around it did ferociously.

'I've never had sunburn this bad in my life,' he winced to the others who were playing cards on the floor. They looked up at his torso in amazement.

'What's that, the shape on your chest?' asked a slightly concerned Will.

'Look it's the shape of your hand, where you must have pressed on the sunblock,' explained Rob.

Conrad continued to look at himself in the mirror and realised that Rob was right. The white blotch of unburned skin was the perfect shape of his hand. It was where he'd simply pressed on only one handful of sunblock and not thought to massage it all over.

THE DEVIL'S DUST

'But we were in the water a lot of the time!' Conrad protested.

'Yeah so what? The water wouldn't stop you getting sunburnt. It proves that sunblock does work. Look everywhere that's not red is precisely where you put it on.'

Seeing the state of Conrad and feeling his own shoulders starting to itch, Rob removed his T-shirt and realised that he was almost as bad. He was next in the shower to rinse away his minced hair and learn just how sore washing would be for the next few days.

'Anyway how's your friend? That girl with the red hair you were talking to in the library?' Paul asked Will who had since returned to his trusty PC.

'She's Australian, that's all I got to know. I came up here virtually straight after you ran out of the room. What was that all about?'

'I just read something on the BBC website that I had to go and think about.'

'I've never read a lot on that site that says much to me about my life. There's always a lot of attention on foreign policy and all that, so a lot of the more national and local news doesn't get covered. It's always about wars that may as well be on different planets as far as I'm concerned.'

'I could be in that war, man. My old regiment got mobilised and sent to Iraq. I could be dead. That's what I was reading.'

Now brushing his teeth Conrad couldn't help but listen in on what was becoming a rare serious conversation between Will and Paul. Will meanwhile discreetly linked over to the webpage that had caused Paul the distress and began silently reading it. Paul continued playing with the cards; not wanting to react and embarrass him for saying how useless the war coverage felt.

'Come on Paul,' said Conrad now trying to carefully place in a contact lens, 'I picked Memphis, what's your nomination? Where would you like us to go?'

It was of course a deliberate attempt to lighten the mood but still a question worth asking. Paul seemed passively uninterested though; seemingly only able to just agree with everyone else's ideas: 'I wouldn't mind seeing Graceland while we're in Memphis of course....'

'Obviously – we have to don't we? Elvis was The King. Wonder if we'll be able to see the bathroom where he left us? Anyway listen I've got to get the directions to the venue tonight. I'm going to ask the information guys downstairs. Back in a minute.'

Washed, dressed and lenses inserted Conrad headed downstairs as Rob stepped out of the shower and took a first real look at his new haircut.

'Pretty good don't you think?'

'What?' said Paul.

'My hair.'

'If you say so mate.'

When Conrad re-entered the room he ushered everyone out: 'Everyone ready? Come on. The guy on the desk told me the venue is just one ride on the train that we get on one block from here. Just round the corner.'

★

IT WAS EARLY evening as they left the hostel and on the way to the CTA stop Will happened to see that they were walking past an electronics store that was by the looks of things just closing up for the day.

'You can get a phone in there, remember you two wanted a mobile?' he said.

'Nar they're closed now, we'll wait until tomorrow,' replied Rob.

Conrad tried the door and it was open. He asked whether they could do business and gestured everyone in.

'What's the cheapest cell phone we can get here?' said Conrad to the assistant.

'The cheapest?'

'We're on holiday see and all we want is a simple phone while we're in the country, you know nothing fancy..?'

'Oh right let's see then.'

As Conrad followed him round to one of the many wall units covered in mobiles the others walked round amazed at how much cheaper things were than at home. Not just phones but iPods, portable DVD players, laptops and computer software, some if which they even recognised as being less than half the price they were used to.

'If you really need something it wouldn't be a bad idea to buy it in LA just before we fly home,' Will said to Paul.

'Why LA and not right now?'

'Well if we buy stuff as we're leaving the country it's less luggage to carry en route.'

'Yeah maybe, but I'll probably be skint by then.'

While another member of staff was advising customers to make their final purchases Conrad was talking with his assistant.

'Well if you just need a basic phone then I can recommend this handset that offers nationwide coverage. It can send SMS messages, has a calculator, tip divider, calendar and alarm clock etc.'

'So how much is it?'

'Since it's on a promotion this week the price is just twenty dollars.'

'Right. And it's a top up phone? You know pay as you go?'

'That's correct.'

'I'll take it – though one moment please,' said Conrad before walking over to find Rob who was by the webcams. Rob handed over cash. Conrad walked back to the assistant who was rummaging under the counter.

'Here we are,' he said placing a box on the counter and flipping open the lid to run through its contents. 'Okay phone, charger, battery, instructions, warranty form. Right then that'll be twenty dollars please.'

'We want to buy twenty dollars worth of call time as well. Can you put it on the phone for us?'

'Oh no problem. Let's have a look then...'

Will and Paul were now waiting outside. It was still a sweaty evening but clouds had started to gather. Looking up at the tops of the buildings they could see a threatening pink sky and very occasionally a drop of rain would land on the back of their necks. The streets were less busy than they had been all day and that made a big difference to how the city was beginning to feel. The buildings, cars, roads and CTA facilities all still looked as overwhelming as they had but with more and more people having left for their suburban homes downtown Chicago felt less welcoming, dirtier and perhaps scarier than they'd experienced on their first night.

'People are all off home to get their rest before another day at work,' Paul commented.

'That's the good thing about being on holiday – you don't have to get up in the morning.'

'Yeah but you should – who wants to waste a day in bed? We can sleep just the same at home and at much less cost.'

Conrad and Rob walked out with the new phone. Conrad led the way to the train stop that was high above the street on a junction spread across two thin lanes of traffic. 'Right,' he said as they approached the sign steps leading up to the station. 'Let's have a look. We need to get on the brown line and stay on until Southport. The club's website says it's the nearest CTA stop; only about five hundred yards from the venue.'

On the train rattling briskly above the streets they saw that their destination stop was way down the line and the rain that had merely threatened just minutes ago was starting to slam against the carriage while the sky was now a menacing but undoubtedly beautiful red.

'So who are we going to see again?' Rob asked Conrad.

'Grant-Lee Phillips, at a club called Schuba's Tavern. According to this we're heading up to north Chicago where the club sits on the corner of Belmont Avenue and Southport - close to the Southport stop on this line.'

'What sort of music does he play?'

'He's a singer songwriter. Imagine Bruce Springsteen with Johnny Cash's voice...'

'Not my type of music.'

'I assure you it will be after tonight. Grant-Lee is the man!'

'Is your sunburn sore?'

'Yes, and so are my feet. It's getting a bit hard to walk comfortably.'

'Your feet?'

'After burning them on the sand today.'

Will and Paul had been quiet looking down at parts of Chicago that had none of the glitz of downtown and were now rain slicked and by the looks of things probably quite chilly. The turn in the weather had been instant and from one extreme to the other with even a flash of lightning adding to the turnaround. Northern Chicago looked a lot like the Manchester they knew; industrial and at that moment sparsely populated.

'I like the way the voice tells you where you are before every stop' said Paul.

This is a brown line train. Next stop is Southport. Please stand clear of the closing doors.

'See, it's very clear isn't it?'

Getting off Conrad slipped and nearly fell coming down the wooden steps of the station such had been the amount of rain that had fallen in the time since they were last down on the street. Not knowing where to start looking for the club he decided it best to ask for directions.

'Sir, can you please tell me where Schuba's Tavern is? A club somewhere round here?' he said to the first pedestrian he saw.

'Excuse me?' said the man.

'Do you know where Schuba's Tavern is?'

'Er no sorry I don't.'

'Oh well,' thought Conrad, 'someone round here must know where it is,' as the other three skipped under a nearby canopy to shelter from the increasing rain.

'Oh Schuba's!' said the man soon returning with a different, clearly more American pronunciation of the word.

'Yes.'

'Right sure. It's just about eight blocks down here on the left. Straight down you can't miss it.'

'Okay great thank you. Come on guys.'

The rain was now hammering down on the blackened streets that made it impossible to progress more than a few feet without getting soaked. Huddling in the doorways of cafes, theatres and dance studios many people, in what was, by the looks of things, quite a happening part of town, joked at how quickly the conditions had changed.

'Would you look at this,' Rob overheard a young man say to his girlfriend as they joined a cluster under a porch.

'And I left my washing out as well,' she replied.

'Paul what time is it?' asked Conrad.

'Nearly eight o' clock. What time does the concert start?'

'Doors open at eight.'

'Well it's not going to start for a while is it?' said Will, who had now pulled his arms inside his T-shirt to keep them from the rain. 'Anyone fancy coming for something to eat?'

'Are you hungry?'

'I am a bit, and I fancy being indoors right now and conveniently enough there's a restaurant right across the street…?'

They all stepped out into the bouncing rain and dashed over into Franco's where they were quickly shown to a table that was, luckily, pressed against a hot radiator and some way down from the door. A waiter came over and from a tray instantly placed four ice waters on the table before anyone had muttered a word.

'Decided what to order yet?' Paul asked Conrad, 'well I have; I'm going for the ravioli with parmesan cheese.'

'I'm taking the meatball sauce with pasta spirals,' offered Will.

'I'll take one of the pepperoni pizzas,' announced Conrad while Rob mentioned some kind of spaghetti whilst stripping the phone of its box and instructions.

'So you're ready to order then,' the waiter smiled down.

Everyone repeated their choice and this time all agreed to a bottle of the same beer. It was an easy decision since the waiter explained apologetically that due to a mix up at the supplier all they had to go for was Samuel Smith's Ale.

'Wonder if that's the same Sam Smith's I serve in my mum's pub?' remarked Rob.

'Could be,' said Paul, 'all the way over here. Does anyone know anything about renting cars?'

'I'll look it up later,' replied Will, 'I think we might be best off going back to the airport because all the companies will have branches there. There are so many googled on the net that we wouldn't know where to start.'

'If we drive we're going to need a big vehicle and I can't imagine it'll be cheap.'

'It might be,' offered Conrad. 'Remember loads of people are going on road trips across America this time of year so the companies will be undercutting each other to stay competitive and keep prices down, though I am curious about the price of fuel. If we drive all the way to LA and take the odd detour we're going to need gallons of it. I wonder can we study which cars we can get that gets the best value out of the fuel we'd need…?'

'Let's just splash out, that's what I say,' said Rob. 'I know we've all worked hard for this and been very careful to save up but look at people's lives at home. Some people who we knew at school have now got kids and all kinds of crap holding them back. We're lucky to be here and have this chance to see this country while we can. These are the days of our lives! Next thing you know we'll be thirty and I'm not looking forward to that!'

Paul raised his eyebrow upon hearing that last sentence.

'Oh sorry Paul!' apologised Rob for his slip.

'Hey I'm not that much older than you you know! Our age difference won't matter when we're all pensioners.'

'You're right,' agreed Conrad. 'Everyone gets old and life treats different people in different ways. We just have to learn to deal with it and a good way of doing that is by making the most of our time while we've got it. No matter what I'm going to spend and no matter what I'm missing in England I've no regrets about being here. In fact after just one day can tell it's going to be well worth it.'

'Anyway, we're definitely going spend a bit of time in Vegas right?' casually announced Rob as he sipped his water.

No one responded with any kind of enthusiasm. Rob took mild offence: 'We're booked onto a flight leaving LA and last time I looked Las Vegas was in that general direction so you know it wouldn't be a bad idea would it?'

'Hey I'm easy,' admitted Conrad. 'I picked Memphis next so when we've been there I'll go anywhere and be happy, though I've got this fear you'll get wiped out in Vegas.'

'Never. Honestly I'll bet small. Though we could win a bit if we employed say a tiny bit of our usual gamesmanship. The World Series Of Poker is happening out there this month and I tell you I wouldn't mind taking home a slice of the town's loaded economy anyway we can.'

Paul laughed, believing that the consequences of such tactics would be too horrendous for them to contemplate: 'Cheating in Sin City wouldn't just tarnish your visa but probably condemn you to one serious beating from the heavies!'

'Hey it's only cheating if you get caught,' assured Rob with a swaggering nod.

'Who wouldn't want a big jackpot?' agreed Conrad. 'Though I don't think either me or Rob would have a much of a chance playing straight against even half of Vegas. The best players in the world will be there preying on dumb tourists.'

At that moment the waiter returned with the drinks and Rob's eyes lit up with obvious pride since it was indeed the same Sam Smith's that he served in his mother's pub: 'Oh man you've got to get a picture of this. Will, come on get your camera out...'

THE VENUE WAS busy, though Conrad couldn't be sure if this was due to the popularity of the performer or since any passer by would have had to seek shelter given the continuing downpour.

'It's like an English pub,' Rob told Conrad, as the pair of them stood

THE DEVIL'S DUST

back from the bar having sent the other two for the drinks. 'It's quite a nice little venue,' he went on, now in the corner of the room nearly sat on a heater; a position that prompted him to point out a figure who in appearance blended together a cowboy, Indian and busker as he carried an acoustic guitar through to the performance room.

'Is that him?' he said with a nodding gesture.

Conrad turned and saw Grant-Lee Phillips hotfooting it alone to his set. 'Have a good show,' he shouted, half star-struck at such a sight.

'Thank you' replied Grant-Lee over his shoulder.

'Right here you are,' said Will as he handed Conrad his bottle which he took and rapidly headed into the audience as Phillips was plugging in and instructing his drummer. Will followed as the house light dimmed making it tricky for him to not spill any of his pint on the wedge of cheering bodies.

'You should have got a bottle, so you don't spill any standing up' Conrad shouted in his ear.

'I'll manage.'

On stage tuned in, amplified up and under the spotlight, the opening number from this quintessentially American artist originated in Manchester of all places; it was his folky cover of New Order's 'Age Of Consent'. Phillips's strumming of his Takamine twelve-string coupled with his honey-coated voice had the hundred and fifty or so paying customers instantly gasping since his sound was both gentle but sharp, soothing yet striking.

'Where's the other two?' Conrad shouted in Will's ear.

'I think they're still back in the bar. I'll go and see.'

Will crept back to the barroom and saw Rob looking worse for wear and Paul not much better on a bench together outside the hall.

'There you are. You two not coming in to see the show?'

'Yeah we'll be through in a few minutes' replied Rob sniffing and shivering.

'Okay.'

Will returned to the audience.

'Are you not feeling right?' asked Paul.

'I can feel a cold coming on and my head's starting to bang. You know when your eyes are watering and your nose is getting heavier and you want to carry on as normal but you just can't?'

Paul nodded.

'I mean I can hear from here that he's good, I just don't think I've got the energy to stand up in there for an hour and a half. Anyway, what were you doing before on your own outside the hostel?'

'Nothing really. Well I'd just read on the Internet that my old army were in Iraq and apparently a lot of them had been killed. Imagine that suddenly. What was I supposed to do?'

'I couldn't imagine it really. Well I can't. Why should I not take my life for granted?'

'When you were in and they made you declare that you'd give your life for your country did you ever think that you literally would? Even at that moment?' Rob asked.

'No. Honestly; I only served three years and never felt in any danger. Losing my life has always been a million miles from my mind. All that was years ago and I'm out now and what's going on over there has nothing to do with me and I can deal with it.'

'That's easy for you to say because you don't know if you would have been sent over, but I saw very clearly that my old regiment were there and the report wasn't good,' Rob looked concerned again.

'What can we do about it? Shall we go in and watch the show?'

'In a minute. Wait until I've drunk this.'

On stage Phillips was hitting his stride and Will was impressed enough to hold aloft his camera and film parts of the set for a video souvenir. The performer was intensely projecting his act and everyone absorbed it all; his guitar, voice and passionate physicality.

'He's good isn't he?' Conrad shouted to Will.

'Very.'

Phillips was now slashing at his guitar and singing in drawl and falsetto with what was obviously his every last drop of energy as the sweat poured from his brow. 'Lone Star Song' was his final number before an inevitable encore. Will stopped recording as the ovation began and went back in search of Rob and Paul who hadn't moved.

'This guy's great,' he said.

'We can hear that,' replied Rob.

'I'm going for another drink.'

Still worrying about international affairs Paul was unable to control his tongue, not helped by his evening's alcohol consumption that only quickened the slipping of his usual reserved personality: 'Have you noticed that the people who decide to go to war are never the ones who put their lives at risk, and they never put their family's lives at risk either?'

Though Rob was in need of some peace he tried to appear as though he was paying attention: 'Remember war is good for loads of people. Lots of businesses do really well from the repercussions of conflict and it stirs up everyone's patriotism. That wins votes for politicians and gives the servicemen a reason to wear the uniform. I mean many people say "what's a soldier that doesn't fight?".'

The pair of them continued to debate the merits of the war while Conrad watched the final few songs of Phillips's set and got chatting to him afterwards. Will meanwhile wasted no time announcing himself to drinkers standing around the place, the number of which had swelled even further since a nearby baseball game had been rained off. Two of his victims were a young couple who were not too disappointed to have not seen the game. The others were finishing their drinks and arranging to head home. It was getting late and having not made any return arrangements they each decided to try and get back to the train since there was a chance they couldn't get one into the early hours. Will though had other ideas once he'd been called away from his new friends.

'Come on guys, let's stay out,' he said. 'The night's just warming up.'

'Look Will it's been a long day again and I'm feeling a cold coming on,' Rob tried to reason. 'We have no idea where we are and it's getting late.'

'Well I'm staying out – you know talking to people, who I get on with.'

'Get on with people? They just think you're an annoying pisshead!'

'Look you stay right but we're going,' said Paul.

'Conrad you'll stay out with me won't you? Come on man we'll have a top night. Let them two go. Why they decided to come on holiday I don't know if they're just going to be tucked up in bed every night.'

Conrad frowned at Will: 'I really would stay out but I can hardly stand because of my feet. I burned them pretty bad today on the sand. Plenty of time tomorrow for more fun - come on.'

'No. I want to stay out and mingle with all these lot. You three are well boring.'

'You're annoying me now mate,' half shouted Rob. 'Me and Paul are definitely leaving when the rain stops end of story.'

'Conrad, come on mate.'

Will was making Conrad choose between him and them.

'We're not robots you know,' Conrad told Will. 'In other circumstances I would love to stay but we're going to miss the last train and I don't fancy just the two of us paying for a taxi all the way back to the city.'

Will walked off in disgust.

Rob and Paul got up and headed for the exit but since the rain was as heavy as ever they couldn't step out but smugly stood together in the doorway and proceeded to badmouth him. Conrad saw this and told them he'd have Will safely convinced and ready to leave in a few minutes. He hobbled back into the performance room, said his final goodbyes to Phillips and found Will again chit-chatting, this time with a roadie coiling up leads.

'We're going now. You know the address of the hostel, see you back there,' Conrad announced before turning to catch up with Rob and Paul who were now ten yards down the street. 'He can stay out if he wants; he knows where we're staying,' he told them.

'Oh well' said Paul, 'he can suit himself.'

Rob was silent and stone faced in his mission to quickly get back and try and rest his cold though Conrad did keep a concerned look over his shoulder almost knowing that Will would change his mind.

'Do you think we have already missed the last train?' asked Paul, as if Will's absence was the last thing on his mind.

'Let's hope not,' replied Rob who was now walking so fast he was almost skipping.

'Remember we're going back downtown, so we'll need the steps up to the opposite platform. There it is over the other side of the street.'

As they were about to disappear from Southport, Conrad turned again and finally saw what he wanted.

'Wait then,' they heard Will shout many yards behind, 'I'm coming.'

Conrad was relieved his bluff had worked since he didn't want the guilt had Will chosen to stay out alone. He dropped his walking pace to allow him to catch up and have company away from Rob and Paul, both of whom had unstable temperaments that could easily slip if Will got any closer. In two pairs the four of them jumped on the first train back during which barely a word was spoken.

The door of room fifty four was opened and the light flicked on. Paul got first look and was alert enough to spot another bed taken above Will's place. Someone else was trying to sleep in their room. After the surprise he instantly switched the light back off and closed the door without letting anyone go in.

'What?' asked Rob.

'There's someone in there trying to sleep.'

'Where?'

'On the bunk above Will.'

'Right. Everyone just be really quiet and go straight to bed. Let's show a little consideration.'

THREE

IT WAS ALMOST MIDDAY when the first signs of life emerged. Rob's feet hit the floor first and he was off into the shower. Will and Conrad were coming round while Paul, who had created a wall down from Rob's bunk with a sheet pulled from his mattress was slower to wake. Since nobody could see him this fact was made obvious only by his snoring.

'Morning Paul,' shouted a mobile Conrad pulling aside his wall. Without opening his eyes Paul gave Conrad the V sign: 'I'll get up in five minutes.'

With a yawn Will emerged from his duvet and pulled on his T-shirt and like a shot had his laptop powered up and logged on to the hotmail site. Conrad looked at Will on his first level bunk and silently pointed his toothbrush upwards.

'What?' asked Will.

Conrad tiptoed from the sink and saw with relief that all that was on the bed above Will was a tousled duvet.

'Wasn't there someone up there last night?'

Will jumped up and looked to see that the second level was empty.

'There was oh yeah; up and out then, nice and tidy. I didn't hear or see a thing. Paul, did you hear that guy go out this morning?'

'I'll get up in five more minutes.'

Rob stepped from the shower as Conrad had finished at the sink: 'I hardly slept last night,' he said, 'my nose is still blocked and that Japanese dude kept cracking his knuckles all night. I was going to twat him.'

'Did you see him then?' asked Will.

'He got up and went out at about eight o'clock this morning. Why's Paul done that with that sheet?'

'Perhaps he's up to something in there that he doesn't want anyone to see.'

'Because the air conditioning was freezing all night, blowing right in my direction,' moaned Paul. 'What time is it?'

'Nearly twelve,' said Conrad looking through his bag for clean socks. I'm going to need some of your aftersun for my feet. My shoulders are starting to peel now.'

Paul sat up, emerged from his den in a slinky robe and flipped open his immaculately tidy case and threw his aftersun in Conrad's direction. Conrad threw it back.

'I can't really spray my own shoulders now can I?'

'Okay come here. It's a good job I thought to bring all this stuff.'

'So we're going to find out about trains today?' said Rob.

'If I remember rightly the Amtrak station's not far from Sears Tower,' said Conrad as Paul was squirting his back with the lotion, 'it's apparently the tallest building in America so if we're in the area I wouldn't mind having a look...?'

'You know my dirty washing's building up and my bags are starting to stink,' announced Rob, as if anyone needed reminding of that odorous fact. 'I need to hit the laundrette and sort all my stuff out before we set off tomorrow. We could do with putting together to get a box of powder because we're all going to be doing a lot of washing remember...?'

'I'd rather just buy packets at the laundrettes,' said Paul, 'it's not dear is it? For now though why don't you just have one of your bags for clean clothes and the other for dirty ones?'

'I might just throw away dirty socks and cheap T-shirts,' said Will. 'I'll be too busy enjoying myself to do anything that's neither fun nor necessary.'

★

DOWN AT RECEPTION there was a trickle of new arrivals queuing up but it wasn't too busy. With Conrad queuing to get directions to the station the others sat by the pool table.

'How did you know that guy who stayed in the room last night was Japanese?' Will asked Rob.

'I didn't. I just assumed Japan because he was Oriental.'

'Could you not tell exactly?'

'What?'

'Could you not tell if he was from Japan or China or wherever?'

'Are you serious – just by looking at him? I saw him when I was half asleep in a darkened room for about ten seconds. What a stupid question.'

'You can tell what country Orientals are from,' Will persisted.

'I've heard you talk some nonsense over the years but that just about tops the lot. Paul have you heard this?'

'I'm speechless.'

'Alright then tell us, those two girls,' Rob said pointing across the room to the pair who organise the bus tours from their first day, 'they're Oriental right so which country exactly?'

'They're too far away for me to tell.'

Much to Rob's delight they started walking in their direction. 'Come on, tell us now.'

Even if Will was brave enough to stick his neck out the girls were so close now they would probably overhear anything he said.

'Hello again,' said the one with the father in English football PR. So are you guys looking for something to do today?'

'Yeah I suppose so,' said Rob.

'Okay right do you guys know of the Sears Tower at all?'

'We were just talking about that, the tallest building in America?'

'Yes that's right,' said the other girl.

'What about it?'

'Well since it's the tallest building and people want to go up there and see the view, if you guys would like to go you can get discount tickets from reception here. Though if you do want to go you have to be quick because there's only a few left for today.'

'Oh right okay thanks, we'll certainly think about it. Can I ask you girls a question?' Rob politely enquired further.

'Certainly, you can ask us anything you like,' replied the first girl.

Will, knowing what the question would be was already deciding the answer.

'What's your nationality?'

The three of them held their breath as the second girl answered: 'We're American, we're sisters but our parents are English. See you later.'

Conrad walked over with yet another map fully marked up and

saw the three of them sat there speechless after having been wrong-footed again by people who were younger, female and even worse, foreign.

'Everyone okay?' he said.

'Just about. Those girls told us that we can buy cheap tickets to the observatory at Sears Tower here, shall we get them?' asked Rob.

They all got up and found that tickets were a very reasonable ten dollars and each made a purchase, especially upon leaning that they could go up and look until ten at night.

Outside it was a fairly grey day with still some evidence of the previous night's downpour. Nonetheless heading north up South Wabash Avenue and west along Adams Street four travellers now confidently followed their directions over the river, carefully crossing all roads and this time had shrewdly thought to cover all their exposed skin with sunblock just in case.

From the outside Chicago's Union Station looked like a government hall with a majestic stone shell disguising the start of a huge four lane escalator that disappeared deep into the Earth. They had likely been walking above the platforms for some time. Following a further underground walkway clearly signposted for enquiries they almost had to cut across the platforms where the trains themselves were far bigger than their British equivalents; double deckers in fact. They continued walking along the pathway and often had to step aside for railwaymen to proceed with their safety checks. Whistles were blowing, digital clocks were counting to departures and engines were exhausting odorous steam while purring with fuel. Coming to a brightly lit information desk it was time to enquire about prices and times down to Tennessee.

'Who's going to ask?' said Will.

'I'll go,' said Paul turning to approach the desk.

'Can you please tell me how much are one ways to Memphis? There are four of us and we would like to set off as soon as possible.'

The guy started typing into the computer.

'Four to Memphis. Well one's leaving this evening but it looks like that's fully booked but, I can tell you that there's also one leaving tomorrow at the same time; 6pm. Would that be good for you?'

'Yes.'

'Economy travel on the New Orleans bound and alighting at Memphis…that will be a total cost of nine hundred and forty dollars.

That's for seats in an eight man carriage.'

'And how long is the journey?'

'It should take about ten and a half hours.'

'Okay thank you very much.'

Paul walked back and told the others to which there was a mixed reaction: 'Nine hundred and forty for four?' said Conrad. 'What's that? About two hundred and thirty dollars each?'

'I think it's too much,' voted Rob, 'it's a lot for nearly a whole day sat on a train with strangers don't you think?'

'Right well let's not pay for anything just yet,' said Paul, 'we'll just make a note of it and when we know about car prices we'll decide then.'

'I say we just forget about the trains altogether and take a car all the way' announced Conrad, 'there's more chance of us getting lost if we take a car..?'

'Obviously that's a good thing,' quipped Rob.

'For the last time - it's the whole point!'

Though Sears Tower was the tallest building in the country it may as well have been a needle in a haystack for someone unable to see the city's skyline. According to Conrad's map the Tower was only three blocks away and, never out of his depth he announced that they had actually walked past it on their way to the station; they had in fact passed the corporate side that wasn't marked for sightseers.

'Do you think a place in the Sears Tower would be expensive to rent?' asked Will.

'Are you thinking of relocating your business to Chicago?' asked Rob sarcastically munching on a hotdog he'd just bought.

'Since it's the tallest in America the landlord can probably charge a couple of hundred dollars just for that.'

'I wouldn't pay any extra just for an office in a high building, though now that you mention it they're charging us just to see the view, so I suppose I would' observed Paul as they wandered back over the river.

Counting the junctions Conrad was determined not to miss the base of the building though to correctly identify it he did have to compare what he saw when tilting his neck to the images he remembered from his books. 'I think that's it' he announced.

The others looked up and saw a topless tower that looked like a cluster of square chopsticks racing up past each other. Walking round past revolving doors and top-hatted doormen they came to an entrance that had anyone not been looking carefully could easily have been mistaken for a service door. Proceeding in, Conrad led them to the visitors' desk where they were met by two smiling women and a security guard.

'Hello, we have tickets to go up today.'

'Okay the next elevator departs in fifteen minutes. Can we take your tickets please?'

'Sure.'

It wasn't an airport but airport security was in full effect, complete with an X-ray door and conveyer belt for belongings and loose clothes. Conrad even had to take off his belt. With shoes back on and following a young female escort they stepped into a roomy elevator and waited patiently to see what all the fuss was about. A dozen people were squeezed in when the doors closed and only seconds into their ascent their ears began popping at the altitude. The express elevator took less than a minute to travel over a thousand feet and once the doors opened, their eyes almost popped from their heads.

'Alright then,' said Will stepping into the enclosed observation deck. It was of course very uncool to appear awestruck but staring through the glass far out across Illinois, Indiana, Michigan and even Wisconsin couldn't fail to move even the most passive observer. Looking down to the street, pedestrians looked like ants and the surrounding family of skyscrapers couldn't have been more stunning had they been a daydream. Though it was an overcast day down on the street, Chicago from its highest point again looked sunkissed and amazingly peaceful.

'Let's just get a couple of photos then,' said Rob handing Conrad his camera and posing in front of the glass with his back to the east side and the lake. Conrad took the photo but was doubtful that the imagery would show up well considering the bright exposure and the notoriously unreliable quality of cheap disposables, the like of which he too had to use.

'Too bad we didn't think to get digitals,' said Conrad, 'We'll have to get Will to snap us with his. Where's he got to?'

Will was attempting to shove a quarter into one of the metal telescopes round the other side with which he could probably see Stockport.

'Will, can we borrow your camera for a while?'

'Okay.'

Paul was busy deciding what souvenir to buy from a shop that was well stocked with shirts, caps, key rings, photos and all kinds of miniature Towers.

'Impressive don't you think,' he said, catching up with them having decided on a modest but still shockingly expensive key ring.

'That it is' said Rob. 'America looks brand new doesn't it? I mean especially from up here. I can tell now how old and dirty England is. Honestly there's nowhere really in the UK that can offer a view even half as spectacular as this is there?'

'Maybe not, but according to some history and tradition is worth celebrating just as much as growth and development.'

'Anyone who thinks that is scraping round for second best. This is absolutely incredible. There's no comparison for me; we're light years behind.'

'What is Sears anyway?' asked Conrad.

'I don't know. I only know of it because of this tower. It's probably a computer company or something.'

'If you jumped off the roof here it would seem like you're flying like a bird,' said Paul. 'I mean it would be a good height to skydive from, especially if it's windy.'

'This is the middle of a city, not exactly your traditional skydiving location is it?' replied Conrad.

'That's not what I'm saying. I mean it would seem like you're floating round on the air, even though you would actually be dropping like a stone.'

'Would you like to skydive?'

'The thought has crossed my mind.'

'Well why don't you just have a word with security over there. I'm sure he could open the door for you. And who knows, he might just have a prepared shoot for you all ready to strap on and jump out?'

'I will if you will?'

'I bet he'd take his baton out and beat us raw on suspicion of terrorism, you know judging by the level of security here.'

'You've got a point.'

After making sure they got all the pictures they wanted with everyone's cameras the time to leave came when the next elevator of punters arrived and made the already small deck seem even smaller.

'I want to phone home and tell my mum that I was just at the top of the tallest building in America,' said Rob stepping into a descending lift past the photographer without posing for his blue screen souvenir.

'Have you done that yet on your phone?' asked Paul.

'I haven't actually. Before I forget Will what's your number there?'

Will told him his number which Rob stored in the address book and then instantly rang. Will received the call and likewise stored the incoming by the time they were back down on the street feeling both dazed and confused.

'This is our last full day in Chicago remember, the last night we've paid for at the hostel and I'd like to make the most of it' said Will. 'I think we should head back and get our things packed before tonight. I don't want to be rushing tomorrow before kicking out time.'

Walking back around town the sunshine had come out once again as the city was approaching rush hour. Passing a newspaper seller Paul was compelled to pick up a copy of the *Chicago Tribune*. Though the heat wave was the headline there was a sidebar article about the situation in Iraq that typically caught his attention. '*Bush stands firm over Oil Dispute*' was the sub heading that led into another distressing report about the hardships the servicemen were suffering in the line of duty. Paul began to lag behind reading the article; missing green walk lights and banging into fellow pedestrians, some of whom were bold enough to tell him to watch where he was going.

'Where's Paul now?' said Conrad looking around to see him nowhere in his sight.

'There he is still across the road,' replied Rob. 'Hurry up,' he shouted above the traffic. Paul tucked the paper under his arm and caught up wearing a straight face though he was again hurting about what was probably happening to his former colleagues.

'Alright?' asked Will.

'Yeah – just picked up a paper that's all.'

Arriving at a pedestrianised square not far from the hostel they saw several wooden huts positioned in neat squares selling barbecue food, vegetables, milk and cheese. It was a farmer's market in the middle of the city and some thought it worth a look. Will and Rob took a wander as Conrad and Paul sat on a nearby wall.

'Do you feel American yet?' asked Conrad.

Paul didn't respond, instead choosing to unfold his paper and carry on reading about the war.

'Good to see the sun back out..?' continued Conrad.

'What? The sun? Oh yeah it's good. The guys who make the

decision to send people to war, where the hell do they get their motivation from?'

Conrad didn't want this conversation but played the diplomat: 'I have no idea. I suppose some people simply need conflict and thrive on it and that's what will get documented in their legacy, which they're all so desperate to secure.'

'A war? Where many people die?'

'Yeah. If a Prime Minister wins a war they'll be remembered as a great leader no matter how poorly they may perform in other areas.'

'It says here that America's profits from the oil trade in the Middle East could quadruple should their militaries' occupation of Iraq continue into next year.'

'Quite possibly, so what?'

'Didn't they say long and loud that there was some kind of terrorist threat to the West that needed to be sorted out and it was time to overthrow dictators and liberate people?'

'Yes they did.'

'Well if it was about oil money then why didn't they say that at the time?'

'What difference does it make? Anyone can do what they want until somebody stops them and no one can stop those guys unless they get voted out, and anyway you shouldn't believe everything you read.'

'And you're an expert?'

'Well I am a reporter and when it's a slow week the editor tells me to just pad stories out with a bit of exaggeration.'

'And you do?'

'Papers all have their own political agenda that caters for readerships which simply become constituencies at election time. The people that vote for pro-war politicians are at no risk and like to believe that they're winning regardless of whether they are or not.'

'So how do they benefit?'

'Well oil money might certainly be one way.'

Looking across the square Rob and Will were spotted talking to a dealer whose business looked to be in meat.

'There they are,' said Conrad with a nod of his head.

'So kids out there are getting killed for oil money then?'

'Is that what the paper says?'

'More or less. When I was a soldier it was the best time of my life and I wouldn't have swapped those years for anything but I could be dead now.'

'Yeah but you're not; you're here. Anyway you should have known the risks when you joined. You didn't think you'd be on holiday for seven years did you?'

'Well I was in a way - since I travelled everywhere and had everything paid for.'

'But you didn't pay any attention to world events that you could have got caught up in?'

'There was a bit of talk about us getting sent to Kosovo but I was too busy enjoying myself with the lads to pay any attention. I think we were in Berlin at the time.'

'Doing what?'

'We were very badly behaved, especially at weekends I'll admit that. Some things are legal in Germany that are not in the UK and we took full advantage of it shall we say...'

Rob walked over looking frazzled and sat down next to them.

'What have you been up to?' asked Paul.

'Nothing. He got talking to this butcher woman and it looks as though she's convinced us to buy some of her meat. There's simply no stopping him sometimes.'

'What the hell's he done that for?'

'Search me.'

'Well you agreed?'

'Well I would have just walked but I didn't want to appear rude when she started talking to us.'

The three of them looked on and saw Will count out a roll of cash while the woman strapped closed a bag full of ingredients.

'I don't believe this! Look he's just spent a fortune. I gave him thirty dollars and told him that I expect plenty of change.'

'What are you going to do? Go back to the hostel now and cook a lovely evening meal together?'

Conrad laughed at Paul's thought.

'I would have just said no but she started writing down one of her recipes and priced it all out before I could say a word. I swear I'm going to knock him out!'

Will walked over carrying his shopping as if there was nothing at all unusual about his recent purchases: 'Everyone okay?' he asked.

'Are you for real?' snapped Rob inspecting what little change he did get.

THE DEVIL'S DUST

'Now what? I just bought us some chops and dressings.'

'We're on holiday and can afford to eat out every night and you go and spend a fortune on cooking ingredients?'

'I thought it might be a nice change. You know a bit more cultured?'

'More cultured? Let's go before I lose my temper,' said Rob storming off with Conrad and Paul hardly able to hold back the giggles. Will remained as thick skinned as ever.

'Which restaurant shall we go to? Paul said loudly to Conrad, 'fancy a nice Mexican at that place round the corner?'

'Not a bad idea there mate.'

'Good luck,' Conrad said.

Paul was gracious enough to control his tongue and not make any jokes about the beautifully domestic situation the other two found themselves in. He and Conrad knew that Rob and Will in a kitchen together would be good guys to avoid and arranged to see them back at the dorm within a couple of hours.

'What are the chances of Rob killing Will sometime time in the next hour?' remarked Paul now that their backs were turned.

'I'd say about two to one. The hostel kitchen contains every appliance a chef could want; especially sharp knives that could come in handy!'

Paul laughed as they entered a dimly lit and almost empty restaurant that had an American South West theme. Spread across the walls were images of the Grand Canyon, Monument Valley, John Wayne and Geronimo. The tables were decorated with candles and menus parodying wanted signs from classic westerns while trumpets cheerily provided the soundtrack. The all-female waiting staff were dressed in full Navajo regalia.

'I'm going to wash up,' said Paul leaving Conrad to study the menu alone. Looking around the dusty room Conrad noticed a large wooden plaque nailed to the wall close to his shoulder. On the plaque was a silver plate inscribed with what appeared to be stylish religious symbols and a paragraph of readable text in a scratched gothic font. He took a closer look:

The man tied to the pole and burned with the hammer was a witchcraft ceremony practiced in New Mexico until the eighteenth century. On the hottest days of the year ancient families would kidnap unsuspecting visitors and offer them to the Antichrist. The four symbols was how this destructive cult was identified and have since been adopted in popular culture by rock groups and graffiti artists

'Entertaining stuff,' he thought.
'So have you ordered a drink?' enquired Paul on his return.
'Not yet.'
'Well what have they got? A nice selection of draught and bottled beers I hope. So do you think the girls in here are hot?'
'What the waitresses?'
'Well yeah.'
'You know if any of them are really from the South West they may be descendants of a family that would torture innocent victims and offer them to Satan you know.'
'What?'
Conrad showed him the plaque as one of those waitresses came over to take orders.
'Alright can I have a bottle of Tiger Beer please,' said Conrad.
'And for you?' the waitresses asked Paul, looking back from the plaque.
'I'll have a pint of Miller.'
Paul returned his attentions to the plaque. When he'd obviously finished reading it by the look on his face he was clearly amused: 'Total rubbish I bet.'
'Well you never know, like history is full of weird stuff and you know how militant some religious groups can be. Anyway what are we ordering?'
The menu offered nachos, fajita wraps, quesadillas and grilled peppers; all the usual Tex-Mex combinations with no shortage of salsas, cheeses and lentil bean toppings. When the girl came back the dishes that got their votes though were the Carne Asada for Conrad and the steak Jambalaya for Paul while they would split a side order of chicken wings with onion relish.
'Did you know there was a Chicago football team?' said Conrad pointing to the small match report on the back page of Paul's paper.
'No I didn't. Is that them? The Chicago Fire?'
'Think so. Why do all the American sports teams have names like that?'
'To make them sound like superheroes maybe?'
'Yes. Our cousins over here clearly prefer to wrap their entertainment in a way different to us – more showbizzy.'

The place was filling up and the clientele was quite cosmopolitan judging by some of the accents. Paul and Conrad were intrigued overhearing a conversation between a waitress and an American couple who'd chosen to go to England on their summer holiday for which they were departing tomorrow.

'Did you hear that?' said Paul. 'That couple over there are from Chicago and they said they're going to see the English Lake District and the Peak District castles.'

'Well yeah, apparently one of our most lucrative industries is tourism. I heard that when watching News 24 last week. I can't imagine why though. When I look around all I see are grey buildings and litter. I can't say I've ever seen much more in Britain in my entire life.'

'That's because you're an urban person. You've got everything you need on your doorstep in Manchester. City slickers live in a bubble with no real need to broaden their horizons. I learned that when I was in the army. All the barracks I was based at were out in the sticks and let me tell you when the weather's nice Britain can be a beautiful place.'

★

SINCE FINISHING UP Rob had taken his dirty clothes up to the laundrette and Will had gone back to the room where the door opened and in walked a young man who introduced himself as Stefan and began unpacking.

'Hello. Where are you from?' asked Will.

'Germany; I'm from a place called Wiesbaden. And you?'

'England; Manchester.'

'Alright. So are you in Chicago on holiday?'

'Yes. Are you?'

'Kind of. Well right now I'm a group leader for some of the students on our college trip. We've been coming to Chicago every summer for a few years now. We like it here.'

'So what do you do at the college during term time?'

'I teach French and English.'

Immediately feeling daunted by Stefan's bilingual sophistication Will thought it best to check that it was just the three languages he was fluent in: 'Right. So you can speak German, French and English then?'

'Yes,' replied Stefan, 'but in Italian and Spanish I'm only conversational and need to work more on my reading and writing before my big exams this year.'

'So you're hoping to become head of languages or something?'

'No,' Stefan laughed, 'I see the teaching as a temporary job just to pay my bills and give me the chance to travel at someone else's expense. I aim to be a politician for Germany's European embassies before the G8 summit in Heiligendamm next year. I think it's important that in such a hierarchical continent as Europe is right now that taxation, trade union power and public spending are all increased before the selfish fat-cats end up exploiting us all using up too much of the Earth's natural resources in the process. Don't you agree?'

Intimidated, Will just nodded his head, totally unable to say anything on an equal level of sophistication.

Up at the empty laundrette Rob had inserted his quarters, bought his powder and sat watching his clothes spin round the drum. Sat with his back to a hot and vibrating tumble dryer and seeing his shirts fall round and round was a situation that just about sent him to sleep. He didn't notice when two tanned guys walked in including one who intended to collect his clothes from that very dryer.

'Look that guy's asleep; I'm going to have to wake him to get my clothes out... Excuse me...' he loudly continued; a speech that woke Rob with a start. 'Can I please get my belongings out of the dryer there?'

'Oh sorry of course,' Rob replied apologetically before standing and stepping aside, 'I've had a long day, you'll have to excuse me. So, you guys on holiday then?'

'Sure are,' said the second guy throwing a basket of clothes into a washer and slamming the door. 'We're here for the festival; our first day is tomorrow, what about you?'

'Me and three others have been here since Tuesday. We're driving across to LA. We're setting off tomorrow.'

'And where you from?'

'England. And you?'

'I'm from Texas and he's from New Mexico.'

'We'll almost certainly be passing through Texas if I remember correctly. I don't suppose you could you tell us anything about it, anything at all?'

'Well Texas is real big. It depends where you go really. Like I'm from San Antonio which has like a huge Mexican influence but other places like Dallas and Houston are very Republican. Do you know which part you'll be in?'

'I don't. We might end up anywhere since we have no set route.'

'So you may also be going through New Mexico then if you're driving to LA?' assumed the native who'd since thrown his still damp clothes back in the dryer.

'I suppose so,' half agreed Rob transferring his own laundry from the washer to a dryer.

'When I'm not at college in San Antonio I go back there to see my mom. I'm from a tiny little town called Tucumcari east of Albuquerque. New Mexico is not really a sightseer State but if you're stopping by there are some neat little places that celebrate the culture and mix of people who live there.'

'The mix of people?'

'You know there's like American, Mexican, Hispanic and Latin people and all their descendants spread throughout the State.'

'Right. And everyone gets on fine I hope?'

'Oh yeah. Well most of the time. There's like the Native Americans who still practice their traditions that some don't agree with but it's usually okay. So you going out tonight?'

'Me and the guys go out every night without ever knowing where.'

'Well we're going to this blues club not far from here, don't suppose you fancy coming along?'

'Er…I don't see why not…I'll mention it to the guys. Anyway what are your names?'

'I'm Mark and that's Ed.'

'I'm Rob. Well my clothes are almost done now. I have to get back to my room and pack for tomorrow. Look might I see you guys at reception around say eight o' clock then?'

'Sure.'

'I can't say we'll make it but I'll try.'

'No problem.'

With that Rob left the laundrette and returned to fifty four to find Stefan stood explaining to a bewildered Will Germany's role in the European Union. Walking across the room he accidentally kicked the small portable fan causing him to trip and drop some of his newly clean laundry.

'This is Stefan from Germany,' said Will, 'and you've just broke the fan.'

'Fancy coming to some blues club tonight? I just met these guys who invited us out?'

'Who?'

'I don't know. These guys are from Texas and New Mexico, and if we're going I said we'll see them at reception at eight?'

'Well let's wait for Conrad and Paul to get back and see what happens,' reasoned Will who, like Rob, had begun to tidy his bed and at least try to pack away his belongings to save the trouble in the morning. Stefan went off to meet some of his students in the TV room passing Conrad and Paul on the landing.

'Who was that guy?' asked Paul.

'That's Stefan,' answered Will, 'he's in here now. He's from Germany.'

'Was it a total disaster then, your romantic meal together?'

'It was quite good actually; I didn't know I was such a good cook,' Will answered, going to look for a phone to call maintenance about the fan.

'It was a nightmare in the kitchen,' contradicted a horizontal Rob, just as they always knew it would be. 'But once we'd got the fryer working we managed. Anyway we've been invited to some blues club tonight by these guys I met while up doing my washing. You both coming?'

Paul and Conrad passively agreed and also set about getting their things together though they didn't take long. It was only Will's heap of video leads that was spoiling the floor.

'Maintenance will be round to fix the fan tomorrow,' announced Will on his return, only to be met with three bodies lay silently on their beds.

'What's this? Everyone having a cat nap? I think I might join you.'

★

THE RECEPTION AREA was bursting with arrivals, departures and revellers waiting to meet up and head out. Hearing all the languages and accents and seeing the different complexions they had to realise that they were experiencing an international leisure culture embraced by many young people for whom it was clearly a way of life. Old friends were meeting up and others were hugging and swapping email addresses arranging to meet again on the other side of the world. It was almost an exclusive community, the like of which everyone knew could never exist in the franchise resorts of Benidorm or Tenerife.

'Not tempted to hang around to maybe see some of this rock festival?' Conrad asked whoever.

'I kind of want to get going now since we've had a decent look at Chicago' replied Rob.

'And how've you found it?'

'Oh good, but we have to get going. My eyes need a new adventure. The thing is about this travelling is that it's only special like this for a short while. Look at all these getting emotional and saying they want to stay forever, but the pain of leaving is only a reaction to the thrill of discovering somewhere and some people new so it's important to keep moving.'

'I'm getting a bit sad actually,' mentioned Will. 'These have all been our single serving friends this past couple of days and sometimes they're the best you ever have.'

'What's a single serving friend?' asked Paul.

'The type that you know for only a brief period and you know you'll never see again.'

'Interesting.'

No one was expensively dressed and many travellers had only minimal luggage. Noting a single black girl flick through the pages of her passport everyone saw that she'd been round the globe and she can't have been more than thirty.

'I need to change my lifestyle,' announced Will. 'I may be stuck in a nine to five soon and I'm dreading it. I'd like to get lost somewhere in the world and not have to worry about time or money like this lot.'

'Would you like some of my Kleenex?' wondered Rob as he identified the guys from the laundrette approaching.

'Hi there, so you guys coming with us?' said New Mexican Mark with Texan Ed by his side.

'Yeah let's go,' answered Rob who proceeded to introduce everyone while they took the short walk to the club.

IT WAS A LARGE dark room with two bars, four pool tables and a small stage on which a big guy with a still head, shades, beard and slide on his fretboard was screeching out some delta blues. Maybe three quarters full, there was a small TV crew filming the performance while ornament guitars, discs and press cuttings were proudly displayed in cases around the walls. While everyone went to the bar Conrad took a closer look at the articles and noted that they all mentioned the great electric bluesman Buddy Guy. The discs were certified sliver, gold and platinum for record sales and the instruments were signed by the man himself. He found a table and somehow managed to hold it with five chairs and called everyone over when they'd finally been served.

'Had I known this was Buddy Guy's club I would have had us here on the first night,' he said to Rob who handed him his drink.

'Is he famous then?' asked Rob.

'Well I know who he is. All the guys like Clapton say he's a total influence on them and has been for decades.'

'Okay,' said Mark obviously impressed with Conrad's knowledge. 'So then, what do you guys do for a living?'

'Well I write for magazines, Rob here is a security guard and occasional barman, Will runs his own video business and Paul's a lorry driver. What about you?'

'Well we're both students in San Antonio. We study Biological Sciences but we also work. I'm a part time usher at a theatre and Ed works in a call centre for a real estate company.'

'What brings you to Chicago then?' asked Paul.

'The big rock festival here in the park this weekend.'

'Yeah we heard. So what do you think of the hostel?'

'Oh it's fine,' answered Ed. 'It's a bit strange having so many people to talk to all the time, like there's always something going on and people to do it with.'

'Have you seen the two Oriental girls yet?'

'Oriental girls?'

'Well they look Oriental.'

'Actually I think we have. They're the two sisters from New York right? They tried to get us to go to a yoga class yesterday. Remember Mark? The leisure organisers?'

'Yeah what about them?'

'Don't ever try and get into an argument with them. They're too clever,' answered Rob to some uncertainty from the Americans though Will slipped a chortle which provoked Rob to elaborate: 'I was never really interested in what country they're from. There's no such thing as background anymore is there?'

'I thought you were once a solider,' replied Will, 'and you always took pride in your background and had a great interest in people's nationality?'

'I was younger then and not as well travelled. I was just a kid from a Lancashire mill town who thought that the only people in the world were English-born with maybe a little Indian or Pakistani dilution.'

Mark and Ed listened with interest.

'Do you now think that's just naivety?' continued Will.

'Yes I do; the world's far too small. We're in America you know; the land of the immigrant and I've seen the benefits already. I mean just look at how hard people work here. Everyone thinks they're going places and those girls probably are.'

'Yeah, but that's because upbringing is probably not such an issue to people over here the way it might be for us.'

'What do you mean?' asked Ed.

Will took a deep breath and began: 'Well I've got this theory that because we have a prominent Royal family we understand that your status in life is hereditary, like who your parents are can hugely influence your life chances whereas here the impression I get is that opportunities are there for the talented and hardworking regardless of background like nationality, ethnicity or social class.'

'I've got an idea then,' suggested Conrad.

'Go on.'

'Let's kill the entire Royal family...? Well it worked in France?'

'Yeah I'm well up for that,' Paul piped up.

Rob could see Will's point but was not convinced: 'Where they can, parents everywhere have always bought their children a flying start in life haven't they? It's a good point but things are never going to be equal anywhere.'

'I think the British Royal family are totally cool,' said Mark. 'You shouldn't compare your life chances to people like that though. My expectations in life are not that high; I just want to make an honest living and have some fun.'

'Well if you just want to make an honest living what the hell are you doing all this studying for?' asked his mate, 'I mean you can do that working at a gas station.'

'I'm just at college to meet girls.'

'Right well then I want at least three wives in my lifetime and many more mistresses. I want four vacations a year, a private jet, a season ticket for the San Antonio Spurs and a big country house with a pool shaped like a guitar. Well it could happen?'

'It could. A guy who I was at school with now turns over half a million dollars a year since he's built up his family's shoe business,' mentioned Mark. 'He lives in mansion in San José now but when he came back he told the newspaper that his success is entirely down to hard work. In just ten years he's gone from rags to riches so it can be done.'

'If it was his family's business then he didn't start from square one himself did he?' questioned Rob.

'No. If I remember correctly the article said that he found a gap in the market: it was the need of women who practise aerobics.'

'I think that's just a bit of luck. Finding and exploiting a gap in the market is not just the result of talent and or application is it? The hardest working people are likely to get exploited if you ask me.'

'How do you mean?' asked Conrad.

'There's this patriotic myth flying around that if you work hard, learn and show some ability you can in fact reach the top and become one of life's winners, but I think a lot of the people who say that were either born into success, incredibly lucky or are bosses trying to temp their employees into working harder for promotions that they simply won't get.'

'Man that's a bit cynical,' said Mark.

'Honestly. The people at the top are ignorant as much as anything,' continued Rob.

'Like how?'

'Well imagine a world where there was no ignorance and ethnicity, experience and the like wasn't an obstacle for progress...what would happen? Obviously a lot of the people at the top would get overthrown so they ignore the threatening application of anyone who might replace them. It's human nature to protect your assets.'

'Something tells me you're not too happy with your life at the moment. You're only in your mid-twenties, you still have plenty of time to catch a break and show what you can do?'

'Mid-twenties? Christ! Time is flying past and I haven't achieved anything. My brother is two years younger than me and he's getting married, having a baby and is doing well in construction.'

'Working construction? That's like a blue collar job right?'

'He's a bricklayer.'

'Like a job that he just took to keep busy and get money?'

'I suppose so.'

'Man, life happens too quickly for a lot of people. Jobs, children, responsibility. It can be too much in your twenties; people make their beds too young, get stuck and miss out on so much.'

'We know that. My brother could never afford to come here since he's stressed out all the time. I've like been taking just temporary jobs in security and at my mum's pub that I can always walk away from.'

'What about education? Did you guys ever try college or ever think of going?'

'Conrad and Will went through college together and after school I went in the army for three years, worked in factories and then tried college last year but had to drop out because it was too expensive.'

'Three years in the army? That must have been cool,' said Ed.

'I was in for seven!' gloated Paul.

'Wow. So what do you think of Tony Blair then? We love him in Texas. He seems a man of real conviction?'

'Tony Blair and the student tuition fees he introduced is the reason I'm now in thousands of pounds of debt,' said Rob, speaking for himself Will and Conrad.

'I don't really care about him to be honest, though at home he's getting a lot of strife at the moment because of this war,' answered Paul as he got up and made for the restroom.

'Get us another drink,' said Will handing him the cash.

'Seriously man,' Conrad said to Ed as Paul was halfway across the room, 'don't be asking him about Tony Blair. He just learned that his old crew are out there in Iraq right now and are coming under some heavy fire. Really. We saw it on the news yesterday. He's been stressing us that had he still been severing he could be one of the casualties.'

Without saying another word everyone turned their attentions to the stage where, according to the flyers scattered around the table, it was the Bryan Lee Blues Band who were singing about being sad, blue and alone but forever loyal to Jack Daniels.

'Bet you don't see this kind of music too much in England?' wondered Mark.

'Have either of you ever been to England?' said Will.

They both shook their heads.

'Well you're not missing much,' interrupted Rob getting up. 'Is it my round?'

Conrad confirmed that it was, before being compelled to find out what he could about Mark and Ed's knowledge of his country: 'When you think of the UK what do you see?'

'When I watch British TV shows I see like tiny little houses and think of soccer hooligans,' laughed Ed.

Rob and Paul returned from the bar with another round but it wasn't everyone's usual order. On their trays were several glasses of spirits and shots, evidence a plenty that suggested what they had in mind was a notorious English drinking game.

'What's all this?' asked Will.

'I recognise the drinks,' Conrad began to explain to the Americans, 'if you chose not to answer the question you're asked truthfully then you have to swallow a full glass in one go okay?'

'And why are you telling us?' asked Mark.

'Because you guys are going first!'

Mark and Ed looked at each other in curiosity. 'What if we just tell lies?' asked Ed.

'Then you'll bring shame on your country. And we'll tease you mercilessly for the rest of the night about how badly you speak our language and how you got your asses kicked in Vietnam.'

Mark and Ed braced themselves.

'Come on guys, right now our countries are allies at war so we should be allies in the pub too,' reasoned Rob handing Mark his glass. 'So Mark, your question first: have you ever dressed up in women's clothing, and if so under what circumstances?'

'What?'

'You heard.'

Five eyes were dangerously staring at him earnestly awaiting an answer. Mark took his time, considering the forfeit of a glass full of he didn't know what.

'What the hell's in this?'

'It's a thermonuclear English poison that has been known to severely paralyse lightweights. That's why we were so long at the bar; we had to tell the girl all the ingredients. All we want is the truth. Now tell us have you ever dressed up in women's clothing, and if so under what circumstances?'

Mark took a deep breath, screwed his face up, closed his eyes and picked up his glass...

'Will, you should film this on your camera,' announced Rob in anticipation. 'It's going to be a moment to remember.'

THE DEVIL'S DUST

Mark threw the contents of his two inch glass down his throat only to open his eyes with slow relief. It was water. Rob and Paul giggled uncontrollably.

'It's water,' remarked Mark in surprise, 'and I only dressed up as a woman in the school theatre when I was thirteen!'

Everyone laughed.

'Ed it's your turn,' said Paul manoeuvring all the glasses round the table like a magician. 'Now tell us, in your opinion who's the sexiest famous man you've ever laid eyes on?'

'Sexiest guy?'

'Yes tell us, and you can't say Tom Cruise because Will secretly longs for Tom and he'll end up killing you in a fit of jealousy.'

'No I won't,' corrected Will, 'not for him. George Clooney's the only man for me actually.'

'Man I'm thirsty,' conceded Ed. 'I just want to drink this anyway. And besides I don't mind admitting that the man I'm most attracted to is the man in the mirror. Cheers.'

Unlike his college buddy, Ed swallowed the drink he was given since it was indeed the vicious cocktail he'd been warned about; a screwball vodka.

'We told you it's pretty strong stuff,' commiserated Paul.

'No I loved it,' said Ed after a pause, 'hold on let me try again.'

Ed slugged another glass, and then another. No one could be sure if it was because he did indeed love it or he just couldn't have his pride taken away by these ludicrous limey hedonists.

'I can match that,' then demonstrated Will with Paul right behind. While no one said anything too serious in with all the laughing it was obvious that they were getting more than just tipsy; they were all moving onto the stage where their intoxication would be getting sickening and shortly after quite dangerous. Then far-sighted Conrad had a sneaky word in Rob's ear.

'Aren't we driving like five hundred miles tomorrow?'

'Ay, as far as I know.'

'Well you know if we have like banging heads and murderous hangovers we're going to struggle a bit don't you think?'

Rob looked at Conrad with horror and realisation. 'You're right we should slow down,' he announced. 'Mark, Ed, you've got more balls than we thought you had but remember we've got a long drive tomorrow so we won't be overdoing it from now on.'

'Who's coming for a game of pool?' asked Conrad.

'Sure I'll play,' said Ed following him to the tables, 'are you good at this?'

'No. My main sport is poker. I never play pool, nor do I know the proper rules but here goes...'

With Rob and Paul watching the band Mark got talking to Will, asking him about his most recent video job that had been filming a school choir in London only a week before. It put Will in a frustrated mood but he was not too sulky: 'The kids were hard work - they just wouldn't do as they were told. They kept asking "is this going to be on TV" and "when can I have a DVD?" Not to mention them messing with my mic leads. What a nightmare.'

'Kids are all like that. So was the money good?'

'Yeah well in the business when you're busy the money is generally quite good but this time when I'd paid for all my equipment I may just about only scrape the minimum wage. It's at least a good stepping stone you know?'

Mark nodded politely - not wanting to appear surprised at how Will was working so hard for what appeared to be so little.

'He got ripped off, as always' interrupted Paul who'd been listening as the band went for a breather.

'I don't always get ripped off at all. Well the money might not be that great at the moment but I get to travel around the country and meet different people doing something I love and as long as I can hold off a standard nine to five I'm doing alright.'

'I'll give you credit for that man,' supported Mark. 'My father says that anyone who enjoys what they do for a living is nothing but lucky, in fact I think he's really jealous of people like that.'

'Why is that?' wondered Will.

'Well he wants us to know that he basically failed in life and became nothing more than a journeyman, not that he says it directly but he's always moping around gloating about how he's give up so much to work as hard as he has - like he wants loads of credit - but I say "If you don't like something you can always try something else".'

'Will might enjoy making his videos but since he's doesn't actually make enough net to live on technically it's not what he does for a living. I suspect there's a lot of borrowing funding his existence,' said Paul.

'Yeah so?' countered Will. 'There's nothing wrong with investing when I'm young and have the time to develop.'

'Nonsense! You should live within your means. That way your life will always belong to you and not some threatening bailiff.'

'Anyone thinking about wrapping up for the evening?' asked Conrad back from the pool table still mindful of the next day's slog.

Everyone looked at each other and without saying a word eventually rallied together and agreed. They headed back to Hostelling International, stopping off for fajitas along the way.

★

SOMEONE'S DRUNKEN MISTAKE saw everyone step out of the lift on the third floor and still wonder why they couldn't find their dorm. Following Mark and Ed who went into the half-full TV room Rob was first to mention a loud cheer they all heard from the nearby dining hall.

'What's going on in there at this time?' he asked Conrad behind him.

'How should I know?'

'I'm going for a look.'

After five minutes away Rob returned full of excitement: 'Man a group of guys are playing poker in there; there are two tables of Hold 'Em going. Let's go in and clean up? How much cash have you got on you?'

Conrad pulled out a fat roll and smiled since it was he who first introduced Rob to poker.

'Same tapping signals remember?' said Rob as they set off for the dining hall, referring to their tried and trusted method of communicating whilst appearing to play fair.

'I don't think we should both play at the same table – in case we slip into old habits...'

'Why not? No one will suspect a thing if I'm the dealer. Anyway what's the risk in here? Looks like easy money to me.'

'I don't care; we may be out of our depth here. You sit at the other table and take what you can. I'll put down two hundred dollars?'

Rob was annoyed but had to accept Conrad's stubbornness.

'Guys can we join in?' asked Conrad.

'Sure. Pull up a seat; you're in next hand,' answered Dylan from their check-in, the spokesperson for the four others sat round his table. 'We're playing limit Hold 'Em where players are dealt two private cards then three flop cards are upturned on the table; these are presented to all players and with additional betting a sixth and seventh community card is available to make the best hand.'

'What are the stakes?'

'The betting structure is ten dollars before and on the flop and twenty dollars thereafter with four raises per round. If you need ten, twenty or five dollar bills you can use the dispenser down in the arcade.'

'Five dollar bills?'

'For when you're the first blind.'

'Sure. We've got plenty of notes.'

After his invite Rob took his place at the second table and was often cocky enough to raise after every new card and even hang around to expensively see the sixth and sometimes even seventh card. Maybe it was too much pride but his inability to fold early cost him almost a hundred and fifty dollars within an hour. Scraping the odd small pot now and again hardly kept him afloat until he was forced to go all in and thereafter disappear with a whimper. Miffed, he turned his attentions to the other table where Conrad had been doing almost as badly.

'Come on man...' one of the players said to Conrad, '...we haven't got all night! Call, raise or fold...'

Conrad's impatient opponent was one of two other players waiting for a decision. There were thirty five dollars in the pot – fifteen from the blinds who'd since folded - and Conrad held the ace and seven of clubs. His two remaining opponents were a guy from Canada who held the king and queen of spades and a guy from Detroit who had two jacks – diamonds and hearts. Conrad was relieved that there were no raises since he now couldn't really afford to pay more before the flop. He called with ten dollars and overturned the ace of spades, the jack of clubs and the two of diamonds and he immediately felt good. With his pocket ace, the one that had just turned over gave him the strongest possible pair so he called. The Canadian had nothing, but since his bankroll was high he would almost certainly pay for at least one more card since he was now in with a chance of landing an ace high straight should a ten appear. Mr Detroit, of course, now had three jacks which put him in the lead so he also called. Seventy-five was now in the middle.

'It's everyman for himself this game,' said Conrad with laugh. He didn't think much of it but his opponents were looking for clues – it could have been an emotional slip or it could have been nothing. 'It's a metaphor for life poker; you know, decisions, decisions, and it helps if you first arrive with a lot of money.'

'But you're English?' said the Canadian, 'you guys all live in palaces right?'

'Oh yeah, course we all do. No one's born poor in the UK.'

Rob was looking on. He may have been wiped out early but with the stakes rising he couldn't help but feel the tension.

Conrad didn't have much left but having a pair of aces he wasn't too worried and like the other two merely called the now twenty bucks to see the turn. A hundred and thirty five dollars was now for someone's taking that could well be helped by the arrival of the eight of spades. It was twenty dollars for no benefit as far as Conrad and Mr Detroit was concerned. The impatient Canadian still had nothing but the new eight was his fourth spade – he still had one card left for a ten that would give him a straight and now one more spade would give him an ace high flush. Everyone was happy but again cautious. Without raising or folding everyone threw in their twenty for the final card, dragging the pot up to a hundred and ninety-five dollars. Conrad took a peek at his hole cards; they were still there - the ace and seven of clubs. The dealer produced the seven of spades. Conrad now had two pair: aces and sevens; it looked like his investment this last hour was about to be doubled but if it wasn't he would be all but wiped out. Again there was no raising – everyone called the twenty to see and bring the grand total up to an eye-watering two hundred and fifty-five dollars. The majority in the room were now preened for the showdown, Rob included. The dealer said 'on your backs'.

'Two pair; aces and sevens,' announced Conrad flipping over his own ace and seven.

Mr Detroit: 'Three of a kind; jacks.'

Conrad was hit with that sinking feeling that all players know. He was beaten by a hand a rank above his own. Detroit was acting cool, as well he might believing he was about to take the pot but of course he too was not to know that Canada wasn't bluffing; he'd got his spade and had made his flush. Winning right up until the river card was even more painful for him and when Canada had the thrill of throwing down his cards, poker, like life, was cruel for some but incredibly lucky for others.

With Rob staring on in disgust at Conrad's unsuccessful attempt to play fair the pain was too much to bear.

'Come on, we're going,' said Conrad as he headed back into the TV room as Rob ran after him.

'What was the point in all that?' Rob demanded as they plonked themselves down on the sofa next to a sleepy Will, Mark and Ed, Paul had already retired to the dorm. 'Suddenly becoming a saint for the night when we could have taken it all, you know, like we've been doing at home!'

'I can't win all the time,' Conrad tiredly replied back, relieved to be out of there. 'You know there's a lot of luck in the game. You got cleaned out early because of just bad luck right? There's not much satisfaction when you win by cheating is there?'

'But money talks!'

Conrad got up and left for the dorm with Rob following him.

'What's happening with those guys?' Mark asked Will.

'They must have lost money at cards again. Listen write down your email addresses for me. I want to drop you a mail to let you know how we get on. Enjoy the festival.'

'Oh sure. Nice knowing you guys. Tell Paul, Rob and Conrad to take care.'

Will shook hands with Mark and Ed and headed back to the room where he found everyone including Stefan sat round on the floor.

'Not bother to say goodbye to Mark and Ed then?'

'No,' dismissively replied Conrad.

Will fell on his bed and kicked off his shoes. He was out for the night.

'So how much did you lose tonight then?' asked Paul.

'A couple of hundred dollars' said Rob.

'Between you?'

'No. Each.'

'Ouch.'

'I'm wanting to go to bed. Don't forget to turn the light off when you've finished.'

With Will and Rob retired, Conrad sat down next to Paul and Stefan and explained what had just happened and neither of them had much sympathy.

'Everyone plays poker in this country,' said Stefan. 'There are some really good players here.'

'But I really could have won. I just got a bit reckless too early. I'll know to be more careful next time.'

'There shouldn't be a next time should there?' Paul said, though he knew that his words would fall on deaf ears.

'It's not a problem. I can easily win the money back if I get chance.'

Not saying a word Stefan shook his head recognising a gambler's addiction as Conrad headed for the bathroom. When he came back they too had turned in for the night.

FOUR

EVERYONE WAS JUST about ready and quietly sat on their beds making an effort not to wake Stefan. Check out time was in an hour and the plan was to jump on the train back to O'Hare where they would get breakfast, rent a car and hit the road. Bags were packed, belongings secured and rubbish was cleared; it was only courtesy to leave their quarters as tidy as they found them.

'Is your head banging?' Paul said to Rob.

'I'm not too bad actually. I'm still pissed off about losing that money last night. I should have sat down with a clear head.'

'Hurry up Will. What's keeping you?' asked Conrad.

'Nothing – I'll be ready in a few minutes.'

Conrad knew full well what was keeping Will; as he predicted as soon as he opened his case on arrival he knew he'd struggle to get it closed again. His video leads were not coiled to fit back where they'd come from and it was his own fault; he was holding everyone up and the longer they waited the more chance there was of waking Stefan and losing precious road time.

'I'll be ready shortly,' again said Will in an increasing panic trying to rearrange things.

It was almost inevitable that the others would start talking about how important it was for them to make good time and began to hint more of how impatient they were getting. Rob made sure that Will saw him looking at the time on his phone and Paul began pacing up and down. Will meanwhile had tried for a third time to repack and still couldn't find the space. Something had to give; it was either carry some clothes or his bulky power supply.

'You've not even used your big camera so why did you unpack it all?' said Rob. 'Guys, perhaps we should try and book another night?'

'We may as well do,' agreed Paul as there was a knock at the door. Conrad, who was closest, skipped to answer it since further knocking would almost certainly wake Stefan.

'Hello maintenance. There was a report about a broken fan yesterday?'

'Sorry?'

Rob and Paul came to the door to see what was happening.

'Oh yes that's right,' said Rob, 'the fan is broken. It was like that when we arrived.'

'I need to take a look,' said the boiler-suited man as he marched passed them and placed his tool bag on the floor.

'Christ, he's finally ready' said Rob as Will was suddenly packed and wrapped. 'Everyone got their key cards ready for dropping off? Let's go.'

'We're leaving now' said Conrad to the repairman as he hauled his backpack onto his shoulder. 'Goodbye Stefan mate, whenever the hell you wake up.'

As they approached the desk Conrad and Rob saw Dylan with a painful chuckle on his face no doubt in commiseration with them about their financial loss the night before. One by one they marched past him dropping their keys into the slot in his desk. 'Come again sometime,' said Dylan in a way that English poker losers knew was blatant sarcasm, even from an American.

'So we're definitely not getting a train down to Memphis then?' said Will, requesting simple confirmation that it was by road that they would travel.

'I'd rather take a car the whole way,' said Rob. 'I just think it's better to be in control of where you go and at what time really.'

'It's no problem,' replied Will heading down into the train stop where they would wait a few moments before boarding a carriage back to the airport.

★

AFTER BREAKFAST PAUL led everyone to the travel section in a huge bookstore that must have contained a map of every major country in the world.

'Good thinking Paul, we need a road map but which one?' wondered Conrad.

Paul picked up two and randomly found a page in one and went in search of the same part in the other. Once he had made a comparison and decided which one to buy it was time to find the car rental offices that lay somewhere round the airport. After getting assistance they gathered that they were all on the outskirts of the complex and required a bus journey to get there. Not that anyone had studied the cost of renting but the mere name of one company – Budget - sounded no worse than any so Budget it was.

Looking out the window of the Budget bus en route to the depot everyone silently said goodbye to Chicago. Those who had wanted to begin the trip in New York now didn't mind having been outvoted since their three days in the Windy City had been a great experience and a practically perfect introduction to America. Zipping across the concrete past the terminals and control towers everyone was excited to move on and see what the next day would hold.

'Remember I won't be driving,' said Rob, 'since I'm still banned.'

'But that's in England man – who's going to find out?' reasoned Conrad. 'I haven't driven in years but I'm not going to miss this opportunity. I think we should share the responsibility between the four of us.'

Rob was adamant that he wouldn't drive. 'Remember you have to pay separately for each driver on the insurance and the cost will add up.'

'Okay. Who's coming with me to the desk then?'

'I will,' said Will as the bus pulled up and they went to join the queue in the foyer.

'Put me on the insurance as well,' said Paul waiting outside with Rob.

Will confidently strutted up to the desk: 'Right we would like to take a car away today and return it on the twenty third of this month at LAX. Four people are travelling and three of them wish to drive. What have you got?'

Conrad was impressed at Will's poise as the woman began typing into the computer.

'All the way to LA...you guys doing Route 66?'

'We may well do.'

'Awesome. Right then we've got a brand new Ford Freestar that's out in the parking lot and ready right now. The total cost for what you want is two thousand three hundred fifty dollars. Would you like to make that rental?'

Upon seeing the picture of the vehicle in the catalogue in front of them Will and Conrad looked at each other and nodded affirmatively: 'Yes, we would!'

'Okay can I see your IDs and licences please? And I need you to fill out these forms.'

They both obliged while Will opened his mouth and asked: 'Do you accept cash then?'

Both the woman and Conrad looked at him in bewilderment.

'Just kidding' smiled Will smoothly unleashing his new credit card which promptly failed. Three times.

'I'm sorry sir but that card's been rejected. Is it foreign?'

'What?'

'Here take mine,' said Conrad handing over his American Express which processed perfectly. 'My flexible friend. Never leave home without it.'

'And where's your first destination?'

'Memphis.'

The woman photocopied a street map of Greater Chicago and with a highlighter pen marked up the route out of the airport and onto the Interstate while they signed the papers and folded the information receipts.

'Who wants the keys?'

'I'll take those,' said Will with a beaming grin.

'The vehicle is out in space D3 with a full tank. Have a good journey.'

PART TWO: THE HEARTLAND

FIVE

THE SILVER FOUR SEATER Freestar had never been out on the road. Brand new and gleaming in the Illinois sun, Will took one look at the vehicle and with a grin clicked the central locking button on the key ring while behind him everyone looked on with excitement. This big machine would be both their wheels and virtual home for nearly three weeks.

'How much is this baby costing us then?' said Rob.

'Two thousand three hundred and fifty dollars' answered Conrad. 'Nearly six hundred each. Is it a lot?'

'Who cares!'

'What are we waiting for?' said Paul opening the back door and throwing his cases in the space. 'Do we know how to get on the motorway from here?'

Conrad gave him the marked-up street map and slid open the side door and hopped into one of the two back seats. Before rotation it was to be Will driving with Paul his map reader with Conrad and Rob in the sightseeing rear.

With all luggage secure Will leapt behind the wheel, started the engine and looked at the dashboard. It was like *Knight Rider*. There were digital clocks and dials for everything. Speed, fuel, engine conditions, door status, radio controls and a lordly air conditioning facility that would clearly be put to great use. The gears were simplified to drive, park, neutral and reverse while the two pedals were simply go and slow. Backing out of the bay gently they pulled out of the lot and onto a one-way road still in the airport.

'Right well what does that street map say then? Which way? Left or right from here?'

'Hold on. Give me chance,' replied Paul in a panic almost as intense as they joined the flow of traffic heading for the junction out to the real roads, 'just go left.' Will did just that; slowly turning the wheel and heading out over a roundabout and onto the correct side of a sparsely busy dual carriageway and to keep pace gently pressed the accelerator.

'Alight,' said Rob, 'away we go.'

'Anyone got a clue where we are?' again said Will in another cry for help.

Paul was squinting at the street map which in his opinion wasn't a great photocopy.

'Look there's even a clock, compass and thermometer' announced Rob pointing to a display in the roof that read 15.10, SE and 92c.

'The woman told us this was a state of the art vehicle' said Conrad. 'It even has a satellite tracking device to find us if we get lost.'

'What do you mean "If we get lost?" It's inevitable we're going to get lost. In fact we're lost right now!'

Everyone laughed except Will who was still focused on the road but was beginning to enjoy the smooth handling and the surprisingly clear road signs which told them they were heading south through an industrial estate, the like of which surrounded airports the world over.

'I think you should just drive straight when the compass says south' smirked Rob. 'At least that way we know we're going in the right direction.'

'Look "Interstate 57 – The South including Memphis"' said Will reading from an overhead sign with pride in himself and disappointment in Paul; who for someone officially appointed 'map reader' was yet to say anything of any use. He was busy switching his attention to the nationwide atlas they'd just picked up in the bookstore.

'Just follow those signs then,' said Paul trying to find Chicago land.

'You're a genius,' Will sarcastically replied.

The traffic was thickening since it was approaching rush hour and unless they got out of the urban sprawl soon there was a great chance they'd be gridlocked in a rough looking suburb. Graffiti was suddenly everywhere and peering out over the edges of the widening freeway lanes, battered project blocks and derelict factories dominated the landscape.

'No problem is it driving on the right?' Conrad asked Will.

'No.'

'Does everyone believe we'll make it all the way to Memphis in one go?'

'Why not?' said Rob.

'Because it's about five hundred miles!'

'Look,' announced Paul pointing up to another overhead sign, 'I-57 straight ahead. Memphis 490 miles.'

Likewise seeing it and manoeuvring into the correct lane, Will put his foot down and pulled away from the sluggish suburbanites in their 4x4s towards the beginning of 57 where with a bit of luck they could eat up some serious road well down into southern Illinois. Accelerating, he saw Chicago get smaller in his rear-view mirror then pressed down on the brake no more than a mile later. 'We're getting into a bit of traffic here,' he announced with curiosity.

Everyone peered through the windscreen and noticed an overhead saying 'Toll Booth ½ Mile'.

'Anyone know what a Toll Booth is?' asked Will since he was the driver and knew that it would be him, if anyone who would have to do any talking.

'Is it where you pay to drive on the road?' asked Paul. 'I think it is.'

'What happens if we just don't go into it, I mean like just stay driving in this lane?' wondered Rob.

'Well it's a tax isn't it?' considered Paul. 'I assume that we'll have to prove that we've paid somewhere further down the line.'

As the lane was splitting into two with right for the booth, no one announced that they should pull over and stump up however much it would cost, even though Will did his very best to slow right down before the fork.

'To hell with it; let's be bad-ass outlaws,' said Rob. 'We're genuine foreigners remember – brand new to this. No one's told us the rules of the road here and anyway, what's the worst that could happen?'

Will resumed with the accelerator leaving many a motorist stationary in the queue. 'I don't like the idea of handing over cash to use a road anyway,' he said now having them speeding well past that particular inconvenience.

'Me neither,' said Rob. 'We're already spending a fortune in this country. I think they can let us off just this once.'

'Alright well you're taking all the blame in court.'

'No problem. Is it alright if I use your laptop for a while? I just want to try and look at something about poker.'

Rob was still hurting about losing last night and wanted to swot up on tactics in preparation for whatever chance he would get to win his money back. He was disappointed but hardly surprised when there was no online connection - though with plenty of battery power he proceeded to keep himself amused by feasting on many of Will's private video files. Conrad meanwhile had a hypnotising view of the scenery that he feared would simply swallow them up before they found their destination. They were inexperienced travellers in a foreign land attempting to tackle a mighty piece of road into the unknown and, while everyone was more excited than scared, the longer they compared their speed to how slowly the road signs were matching the same names down the map line there was most definitely an undertone of apprehension. Perhaps Memphis in one go was too ambitious - perhaps they should consider a pit-stop before then?

'Everyone alright?' asked Paul three hours in and a hundred miles down the line.

'I'm alright,' said both Will and Conrad, Rob though was in a trance watching Will's films.

'Does it say anything in your book about any towns down the Interstate…like somewhere we might consider staying before Memphis?' Conrad asked Paul whose guidebook was different from his own.

'How should I know,' was Paul's tired and can't be bothered reply. 'Anyway my book's buried at the bottom of one of my bags and I'm not going looking for it.'

'We're not staying anywhere before Memphis,' said Will with some authority. 'We only have to take one turning before we arrive so driving in a straight line shouldn't be too difficult.'

'I'm glad you think so,' said Conrad.

'There will be three of us driving remember so the driver will always be fresh while the other two get rest.'

'I'm getting a bit tired right now and I haven't even done anything yet and Rob's half asleep already.'

'I'm just writing an email to one of the guys back at the pub,' Rob answered. 'I'm not half asleep but I'm never driving so it wouldn't matter if I was.'

'Anyway,' Will continued, 'say we do find a cheap hotel it'll be well into the night and with checkout time as early as midday we'll be paying full rate for only the few hours that we'd be taking to just get our heads down.'

'Look I don't want to stop off en route,' said Conrad now on the defensive, 'I'd love to make it all the way in one go. I'm just saying it's something to think about that's all.'

'Why should we not make it, apart from tiredness I mean?'

'I don't know. We might accidentally take a wrong turn and waste hours getting lost somewhere?'

'We only have to take one turning…I think we can just about manage one turning…'

'What if we get a flat?'

'Oh don't say that!'

'Well I'm having another look here just in case. You never know. One of these towns like Kankakee or Champaign may be worth a look. Anyway it might say if any hotels there charge by the hour.'

'What are those places called again?' asked Rob. 'Champagne?'

'That's right Champaign,' confirmed Will. 'It's been on all the signs.'

'Cool.'

Conrad climbed between the seats and halfway into the backspace where he grabbed his bag and hauled it onto his lap. Upon opening it he saw that it contained belongings that weren't his.

'Will, you idiot!' he barked in anger shocking everyone. 'You've sneaked some of your shit in my bag!'

Paul and Rob both looked round to see Conrad throwing Will's jumpers at the back of his head. Will thankfully wasn't distracted from the road and said nothing; obviously accepting that his cunning plan had been discovered sooner rather than the later he'd hoped for.

'When I went to answer the door in the hostel to that repair man you did it then!' Conrad realised.

Will said nothing in guilt. Paul and Rob also said nothing, amazed at such nerve.

'Remember? He couldn't get his case closed when we were packed. Suddenly when I came back from the door he was ready!'

'Alright I'm sorry,' said Will with no alternative upon being hit yet again with one of his scrunched up shirts. He might as well have asked Conrad to pick them up since the car was already starting to look like a tip.

THE DEVIL'S DUST

★

JUST PAST KANKAKEE Will let it be known that after several hours behind the wheel he was tired. He'd had a great innings but recommended that Paul take over and give him chance to rest his weakened legs and fatigued eyes. Conrad was happy to hear that Paul was next up because it put off his big return to the wheel for a short while at least. Not that he didn't want to drive, of course he did - this was an extravagant road trip that he'd paid heavily for – just that his nerves were jangling, that he hoped would be more under control into the night when there may very well be no traffic on I-57 at all. After swapping seats in a slip road Paul turned on the lights, adjusted his mirrors and suddenly wearing a funky pair of driving shades had them speeding south with fresh urgency.

'How's it handling?' asked Conrad, getting the lowdown on the vehicle before his turn in the hot seat.

'Pretty sensitive actually,' came Paul's reply. 'I like this automatic; manual gears have no advantage over this at all. I think all cars should be automatics.'

It was getting darker outside and they were still not even halfway. Both Will and Paul had them virtually at top speed and Memphis hadn't yet appeared on any of the signs they were flying past while an eternal row of cat's eyes was becoming the ever more dominant sight on the horizon.

'I've got something to announce,' said Conrad.

Will and Rob looked at him in suspense.

'One of my secret ambitions in life is to get into a fight with a midget.'

Rob chortled in bewilderment while in the front the other two were equally amazed.

'A fight with a midget?' Rob questioned whilst struggling to speak with giggles.

'Yeah well sort of,' Conrad elaborated, 'I'm not a violent person but what I'm saying is that if I absolutely had to fight someone and a dwarf started on me I wouldn't hesitate to do a thorough job on his head. You know just to prove my manliness once in a while and be guaranteed victory, having a fight with a little guy would quite satisfy me.'

Everyone was laughing at Conrad's violent little fetish. Two of them could hardly believe what they were hearing.

'How could you guarantee victory?' asked Rob now with some intense concern. 'Some of our little brothers I tell you can pack a real wallop so I wouldn't be so sure there mate. You could get caught by an overhand left to the balls!'

'Look I don't care how hard he might be there's just absolutely no way on Earth a four foot man could take me. I would just have too much of a height advantage in the heat of the battle. You know all I'd have to do was land one clean knee to the head and he'd be down.'

'Obviously,' said Will, 'you'd have to fancy your chances wouldn't you?'

'That's what I'm saying: I'd be guaranteed victory! I know but it's still a victory! Hurrah!'

'You wouldn't purposely pick a fight with a midget, then – is that what you're saying?'

'Of course I wouldn't – but if provoked by one of those guys that's when you'd see me in action. That's all I'm saying.'

Everyone thought Conrad was extracting the urine. They were right.

'Anyone fancy stopping off at one of the services for some snacks?' asked Will.

'I wouldn't mind actually,' answered Paul. 'The last sign said "Services Ten Miles".'

The buildings illuminated the blackening sky a long way down the slip road. There were two motels, a convenience store, gas station, restaurant and amusement arcade. After parking up they went into the store and bought crisps, sandwiches and popcorn and sat at one of the many picnic tables in the surrounding gardens.

'Are those guys sleeping there?' asked Will pointing to a row of cars only yards away obviously containing people under blankets in darkness. 'They mustn't be able to afford the motel?'

'They're probably catching up on some sleep,' started Paul. 'I mean driving long distance is probably more common for Americans. Drivers simply nip across States whereas a neighbouring State can be like the entire length of the UK away - which just seems more ambitious to us; so a little cat nap here and there is understandable. I can tell already that driving here is a pretty cool way to unwind; like there are easy to follow maps, roads that all seem to be in straight lines, budget motels, cheap fuel and top scenery. Everything almost encourages you to fill up and hit the road.'

Everyone was pleased to hear that Paul was enjoying himself now; far from the distraught vet that he'd become in Chicago. 'Not fancy a drive yourself?' he asked Rob who he knew wasn't on the insurance but was still keen to spread the vibe.

'I'm banned remember.'

'Thousands of miles away you are..?'

'I'd love to but it's too risky.'

'I suppose like everyone you thought you wouldn't get caught over the limit?'

'Well I was drinking the night before. It was about nine in the morning when I did a U-turn twenty yards away from a cop car that I didn't see. He breathalysed me and I was still a bit over. I got a forty quid fine, three points on my licence and banned for a year.'

'Ouch,' Paul commiserated while getting up for the restrooms back in the store.

'I wish these flies would piss off' said Conrad referring to the swarm of insects that just loved milling around people eating in the hot evening air.

'Clap your hands and see how many you splatter?' challenged Rob though Conrad did nothing but slurp his creamy milkshake.

'Guys, do you think he's over all that coverage about the war?' asked Will right out of the blue.

'Let's hope so,' answered Conrad, 'but don't be mentioning it again if you can help it, right? I started to get the feeling that he'd be stressing about it throughout the whole trip and I don't mind telling you that I don't want that.'

Rob nodded in agreement. 'No don't be bringing it up,' he confirmed standing on the sight of Paul returning with a couple of magazines tucked under his arm. 'What are those?' he asked.

'They're free in the store there,' Paul replied, 'trucking magazines. They advertise like motels and services along the roads at a discount so I thought I'd just pick a couple up.'

'I don't know what we'd do without you.'

'I do, you'd struggle.'

They cleared away their rubbish and clambered back into the car and sped off down 57 towards Champaign with noticeably fewer cars on the road allowing them to make great time. Although once the novelty had worn off it simply became four men sat in a car and conversation eventually slowed and more and more frequently stopped altogether. Will had his eyes closed and was no longer able to listen to Conrad and Rob setting the world to rights for the next couple of hours.

'How're we doing for fuel Paul?' Rob thought to ask over two hundred miles into the journey and never having thought Paul looked at the gauge for the first time.

'Just about empty in fact. We better fill up.'

Turning off at the next gas station he pulled them onto the forecourt but stopped in hesitation.

'What are you doing?' asked Conrad. 'Pull up to the pumps then...'

'What pump? What do we put in it; diesel or petrol?'

No one had a clue.

'Did they not tell you at the rental office?' Paul asked Will and Conrad who both agreed that the type of fuel required was never mentioned.

'Well – now what?' wondered Paul turning off the engine hoping for some constructive discussion to solve this dilemma.

'Are there no stickers or notices on the dashboard or anything like that?' asked Conrad.

'Not as far as I can see.'

'I'll get out and see if it says anything on the hatch,' announced Rob only to soon return none the wiser.

'Well we could just flip a coin?' suggested Will. 'What do you say? Heads for petrol and tails for diesel?'

'Stop taking the piss,' snapped Rob. 'Do you know what would happen if we attempted to run the engine on the wrong fuel?'

'I know that. Can't you take a joke? Shall I go in and ask the guy to come out and have a look?'

'Yes,' Paul quickly voted.

'Hang on wait' announced Conrad with a theory. 'It should say on the paperwork we got at the office. Will where did you put it all?'

'It's all folded in one of the pockets in the driver's door.'

Paul reached down and pulled out a stack of official paperwork that must have been an inch thick and began to list the headings on the tops of the pages. 'Insurance, contact details, receipts...'

'What on Earth's the need in all that shit,' said Conrad in frustration.

'Well if you'd thought to ask what fuel it takes we wouldn't need the form that tells us would we?' said Will.

'Well I didn't know it was my responsibility. Could you not have asked?'

'Diesel, it takes diesel,' announced Paul to everyone's relief before he pulled up to the appropriate pump. 'I'm going to fill her up. Pay us later.'

'Are we making progress then?' asked Will.

'We're nearly at Champaign,' answered Conrad measuring up the distance on the map that he was poring over. I'd say we're about a third of the way there.'

'Only a third?' erupted Rob in disappointment. We've been hammering it for five hours. At this rate we won't get there until early tomorrow morning!'

Once refuelled they were off back down 57 and through the town without saying a word. Conrad was now having trouble keeping his eyes open and his appearance made some reconsider his rejected suggestion that they stay somewhere en route: 'So, might one of these motels offer us an hourly rate then?' asked Rob to no answer.

Paul didn't answer not because he'd fallen asleep thank goodness but because he wasn't too interested and more accurately didn't know. Like a professional he kept them safely moving down towards the Missouri border. They were only forced to slow down upon suddenly noticing a row of taillights at two turn-offs onto another Interstate where for the first time in miles there was a considerable amount of traffic in view that was building up to a considerable jam.

'What's going on here?' Paul wondered.

Everyone woke up, rubbed their eyes and saw the flashing lights of several police cars stopping the traffic up and down and left and right. Paul stopped as close as he could to the car in front and perhaps thankful for the break couldn't help but slip a small yawn.

'Is it a level crossing?' wondered Will.

'Don't think so,' said Paul trying to make out the figure of a uniformed man who was one by one talking to the drivers in the queue. 'He's coming look.'

'Just say we didn't know about that Toll Booth thingy.'

'It's midnight man, and all this won't be about that,' said Rob almost blinded by the lights.

'Maybe it's the State line? If it is I'm getting out and walking across,' said Conrad, 'you can pick me up on the other side.'

'Why?'

'I'm just a bit worried about the ten kilos of Columbian pure in the spare tyre that we don't know about…'

'Stop taking the piss. State lines are unchecked anyway.'

Paul lowered his window ready for a conversation with the guy who as he got closer was easily identifiable as a policeman.

'Evening gentlemen, where you headed?'

'Memphis,' replied Paul. 'So what's happening?'

'Well about an hour ago a truck got stuck under the bridge on Interstate 70 just at the junction here. Because the truck was carrying some kind of chemical the State Highway Patrol decided to call in the engineers to weigh up the damage. They've just arrived now and need both the 57 and 70 closed off while they get in their crane truck to remove the danger. I'm afraid all drivers will be stuck here for a while yet.'

'Was anyone injured?'

'No one at all.'

'How long is the delay likely to be for?'

'I can't say at this time. We're considering arranging a short diversion across the field at Effingham so sit tight and we'll send you on your way as soon as we know it's safe.'

'Well that's just great!' spat Rob in understandable frustration. 'It's the middle of the night — not exactly rush hour is it? Why do they need to shut off the entire junction?'

'The crashed truck contained a chemical remember…' reasoned Paul while sticking his head out of the side window and seeing little rows of red lights brightly piercing the blackened terrain. 'Better to be safe than sorry.'

Rob was in no mood for such caution: 'So they're saying if we just drive on right now we're going to get blown up or something? I don't think so. There's never any need for all this. And they're only holding us here to make space for the cranes to get in and out. So they can use the road but for some reason we can't?'

Will opened his door and took in some fresh air. Other stranded motorists who were also naturally curious to see what had happened had also taken the opportunity to stretch their legs. He wasted no time asking a young smoker what he thought of it all.

'I can't believe this man. I got to get back to St Louis before work tomorrow and get my son to school' he said.

'How far away is St Louis?'

'It's about an hour and a half drive along I-70 here.'

'Did that policeman tell you how long we'd have to wait?'

'No, but I'm guessing it'll be at least an hour and who knows how long for those guys behind. Anyway I need to make a call and explain this to my dad,' he said throwing away his butt and returning to his car. Will turned and saw the beginning of the slip road up onto the winding stack junction. He went for a closer look and even before reaching the ramp saw the horror of the truck's collision with the bridge; part of the trailer had been torn off and several beer-like steel drums had been scattered all over the road below; there was debris in both big chunks and flaky shrapnel being slowly lifted up and away by a crane truck twenty yards in front of him. Not allowed to ascend further he stood with maybe twenty others peering down at the wreckage.

'You getting some fresh air?' Rob asked Paul who opened his door.

'It's the middle of the night and it's still so hot,' observed Paul.

'Man I'm tired, come let's go for a walk; let's see the no doubt tiny little obstruction that's holding us up.'

As Rob and Paul joined the onlookers wandering up the shoulder they too saw the blockage and Paul - the professional lorry driver - soon identified the vehicle: it was a Kenworth Semi that must have had at least fourteen wheels. What little was left of the trailer they also saw was clearly labelled with flammable stickers and only then did they understand the caution of the authorities. They found Will who was talking with more stranded motorists.

'Pretty bad don't you think?' said Rob.

'Yeah, looks like we're stuck here for a while yet.'

'Do you think we could somehow get round onto the other lane and head back to one of those motels for the night?'

'Well it's a thought since this has happened.'

Looking over, the left carriageways were several yards west of the right ones and hardly visible through the trees, and in any case because of the steel barriers a U turn was out of the question.

'Remember the last hotel was maybe only a mile back on the right,' said Rob with quite a cunning plan. 'We might just have room to spin round onto the hard shoulder and be safely back there in about a minute?'

'Driving in a lane reserved for ambulances a hundred yards away from an accident like this is a very bad idea,' warned Paul, obviously not in favour.

'By the time anyone's noticed we're away we'll be off the shoulder which as far as I can see no one's using anyway. I say we go for it?'

Will turned and could just about see a motel sign glowing in the night sky not too far back and virtually on top of the illegal lane. It would indeed be a very quick nip and he was tempted to agree.

'Let's ask a cop if we'd be allowed then?' he suggested.

'No way man, let's just go.'

Paul stayed silent as Will took it upon himself to approach one of the patrolling officers and politely ask if they could use the hard shoulder to get to the motel: 'Look we're really tired and we've been on the road for hours and it'll only take a minute?'

The cop appeared to ignore him; he was listening to his crackling radio while Will felt less than appreciated. 'Come on it'd be okay…?' he continued to plead. The officer was in fact looking past Will at two authority vehicles that had just arrived on the hard shoulder therefore rendering the plan now impossible in any case. When Will saw them his heart sank in disappointment while the cop's first and final words were almost mocking: 'I'm sorry Sir but as you can see the shoulder's now engaged…' Will returned to the other two who were just as annoyed.

'If we'd just gone when I first said instead of you talking to him we'd be there now,' Rob snapped in frustration as he headed back to the car where he found Conrad resting his eyes. As Paul and Will also got back they soon saw more and more cop cars arrive down the shoulder causing a jam almost as big as the one they were in.

'Christ! This is turning into a disaster,' worried Paul as they stared at the convoy of vehicles passing them on their right. No one knew what was happening; maybe half a dozen police vehicles were lining up from which several officers soon emerged and congregated under a floodlight and unfolded what was likely a map of the junction.

'We might as well call it a night,' spat Rob as with the meeting soon over the officers mysteriously all returned to their cars.

Then, and to everyone's amazement the first cop car that had arrived turned off the road just before the slope and with lights on full beam headed down onto the open grassland that surrounded them.

'What's going on?' Paul wondered while looking through his side window at the car now parking up in the dark field to his right. The other three had no idea until it became pretty obvious that all the police cars were following suit.

'They're all driving out and forming a guide for us to drive round the accident!' said Conrad with an astute brainwave, as sure enough more cars headed further out onto the field creating a leader lane with their lights spreading way beyond the junction.

'Finally,' said Rob with a second wind as an on foot officer soon instructed cars one by one to drive out to the first car where they would be likewise pointed on towards the next one. The grass was bumpy but posed no real problems as they made hay around the illuminated vehicles scattered quarter of a mile around the accident to finally arc back onto either the 57 or 70.

'No messing now, let's make some real progress,' declared Rob as Paul hit the accelerator after being reunited with the 57 tarmac.

'Top speed from now on!'

And so it was. It was in fact just before the Missouri border before Paul woke everyone to admit that he was feeling drained and suggested a change behind the wheel. Six years after passing his test it was finally Conrad's turn to operate a motor vehicle again and feeling the butterflies he asked Paul to pull into a gas station to give him the space and light he needed to insert his contact lenses.

'Are his glasses no good or something?' wondered Rob.

'His new contacts are a more recent prescription' answered Will. 'Do you think he's alert enough to handle it?'

'Well there's only one way to find out.'

'It's been nice knowing you' muttered Will as Conrad returned and leapt up into the driver's seat to be given a quick tour of the controls.

'The accelerator's right over in the corner; with your right foot feel it' said Paul now in the front passenger seat, 'and you don't have to worry about gears remember…'

With his mirrors satisfactorily positioned Conrad started the engine and slowly pulled out onto the slip road and picked up the pace before rejoining the empty Interstate without any problems.

'See, there's nothing to it,' he said, 'I know you all thought you were putting your lives on the line by letting me drive and all that… well you can relax now and go back to sleep.'

Everyone was pleased with his confidence but there was still a long way to go. Now well past halfway into Missouri things were going fine. Since there were no other cars on the road and it was essentially a well-lit straight line, virtually all Conrad had to do was stay awake.

THE DEVIL'S DUST

Genuinely getting comfy Rob, Will and Paul could relax and let their heavy eyelids close once again. Although occasionally tempted to unwittingly pull into one of the many disused truck weighing stations unclearly marked along the shoulder, cruising at speed down the open road was a delightful experience for Conrad and his apprehensions soon lifted. The thoughts that were going through his head were ones of great accomplishment and, despite being the last of the insured three to drive he was actually the first to notice that in the hundreds of miles they had travelled, but for a small one back in the airport, they had not seen a single roundabout. Not one. Americans it seemed, just couldn't handle roundabouts; 'maybe it was an inferiority complex?' he thought.

'Christ man, careful!' warned Rob with a start having been woken-up by Conrad's two second scraping of the cat's eyes. It caused a vibration that also took Will and Paul from their dreamland and for a split-second there the three passengers could see nothing but the black Missouri sky and for all they knew could have been flying over a cliff. Not quite asleep and not quite awake, it was a moment of panic that had in fact been caused only by Conrad's sweaty right hand briefly slipping from the wheel. They were all still alive and well but after seventy miles or so it was deemed time for rotation again. One of Conrad's last responsibilities was to have them fly round the one junction onto 55 after which continuing through Arkansas into Memphis would be a formality. Will once again took the wheel for the last leg of the epic all-night drive.

SIX

I-55 WAS COMING to an end. Will was still driving and thankfully fully awake safely getting them down towards the famous old city before dawn. With Rob and Paul snoring, Conrad, unable to sleep any longer during the anchor leg, was fresh enough to strike up conversation: 'Christ man, how can you drive so fast after all this time behind the wheel? Not need a break?'

'I'm alight. It's been quite a nice drive since you were last awake. The countryside and the farms down here are really beautiful looking at night. What time is it?'

Conrad leant his head back and looked up at the clock in the roof.

'It's twenty to six.'

'It's taken us nearly twelve hours,' replied Will, confirming that they were approaching the outskirts of Memphis as rows of motels suddenly started to appear on both sides of the road. 'Any idea if we can stay in one of these?'

'You're feeling tired now aren't you?'

'I'll get us wherever if I knew whereabouts we were going.'

'Hang on let me have a look in Paul's book. Turn the radio on.'

Will flicked the knob and heard the sort of music that had become arguably the South's greatest export. Conrad started nodding his head in approval.

'What is this?' asked Will.

'This is Bluegrass. It's a form of traditional American music. You can recognise it because of the fiddles, banjos and mandolins. We're not in Chicago now. Anyway have you been watching the signs?'

'The last one said "West Memphis Two Miles" on Interstate 40

– which is a left fork.'

Conrad nodded his head with double the approval as there were finally some stirrings in the back.

'What's this noise man?' asked a roused Rob.

'It's Bluegrass music,' replied Will with newfound knowledge.

Rob looked like a zombie. With tousled hair, sleep stuck to his eyelashes and stretch marks on his forearms he'd only half come round and like Will was concerned to find a bed for the day. 'Where we staying then?' he asked.

'I don't know,' answered Conrad. 'I've just been looking through the book and so far can't see a whole lot about accommodation in Memphis.'

Rob reached in the front and took the book from his hands. 'Let's have a look,' he said obviously thinking he could do a better job.

Outside it was just starting to get light. Approaching West Memphis on the rapidly narrowing Interstate, the scenery, like the music from the radio, was nothing like they'd experienced in Chicago. Old churches, battered ranch houses and oblong grocery stores accompanied rows of streetlights and telegraph poles before disappearing behind a wall of early morning fog and dense woodlands.

'Just pull up outside one of these motels and we'll go in and ask,' suggested Rob to which Will had no objections; soon doing just that but without enough skill to turn off the engine without waking Paul.

'Are we nearly there yet?' Paul asked like a bored seven year old on a school trip.

'Morning Paul,' Will said cheerily, just about hiding his fatigue.

'Christ, six in the morning. I've been asleep for nearly three hours. What have we stopped for?'

'We're in Memphis. We're going to ask if we can get rooms in this motel,' answered Conrad. 'I'm just going in and getting the prices.'

'It says here,' announced Rob reading from the book that "you can almost smell Elvis the minute you arrive in Memphis…".'

'What?'

'You can almost smell Elvis the minute you arrive here…'.

'What are you talking about?'

'Hold on a second,' said Rob as the others gave him a puzzled look.

Rob slid open the door, jumped out and inhaled long and hard into both nostrils the chilly morning air and then stuck his head back in the vehicle.

'Yep, he's here. I can smell The King. Come on Conrad, let's go in and ask then.'

Will and Paul laughed.

Walking across the car park Conrad and Rob were hit by waves of a high pitched chirping noise coming from a small forest behind the buildings. The loudness of it was almost deafening.

'I think that's those crickets telling folks it's time to get up' commented Conrad. 'You know for small bugs they don't half make some noise.'

'How do they do it?'

'It might be a scream or they might be rubbing their wings together.'

'They'd better shut up while I'm trying to get my sleep.'

Having passed the rooms they approached the reception building, pressed the buzzer and waited.

'Where the hell are they?' snapped Rob before buzzing again. 'They've got this big sign outside saying "Rooms for Rent 24hrs" and they can't even open the door!'

'Calm down man you'll be in your bed soon.'

At that moment a stern looking man joined them at the door having come down from a second level room. A black guy in a vest, shorts and sandals, he explained that he was a long-term tenant there and the receptionists were known to take forty winks when things were quiet. He also mentioned that the buzzer never worked. Rob and Conrad watched as he leant down and peered through the letterbox.

'Get up you lazy bastard!' he bellowed at the top of his voice. 'There's two white guys here and they want their rooms!'

The Englishmen gasped in amazement as he then started punching the door on their behalf.

'The guy who's on in the mornings is a drunk I tell you. Wake up wake up!' he continued to the equal fascination of Will and Paul who had their faces glued to the windscreen across the car park.

'There's going to be a dawn riot here,' predicted Will with possible wisdom.

Finally the door was opened by a fat black guy who everyone could see had obviously just woken up. He was immediately wrestled to the ground by the angry tenant. Conrad and Rob stepped back and watched in horror.

'My sink still won't work you lazy bum!' said the tenant throttling the front of house.

'You son-of-a-bitch!' screeched the motel guy, 'Get the hell out of here! Martha call the cops...' At that moment a woman, presumably Martha, appeared from behind the counter and immediately started whacking the angry tenant with the tube of a vacuum cleaner she happened to have handy. Just as Will had predicted, things had got out of hand but this was in fact simply another incident between undoubtedly poor folk frustratingly stuck in budget accommodation.

'Are you seeing this?' Will asked Paul.

'I haven't been dreaming for half an hour.'

As everyone stared in amazement the challenge was to understand more of the dialogue which wasn't easy since between the swearwords and grunts they were snapping at each other in a distinctly Southern African-American lingo. As they scuffled Martha was proving quite useful with her weapon; repeatedly smashing it into the head of the tenant to the point that after only a few seconds he began to retreat.

'Leave my husband alone,' she barked and sure enough his assailant soon fled up the steps back to his room. 'Don't let him do that to you again,' she then lectured her man who just about had enough dignity left to haul himself up.

'Are you okay?' asked Rob helping the guy back to his feet.

'Sure. It's nothing; he's my brother-in-law. Don't worry about that little problem there. Anyway what can I do for you?'

'We need four beds,' somehow answered Conrad with a straight face. 'You have the vacancies?'

'Sure I got the vacancies but....'

'But what?'

I just don't got the rooms working fully. Right now we're having a few problems with our water supply and it won't be fully fixed until maybe sometime next month. But I can give you the rooms at half price? What do you say – we got a deal?'

Conrad looked at Rob.

'No thank you - goodbye,' said Rob turning in obvious disgust. 'Sometime next month before they get water!' he fumed in a knackered rage back in the car. 'He should have got an even bigger beating off that guy!'

'What the hell was all that about?' naturally asked Will.

'A tenant here was somewhat annoyed at the service he was getting and done what I'd do,' replied Rob again picking up the guidebook. 'Let's look for somewhere else.'

'Somewhere a bit less dangerous I hope,' smirked Paul as they drove off.

With town now almost fully covered in golden sunshine its ugliness was fully exposed. Far from being a picturesque Southern city Memphis looked like it had seen better days. Driving slowly around town, with the Bluegrass quietly on the radio, battered factories, rotting wooden houses and litter strewn pavements was just about all they could see. Black people were lying on benches and dead rabbits were left on and by the roads. There was no sign of any commerce or civilisation.

'There must be more money in the Sears Tower than there is in the whole of Memphis put together,' commented Conrad.

'It's the crack of dawn, give the town a chance will you,' defended Will putting his foot down.

'"The city of Memphis lies in two parts",' read Rob. '"West Memphis on the Arkansas side of the Mississippi greets motorists from the Missouri Interstate who have to cross onto the Tennessee side to fully appreciate the birthplace of both rock 'n' roll and the civil rights movement..."'

'Well...get across the Mississippi then into Tennessee!'

'Of course, now you tell me!' commented Will. 'Anyone got any ideas on how to get there then?'

'Look,' said Conrad pointing through his side window to a majestic but distant arch overpass carrying trucks across to a shiny looking community that was obviously downtown. Assuming the correct direction, Will followed the road round and had them speeding towards the Hernando Bridge over the vast Mississippi that they saw was already prettily decorated with two riverboats and rows of jumpy seagulls.

Coming into downtown everyone felt safer. Watching the place come to life that Saturday morning the ambience was far more relaxed than the sophistication of modern Chicago. In fact if they didn't know any better they could have sworn they were in a different country altogether. Along the river-front with tramlines cutting up North Riverside Drive morning revellers were leisurely strolling along, milkmen were making their deliveries and people were arriving for work including a group of middle-aged women opening the town's Visitors' Centre which Paul astutely spotted no more than twenty minutes after getting off the bridge: 'If they don't know where we can stay then no one will,' he said.

'Pull up Will because I need the toilet,' instructed Rob with urgency.

Outside the building in the shadow of the famous Pyramid Arena the chill was giving way to an increasing blaze of hot sun that was glistening on the small waves of the river.

'Chill man,' said Will with a yawn before stretching his legs and rubbing his stiff neck.

In the entrance to the Centre there was a statue of a man wearing an extravagant cat suit with a quiffed hairdo and ornament guitar.

'I bet you'll never guess who that is?' said Rob as they walked by heading for the information desk.

'Is there a rest room?' he asked a woman wearing an Assistant badge.

'I'm sorry but we don't provide restrooms for the public,' she answered.

'Well do you know if there's one nearby?' responded Rob with half annoyance since there obviously were the facilities but they just wouldn't let him use them.

'You may be able to use the ones in the library across the street but I don't know if they'll be open yet...'

Rob made a sharp exit in a less than perfect mood.

'Hello. We're looking for a place to stay,' Conrad took over. 'Might you be able to tell us whereabouts in town we can find accommodation?'

'One moment, I'll just get the directory.'

She walked off leaving Conrad, Will and Paul rather puzzled as to why she didn't know from her head.

'What the hell's taking her so long?' said Conrad looking round the room.

'You're a bit snappy this morning?' said Will.

'I'm tired.'

'Aren't we all?'

'I know it seemed like a good idea at the time but let's not be driving at seventy miles an hour all night again okay? We must be crazy for doing that having been awake all day. Crazy.'

Also feeling like a vampire in the morning light Will agreed that it was pretty miraculous that they'd made it in once piece and realised that what he thought would only be a relaxing holiday could quite possibly turn out to be a backbreaking slog across a truly enormous country.

'Look at those leaflets,' mentioned Paul pointing to a wall unit covered in tourist literature as he began wandering over. 'There might be some hotels advertised...' The other two followed him and likewise started skimming through the pages and sure enough saw dozens of hotels in the area.

'Shall we give one of them a ring?' suggested Conrad.

'Go for it,' said Paul.

'This one – The Super 8 Motel?'

'Why not?'

As Conrad was on the phone Rob re-entered the foyer.

'Suitably relived?' Will asked him.

'What?'

'Find a toilet?'

'No. I just added to the river.'

The woman came back with two accommodation directories and placed them on the desk in front of Conrad though when he hung up he thanked her but told her they'd found somewhere but didn't know how to get there. 'West Illinois Avenue...' he said. 'Do you know where it is?'

'Sure. Is it the Super 8?'

'It is. We got the details from a leaflet here on the shelf.'

The woman marked up a map and sent them on their way where taking the short drive down the riverfront Memphis now looked little short of spectacular.

'Are we staying two nights here?' Conrad suggested hopefully as Will steered them to a four-storey building nearly totally hidden by trees, an Interstate junction and rows of obviously well worn railway tracks.

'Two nights here?' Rob wondered at first glance, 'this looks like The Bates motel!'

'We're staying here; even I need my sleep now,' declared Will parking up before opening his door and proceeding to pull his bags from the rear.

'It's a good job the four of us are walking in together,' said Rob. 'You never know. One of the women here might be pretty handy with a vacuum stick.'

THE DEVIL'S DUST

'I've got your back,' assured Paul.

Nicely carpeted the small reception area was empty. Dropping their luggage to the floor without knocking over any of the many table ornaments the four of them nearly fell over each other to hit the bell to which a young dark skinned woman soon responded.

'We need four beds....,' started Will, 'and for two nights?' he asked looking at the guys who nodded. 'Yes. Tonight and tomorrow...'

The total price was two hundred and twenty dollars. As they were expecting their keys they were told that the rooms wouldn't be ready for an hour and that they could either wait in reception or come back then.

'Can we leave our bags here?' Conrad asked the girl who confirmed that she could store them in the motel's security cages without charge. 'There's a great café just five minutes down the road...' she told them.

'Let's go,' announced Rob leading the march.

'It's quite nice out here don't you think?' Conrad asked Paul as they looked out across the sparkling river.

'Yeah. Three nights was enough of Chicago.'

Heading to the front through a small public garden almost directly opposite the motel, they were met by the strange sight of two men in soiled dungarees carrying fishing rods and stacks of coloured paper.

'Who the hell are these guys?' Rob wondered loudly.

They were both middle-aged and short in stature. As Rob was first past it was him who was handed the flyer; it was in fact a promotion for a speech to be given by a politician the following day.

'Thank you young sirs. We look forward to your attendance,' said one of the men.

'They look more like car mechanics than political campaigners,' said Rob in surprise.

'Or farmers,' suggested Paul, following him into a kitschy rock 'n' roll themed diner where they sat in a corner booth.

'Outside your skin burns but inside you're shivering,' was Will's way of acknowledging the air conditioning. 'It's too cold.'

'What's grits?' asked Rob reading from the menu. 'It says here that "all breakfasts come with either grits or beans".'

'There's only one way to find out,' smiled Paul as the waitress came over with her notepad.

'What's grits?' again asked Rob when asked for his order.

'You don't know what grits is?' she said in a thick Southern drawl.

No answer.

'Right well grits are a simple corn dish like porridge or rice pudding that we take great pride in serving in this part of the country. You should try it. I've been eating grits for forty years and they've never done me no harm.'

'Okay,' submitted Rob. 'I'll take the breakfast with grits.'

'Great, anyone else ready to order?'

They all took the same with coffee and toast.

'We would like our food ASAP!' Rob announced before a strange look back from the waitress.

'He means as southern as possible,' Conrad quickly explained with a charming smile.

THE RELENTLESS AIR conditioning was partly responsible for waking Conrad. It was five thirty in the afternoon and he was almost fully refreshed having slept from almost the second his head hit the pillow. Trying not to wake Paul he wandered across the room, turned down the intensity of the fan and opened the front door. In surged rays of sunshine that cut the room's darkness so sharply that he could almost note the contrast in straight lines. In only his vest and shorts, he stepped onto the balcony leaving the door ajar and took a wander round the deck and noted that tenants had hung their laundry over the wall and round the back was a laundrette and swimming pool. With his feet being burned by the concrete, he meandered back into the cool, carpeted room as Paul slept. At low volume he switched on the TV and was met by endless commercials on countless channels. He noted that his bedside cabinet contained a bible and a two year out-of-date Yellow Pages. The phone was fully charged and his backpack untouched. There was nothing to do except answer the door when Rob came knocking.

'Alright?'

'Yeah. I've just woke up. Is Will up?'

'Yeah; he's in there fiddling with his computer again.'

Conrad went for a look, and seeing Paul still asleep Rob followed him back to his room and joined Will reviewing the photos that he was transferring to his laptop.

'They're really good quality; well better than cameras that use film,' said Conrad who was now actually thanking Will for having taken so many snaps in Chicago.

'I don't like seeing pictures of myself,' said Rob. 'It's because I don't like the realisation that I'm not quite as good looking as I think I am.'

'Yeah, but you're obviously still very good looking you mean… like, compared to the rest of us?' sarcastically countered Will.

'Have you closed our door?' Conrad asked Rob in a mild moment of horror.

'Yes.'

'Oh well; I'm locked out now then in my underwear until he wakes up.'

'Let's wake him then, let's just give the wall a few knocks?'

'Let him sleep. May I suggest a game of poker?'

Rob emptied one of his bags over his bed and found the cards and began scraping together his coins. The quarters were the bigish silver ones and he'd now gathered quite a few of them. Looking at them glisten he saw that they weren't identical but were in fact slightly marked after different States. In his hands he had Oregon, Rhode Island, Ohio, Vermont, Georgia and Kentucky.

'It'll be worth seeing if I can get all the States before we fly home,' he said as Conrad sat on the floor.

'I don't think you'll get them all,' was Conrad's cynical opinion, 'assuming of course that every State has a coin. There are too many. Anyway why don't you spread your damp clothes over the wall outside to let them dry off?'

'There's an idea,' said Rob picking them up and carrying them out giving Conrad time to split the pot, shuffle the deck and deal on the duvet.

'You playing?' he asked Will.

'No thanks. Try not to make too much of a mess over there will you?'

'Yes, father.'

Rob sat down and threw in his blind. Conrad did the same and considered his pocket cards. Since there was no real money at stake the only challenge for them was to read each other and note any aggressiveness when betting in reaction to what turned over on the board.

'It's been a while since we played each other,' said Rob.

'We're not really playing each other; this is a pittance that we're just going to put back in our Pringles tube. Do you think you could beat me for real though?'

Rob looked as cocky as ever: 'I know you're a cautious player, often reluctant to make moves when you've got the chance to really cash in. I may struggle to play for a long time against you but I honestly think I could dominate you early and soon finish you off.'

'Oh really?' replied Conrad, surprised at both Rob's assessment and confidence as he was getting into his stride with his raising and bluffing; taking three of the first five pots. 'If we both started off with the same amount playing no limit you reckon you could clean me out inside, say an hour?'

'Easily.'

'But you're not so good at playing straight,' snapped Conrad obviously referring back to his big loss in the hostel.

'Well you didn't do much better did you?'

'Yeah but I was drunk and not playing my usual game. Luck - and that's all it was - wasn't on my side.'

'Yeah, right.'

Will was well used to this macho competition. For years he'd watched them go from poker novices to aristocrats and, eventually, outlaws. Though he found their egos entertaining he had no desire to indulge in their sporting obsession, especially since a natural greed had taken over and their temptation to cheat routinely became irresistible.

'The problem with you two is that you know each other's game so well. I reckon one on one there would be no winner,' he said.

'Arrh thanks mate,' said Rob fighting back with a considerable victory of his own.

'Yeah, we don't know what to say,' agreed Conrad. 'If we're sat at the same table against a couple of suckers we're gonna cheat. I mean seeing a fat pot in the middle is just too tempting. I can't risk the luck in this game. It's like a metaphor for life. Nice guys finish last and if your opponents are down then kick them until they're dead.'

Rob laughed, finding it hard to take the toy game seriously: 'Right, so the old determination is back then? Well I hope it stays and doesn't piss off on me like it did in Chicago. Playing apart and playing fair; what was all that about?'

'I thought it wise to just test the water.'

'Well that was an expensive thought.'

THE DEVIL'S DUST

Finished with his computer, Will was off into the shower having decided what to wear for a big night on the town. It wasn't a difficult decision since he'd all but run out of clean clothes and for someone who'd recently been concerned about tidiness left his bed covered with cameras, phones, maps and sweaty shirts.

'This room was immaculate when you checked in,' said Conrad. 'These chain motels don't have big rooms do they? I mean with the two beds, and that means two people and all their luggage, things are going to get cramped.'

'I'm not complaining. I could ask for no more,' said Rob as he stood up on the bed, wrecking the layout of the coins and cards and started knocking on the wall.

'Nah, let him sleep man' said Conrad, annoyed that their little game was obviously now over.

'I'm going to knock on the window,' announced Rob and out he went where after two knocks Paul opened the door, wide awake and fully dressed.

'How long have you been up?' asked a surprised Rob.

'About half an hour.'

'Conrad locked himself out and has been in our room.'

'Like I couldn't have guessed?'

Conrad arrived and like Will took his shower. Rob took note, gathered up his now fully dry clothes and also went to get ready. Paul headed down to reception and the same girl from the morning emerged from a backroom.

'Hello. We checked in this morning,' he began, 'I was wondering if you could tell us where we can go tonight to enjoy ourselves?'

'Oh sure' answered the girl. 'You guys on vacation?'

'We are. We've been in the country for four days.'

'So where you from?'

'England.'

'England! Wow! Oh I'd love to go to England. You know to see those big stone rocks…'

'There are flights to England everyday,' Paul told her, by now growing tired of playing ambassador for his country.

'So what brings you Memphis?'

'Well why not?'

'Cool. Right well then the main part of town for going out is Beale Street. It's got like bars and clubs and you'll have a really great time. The motel provides a driver service to downtown so you can get there in about ten minutes.'

'Okay. And there's always a driver waiting?'

'Not always but we have two guys on tonight so you wouldn't have to wait long. There's one of the guys pulling in now,' she gestured through the glass doors to which Paul turned to see for himself. 'So how've you found town so far?'

'We've not seen any of it! We arrived first thing having driven all night from Chicago and we've been asleep all day.'

'Oh of course sorry,' laughed the girl in a most flirtatious way. 'Have a good time then.'

Paul laughed along before returning to the rooms to find everyone just about ready.

'Is it getting chilly?' asked Will locking up and pocketing his key.

'The breeze is quite nice,' said Rob.

'It is,' agreed Conrad following Paul into the car he'd just seen pull in.

'Where you guys headed?' asked the driver.

'The girl told us Beale Street?' answered Paul suggestively.

'Sure thing.'

ROB, WILL AND Paul were quick getting out of the cab, so it was left to Conrad to cover the steep bill which he claimed covered the cost of his meal in a diner just off Beale since the taxi couldn't get them close enough. No longer peckish they followed the crowds and were instantly overwhelmed by the carnival atmosphere and eye-bright neon signs illuminating the street beneath the darkening sky. Like walking to a football ground, the flow of people was a grand sight and a special feeling. Young and old, black and white, thin and fat, everyone was frolicking and drinking seemingly without a care in the world. Almost every doorway was a bar with live music; top entertainment that was also provided by talented street musicians. Banging into people whilst trying to get their bearings, no one knew where to go; every place looked as good as every other so without discussion it was assumed to just keep walking and simply arrive somewhere and maybe fraternise with any of the Elvis impersonators or the equally dressed up Tinkerbell women in low-cut tops and tiaras. Beale Street was absolutely heaving.

THE DEVIL'S DUST

'It's like an Ibiza street,' said Will tiptoeing round numerous plastic beer glasses that had overflowed from a nearby bin.

'I need to get to an ATM,' said Conrad joining a queue close by.

'You don't know where to start do you?' asked Paul, no doubt feeling a dry throat already coming on.

'Anyone oppose that place?' asked Rob pointing to no objections when the illuminated sign reading 'GIRLS DANCING' was also noticed by Will and Paul. Conrad caught up with them and once inside saw a brand of showboating that he knew would never catch on in Britain anytime soon. Though the Englishmen were hardly alcoholics they thought they knew what a bar was for and were stunned to see this one not serving drinks but being used as a bouncing all female dancefloor. The women up there looked like tomboys; many of them were wearing leather trousers, stetsons and tight T shirts with the sleeves fashionably torn off. Their heeled boots were hammering down on the wood as they spun up and down while the sight of a drunken man attempting to get up ended with him being punched away and then dragged out by a not exactly fragile looking bouncer.

'I think it's pretty obvious in here then that the policy is look but don't touch,' said Paul in search of the real bar that was in fact several huge tubs of bottles in ice water spread round the opposite walls. He wandered over and ordered four Millers from the cowgirl on patrol. 'Coming right up,' she said before bending over to whip out the beers.

'There appears to be no shame in dancing and not just in a bar but on a bar,' said Paul, still amazed at what he was seeing as the women were bopping away and spraying them with exploding bottles of liquor. 'That's what you were like in that Irish place the other night,' he continued in Will's direction.

'I love it in here. These people are enjoying themselves without the reservations of British people and they're drunk relaxed and not drunk dangerous like they get in England. I think I could have a laugh with all these without risking my life if you know what I mean?'

'You've got a point,' said Rob noticing an even stranger sight in the middle of the room: 'What's going on there?'

They all looked round to see.

'I don't believe this,' he said to everyone who most definitely agreed on sight.

Three bouncers, who could have been wrestlers had they looked less intimidating, were absurdly executing a foot perfect linedance with camp twirls and handclaps neatly in time with both each other and the house PA. They'd obviously rehearsed the performance.

'You know when applying for a job as a bouncer, to be in with a shout you evidently have to meet certain criteria...' said Rob. 'You have to be at least seventeen stone. Check. Have a shaved head and goatee beard. Check. Throw guys out for climbing on the bar. Check. And most importantly you have to be able to cut a mean figure doing the Macarena. Check.'

Finishing their bottles everyone laughed. Conrad left for the next round and just having to get a souvenir Will took out his camera but upon sight of it one of the beefcakes immediately marched over with some strong words. While no one was especially worried, it turned out that though there was no problem filming the bouncers, all images of the women was in fact a breach of the bar's copyright.

'And you have to enjoy being filmed and having your photograph taken,' Will told Rob adding to the criteria.

'Camp bitches,' were Rob's concluding words of assessment.

Conrad returned and looked round the tables and saw that many of the people there were middle aged women with short hair and tacky jewellery; all slouched over tables and propped against the walls.

'What you looking at?' asked Rob.

'This lot; half of them look like they're on a cheap hen night and the other half look like divorcees back on the shelf.'

'Maybe it's not too different from Manchester then after all?'

With Will snapping away he caught the attention of a squalid looking young black man who on approach initiated some friendly chit chat.

'Where you guys from?' he asked.

Will didn't hear him at first but Conrad did and said 'Memphis', having by now clearly grown tired of telling the truth though he didn't make himself heard over the music.

'England' Will then answered after he repeated the question.

'Oh great! So what are y'all names then?'

Leroy, as he was called, understandably took an interest in all things new and that included the background of travellers passing through his town. They introduced themselves and assumed that he was a friendly local rightly proud to tell them about Memphis.

'You got this in Manchester then?'

'No. Strip joints are the closest we've got.'

'Alright!' was Leroy's response in a slow, slightly sinister tone. 'You guys feel the same as you do when out back home?'

'We feel safer actually.'

'Safer?'

'Yeah,' Will explained, 'if this was Manchester on a Saturday night there would be like hundreds of drunks in the street, vomit everywhere, fast food wrappers thrown all over the place, fights over taxis, police all over and half naked women running around barefoot whatever the weather.'

He suddenly looked like a shrinking violet; his chequered hoodie and baggy jeans almost swallowing him up. 'Man. I always thought England would be like real classy. Listen you guys fancy a drink across the street?'

They all submissively agreed and followed him back outside.

'So who gonna pay my five bucks entrance to the club there?' Leroy asked to some surprise.

'No change mate,' prudently said Rob.

'Me neither,' answered Paul.

Since Will was keeping his distance it was Conrad who submitted to his perseverance and handed over a five dollar bill and told him to lead the way to an establishment where they could continue drinking. Leroy ushered them to another place further down the street where they were required to join a small queue.

'This place is real cool,' said Leroy approaching the door where he did not hand over any money but merely received a hand stamp. Once inside Conrad politely confronted him for an explanation: 'If this place is free then why did you ask for money?' he said.

'Look I didn't know, I'll get you a drink. Wait one moment while I get to the men's room.'

Looking over his shoulder Conrad saw Rob, Will and Paul getting their hands stamped and strolling to the bar. Leroy had disappeared somewhere round the building and a moment or so later a shamefaced Conrad realised he'd been had.

'Next time someone asks us where we're from just say wherever we are in America, and you' he gestured angrily at Will, 'stop flashing your camera around so often.'

'Don't take it out on me,' Will answered back. 'Someone exploited you and took your money. Get over it. If he'd stayed with us we'd have bought him a drink for the same price and you wouldn't have minded.'

They all carried their drinks out to the beer garden and began to brood, though it wasn't too long before the piss-taking began. Conrad could soon take no more and drank up before wandering off alone down to the riverside.

'Come on it was only five dollars,' said Paul. 'It could have happened to any of us.'

Rob agreed and upon emptying his glass went to console him out on the corner.

'Alight?' said Rob.

'Yeah. I just need a bit of space from the crowds that's all.'

Staring out over the river the pair of them saw the strange sight of what appeared to be a man perched high on the metal bars of the Hernando Bridge. 'What could anyone be doing up there at this time?' they both thought.

'Come on let's go and have a look,' said Rob setting off in curiosity. Quickly walking along with one eye permanently on the climber, the closer they got the more they realised he was at some risk up there and saw that if he was to fall he would almost certainly fall to his death. Now out well away from the crowds Rob and Conrad were nimbly able to climb across the traffic barriers and illegally proceed along the road to the point where they were almost directly below to see him continue climbing.

'Hello!' shouted Rob to no reply. 'Why are you up there?'

Conrad started to worry. Interstate 40 that was being carried by the bridge had no pedestrian walkway and should a vehicle come along they would be in almost as much danger as the daredevil who was still moving.

'What are you doing up there?' again shouted Rob.

The man looked down but did not say anything. Taking matters into his own hands Rob himself clambered onto the girders.

'Don't be stupid man,' shouted Conrad.

Putting himself in the same danger Rob continued climbing and was soon almost level with the man, a young African American who it seemed was in no mood for conversation.

'Are you okay?' shouted Rob who had difficulty projecting his voice through the wind that was three times what it was at ground level. Again he received no reply while Conrad was horrified at Rob's stupidity, especially knowing that his senses wouldn't be a hundred percent with his evening's drink.

'Get down you idiot!' he shouted whilst just about avoiding a taxi honking him in the middle of the road.

'Look it's dangerous up here...,' Rob began again with obvious truth.

Conrad pulled out his mobile and rang Will back on Beale Street. 'Rob's gone mad,' he said with half worry and half astonishment.

'What's he done now?'

'Well he's climbed up to the top of the big bridge over the river and is talking to a guy who's probably going to jump.'

'What?'

'You heard!'

Will dragged Paul down to the riverside and in a curious half-panic scanned the horizon. To his right he saw the bridge and could just about make out Rob's figure high up on the bars. He started shouting down the phone but the signal was breaking up. Paul too couldn't believe his eyes.

'Is he out of his mind?' said Paul. 'Should we tell the police?'

Will approached a police officer marshalling the traffic around Beale and calmly told him the situation. The cop took some convincing before he followed them to the river but upon sight wasted little time getting on the radio. Will modestly tried to downplay the situation but there was no point; the ball was rolling and within minutes two cars with sirens blasting were careering onto I-40 where on arrival Conrad attempted to tell them the circumstances. In a flash the bridge was closed at both ends and the whole thing was turning into quite a drama.

'Look I'm gonna jump,' the guy finally told Rob beside him in the danger zone.

'Why would you want to do a thing like that?'

'I owe too much money man.'

'Don't be stupid; let's climb down together,' answered Rob with a cool confidence, clearly beginning to enjoy himself up there while half a dozen officers were now on the scene and diversions had been set up for traffic. A powerful spotlight was turned on that momentarily blinded Rob who for a second caught its full beam square in the eyes. Thankfully his grip was solid, and though he knew he was getting into trouble he thought it best to try and communicate with the poor soul who had not yet been seen by the police.

'Please climb down,' announced a cop through a megaphone.

'See,' said Rob to the guy who was seemingly determined to go through with his plan. 'Anyway, who do you owe money to?'

'Everyone man, everyone!'

'So what do you do for a living?'

Now that the guy was talking Rob expected to hear that he was a tramp or something.

'I'm an Investment Banker for an airline.'

In his moment of his supposed heroism Rob now struggled for something to say. 'Well it can't be that bad surely? You might die if you jump. Tell me who do you owe money to?'

'Banks and credit cards.'

'Please don't jump,' said the policeman who was unaware that Rob never had any intention of letting go despite what Conrad had been trying to tell him.

'Listen mate,' Rob began, 'Business money's insured, it's just materialistic crap created by bullies.'

The guy looked back at him with full attention. Their conversation was becoming quite enjoyable considering the circumstances.

'Imagine right if you were in a desert,' continued Rob 'and you were about to die of thirst, what would you rather have: a million dollars or a jug of water? Know what I'm saying - money's man-made crap!'

The guy said nothing but judging by the look on his face he could see Rob's point and Rob knew that he was making progress. The pair of them began to share a peaceful moment. From up there the river looked awesome and the city even better. Despite the minor circus below they could have been the only two men in the world just then and soon the no doubt intelligent Investment Banker made a move to climb down to safety.

Will and Paul meanwhile had jumped passed the barrier and found Conrad dazed by the drama. 'Is he coming down?' asked Paul.

'He is! Look!'

They both arrived safely back down on the road and were each immediately escorted ever so politely into separate police cars and whisked off to a nearby station. Conrad explained to the officers that Rob had done no harm and was asked with Will and Paul to go along and provide a short statement.

'A nice bit of excitement there,' said Conrad with relief. 'Did you call the police?'

'What were we supposed to do?' said Will. 'He looked in trouble from the bottom of Beale Street…'

'I've never been in a police van before,' remarked Paul, implying that it would take the impending trip for him to start enjoying himself as the three of them hopped in and like Rob were taken to the local headquarters.

SEVEN

'I SUPPOSE YOU THINK you're funny?' said Paul chewing his bagel in the motel's small dining room about half an hour after they'd all awoken with headaches.

Refusing to accept any blame, Rob replied: 'Hey, I saved a life...'

'Well what did they say to you in the station last night?' asked Conrad. 'They asked us all did we know of any criminal history you may have...'

'Nothing much really. I just got a slap on the wrist for putting myself in danger and all that. The cops acted as though they'd seen it all before.'

'You didn't get charged with planning an act of terrorism or anything? I had this fear you'd get sentenced to ten to twelve in San Quentin and Tony would have to negotiate for months with George to secure your release and all of Rochdale would be on the verge of hysteria, you know all out on marches and stuff...'

'Oh yes. It'd be nice to think they would. Apparently I broke two laws but they're going easy on me because I'm a visitor. I just got a telling off. Not even a mug shot which I'm a bit disappointed by actually.'

'What happened to that black guy?' wondered Paul.

'I don't know; I never saw him again. He said he was going to jump and I talked to him and he changed his mind, so I think I deserve a little credit..?'

'He was probably just fancying a sporty dive into the river. I bet loads of people do it round here and it's perfectly safe. You know - splash!'

'Never. I saved his life and he'll find me and thank me one day. So, a Sunday in Memphis then? Anyone got any ideas?'

'I know let's climb a hundred foot up a bridge, cause a big road block and go on to waste several hours of police resources in the process? What do you say?'

'Alright leave it out.'

'We have to go and see The King don't we?' said Will. 'You know – Graceland?'

'Yeah okay,' agreed Rob appreciating the change of subject though he wasn't really interested.

'It's a bit touristy don't you think?' mentioned Paul while Conrad again thought of his mother: 'I need to send her a postcard, she'd love mail from his house. Has anyone got any change to get some stamps from reception?'

Rob emptied his pockets and gave Conrad some coins and asked him to pick up a map while he was there. A piece of yellow paper arrived on the table that Paul picked up and began reading.

'That's what those guys gave us yesterday morning,' said Rob thinking no more of it. 'Remember just after we checked in?'

Paul didn't reply; something on the flyer was obviously holding his attention. 'It says here,' though he soon announced, 'that today Republican Senator Jim Douglas will be addressing local people about the benefits of military service in front of city hall at 3pm…shall we go?'

Will didn't know what to say; he knew that Paul could well revert back to his depressed self if he went anywhere near anyone preaching anything pro-military and no one wanted that, though Paul seemed adamant: 'If it's a waste of time we can always go to Graceland afterwards?' he said.

No one dared disagree.

'Right, well let's go then,' Paul said with total conviction. When Conrad came back everyone finished up and headed back to their rooms to pick up essentials on what was already feeling like their hottest day yet.

'Look, if this guy's speech begins at 3 and the last tour of Graceland is at 5 on Sundays then we'll hardly have time for both,' said Will, 'and I'm not dying to go and listen to some guy talking about the Army.'

'How do you know the last tour is at 5?' asked Rob.

'It's in one of the books. I think Graceland's not to be missed.'

'You've got a point,' agreed Conrad before going in with Paul to pick up his wallet.

'Look well I'm going to see this Douglas guy,' confirmed Paul as he pulled the door firmly shut. 'Are you coming with us to see this speech?' he then turned to Rob who to his surprise showed an interest: 'Since we've got to find both places we're not going to have time for both and I'm not too interested in that guy's house,' he admitted on the way to the car.

'Right well me and Will will go to Graceland and you and Paul go and see this guy then?' reasoned Conrad. 'We'll meet back here before dinner tonight okay?'

Will pulled out of the motel yard and after dropping the other two off as close to city hall as he could continued on with Conrad trying to find Memphis's top tourist attraction: 'I don't see what's so good about some old guy giving a speech about the army,' he said.

'Well it's better than nothing, though I'd rather go and see The King's bathroom you know? Look, "Graceland – Elvis Presley Boulevard" next left,' Conrad announced as they crept along in the traffic crammed round the specially set up diversion zone.

★

THOUGH DOUGLAS WASN'T due for a half hour, the crowd in the car park outside the Government building was already swelling. There was a marching band in full cry, stars and stripes banners at all corners and up front a podium and a dais heavily surrounded by security. Up behind it all was a large video screen and to one side was a tent set up labelled 'Recruitment Application'. Approaching from the rear Paul and Rob – even being two ex-soldiers themselves – couldn't quite grasp how the mood could be quite so carnival.

'Have you heard of this guy then?' asked Rob.

'No. I'm just curious to hear what he's got to say.'

Fifty yards from the podium Douglas's audience looked somewhat different from the suits upfront. Baseball caps and jeans seemed to be the uniform while even the church goers and less affluent blacks seemed full of fever and excitement about what they were about to hear. Unlike in Britain, the political rightwing here was loudly celebrated, and even by the less sophisticated folks of a beautiful but undeniably hard-up Southern town. The fever only heightened when the band stopped and Senator Douglas was introduced.

'Here we go then,' said Paul as if he was about to witness a comedy concert.

Douglas was, as expected, formally dressed in a suit decorated with so many war medals it was a wonder he could stand. A WASP well into his seventies, he regally waved to his adoring supporters with all the authority of the President to whom he was only a dozen positions away from in Congress. He took the microphone and began.

'Thank you! Thank you!' he said with his wrinkly grin stretching from ear to ear beneath his sweating brow.

'It's such an honour to be given this great welcome by the good folks of Memphis…'

'Knob head,' immediately snorted Paul.

'Ladies and gentlemen, I can't tell you how much I appreciate such a reception this afternoon and it's wonderful to see so many of you here showing your support in these trying times for our country, both at home and oversees…'

Silence.

'…but even so I must say that it is of utmost importance that we do pull together and try and understand that despite the struggles our country is going through, The United States of America is still a great nation and will continue to be a great nation!'

Cue rapturous applause, though not from the two young Englishmen who were still more amused by the spectacle of it all than anything he so far had to say.

'Now I fully understand that serving overseas in our country's military is not for everyone but the brave men and women who take that step forward can take great pride in themselves and I can't make it clear enough that each and every one of them – from a new recruit right up to the most senior officer – should know that me and you, honest hard-working Americans are all very proud and will continue to give our total support until nothing but a comprehensive victory is secured!'

'He thinks he's a rock star,' remarked Paul, rather dismissively.

'Now when I was a young man I served my country out in Vietnam…'

'Oh here we go…'

'…and as I'm sure you can imagine Vietnam was tough, but let me tell you; what kept me and my unit going more than anything else was the incredible messages of encouragement and love we frequently received from our families and people back home, so I urge you all to make every effort to send messages, money, gifts, anything at all to our soldiers who are without question doing a tremendous job out there in the quest for world peace.'

'He's high on sentiment I'll give you that,' Rob interrupted.

'Now I know an old friend of mine, George W Bush…'

Applause.

'…took the hardest decision of his life to send our troops into Iraq and it was a decision that I too would struggle to make but as the democratically elected President we must respect his decision, and while the dangers of this and any conflict are only too obvious, here today it is my desire to remind people that being a serviceman also offers a truly wonderful sense of unity and honour, the like of which I have never found in any of my jobs since being discharged…'

'He's probably never had another job,' was Paul's latest smirk.

'He's a politician now isn't he?' rebutted Rob.

'Since when's that ever been a real job?'

'Now if I may I would like to introduce to you a young man who's just returned from serving in Iraq to say a few words and help us understand that what's happening over there is not just struggle and hardship as media would have you believe, but as I'm sure he will explain equally about other beliefs and values that I'm certain are going to see the United States prevail through this most unfortunate situation. Please will you welcome Mr Scott Fletcher!'

As Douglas took a seat, a skinny man bound to a wheelchair rolled up to the dais and after the microphone's awkward adjustment began by likewise giving thanks.

'He's just exploiting that poor guy,' Paul quickly snapped, 'he's only a kid who probably just signed up to pay his way through college and now he's got his legs shot off…'

Though he didn't reply Rob agreed and was starting to notice Paul's temper slipping; he had been cat-calling Douglas at virtually every opportunity and had watched him push further forward in the crowd to the point where they were almost in the golden circle reserved for the TV crews.

'Now I must say,' started Fletcher in a clear-cut Southern twang, 'that although I've been unfortunate I've learned many great things whilst being a serviceman and certainly do not regret my decision to sign up. I may come from a family that sometimes struggled to find work but I attach no blame to anyone other than myself for my injuries. I volunteered, I knew the risks but the United States military has still given me both the opportunity to see many amazing places and taught me a skilled trade…'

'You're a cripple mate, not much use now,' Paul called out, perhaps too loudly.

'Leave it out,' Rob tried to reason.

'They just took his life away and the poor kid's obviously too dumb to see it…'

'But more than that I learned a good number of core values that I wish to explain to you here today, and especially to any of the young men and women who may be considering joining the Tennessee National Guard, a step of bravery that I both still admire and fully encourage.'

'Christ, it's a recruitment event now as well,' said Paul now burning up.

'There are seven main values that I learned while serving my country, and those are duty, respect, loyalty, self-service, honour, integrity and personal courage…'

'You're lucky to be alive little boy,' shouted Paul in another outburst that was surely heard by the speaker. Then in a moment of overly sentimental pride Fletcher began to elaborate on his supposed core values.

'Duty. I fulfilled my obligations as a part of my unit every time I resisted the temptation to take shortcuts that would have undermined the integrity of the mission. Respect. Respect is what allowed me to appreciate the best in other people. Remember the Army is a team and each of my unit always had something to contribute…'

'He's almost got tears in his eyes,' Paul told Rob. 'Not because he believes in all that stuff but because they're probably forcing him get up there and say it, you know just so his poor mother can have an extra day's groceries.'

'Hey that's cold.'

Fletcher claimed that personal courage 'has long been associated with the Army. Facing moral fear may be a slow process especially if taking those actions is not popular but will be most honourable in the end…'

'He's basically a vegetable and yet trying to sound like a commercial.'

As Fletcher finished Douglas returned to the dais, Paul loudly claimed 'a couple of thousand dollars richer,' and continued to spout more Republican patriotism. Looking around as Paul got evermore animated Rob noticed that more than one security guard was talking into a headset and possibly keeping an eye on him as a potential troublemaker.

'Relax man,' Rob warned as Paul was clearly about to blow. He was talking loudly to himself with his fists clenched and teeth grinding. Rob knew he was passing the point of no return but there was little he could do. Douglas then asked everyone to spend a few moments looking up at the video screen that began showing images of formal military celebration like marching soldiers, medals and flags. For Paul it was the final straw.

'It's funny how they never show any pictures of loaded coffins or lads burning to death?' was his final rant as he leapt onto the platform where he was too quick for the first guard during his attempt to highjack the microphone. In a flash Douglas was surrounded and frogmarched backstage and along with two thousand others Rob watched helplessly as Paul was wrestled to the ground, though not before landing a hammering right hook to one guard who was well and truly sparked out in the five-second mêlée. The photographer's flashes exploded and the news cameras all got crystal pictures of the incident. Getting as close as he could, Rob could just about see six guards carry Paul kicking into a portacabin behind the stage. After a few minutes of confused mutter the promoter announced that Douglas would be returning to continue his address which he did, though Rob now clearly had another much more serious concern.

★

BACK FROM GRACELAND, Conrad and Will went for a swim in the motel's pool. It was early evening and still warm enough to be splashing about without worrying too much about the other two who they'd gathered were running late.

'Well I'm going to the laundrette,' said Will getting out and drying himself on the patio. As he was pulling on his shirt his phone fell out and he thought he'd give Paul a ring to find out what was keeping them.

'No answer from Paul, I'll try Rob,' he said. With his ear to the receiver he heard the phone ringing next to him; it was still in Conrad's jeans at his feet. 'Why didn't you give Rob the phone you've been sharing?' he asked in disappointment.

'Sorry mate, I forgot,' Conrad shouted while executing a nifty backstroke.

Picking up his things, Will thought it might be a laugh to take Conrad's glasses that he'd left in his shoes and then left to collect his washing. It was nearly another hour before Conrad got out and just about managed to squint at all the door numbers along the first level where Will knew the joke was wearing thin.

'Alright! Alright,' Will said with a snigger from his chilled out position watching the news. 'Your glasses are in this room somewhere, you're getting warmer…'

'Stop being a knob.'

'Catch,' said Will throwing them at him.

'You idiot, do you know how much these cost?' Conrad snapped as he put them on in time to see a news report about 'an incident' at the day's political rally in downtown Memphis.

'Isn't that where they went today?' he wondered.

'It is, what happened?'

'Quiet.'

Will clambered for the remote and turned up the volume to hear that Senator Jim Douglas was 'put at risk by an unidentified protester who is currently being held in police custody…' The pictures left nothing to the imagination.

Silence. Shock. Disbelief. Horror.

They looked at each other stunned after the third replay of Paul fighting with security was broadcast all over the South.

'Well I think we know where they are now,' was all Conrad could say.

'Well that's the holiday ruined,' a disgusted Will announced. 'Why can't he just get over it? He hasn't been a soldier for years but suddenly he's all distraught and spoiling everything.'

Conrad went to get dressed and told Will to do the same. It would be responsible of them to go down to the station for an update and probably see Paul for the last time. As Will was getting ready his motel phone rang. It was reception.

'I took this note for you…' began the girl.

Rob had called and asked them to come down.

THE DEVIL'S DUST

★

'WERE YOU GUYS not listening last night?' said the policewoman to Rob, Conrad and Will who could all understand her disappointment. 'You British people always seem to do little here but get drunk and cause trouble…'

Though she knew those three weren't in bother it still didn't look good, and whereas Rob merely got a chiding the night before, there could be no doubt that Paul was in serious trouble. As they sat there waiting for news they couldn't help but fear the worst. He did, after all, attempt to penetrate the security of one of the county's top politicians and everyone knew that the price for such a crime was pretty high. All they could do was sit in the waiting room and hope that behind bars Paul was being dealt with leniently.

A meal and eight hours later Paul was finally released and found them still waiting with the cards out. He joined them at the table looking ashamed of his behaviour and no one knew what to say. It must have been a full minute before Will broke the ice: 'So what's happening?'

'I'm being deported in a week.'

'What?'

'I've been given a criminal record, won't be allowed to re-enter the country again for two years and have had an electronic tag strapped to my ankle.'

'You're shitting me?'

Paul lifted his leg and showed them.

'Deported in a week… from where?'

'Anywhere. Security at any airport in the country will expect to collect it before next Tuesday when it's confirmed I'm to get on a plane and leave.'

'And what if you don't leave by then?'

'Then I'll be arrested and sent to prison. Probably.'

'And who's fault's that?' asked Rob.

Paul got up and walked out. The other three followed, helplessly wondering what this meant for the rest of the trip.

'Did you not argue any of that?' asked Will chasing after him. Paul said nothing.

With the morning sun coming up Will drove them back to the Super 8 where Paul immediately retired while Conrad accepted an invite for a drink next door. The three of them sat pinching themselves;

a criminal record, deported. It was nothing short of a disaster; almost all their worst fears had been realised. Will turned on the news in an attempt to show Rob what they'd seen and the incident was still on the bulletin's headline loop. Upon seeing the pictures Rob wasn't surprised and began to think that Paul had got off lightly.

'Well?' he said.

'Well what?' answered Conrad.

'What's happening?' Are we going back in a week with him? What's the new arrangement with his flights?'

'How the hell should we know? Could you not have stopped him from going mad?'

'Hey don't be blaming me! He's an adult and you know what he's like when his buttons are pushed.'

'Why didn't you vote for Graceland with us? If three of us wanted to go, he wouldn't have gone there alone and this wouldn't have happened!'

'Look, if you're just going to be whinging all night then I'd rather you piss off to your own room and let us get some sleep.'

'Alright then I'll go. See ya.'

Conrad stormed out but rather than face Paul went for a walk at nearly five in the morning. It wasn't just Paul's incident that he needed a break from – it was all of them. They'd been in each other's pockets for a week and he was absolutely sick of it; all the egos, bickering and the chronic lack of privacy. He was starting to think that he'd had enough of America and in a way he didn't totally object to the idea of leaving a week early with his felon roommate. Walking along the river in the city that had caused them so much bother this past two days he saw that it was still much better looking than Manchester and after a mile or so began to cool down. He was just unlucky to have been hustled out of a paltry five bucks on Beale Street, Rob may well have saved a life up on the bridge and Paul, well, in a way he could just see it as a form of direct action that showed that he still had a passion that was lacking in far too many downtrodden people the world over, the like of which were lying homeless on the benches he was currently walking past. Tramps and vagrants were curled up under newspapers having been denied a home no doubt by the likes of Jim Douglas.

'Spare a few bucks please!' called out a big man jumping up from a doorway that scared the shattered life right out of Conrad's aching body. Since he'd been virtually sleepwalking for an hour the shock was instant forcing him to fall and, in reaction made him well ready for a possible fight.

'Just a few bucks man that's all…?'

Having got his breath back Conrad saw that the guy was some kind of ethnic minority; he was wearing a leather waistcoat that along with his long black curtained hair half covered his marked torso. He may well have been homeless but was at that moment no scruffier than the English tourist accidentally sitting on the ground. Not that there were any passers at six am but if there had been the poor man and the holiday-maker would have been difficult to tell apart.

'Jesus Christ, man,' barked Conrad climbing to his feet, 'you scared the life out of me.'

'Look I gotta get home, whatever you can spare please…'

Conrad had twenty dollars on him. 'So where's home?' he asked.

'Huh?'

'Where's your home?' persisted Conrad in an attempt to see if he was honest or not: 'Why do you need money?'

'My family's from New Mexico,' said the guy. 'I've been living rough since Knoxville last week. I'm looking to get back for my mother's birthday this month. I haven't seen her for more than ten years.'

Conrad put his hand in his pocket but kept it there; he needed more confirmation that it wasn't just a sob story by a seasoned junkie. 'So you're heading to New Mexico right, whereabouts?'

Surprised by Conrad's stubbornness but nonetheless quite genuine he elaborated that he was from Quay County before having the cheek to ask what an Englishman like him was doing in Memphis.

'Me? I came to see Elvis's house, I was there yesterday.'

'I ain't never been to Graceland. I've heard all about it though. The study, the jungle room, the living room. Did you see it all?'

'I did.'

Convinced, Conrad handed him the money, turned and headed back to the motel where if he was lucky would get four hours rest before they would be required to rebook or move on.

EIGHT

'Well where shall we go to next then?' said Will as the four of them sat on his bed looking at the atlas. The original plan was to get to LA by the twenty-third but since Paul was now expected to be out of the country before the fifteenth the itinerary likely had to be revised. 'What about further south like Jackson or Baton Rouge?' Will continued to still no suggestions. Everyone was looking at Paul.

'You've only got a week left,' Conrad reminded him, 'so are we going to get you to an airport where the airline might renegotiate your ticket, or should we all just hammer it straight to LA this week…I'm sure we could make it?'

'Of course we could, but that wouldn't leave us much time to stop over anywhere would it?' replied Will, still rightly wanting his full break that he'd paid top whack for.

'I suppose you'd better just drop me off at an airport then on the way,' conceded Paul.

'So you're not bothered then if we stay until our full three weeks are up?'

'No, why should I be?'

'Well remember you still owe Conrad five hundred and ninety dollars for the car - that's your payment that you now won't get full use out of.'

'It's alright I'll pay him the agreed full lot.'

'Okay then, you choose – where are we going next?'

Paul pondered the map. Since the others were due on the west coast he thought it considerate to begin the journey, and as they were virtually on Interstate 40 that was by the looks of things all they would need, he nominated Oklahoma City as their next destination.

'I personally don't mind,' said Rob, 'but I want to make sure you get the most of your time left,' he said in an attempt to console Paul while picking up his gear. Paul didn't want any sympathy and stuck with Oklahoma.

As they were about to exit the motel phone rang; it was reception asking if Paul from next door was able to come and speak with police officers there who wished to have a word.

'Did you tell the police where we were staying?' asked Will with his palm over the receiver.

Paul nodded.

Will, Rob and Conrad threw their bags in the car and followed Paul into the lobby where he identified them to two waiting officers who asked for half an hour. They agreed and were all led to the motel's small conference room and were told that while the situation was unfortunate, it was simply a necessary precaution to keep them all under low-level surveillance. They were questioned about their destination plans and were asked to provide their passports which staff were sent to photocopy. Paul was kept for a further few minutes and told that his tag was to be kept within roughly a mile of a tracking device that would now be fitted to the car. Outside everyone stood silent as the two cops efficiently placed and secured a small antenna like box on the dashboard that displayed a flashing green light in conjunction with the bracelet strapped to Paul's ankle. While everyone felt violated no one could refuse to co-operate considering the circumstances and compliantly waited until told they could go. Holding his veto forms Paul was struggling to say anything though everyone knew he wanted to apologise so didn't feel the need to bring it up. What was done was done. Will, now quite familiar with Memphis's roads, soon had them over the river where Monday brunch was immediately provided by another chain food bar.

'It's not so bad...?' said Will to no response, implying that yes, it was still a total disaster. Whole minutes went by before conversation started and only then on understandably safe ground: 'How many miles is it to Oklahoma City then?' asked Rob having finished eating.

'Don't know,' said Conrad struggling with the map on the table, 'though we should make it there sometime this afternoon.'

Conrad looked out through the window and after a second or two saw the homeless man he'd briefly chatted to earlier in the morning:

'See that guy, I gave him twenty bucks...'

They all looked out and saw a tall man in dark leather with shoulder length black hair and spurred heels stood at the end of the estate's slip road holding out his thumb.

'What him?' wondered Will.

'This morning I went for a walk and he jumped up from a doorway and asked me to spare a few bucks to help him get home to New Mexico. He's homeless.'

'Right...so he's hitching a ride then?' assumed Rob pulling the map from under Conrad's elbow. 'Right, we're just into Arkansas on I-40 and New Mexico is....there; this road would take him all the way actually.'

'Really?' said an inquisitive Conrad, 'let's see.'

'Don't even think about it!' said Will hoping that his thought was just Conrad's fantasy. Though he didn't say anything Conrad was curious as to what harm it would do to give a poor guy a lift.

'He's probably another sneak thief like that guy on Beale Street,' Will continued.

Conrad, still looking through the window at him being ignored by car after car believed that it wasn't a totally crazy idea. 'I'm going out to talk with him,' he said getting up and throwing down a tip.

'What is going on?' said Will. Rob laughed while Paul said nothing.

Outside Conrad approached the man who recognised him. 'Hey how you doing there?' he said with a smile, 'thanks for the money this morning.'

The other three looked on wondering if he could actually be offering a six foot drifter a free ride with them halfway across the country and, by the looks of things their conversation was really developing.

'Indeed, what harm would it do to give a poor guy a ride?' suddenly asked Rob.

'What?' barked Will in increasing dismay, 'don't tell me you're serious?'

'Homeless people are not all druggies you know. Maybe he's a good guy who just got made redundant? And anyway I know he's big but there are four of us - so if he started we could all take him.'

Rob went outside and was welcomed by Conrad to the little soirée with his new buddy.

'Where you from man?' asked Rob.

'Well originally I'm from Quay County in New Mexico, but I've been around here in the Tennessee area for the last couple of years. I'm looking to get back there now to see my family.'

Rob was surprised at how well spoken this homeless guy was and like Conrad took a strange interest in the fact that someone who was obviously in such an unfortunate condition could be so open and polite. They stood chatting at the roadside as he again extended the thumb on the end of his aching right arm and continued to be ignored by every passing vehicle. The Englishmen went back into the diner and announced that they should give him a ride: 'Just to the next big town?' said Rob.

'Are you crazy?' said Will while Paul again said nothing.

'He's a top guy, we've just been talking to him,' Rob continued, 'come on we'll all go to heaven for this, even Paul!'

Paul slipped a smile while Will took another look at the homeless guy, though he was pleased to see him nowhere in sight. 'He's gone now, look' he said with private relief.

Back in the car Conrad and Rob were pondering missed opportunities saying that it might have been good to have a bit more company every now and then, and they soon could have since Conrad spotted him again only yards down the highway where his hitching was now illegal. 'Stop let's get him,' he said.

Will pressed the brake having overtaken his thumb by maybe fifty yards. 'What are you getting us into?' he sighed.

Rob, sat in one of the two back seats with Conrad, climbed into the back space and was able to open the hatch. Will was clenching his fists in anger as a total stranger then hopped in and took great care not to crush anyone's luggage as he settled down and shook Rob's hand. They all peered round.

'So what's your name?' asked Rob.

'Wimbush, Charlie. This is great. I can't tell you how thankful I am for this. So where you guys headed?'

'We're heading west. Three of us are flying out of LA in a couple of weeks.'

Luckily without having held up any traffic Will set off again and like everyone else had his ears peeled listening to this new arrival.

'So what are all your names?'

'I'm Rob, that's Conrad and in the front there is Paul and driving is Will.'

'Great. All the way to LA huh? Staying on the 40 the whole way then?'

'Probably not, but we're on until Oklahoma City.'

'Great. Little Rock's fine for me.'

'No problem, we could use some new company; I tell you the same four guys in a car together can get tough after a while. So what about you?'

'Well until last month I was dealing the whisky up in Knoxville but the revenue man got too close and I had to run. I figured if I was ever going to get a chance to get home it would be now.'

'Right. So you're illegal?' Rob rather cheekily assumed.

'Selling my whisky was illegal.'

'I see. Moonshine.'

'All the jobs have been disappearing so mixing the liquor became my way of surviving and I found some demand near Knoxville.'

'So how long have you been in Tennessee?'

'About fifteen years. When I was about twenty I got forced out of Quay County by a family called The Orendas from the other side of our town, see they wanted to take over the business.'

Rob was slightly bewildered. 'You were mixing whisky at home then?'

'No, we made pots and rugs. My family had for decades produced furniture that was doing quite well until they attacked our store. They destroyed it; four of them smashed up all the jugs and set fire to the place. My mom tried to stop them and got knocked over, so I took one of them out. After that I had to flee.'

'Took one of them out?' said Rob, obviously wanting an elaboration.

'I didn't intend for him to fall that way,' said Charlie without actually declaring what had happened.

Rob was playing along, though whether or not he believed this personal horror story was anyone's guess. At the wheel a cynical Will wasn't surprised hearing all this. Paul sat in shame yet Conrad was fascinated by this little tale and made an effort to face them squashed in the back.

'Thanks again for the money,' Charlie said to Conrad who soon couldn't take his eyes off what appeared to be an elaborate tattoo poking above his V-necked waistcoat. He could make out four symbols that he knew he'd seen somewhere before.

'Could the police not have done anything?' wondered Conrad.

'The police know not to bother either the Wimbushes or the Orendas and both families are fine with that. We like to be left alone.'

'This is some pretty personal stuff you're telling us here?'

'Hey I don't mind. You're only single serving friends,' Charlie smiled.

After nearly a week in the country, once the novelty had worn off, it was only when cruising west along the spectacular I-40 that their long planned road trip commenced. Only an hour since touristy Memphis everyone was feeling better about this part of the land and, by the looks of things, Arkansas hadn't been spoiled by property developers who might have thrown concrete over its stunningly thick woodlands that hugged the road. They were making hay as they glided over lakes, alongside big rigs and bandana wearing Harley riders. Today was a new day and the more they listened to him, the more their new passenger appeared to be quite a nice guy.

'What you doing there?' Rob asked Charlie who had begun writing something on some scraps of paper that he'd pulled from his bag.

'I'm making a note for one of my buddies – he owes me a lot of money,' Charlie replied. 'I know this backwoods man from near Little Rock who was one of my customers. He usually took a big load and told me to look him up if I ever came to town since he said he might be able to get me some work in the speakeasies where he deals. Worth a try…'

Rob was fascinated. He leaned over to look at Charlie's page and saw that he wasn't writing in English. It was like Chinese; he gathered most likely some kind of Native American text; he was suddenly being exposed to a different way of life, prose and culture that he never knew existed.

'What language is that?' he asked.

'It's just a code I use…'

'A code?'

'Well to be able to communicate and keep the cops and tax people in the dark while we get on, many of us travelling and working round the country have over the years devised a written code to use. I'm gonna leave it at the shelters. See this guy owes me about ten grand for some liquor he took and I'm hoping that if I find him he'll be able to sort me out, and I'm writing a request for other work – later at one of the forests I've heard about; I'm looking to be cutting down trees...'

'Really?'

'Lumber-jacking on the side round Little Rock I hear pays really well. Apparently it's a hundred dollars for three foot of pure mature log, cash in hand.'

'Go for it man!'

'Providing you don't get caught that is!'

Rob was still peering at the secret code.

'Here let me show you,' Charlie said as he began showing them how he wrote his name in the signs. Paul looked round and saw a sophisticated homeless man spread his wisdom to Rob who was awestruck and Conrad who was again looking at the distinctive four marks on his torso that he soon suspected may have actually been scars. Conrad couldn't for the life of him remember where he recognised them from and it began to bug him but he decided not to ask, since he was starting to feel that their new friend had already opened up far too much and was in danger of getting everyone concerned for his welfare.

Instead it was Rob who was confident enough to make the increasingly necessary enquiry: 'That's one kick ass tattoo you've got there..?'

'You like it?' Charlie replied as they listened in suspense. 'The symbols are a type of ancient Latin. I'm not too sure myself but if I remember correctly I think they mean 'sacrifice', 'honour', 'worship' and 'eclipse'.'

'You know I once knew a guy who thought he had his daughter's names tattooed on his forearms in Chinese,' Rob started, 'and after twenty years wearing them he was in a take away one time and the woman thought that was his order. He actually had egg fried rice spelt out and he never knew...'

Perhaps not surprisingly Charlie failed to appreciate this English wit since where he came from it was a most honourable thing to do to decorate one's body with family names and crests.

'So those meanings,' began an assumptive Conrad, 'are they what your family believes in then?'

'No actually. I think the Orendas celebrate these signs,' he replied to some confusion, 'but it was done a long time ago and I didn't have a choice in the matter.'

To Rob and Conrad that didn't make a lot of sense; someone having their body decorated in such a way against their will. What could it have been? Some kind of ritual confirming his acceptance into America's above-the-law hobo culture? This guy certainly had a few strange tales to tell and by now he'd realistically lost more than one of his hosts. Moonshine, feuding families, secret writing and now reluctant tattoos? He could quite easily have made it all up and Will, who sat silently driving them now through the east Little Rock suburbs, was already planning his big 'told you so' speech upon the entertaining traveller's departure.

'What happened,' Charlie elaborated with quite a smug smile, 'was that one day, in a revenge attack for what happened at our store, the Orendas got me, tied me up and gave me these marks, and said that if I left Quay County for good then my family would be allowed to live...'. He then mischievously nodded, obviously enjoying his role of storyteller to these wide-eared foreigners who he knew were playing along with his amusing yarn. In the front Paul smirked, as he was probably expected to, while Charlie went back to his note and didn't say anything more until Will announced that they'd have to fill up and pulled into the next gas station. It was Charlie's cue. 'This is me...' he began as he made an effort to open the door. As the other three went in the store Rob asked for a photo. Charlie agreed, and on his return Will had them all in the frame and set his camera to auto-take a shot of the five of them looking solemnly at the lens.

'Thanks again,' said Charlie.

'Good luck getting home,' said Conrad as they shook hands.

'Yeah, and hope everything works out with the lumber-jacking and the whisky...' agreed Rob. Paul and Will shook his hand out of courtesy despite them having never actually shared a word.

'Did you fill her up?' asked Conrad.

'I did,' answered Will.

'Okay well write down how much I owe the diesel kitty, since I haven't got any change.'

'Yeah I'll owe as well,' said Rob as he curiously watched Charlie disappear on foot.

'You two have never got any change! Does anyone else want to drive? My back's starting to ache.'

With Paul at the wheel they set off again; back on the 40 which looped round the north of Little Rock since no sooner had they arrived in the metropolitan area than they were gone again, leaving with little recollection of the Arkansas capital aside from it being the place where their entertaining hitchhiker got out.

'That was all crap what he was saying,' Will concluded. 'Someone like him has probably never seen ten grand in their life! Don't be getting any more stupid ideas you two…'

'Remember he was our single serving friend,' said Rob, 'we'll certainly never forget him!'

'Why were you talking about his tattoos?'

'Did you not see them? His chest was embossed with these four marks. A rival gang apparently gave them to him – he obviously thought we were just another bunch of dumb tourists looking to be entertained. Bless him!'

'Why can't the government pull people like him into line?'

'I think that kind of lifestyle would be pretty cool actually, you know thumbing it round the country, doing odd jobs and spending nights under the stars. I wouldn't mind getting away from it all like that every now and again…'

★

THE INTERSTATE SEEMED to widen the further west they travelled. It appeared to be a relatively new road and traffic free that particular afternoon. For those used to driving back home, it made a pleasant change – in the States there seemed few concerns about parking, congestion, road rage or any of the other crimes regularly visited upon the British motorist. In other words, everyone realised that with the money and time there could be little better way to see this huge country. As they drove on they noted the landscape changing into Oklahoma.

'Chicago seems like a million years ago,' said Rob looking through his window at the miles of golden grasslands and perfectly blue sky. Everyone agreed; The Windy City had dazzled as an example of a metropolis, yet this landlocked heartland had a character to cherish. There were huge water towers only slightly poking above the tiny green forests to the far left and right while glorious hills smoothly carried them almost directly into the gorgeous sunshine which had everyone guessing how much more beautiful the rolling scenery could become. Conrad took the wheel after fifty or so miles and did his best to dodge the dead animals and blown up tyres on the road.

'So when are all you bitches going to hand over the money for the car?' he asked. 'You all owe me five hundred and ninety dollars each...?'

'Next town, you're driving for your money right?' laughed Rob.

'Too right I am.'

★

OKLAHOMA CITY WAS much bigger and more modern than anyone expected. Getting into heavier traffic Conrad asked for suggestions. The question was should they stay in one of the motels along the Interstate and like Memphis get a cab into town or get as close as they could and take it from there. It was after seven at night and, as was now familiar, everyone's legs were aching having been scrunched up for most of the day. Conrad was losing confidence in his eyesight in the darkening sky and mentioned that he wouldn't mind a break. The smooth, straight drive was over and he didn't want to be the one negotiating inner-city traffic. Will volunteered and soon wished he hadn't; driving in Chicago hadn't been too difficult since the rental offices were outside the city and Memphis wasn't big enough to get lost in but Oklahoma City and neighbouring Bricktown were confusing; there appeared to be no centre and few places open. It was a Monday night and the apparent lack of attractions was mysterious while accommodation was also nowhere in sight. Driving round in circles everyone's patience was soon wearing thin.

'Look, let's just hit one of the motels outside the city?' suggested Rob, now thoroughly pissed off with being lost without a clue where they were going. Will gave up the chase and briefly headed them back east to an Encino Lodge they'd passed on the road coming in. Everyone took their time changing before meeting up to head into town for what was their least eventful evening so far. A steak, two drinks and an early place to get their heads down: that would be Oklahoma City.

Back in the motel before midnight Paul was wringing his socks in the sink while Will was charging and testing his video camera. His monitor and trailing leads were out and all set up.

'There's no need for all that is there?' Paul asked, 'you've not even used the damn thing!'

'Oh don't start that again,' replied Will wiping his lens with his T-shirt. 'Maybe if you took an interest in how this thing works and what it can do you wouldn't be so dismissive of it. Come here I'll show you…'

Paul dried his hands, wandered over and sat on Will's bed and his lesson began.

'What I do is film on this Canon XL2 which is a digital format...'

Paul tried to listen as Will placed the camera on his lap and went through the controls. 'You turn it on here,' he demonstrated, 'and turn this wheel to adjust the focus, here look through the viewfinder…'

Paul peered down and saw the sharpness of the room's curtains increase and decrease as he rotated the wheel left and right, splitting his attentions between the black and white viewfinder and the colour monitor showing the image down on the floor. "Why does the wallpaper look blue?' he asked.

'That's because the white balance hasn't been set. The camera has to know what white is and from that it can identify every other colour, watch...'

Will showed him how to set the balance, open and close the iris and Paul was soon well into it; playing around with the zoom and even asked about recording. With plenty of tape to spare Will was thrilled to show him. For the next half hour Paul appeared to be having the time of his life with Will's XL2 on his shoulder, inside and outside the room; filming the traffic fly by and even grabbing a few seconds of Rob and Conrad in their room opposite. Will showed him his lead to his laptop and emailed Paul's footage to his sister with a quick piece to camera as a sort of video postcard. 'My email address here is wills the man at empire dot com,' he said. 'I just need the wire here to take the file from the camera to the computer, attach the icon to the mail and click send!'

'Awesome,' said Paul, impressed at how he could instantly watch what he'd just filmed on the computer screen. 'Wills the man at empire dot com,' he distinctively repeated and remembered.

'Anyway, is your tag comfortable yet?'

'It's okay, though to be honest I'd rather go without it.'

'So you have to stay within a mile of that thing in the car?'

'That's what they said….'

'A mile's not very far is it? We won't be able to go on any hikes or anything?'

'I won't you mean.'

'What if you just leave it in the car?'

'Police could come and check on the tag or the car at any time and if I'm not there then I'm in trouble. Anyway, can I use the net for a while? I want to see what airports my airline use on the way west…'

'If you want. I'm going to bed. When you're finished will you tell me a bedtime story?'

'No.'

NINE

'LOOK, CAN YOU just get me to the airport in Las Vegas by Monday?' said Paul with the atlas.

'Is that when you're going?' suspected Will.

'I think it is yeah. Vegas has the nearest International airport we can be at by Monday and my airline use it, so it's probably best. We'll have a weekend in Sin City?'

Will had no problem with that. While waiting for the other two he googled a currency converter and to the very nearest cent learned how much he owed Conrad for the car just as he and Rob arrived ready to go.

'Conrad, what's your sort code and account number?'

'What for?'

'So I can transfer the money I owe you.'

'Yeah I need that as well,' Paul chipped in.

Conrad began telling Will who started typing away.

'Hang on' said Paul scribbling on motel stationery, himself considering this new way of transferring sums of money.

'Internet banking's well top,' began Will, 'no messy cash or clearance times. All I need is my bank's website, my username and password.'

'You can gloat when I know the money's in my account!' responded Conrad. 'I'll have to get my balance over the phone in the next hotel.'

They all watched as Will instantly transferred the funds over while Paul folded his note and safely put it away.

'I'll give you what I can...,' started Rob.

Conrad immediately feared the worst; Rob had let him down many times over the years with money and he wasn't surprised at him putting off his contribution but, no matter how far out of pocket he'd been left – and at times he'd been left very far indeed – he always liked Rob's roguish character and how he was eternally able to exploit his own soft spots; money was just money, but two mates covering each other's backs, was priceless. He just never said anything so as not to look a walkover in front of punctual Will. All he could do was nod as Rob continued with his half-assed explanation: '…but the machine's probably going to give me the finger soon so it's unlikely to be the lot. I can always pay you back fully when we get home can't I?'

Out they went. Will started the engine. 'We're leaving Paul to fly out of Vegas by Monday?'

Conrad and Rob agreed as they set off.

SHORTLY BEFORE A town called Clinton they began to notice signs reading 'Historic 66' at virtually every junction.

'What is Historic Route 66 anyway?' Paul asked.

'I don't know but we're obviously on it,' Will proudly announced as if to acknowledge that he'd 'done Route 66', though he wasn't entirely sure what acclaim that carried. They were as usual driving west in the sun underneath a spotless blue sky. It was yet another unspoiled, picturesque day on I-40 that was suddenly accompanied by a bare, almost cobbled pathway running alongside the shoulder on their right.

'That might be it,' suggested Rob which was an underwhelming thought to believe that that little dirt road had been America's main street back in the thirties, and all could understand that replacement with the new highway had been necessary. With everyone else peering at the boarded-up motels, diners and gas stations just behind both the old and new road Will was quick to suggest that they take half an hour to visit the actual Route 66 Museum that he'd coincidently just spotted across a Clinton junction. Without getting a vote he pulled them into the car park and turned off the engine. 'It won't cost a lot,' was his reasoning.

'Here are your headsets,' said the woman handing them their boxes and earphones. The museum was the size of a small warehouse, polished to the shine with a convertible red car in the foyer. All over the walls were plaques, posters and ornaments of jukeboxes, coffee cups and tacky memorabilia obviously celebrating what foreigners could be forgiven for thinking was a symbol of a golden age in American history.

'After the financial turmoil of the late twenties...' began the audio tour, 'America was in steep economic recession....'. In the first room was more of the same; it was obviously encouraged that punters wander round the rooms at their own pace since looking at the walls, watching the documentaries and listening to the audio tour and its explanations of the neatly numbered artefacts was too much to take in at once, even for a tech whiz like Will who was often left two whole rooms behind the others.

The audio tour continued: '...and this combined with unexpected and devastating windstorms in many parts of the Midwest, countless Americans were faced with the prospect of losing their homes and livelihoods, so heading to California was seen as the only option and the legendary status of Route 66 was born as migrants headed west in their thousands...'.

'So these towns survived because of the travellers passing though?' Rob asked Conrad who was thinking much the same thing: 'You know, this country's so regional and with so much mobility and immigration, being merely an American is not very specific is it? Like, "I'm moving from Chicago to Los Angeles", it may as well be a new life in a different continent..?'

'It's something that coming from a tiny island we'll never fully understand,' agreed Rob. 'The tape said that even the weather out west was one of the reasons the homeless moved – so they wouldn't have to worry so much about the winters.'

'Now that I can understand! I think my body's used to this now. I bet it's pissing down at home and I don't miss it one little bit. Satisfied?'

'Yeah. Where are those two?'

'I'm sure we'll see them in the gift shop. I'm getting a t-shirt – come on.'

With Paul driving they were again making time towards Texas and with a new interest in the most famous road trip in America Rob suggested that 'just for authentic reasons' they should pull over onto the old road and do a couple of miles. It would be slower, was unmarked and often not wide enough Paul reasoned, but agreed that it would be worth it. After the ten yard hop onto Steinbeck's mother road Rob called a stop, opened his door and picked a stone from the road. 'I need a piece of 66,' he said, 'this reminder's real, and free, unlike that tacky T-shirt you just forked out for,' he told Conrad who didn't mind another of his eccentricities.

Paul hit the pedal while the others chatted away. He hardly said a word, enjoying the flat glide towards the Lone Star State. He only had five days left and that was a shame since whatever Texas, New Mexico, Arizona and Nevada would present, without California and not least the finale of the celebrated highway they were currently driving on it wouldn't be quite the same. Paul privately realised that he could spend a lifetime travelling this fascinating country and barely scratch the surface. He realised he wanted more: 'I read somewhere that many Americans don't have passports…' he began as they flew through Elk City.

'Yeah so?' wondered Rob putting the rock in his pocket. 'It's obviously because they're all unsophisticated slobs responsible for little but fast food and people like Dubya.'

'A bit of a stereotype don't you think?'

'I do apologise, I really love our cousins here across the pond.'

Will and Conrad laughed at Rob's retraction since respect had never been his strong point. Paul though was still in mid speech: 'I can understand it in a way…'

'Understand what?' Rob probed with unusual seriousness.

'Right, well travelling does people the world of good, everyone agrees but what I'm saying is that you wouldn't really need to leave this country to experience plenty of different cultures.'

'We've been realising that since we got here. You want to stay longer don't you?'

On the spot, Paul didn't answer. Not immediately.

'Come on admit it. You regret being a naughty boy in Memphis don't you?'

'Possibly.'

'Definitely. You tried to twat a top brass politician remember?'

'No I didn't. Honestly, I just tried to get to the microphone and 'slightly contradict' some of that shit he was saying. That's all, I never wanted to attack him, only say something about what the real situation must be like over there in Iraq. If they want me for hitting that security guard then they can have me but I say it was partly in self defence. Just because they're protecting some guy in a suit shouldn't mean they can be so heavy handed. It was total brutality the way they just dived on me…'

Paul was bleeding now, feeling most hard done by, and typically it wasn't an opportunity Rob was likely to pass by: 'All the leaves are brown and the sky is grey…' he sang.

'What's that?' Paul wondered.

'Just a song I know. "I've been for a walk on a winter's day…"' Rob continued in his best voice. "I'd be safe and warm if I was in LA…".'

'What's it called?'

'California Dreamin',' he teased, despite Will visually warning him not to. Paul though had his eyes on the road and though still feeling bitter understood that they were entitled to be excited about the rest of the jaunt that he wasn't allowed to experience, and everyone naturally assumed that he duly wouldn't until he suddenly spoke up again: 'I could just stay until the end with you..?'

Ten seconds of silence.

'What?' Conrad was first to ask.

'I'll only be ten days late…?'

'Ten days! If you're ten minutes late they'll send the Department Of Homeland Security after your ass and deport you via lethal injection.'

'Might be a risk worth taking?'

Sat in the back seats Rob and Will didn't know what to say; obviously no one wanted any more trouble but it was essentially Paul's call since they gathered that he was in fact quite serious about hanging on until the full three weeks were up. Conrad though, wanting to cover his own back if no one else's, was quick to ask Paul to consider the consequences of breaching the condition: 'We'd all be liable if you stayed past your deadline,' he said. 'Remember if you and your tag stray from that thing or aren't passing through departures by Monday they'll be on us like lightning..?'

'Not necessarily; I'll just leave the tag in the car and it'll take until my passport gets scanned when we're flying out of LA for anyone to find me – I'll make it onto the plane and be gone…?'

No one agreed or argued, not even as the old road became a muddy terrain far too unkempt to continue driving on. Indicating, Paul swiftly moved them back onto the Interstate as he contemplated staying.

'Have you told anyone back home about what happened in Memphis?' Conrad asked.

'No. Everyone expects me back on the twenty-fourth with you.'

Hearts were beating in the back. Being an outlaw for not paying at the toll booth back in Chicago was rock 'n' roll cool but flouting your impending visa laws into real criminality was deadly serious. The car was silent as everyone was wrestling with their thoughts on the matter well into Texas.

★

BY THE CITY limits of Amarillo no one was yet tired. Snacking outside services the subject of Paul staying was ignored for now, like the elephant in the living room. The place looked beautifully elegant; buildings were short, square, spread out and mature looking - appearing untouched from any Texas western that could have been filmed there half a century earlier. The sun cast long shadows over the streets while the temperature was breezy enough to enjoy watching the locals drive home during a typical weekday rush hour.

'Where's Dodge City?' asked Rob. 'I want to go to Dodge City!'
'Why?' replied Conrad.
'You know, just so we can "get the hell outta Dodge!"'
'What's that from?'
'Is it Bonanza? Or is it Gunsmoke?'
'I have no idea. Did you read that from that sign?'
'What sign?'

Rob looked round to see what Conrad had nodded towards. Other than Rob no one knew that Gunsmoke had been a TV series and when they saw the billboard across the road they assumed that that was what he was referring to. 'GUNSMOKE SHOOTING CONTEST' read the letters in bold capitals. 'ANYONE CAN ENTER...' They could have taken an interest in any of the dozens of signs along the road, including one that had been advertising a 100lb steak for the last fifty miles, but since they were now finished eating a shooting contest was a lot more likely to catch Rob's eye. 'When's it happening then?' he said squinting at the words as moving traffic cut up his view.

'What you bothered for?' asked Will, again getting that 'Rob's gone mad' feeling.

'I was a bit of a hot shot with the old rifle you know, back in the day...' Rob nodded with pride.

'I'm sure you were. But apart from paper targets what did you actually shoot?'

'Well nothing sadly.'
'Sadly?'
'Well we did have permission to shoot people you know...'

'I bet only in extreme circumstances?'

'Of course, but I tell you if I had been in any danger that I considered threatening to my life and I was locked and loaded I wouldn't have hesitated to pop a cap in someone's ass. Oh yes.'

'So you'd kill someone?'

'If that's what it took. Like Conrad and his long desired fight with a midget, I would never go round just shooting people – as tempting as it may be, but you know I believe in kill or be killed. As a serviceman in the line of duty I wouldn't have hesitated to exercise my rights. Rights sadly above the law for a civilian like I am now.'

'So you were well trained in the usage of guns?'

'Weapons, they're called weapons. The SA-80 was the baby.'

'It's all this week,' said Paul, 'that shooting contest.'

Rob looked back at the billboard and read on with interest. Apparently Gunsmoke was Amarillo's most prestigious shooting contest with a first prize of up to five hundred dollars every game. The poster showed a wholesome looking American family all lined up smiling with their rifles at the ready; mum, dad, kids, everyone. The target audience then was not just macho young men but anyone it seemed with a bit of competitive pride. 'Well what else we doing?'

Will wasn't surprised, Conrad was curious and Paul privately fancied his chances like Rob and admitted that he too wouldn't mind picking up a rifle again provided they could find the place – so off they went.

If Gunsmoke was the city's top shooting contest then it must have been because it was the only one. Cordoned off in one of the expansive yellow fields north of the city, with a two pence budget and on first sight nothing but a handful of yokels standing around drinking coffee, the whole thing looked distinctly amateurish. Young men were discussing weaponry while officials in orange jerseys were handing out numbered bibs to entrants who had completed their five minute tuition course. Everyone queued up for their lesson which they were given with five others, three men and two women. Their teacher was an older man who jokingly explained that he'd already been through the instructions ten times that day. It was an old fashioned M1903 Springfield rifle that would be used with a spotting scope, sling, glove, eye and ear protection. It may have looked funfairish but standing there listening to instructions on how to load, aim and shoot everyone was well excited.

'I can't wait,' giggled Rob.

'You gonna kick some ass?' enquired Conrad.

'Oh yes.'

Rob was cracking his knuckles psyching himself up for what he told everyone would be certain victory and that the prize money would be his contribution to the car bill. Everyone looked out past the issue desks and saw a row of ten multi-coloured targets, maybe fifty yards away from the shooting line. They got their numbers and spread out in their allocated lanes while officials kept everyone safely away from the shooters. One by one they would be given ten shells at the line. It looked easy as they watched those at the front clatter through round after round.

'Win? If you think you're going to win any money then I'm afraid I have to disagree,' Conrad shouted to Rob whose lane was one to the right of his.

'I thought you'd have a little more faith in me than that mate.'

'Well I feel out of my depth here.'

'Relax man. You're in Texas, so you're at least an honorary Texan now so you should act like one. To people round here being able to shoot is a natural responsibility. Attitudes are different to guns in this part of the world.'

The sun was blinding but at least there was a little wind. In lanes next to each other they all watched as those in front were green flagged permission to shoot. From where they were standing no one could see how close the bullets were to the bullseye or even if they had hit the targets at all. Once finished the officials flagged red to their colleagues down at the targets who totted up the scores and announced the results over a Tannoy. Looking at the scoring charts it was marks out of a hundred, though no one had a clue how many points the coloured rings were worth, but it hardly mattered since the bullseye was really all anyone was interested in. While Rob and Conrad were hyper the other two were almost motionless. Paul, in particular, was quite taken by the sight of the guy next to him. Tall, skinny with a ginger ponytail, soiled denims and cheap baseball cap he was quite a sight. He appeared unemotional about getting up to shoot, different from everyone else animated about their date with Texas destiny. Rob was first up. His number was called while his fellow Englishmen naturally had their eyes glued.

'He's going to do shit,' Conrad predicted to Will who nodded in agreement: 'This is going to be funny.'

Rob stepped up and was handed his glasses, ear protectors and grabbed the rifle, though with some trouble. The official gave Rob his bullet box, the first from which he was able to slot in without problem. Putting on his trigger glove and peering through the sight Rob had to circulate the barrel to find the target. Evidently he was having difficulty. He got sight of the board and removed the safety. With arms already aching he got the green flag and pulled the trigger. He shook with the vibration. His shot was way off target. This was harder than he thought. Another round of lead was projected towards his target that was closer and after a while he thought he was getting the hang of it. Having got through his ten shots he stepped back and the counters were given their flag to announce: 'Thirty-three' to a rather hushed applause.

Thirty-three? Rob was shamefaced as he stood back rubbing his aching shoulder. He could see the others laughing at his tally. 'Let's see how you do,' he shouted in a huff over to Conrad who took his walk forward.

Conrad didn't do much better, likewise underestimating the weight of the M1903. He gathered it was harder to hit the bullseye and aimed for the bigger yellow ring outside the centre and saw his tally slowly but surely overtake Rob's but still never trouble the leaderboard. Though it hadn't been explained it was etiquette to keep quiet and respect the shooter's need to concentrate, Rob was in a less than considerate mood, having been shouting bile in Conrad's direction whose applause was almost as muted as his own, despite scoring fifty-seven.

'Do you think Conrad was ever tempted to turn it round and blow Rob's head off?' Will asked Paul.

'You're up.'

'I've never fired a gun before…'

'Enjoy yourself.'

As Will was blasting away Paul again noted the ginger guy to his left. He was doing some kind of exercise with his arms like an athlete before a sprint. Not paying too much attention to Will's effort Paul was very surprised to hear them announce that he'd raked up an impressive seventy eight. Will sighed with a grin as he stepped back and rather than gloat decided to gracefully keep quiet and enjoy the forthcoming excuses from the others that he could almost hear already.

'Pure luck,' Rob was possibly heard to mutter.

It was Paul's turn. He set up and took his time. He got the green flag, pulled the trigger and tore the paper board to shreds with a fire so rapid everyone had to stop and watch, no bitching from Rob or coaching from a steward, nothing, just stunned amazement all round. His concentration was perfect, his execution precise and accuracy virtually spot on. Will's victory parade was suddenly looking less likely since his mate was giving a display of shooting so breathtaking that hardly anyone in the range could believe it. By the looks of things not only would he be by far the highest scorer of the four but quite possibly even the winner of some prize money. When his final score was announced - ninety-four – his applause was rapturous while he took his place at the very summit of the leaderboard. Even Rob managed a couple of claps as Paul strutted back from the line and may have even slipped an embarrassed smile.

'That was incredible,' said Conrad.

'I knew what I was doing from the start; it was the same as the army.'

'So Rob,' Conrad asked, 'since you were also in the army how come you didn't do quite as well...?'

'I would have got it in the end,' he snapped in quite pitiful self defence, 'and anyway he was in for a lot longer than me and had more practice with that kind of rifle.'

'Yeah, yeah, yeah...'

As they stood discussing their performances everyone was expecting to hear that Paul would indeed be picking up some of the prize money; they watched as one by one people came up to him and congratulated him; shaking his hand and asking him where he learned to shoot like that. Of the thirty or so people on the sight no one had any reason to believe that he wouldn't claim the top prize since he was even told by some of the officials that that was up there with the finest performances they could remember. Rob, Conrad and Will almost got killed in his stampede of acclaim though the chatter was soon interrupted by the now familiar sound of brisk shot reload and shot again. Heads were turned.

Everyone back at the range saw the guy after Paul match his accomplishment with another showing of confident shooting. Though everyone recognised the sound of a self-assured marksman, they had to wait for confirmation of his tally: 'Hang on a minute,' announced Rob, naturally quick to try and take the shine off Paul's performance. 'That badass looks as though he knows what he's doing.'

THE DEVIL'S DUST

He was right, especially when the words 'ninety-eight' were announced to even further amazement. For the regulars there it was like seeing two hole in ones in succession. Paul was suddenly yesterday's man as all the high fives were now being given to the new kid on the block, not least when an official arrived in the pack with the remains of his target – the red bullseye had been completely shot out leaving some to wonder why he hadn't been awarded a perfect score. Not that Paul ever wanted the attention but deep down he was a little miffed to have just seen defeat snatched from the jaws of victory. He suggested they be on their way since everyone had no doubt had fun and certainly got their fifty dollar entry fee's worth. It was after six before they left Amarillo to resume their race with more Hell's Angels, tanker trucks and motor homes towards the western horizon.

With Paul driving everyone was starting to ache. It was hard work just sitting there, and while no one was pulling up trees, taking on America like this was never a stroll and the condition of their once gleaming Freestar finally caught some attention: 'Look at the state of this car,' Will said suddenly, and it was a point worth making since now lying all over the interior were dog-eared maps, dirty clothes, fast food wrappers and stacks of motoring magazines. 'If the rental company are charging us for condition on return we may just be running up another neat little bill…'

'We'll sort it later,' Rob assured him. 'Where are we?'

'Near some place called Vega,' answered Conrad, 'and it looks as though we're running low on fuel.'

'Yeah we better fill up,' confirmed Paul.

Having collected everyone's cash Paul stood there holding the pump watching Rob and Will argue as usual. Whether either of them had a point was not the source of his amusement but the fact that somebody always had to have the last word, be it conclusive or not. There was often too much testosterone in the vehicle and at times even five minutes out replenishing the gas was a welcome relief. Paul was surprised to see Rob get out but since the topic of their debate was likely still the comparison of their performances at Gunsmoke it was kind of inevitable. Rob's macho pride had been dented seemingly beyond repair and part of Paul still thought it was pretty funny.

'He's being his usual self,' sighed Rob which Paul took as his final surrender. 'I'm going in for some chocolates.'

As the pair of them stood waiting to pay, the kid at the till was busy listening to the news on a small radio in his hand. They could tell because he had his head slightly tilted next to the speaker and was wearing a determined frown. 'That's just happened not far from here,' he said.

'What?' asked Rob.

'Another double murder...'

Rob and Paul looked at each other. 'What?'

'They're saying that there's been two people shot and killed in Amarillo.'

'Amarillo? We were just there!'

'They're saying it was outside that Gunsmoke competition...'

They thought he was kidding.

'Gunsmoke competition? What's that?'

'It's this shooting contest that goes on there...Oh sorry no, only one has died – the other's been taken to hospital wounded...'

That was of little relief. Too stunned to say anything the Englishmen just waited for more news that didn't come since apparently that's all police knew and the boy was no longer that interested anyway. He just asked them for the money.

'That's bad news,' imagined Rob putting down the bills.

'Yeah but there were over fourteen hundred murders in the State last year and unless we suffer a bout of genocide before January this year's figure should be much lower. Thanks.'

They walked out not knowing what to say to one another.

'How the hell did he know about the murder rate?' asked Paul.

'It's probably crap. Thirteen hundred murders a year in a single State, as if!'

'Did you actually hear what the news was saying?'

'No.'

'It's just been on the radio in there that two people had been shot at Gunsmoke,' Rob told Conrad and Will who were also less than convinced. 'Honestly that's what the guy in there told us..?'

'Come on let's go – it's getting dark,' said Conrad. Paul started the engine.

'He said that one had been killed and the other was in hospital...' continued Rob.

Conrad turned on the radio but found nothing but swinging honky tonk on the only stations the tuner could find. No one had heard of Steve Earle, Charlie Sexton or Ralph Stanley but according to the DJ they were legends in these parts for having topped the country charts.

With Paul at the wheel and the other two puzzled by this very regional music, Will sat reading the papers they'd collected from Gunsmoke and found it hard to believe that there could have been any kind of incident there. Then again maybe shootings were commonplace in north Texas. 'I'd like to make a documentary about something like that, you know it could be good for the business,' he mentioned… 'I could well get a film about a killer into the festivals…'

'Dude, if two people have just been shot and one of them killed the last thing you should be thinking about is your video business,' Rob answered in typical disgust.

'It's not our problem. It's probably crap anyway.'

'You and your films. You need to develop some more interests 'cause I'm getting a bit sick of hearing about it virtually all day long. Do you honestly think anyone's interested?'

'Getting a bit snappy there aren't you?'

'Did you not hear me? Two people may have just been shot and as far as I'm concerned that's not something to help anyone's career.'

'I'm just saying. I don't see why you're so bothered anyway.'

Rob sat with a frown while Will went back to relaxing with his thoughts until they were suddenly interrupted by the flashing lights of a State Trooper that arrived out of nowhere. Paul pulled them over and wound down his window.

'Where you guys headed?' asked the blue suited cop.

'We're stopping in the next town,' answered Paul. 'What's this about?'

The officer was slow to answer. He'd spotted Will reading the Gunsmoke brochure and eventually told them to sit tight while he returned to his car and obviously got on his radio.

'What the hell's going on?' sighed Rob. Nobody had a clue and got worried when the officer returned a minute later and asked them all to step out of the vehicle with their IDs. Some felt violated and others worried.

'So you gonna tell us what this is all about?' said Rob.

'You guys on vacation huh?'

'Yeah so?' Rob answered, taking back his passport as the lawman moved his attentions to Paul who likewise handed over his.

'Enlighten us man!' Rob was losing his temper, especially when he was unhurried to respond upon seeing Paul's photo. He suspected that he'd been on the radio and got word about Memphis two days ago and was checking that Paul was wearing his tag. After a good look at each of them the officer didn't bother checking Conrad and Will's passports. There was a moment of uncertainty.

'I'm sorry about that gentlemen but as you may have heard there's been an incident back in Amarillo at a shooting contest within the last hour and I see you guys attended. You know anything about what I'm talking about?'

'No. What incident?'

'I don't want to alarm you. There's no problem. You can be on your way.'

They knew what he meant and that the kid in the gas station hadn't been fibbing at all. It was confirmed when the country station they'd been listening to broke off for a news bulletin and explained that the suspected shooter was a scruffy looking man in his thirties with a baseball cap and long ginger ponytail. Police told the press that shortly after stealing a rifle he shot two people and is still at large. A manhunt was apparently underway.

'Christ! He was stood right next to me remember; the guy who scored ninety-eight!' erupted Paul. 'I knew there was something about him!'

'Who?' asked Conrad.

'The guy they just described, it was him remember, the winner of the competition?'

'Oh yeah, it might have been!'

'Trust me it was him. Filthy redneck.'

Paul put his foot down but after a while admitted his concentration was affected and he wanted a break to get his head round the situation. Will took over and turned off the radio. There would be no overnight in Texas.

PART THREE: THE SOUTH WEST

TEN

'IT'S GETTING LATE, we're staying in the next town right?' said Will with a yawn. The dusty road across the Texas Panhandle had been incredibly flat; since Amarillo many miles back there had hardly been a single bump, while busy wind farms, occasional ranch houses and miles of yellow grass surrounded them beneath a darkening pink sky. There was almost a feeling of reverse claustrophobia; for urban folk to have hardly seen any concrete buildings for hours, just natural land that the map told them would soon present a place called Tucumcari just over the New Mexico border.

'Has anyone ever heard of Tucumcari or Quay County?' wondered Rob. Not surprisingly no one answered. As they approached first impressions were not great but after another long day on the road all everyone needed was a bed, and there would clearly be no problem finding one since both sides of the highway were lined with motels. Walking to their rooms this time in a Microtel Inn they saw the black Tucumcari mountain in the distance and after throwing in their bags went for a stroll.

It was after ten on a Tuesday night and the four of them wandered slowly along as the wind picked up the dust providing a pleasant cool in the sultry air. They were obviously in another 66 pit stop; more gas stations and derelict diners were visible, as were old trucking yards containing long rusted buses and caravans. Tucumcari looked like it was stuck in the 50s and, pausing to peer at a street-corner map, everyone saw it was maybe only a mile long with buildings roughly just twenty blocks either side of the main road. The rows of bright signs may as well have said 'rooms for rent (but little else).' This was isolated small town America and almost totally silent. The population then was indoors, but surely a few people, everyone hoped, would be in Angel's Billiards at the end of a block opposite.

'What have we got here?' pondered Rob leading the way into the building and down a narrow tunnel lit with lanterns while strings of chilli-peppers and what appeared to be bull skulls hung from the walls. '…my kind of place,' he continued, 'where the hell's the bar…?'

When they found it, it was as dead as the rest of town; it could have been the props room to an old Mexican horror film; there were more of the skull ornaments around the walls while burning candles and the surrounding mirrors reflecting them gave an almost requiem like feeling. Will went in search of the men's room while Rob, Conrad and Paul joined just two other customers; one was shooting pool and another, a middle aged Caucasian man in smart denims, sat quietly sipping at the bar.

'I was stood next to a crack-shot guy carrying a loaded gun just before he shot two people,' said Paul, realising the fact that he could well have been one of his victims. Rob immediately identified the same Paul who'd read about his old army in the war and had reacted so badly.

He and Conrad again tried to lift him: 'Forget about it - it was miles back. Anyway you've still got five good days till you fly out of Vegas,' said Conrad, though Paul just nodded, leaving them to believe that there may be little point trying to cheer him, and perhaps the sooner he left, the sooner they could have fun again without his brooding presence. That was if he did leave when he was supposed to and not stay as he earlier suggested he might. No one was brave enough to bring it up. They just sat there, this time on the whisky.

'So, you guys in town for the celebrations?' the blue-jeaned guy suddenly enquired from along the bar.

'What celebrations?' asked Rob, half to make sure it was them being addressed.

'The Day Of The Dead parade, you know, tomorrow?'

'No, we're just passing through. You?'

'I'm a trucker from North Carolina – that's my rig parked outside. I do the 40 all year long and have done for years, and tomorrow every year many round here present gifts to their departed. That's what all these dolls are for,' he explained, pointing up round the ceiling. The three of them looked and saw many beautiful wooden figures streaming from the rafters which were in fact smiling skeletons in traditional female dresses and sombreros; striking toys that he told them were called 'Catrinas'.

'How many people are expected here tomorrow then?' asked Conrad, hoping that in just hours the town could go from dull to possibly quite full.

'A couple of thousand were here last year,' the trucker replied. 'I seen lots of people arrive this afternoon. If I remember correctly they go indoors the night before and prepare their gifts. The Day Of The Dead is the most celebrated time of year for this town, one of the reasons why there are so many motels along the road here...'

'He's right,' said the barman, 'I've been doing my poems for my brother who died just last year and I'm going to read them to him and maybe give him sugar bread. He loved that stuff.'

'Where's all this happening?' said Rob.

'In the desert, right out the back here.'

'Is there a burial ground then?'

'There sure is, the burials will take place there on the island in the middle of the lake. There are usually a couple of funerals that I hang around and watch – and those expecting visits from people who've been long gone put down their crosses and candles...'

The English were intrigued, while on his way back from the restroom Will got his drink and typically got talking to the only other guy in there and managed to hustle in on a few games of pool, and with nothing better to do but listen to truckers and barmen talk about dead people everyone else just nodded along though with a strange jot of genuine interest.

'You decorate this place?' Conrad asked the barman, still looking round the room.

'Over the years the owners here have built this place up yeah. You like it?'

'It's amazing.'

'What are those jars?' asked Rob, pointing to what appeared to be bottles of sand behind the bar.

'Jars of Devil's Dust.'

'Devil's Dust?'

'Yeah. Well round here dust devils – you know whirlwinds of sand that spin out in the desert – they're considered lucky charms so the owner keeps a few pots and has them on display. It's just a little thing.'

'Right... anyway, might you guys have heard anything about a double shooting in Amarillo tonight?' naturally asked Paul.

'No not tonight,' said the barman.

'Not tonight?'

'Well I think I remember reading that three or four people were murdered around there at the weekend but I haven't been able to keep up. We're kinda slow getting the news round here, being so far from the cities but I wouldn't be surprised if there had been a shooting.'

Clearly gun crime was routine in these parts and it wasn't really a concern for most. For all they knew everyone walked around armed and as fascinating as it was, Conrad was hardly able to keep his eyes open. What he was hearing could by then have slipped into a dream or more accurately a nightmare.

'Look I'm tired,' he said to the guys, 'I'm going back to the motel. Anyone coming?'

'Yeah, come on let's watch the poker,' agreed Rob, 'Paul, you coming or playing pool with Will?'

'I'll stay here with him for a bit.'

It was around one before they headed back. Paul was still seriously tempted to stay on with everyone else. Strolling along the silent empty road looking up at the New Mexico sky he was feeling the thousands of miles from his claustrophobic life back home. Even allowing for the Memphis 'incident', America had been liberating and, being in a silent desert town far from any media he could breathe out, safe in the knowledge that he wasn't pigeonholed as just another rat in a crowded urban race. Here Paul felt tranquil and everyone's equal. He and Will laughingly stumbled along talking nonsense and actually walked past where they were staying, only realising when they saw no Freestar outside any of the similar motels along the road. It was only when they got directions - a full hundred yards in a straight line - from a rare passer-by that they were able to get back on track.

'Hey thanks a lot man,' said Will appreciating the assistance.

'Don't mention it,' replied the helpful citizen. 'Get home safely.'

'See that tattoo on that dude's chest?' asked Will, 'I could never get one like that since I'm too hairy.'

'I think it's time for bed...'

Will was rooming with Rob who had consumed a few strong whiskies and not unrelatedly thought it might be funny to play a minor practical joke on him when he arrived back. All he could think of was to vandalise some of his clothes. He gathered it would at least save him some washing so after the poker he'd begun his preparations.

'Open the door man' said Will absolutely aching for his bed. He continued to knock but Rob didn't open. After a minute or so Rob pushed open the window and poked out a pair of Will's jeans hanging on a wooden cane.

'What you doing?'

Rob grinned as he revealed a cigarette lighter with the other hand and lit the pants that soon caught fire. It was surreal. Conrad and Paul heard Will shouting and rushed out to see the commotion. Rob started swinging the ignited clothes round like a sparkler. It was an eye-catching sight as the fire flew round and Rob was looking thoroughly pleased with himself.

'You're gonna pay for that,' Will shouted.

As the joke was coming to an end a gust of wind blew the flames back in Rob's direction that forced him to throw the rags but it was too late: the smoke had gotten into the room and almost instantly set off both the alarm and sprinklers. Rob's white shirt was quickly covered in soot and he was soaked, as was much of the room. If that wasn't bad enough five or six guests from along the row rushed out in their nightwear in a confused panic. Rob's stunt had rather backfired and when the manageress duly arrived in her slippers she told them in no uncertain terms that they would have words in the morning.

ELEVEN

SHE WASN'T THE only one angry. As if having his clothes burned wasn't bad enough Will had had to sleep in a wet bed as well as being concerned that his equipment might have been soaked. From Rob there wasn't much remorse; when summoned at dawn to the office he agreed to pay for whatever damage, and that, he figured, excused his behaviour but Will was having none of it, especially when told that as an occupant his presence was also required.

'You've been a knob since Chicago,' he fumed during the walk of shame to reception where the bosswoman was waiting for them, probably with a gun. It was to be one of the hottest days of the year and Tucumcari was bursting into unlikely life. They could see dozens of people, young and old skipping along carrying flowers, food, toy skulls and big pictures of people all along the road. They wondered if this was really the same town of only a few hours earlier.

'What's all this about?' continued Will, his fury on hold for a second as he packed his computer and its leads in the car and saw what must have been entire families walking out to the fields behind the buildings opposite. Next to the Freestar were several more cars, pick-up trucks and motorcycles that had been nowhere in sight the night before. Rob remembered the trucker telling them it was The Day Of The Dead and it may have been their day of the dead as they arrived to face the music.

'Go in there,' said the woman pointing to a back office behind the desk, 'I'll see the two of you in a minute.'

'What the hell were you thinking?' started Will as they sat down. 'If you can't pay for your car I don't know how the hell you're going to be able to pay for this. You know I'm not paying a penny..!'

'Look I was drunk. How much did those flares cost anyway…they were filthy; I bet it would have cost you more to wash them.'

'That's not what I'm worried about; did you see the damage to the room?'

'So the sheets and carpet might have got a bit wet?'

'Oh so you didn't notice all the smoke that's stained the walls?'

Half an hour had passed and the manageress still hadn't returned. The reason for the delay was that she was out inspecting the damage. When she finally showed up it was too late for the free breakfast but thankfully the damage was actually only minimal; they were told that sixty dollars would cover it and on the spot Rob handed over the cash.

'I've just spent nearly an hour apologising to my guests for last night's alarm,' explained the woman. 'And especially a lady from one of Quay County's most respected families who was deeply upset by the disturbance and thought she was being attacked by some gangsters…'

'Why is she telling us?' thought Rob '…she's sending us on a guilt trip!'

'I think you young men should make an effort to personally apologise to her since she's still very upset…'

'What?'

She wasn't joking. Middle-aged and clearly of a middle-class respectability, she thought that an incident at her motel was a stain on her character and that was unacceptable, and so those responsible should do the honourable thing and personally clear her name.

'Look lady we're sorry but we've got to get going….' Rob declared.

'I tell you Mrs. Wimbush has been a close friend of mine for many years and now you've made me look foolish…' Rob heard the name Wimbush and immediately remembered Charlie Wimbush, the hitchhiker they took from Memphis to Little Rock two days ago and, since they were also in Quay County that he mentioned he thought it could well be a relative.

'So, will you go and apologise?'

'Oh sure.'

They were escorted through to the dining room and shown to a table where they were introduced to a seated older woman and her teenage granddaughter. Like many of the people they'd just seen outside and again like Charlie they were visibly of Native American ancestry; both had dark skin and black hair, though in the elder woman the greying signs of maturity were naturally evident. Conrad and Paul were across the room having pancakes and cereal.

'Mrs. Wimbush,' began the manageress, 'these are the guests who accidentally set off the alarm last night...'

'Oh don't worry about that...'

'They've come to apologise...'

'Really dear it's nothing...'

While Will was going through the reluctant but short formalities of saying sorry, Rob thought it no harm to ask if they had any relatives who ran a moonshine business in Tennessee.

'Moonshine in Tennessee?' asked Mrs. Wimbush with a most quizzical look, 'No love, of course not. Should I?'

The manageress told them to rebook or be out by midday and off she went.

'Charlie, Charlie Wimbush he's called...?' probed Rob figuring it was still a possibility since he believed that there couldn't be that many families named Wimbush there in Quay. She raised a curious eyebrow but didn't say anything.

After assuming no for an answer they began heading over to the others as the girl spoke to her grandmother in Spanish and something changed. 'Charlie Wimbush...?' began the woman calling them back, 'why do you ask?'

'Well it's just that we met this guy who claimed to go by that name when we were in Memphis a couple of days ago and he told us that he's from Quay County in New Mexico, and since you're also called Wimbush I just thought you may know someone like that since it's quite an unusual name...?'

Mrs Wimbush was becoming intrigued: 'What might he look like?'

Rob sent Will to make the one minute dash to the room from which he returned with his wire and camera. Flicking through the pics he found the one of them and Charlie and showed her the screen. After a moment of unmistakable emotion visibly passing over her she looked back and gave them the warmest smile.

Rob was right. It was Charlie's mother.

★

THE WIMBUSHES LIVED close by in a historic pueblo adobe

building. Next to the shell of yet another old motel, it was a huge house above the family's pottery store, a business generations of them had been running for more than a century. There were five of them living there at the moment; Rosa, her son Ryland, daughter Anna and Anna's teenage children James and Nikki. Having been invited to the house the four Englishmen sat round the kitchen table – Rosa had gathered everyone together to hear anything they could tell them about Charlie, her long lost son, uncle to James and Nikki and brother to Anna and Ry, who asked the first question.

'Er, he's on his way home,' optimistically offered Rob being offered more nachos that had been quickly prepared. With five Wimbushes staring at him he naturally felt under some pressure to deliver. 'Just two days ago we saw him, he was in Memphis and we drove him to Little Rock.'

'Little Rock, Arkansas?'

'That's where we left him. We said he could ride with us for as long as he liked but he insisted on getting out at Little Rock – where we took that photo.'

'How's he doing?' excitedly asked Anna, in her early forties with different coloured beads neatly tied into her braded black hair.

'Well he told us he'd been mixing whisky near Knoxville but when he left us he said he was looking to work in the forests around Little Rock as a Lumberjack.'

'A Lumberjack! Man we assumed he was dead,' Ry continued as he gawped at Will's camera. 'Look he hasn't changed a bit. Damn it, I wish he would just phone! Thank you so much!'

'Do you have a computer?' asked Will, 'Because if you do I can copy the picture for you?'

'Oh would you? The PC's through in the living room. Let's step this way.'

'Our day has changed now,' said Anna now happily passing round spicy rice wraps, 'we were going to put things on the altar for Charlie at the festival this afternoon.'

'The festival?' asked Conrad.

'The Day Of The Dead, today.'

'We can assure you, Charlie is alive and well.'

Conrad chose not to tell Anna that her missing brother was living homeless; he and everyone else just sat there amazed at the coincidence of it all. The four of them looked round and were most impressed with the decorations they saw. There was pots, ornaments and rugs everywhere; incredible pieces of work.

'Do you make these?' asked Rob.

'Of course,' answered Rosa. 'Everyone here can sculpt, paint the jugs and knit the rugs. Both the boys and girls. Charlie was the best at the sculpting. Would you young men like to see our store?'

'Well I would…'

As Will and Ry returned, the teenagers were asked to tidy up while everyone followed Rosa down to the store which, like many businesses in the town that day was closed for the festival. Rosa explained that she and young Nikki stayed at the Microtel along the road to finish knitting a banner they'd been working on while Ry and Anna stayed home and put together a wooden altar to put it on. No one at all minded the wasted effort now that they knew Charlie was still alive: 'I can still go and talk to my husband. I know for sure that he's dead!' said Rosa as she and her grown-up children escorted them downstairs.

The store was gleaming. The pots and ornaments were spectacular; gondola shelving units were glistening with jugs, candlesticks, photo-frames and lamps; many of them patterned with the family crest. There were likewise woven hand baskets and patterned rugs hanging from the walls and colourful wooden Geronimo figures standing a foot high on the floor. Stunned at being given this exclusive tour, the four of them each noted that for all the craftsmanship on show the prices were surprisingly low and in many cases virtually rock bottom. Will couldn't keep his curiosity quiet: 'Do you do well from your sales?' he asked, business-minded as usual.

'Well just enough for us to live on!' answered Ry laughing as he scanned a few barcodes of some vases that were left on the counter. 'Most of our income comes from passing trade. Many folks, like you guys, are just staying in town between nights in Amarillo and Albuquerque and buy something before they move on.'

Ry was a big man and could easily pass as Charlie's brother. Watching him use part of his morning off to catch up at the tills, it was clear that the family business was his passion. The man of the family was proudly telling the visitors about his favourite jugs and they weren't just the ones that he'd sculpted and peering round everyone saw a good number of them were mysteriously full of sand. He was only too quick to explain that it was for luck.

'Luck?' wondered Rob, 'is it called Devil's Dust?'

'It sure is. I believe that many years back a couple of guys from these parts were up in Reno to do some work and they had to paint the floor of some big casino. I think they mixed the sand in with the paint. Two nights later they were playing cards on that floor, had a big win and with the money opened the motel that restarted our town's economy.'

'Excellent. You know I'm a bit of a card player myself...'

'I'm hopeless at cards! People will tell you different why sand is lucky but that's the story I know. And this one is something that Charlie designed...' Ry handed one of his preferred pieces over to Paul who was so careful with it, it was as if he was holding a newborn baby. It was another work of art that was surprisingly cheap. Like Will, Paul had to mention the price. 'Well worth the money...'

At the potter's wheel round the back Anna defended the prices: 'Since we don't employ anyone else we don't have many overheads, and besides, having more money than you need makes you greedy. When I watch the news and see all the trouble that goes on in big places it's all because of money. We're happy with what we've got.'

This was strange. Here it appeared were a family at peace, happily running a small business and apparently not interested in making all the money they could quite easily get: one of their pots in Chicago would easily go for twice as much. No one was chasing their tails then; the Wimbushes were content in their world and also it appeared, only interested in what went on within its close-knit boundaries.

'Would you young men like to come with us to El Día de los Muertos?' asked Rosa.

'Excuse me?' said Rob, half embarrassed that he didn't know the Spanish.

'Would you all like to come with us to The Day Of The Dead?' translated Anna, fully embarrassed for her elderly mother who'd forgotten that they wouldn't know.

No one refused.

AFTER HEADING BACK to the motel to refresh and re-book they returned to find all five Wimbushes smartly dressed holding the gifts. Rosa and Nikki were holding their banner; Ry had the altar while Anna and James each had handfuls of jugs, flowers, toy dolls and chocolate boxes. Everyone was clearly happy but since they were still heading to a bunch of funerals the English were naturally confused. Should they try and join in with the 'celebrations' or should they quietly pay their respects? The nine of them joined the flow of people through the streets and eventually out past the last buildings north onto the harsh landscape that was only broken by a small lake around which a number of people were gathered.

'This morning I'm so sorry for not understanding when you were talking about Charlie,' Rosa told Rob. 'It was completely unexpected that you would know about him…'

'I understand; it's an amazing coincidence. Here let me give you a hand with that…'

On arrival Ry placed the altar down next to that of another family and everyone duly began placing the gifts on its shelves. 'We believe that once a year our relatives who've died return from the afterlife to visit us. They eat, drink and have a good time,' he told them.

There were perhaps two dozen altars on the dirt with people sat round both laughing and praying. Though the candles would serve no purpose in the daylight it was still a sight. The manageress from the hotel was there, as were the trucker and barman from the pool joint the previous night - all eating and drinking from a buffet that had been set up to one side. Everyone seemed to know one another; police, town officials and funeral directors were all embracing while age, nationality or ethnicity was clearly no issue; there, miles from any skyscraper, nightclub or sports stadium, Tucumcari was united in celebration.

'The ancient people of Mexico - the Aztecs – believed that the souls of the dead went to a place called Mictlan…,' Ry continued as he and young James were carefully placing down chocolates and sugar bread, '…and Mictlan is where the souls finally rest and later tonight the recently deceased will start their journey.'

They watched as the Wimbushes sat on the gravel and invited visits from their departed. Unlike any place of worship they were used to, all around was gaudy colour and whatever the noise, nothing would interrupt these special moments.

'Please, sit,' smiled Rosa.

Everyone did as they were told. Looking at their altar now decorated to completion it was as beautiful as the next while conversation was surprisingly encouraged; Rosa, sat at the front chatting away to her late husband while Ry continued telling them what he knew about the day as more and more people arrived by the lake, in the middle of which was a long flat island where several new graves were being prepared. 'The boxes are coming...' he pointed.

They looked over and saw two coffins being carried towards the waterfront. Everyone stood and began to casually wander to the site.

'Listen, James and I are going back to get some lunch. You guys coming?' asked Ry. 'Anna, Nikki and my mom will want to stay and chat for a while but we'll be back for the burials this evening, what do you say?'

Arriving back on the concrete Ry showed them the town's bus station as one of the frequent I-40 Greyhounds was pulling in with even more people. He told them that some even got connecting busses from as far away as Colorado. That trucker had been right; Tucumcari was suddenly a magnet for people and, inevitably, for what was no doubt originally intended as a deeply religious event, things were turning commercial with street vendors spotted charging for shirts, masks and fancy hats. They needed shelter from it all and were taken to a café bar and given a local dish and as many beers as they could handle.

'It's amazing that you found my kid brother,' Ry announced while waving away everyone's offer to pay for the order.

'Why did you think he was dead?' asked Rob pulling up a seat.

'Well he got into trouble with these guys from the other side of town and after an incident we never saw him again. We assumed they murdered him.'

'An incident? Was your store attacked?'

'Charlie told you then?'

Rob nodded.

'It was many years ago – we were provoked one night and Charlie reacted, and, fatally we believed, so did they, since police tell us there's been no trace of Charlie since. Until now - thanks to you guys!'

'Are you going to show the police the photo then?'

'What's the point? The police are damn useless in this town. There are now six full-time cops here and they've no time for the case anymore – they want it closed.'

Rob and Conrad remembered Charlie telling them about this. If they didn't believe him then, they did now as Ry confirmed that a long running feud between his family and another family called the Orendas came to a climatic head; 'They've always been jealous of our success with the pots; three generations have now been taught to hate us. And we feel the same way about them.'

'They're still around here?'

'They run a big blacksmithing shed just outside of town but apparently they aren't doing too well. I heard that with some insurance money they got from losing their clients recently they're preparing a bid to buy the old motel building round the side of our house. If it's true, no doubt their endgame is to be in a position to put in a bid for our house, since by law it's on the same land. We've been in dispute with them for decades over the house.'

'Do you not own the house then?'

'No. We've only ever been renting from the town. Bosses have suddenly told us that we can buy the house now because they're putting it on the market. See here, thanks to stiff hundred-year-old laws that they've only just told us, by owning buildings you can also have first refusal on those nearby if they're not privately owned, and since what we believed was the house's yard is in fact in the motel's grounds we're at risk. Local government has just put up a sign outside announcing that this Monday is the earliest anyone can put down their deposits; ten thousand dollars is all for both the house and the motel. I've got about half that right now.'

'How long have you been renting?'

'All the way back to my grandfather - the family has been renting the house since 1900 - and they tell us that that counts for nothing! It's unbelievable.'

'Nineteen hundred? Jesus Christ! All that time and only now they've told you about this?'

'Before he died my father never told us that we'd only been renting – we could have easily bought the house outright; the old fool. Even still my mom doesn't know. I can only hope that I can get the full deposit down before anyone does so for the motel.'

'Relax, no one's queuing up for that. Surely the town already has enough places to stay?'

'The Orendas aren't interested in owning a motel, it's our home they want.'

As they chatted away it became clear that the Wimbushes, like everyone else, had had their own troubles beneath the peaceful façade that had first met their visitors. Ry's loosening tongue told them that his people had over the years been oppressed by everyone from the Orendas to Lincoln's Yankees. He went on to explain that due to political bigotry many young people were forced to leave for the likes of California in order to build their lives and few ever returned; they often married Caucasian and ultimately reduced the population of the indigenous people. At his most bitter he estimated that the Native Americans had less than a century left before total extinction.

Having been sat there not able to listen with full attention Will and Paul slipped in an interest in moving on but agreed they could handle staying; their succumbing no doubt partially thanks to the endless supply of free beer. They spent much of the afternoon playing the arcade games in the bar while Conrad, Rob, Ry and James all opened right up and drank away. James was particularly pleased with the pumpkin mask and black sombrero he'd just bought; one of the many topics of conversation that occupied them until they stepped back outside at dusk.

The desert was stifling but what a sight. The candles and torches were lit presenting everyone in virtual silhouette under the red sky while many women dressed up as Catrinas held their purses at the water's edge. It was obviously the Latin American Halloween and the spirits were well and truly present. Worse for wear the six of them eventually found Rosa, Anna and Nikki watching the coffins being taken across to the island; one by one the open-topped boxes were lifted onto canoes after a coin was given to the ferryman who placed it in the mouth of the deceased before pushing off.

'What's happening?' Conrad asked Ry.

'The family has to pay for the journey to the afterlife – the cost is a coin. The Charon puts it under the tongue, stands on the stern and paddles over to the Island Of The Dead where the souls are sent on their journey to Mictlan.'

'What if they don't pay?'

'Well the legend says that while the bodies still get buried the souls cannot enter the afterlife and have to wander alone in a nowhere land for all eternity.'

'And who're the ferrymen?'

'Organising and playing Charon is the job of the local funeral directors. Once a year it's their chance to be in the school play. They're the only ones allowed over to cement the boxes to the ground.'

While most were in good spirits, there were one or two opportunists there who could spot tipsy strangers a mile off. As Conrad and his beer breath stumbled along to get a better view he got engaged in conversation with a beautiful young woman who appeared to take an interest in his accent. Playing the drunk for solidarity she simulated falling over, after which he naturally helped her up. 'Oh thank you. Excuse me,' she said back on her feet with his phone now neatly tucked into her bra.

'Did you get her number?' asked Rob, likewise blind to the scam.

'Nar, I was just being a gent.'

Everyone noted that it was a good job only eight burials were scheduled since the Island Of The Dead was looking rather full judging by the number of headstones they could see. Watching the canoes sailing over under the moonlight was picturesque and a rather inconsiderate Will thought it okay to start snapping away and duly received some frowned looks from those around him.

The pictures he took would pretty much be everyone's only reminder of the event since the next day's hangover would almost certainly erase all memories for sometime. Responsibly the Wimbushes offered only coffee back at the house and as they were leaving Ry presented them with two of their finest pots filled with Devil's Dust. 'Thanks for the picture and enjoy the rest of America,' said Rosa, eyes filling up as she stood in the front yard.

'You'll find Charlie,' Conrad assured Ry with a friendly handshake, 'remember he's working in the forests around Little Rock.'

'I'll be heading off there next week don't worry.'

'That's right, and you must drop me an email when you do find him,' said Rob, going round kissing goodbye - Rosa, Anna and even young Nikki who like James had never even known her lost uncle. No one had been expecting much from a tiny town where they would just get their heads down but Tucumcari - with both Will's photos and this family - would be for great reasons as memorable as anywhere.

'I could have made a good film about that,' boasted Will as they strolled back to the motel.

'No you couldn't,' Rob replied dismissively.

'Alright then I couldn't. You know best.'

'Why do you always talk about your business – do you think anyone's interested?'

'It's not just business, making films is my hobby and anyway you're just jealous because I've been able to earn a living doing something I enjoy.'

'Jealous of you? Run that by me again…'

'You heard. You're a barman who if you're lucky is going to get promoted to a minimum wage security job.'

It was business as usual. Since Rob and Will had known each other for roughly half their lives perhaps they were allowed to routinely snipe at each other without any moral boundaries though the other two kept well back.

'And what's wrong with minimum wage?' wondered Rob, increasingly confrontational.

'The people who accept it are just losers with no ambition.'

'And who do you think you are?'

'I'm a businessman…'

Everyone sniggered.

'….and one that's honest enough to try and take every penny I can get. Just what have you got against profit?'

'Do you earn every penny you get? I mean do you really graft for it?'

'That's not the point. If there's an opportunity to maximize my profits naturally I'm going to nip in and take it. It's not about working hard - it's about working smart. Who wants to work for someone else and be a slave? See how happy they are running their own store?'

'Yeah, but employees don't have to cut throats to stay competitive. Unlike employers, they do an honest day's work for an honest day's pay. Their morals are intact.'

'To hell with morals. It's every man for himself in this life and unlike some I'm not just honest when playing cards, I'm honest where it really counts.'

Just before the motel Rob went to the gas station's ATM while the others bought cokes. Conrad and Paul noted that things were getting unusually heated and imagined quite a tense night next door. Conrad had an idea that they should sneak in while they were asleep, nick their keys and phones, lock them in and head off to Albuquerque early in the morning. At least they'd get some peace.

'I'm just going straight to bed before I end up knocking him out,' murmured Rob as they entered the yard. His murmur wasn't quiet enough; in a snap Will threw his can at Rob and soaked him with drink. Rob reacted by wrestling him to the ground. In all the time they'd known each other it was the first time they'd ever got physical.

'Behave yourselves,' shouted Paul who after quickly putting down the pots jumped in to drag them apart. 'You don't want the manager out two nights in a row!'

The scuffle was over in a matter of seconds with Will storming into their room and slamming the door, leaving Conrad and Paul with a new roommate for the night. Rob was fuming, though there was little anyone could say. The air had been cleared. Paul went about his nightly business as if nothing had happened; he switched on the TV and began shaving. Conrad also rather nonchalantly lay down and began to read. Rob sat on the floor and called Will every name under the sun before eventually going silent.

'You want to take a shower?' asked Conrad, 'I'll give you a clean shirt…'

Rob took his shower and attempted to share head to tails with Conrad but didn't sleep such was the anger cursing through his veins. Tomorrow everyone hoped the incident would be forgotten. It wasn't because no one slept; the three of them were looking to quench away their post-alcohol thirst. Rob got up and knocked Will's door. Will opened and he marched in, collected his bags and left again without saying a word.

'Is he still awake?' asked Paul lying there in the dark.

'He is,' said Rob throwing down his retrieved luggage.

'Right well I'm moving in with him. You take this bed.'

Up got Paul with his belongings only to find Will next door putting on his shoes.

'Where you going?'

'I'm going for a walk. I need to clear my head.'

'Don't be stupid man. You need some rest.'

Will continued to dress as Paul put down his stuff to complete the switch. 'Right well I'm coming with you then,' he said.

'I'm stuck with him until we fly home. In fact I might just leave with you,' he spat as he and Paul began wandering along the road. They walked south and again out onto the roughly hewn gravel in the direction of the Tucumcari mountain.

'Where the hell we going – it's five in the morning…' Paul moaned.

'I don't know, anywhere.'

The sun was arriving as they walked out a half a mile from anyone and shortly reached the rock that made up the base of the four hundred foot high hill. 'Can we go back now?'

'I'm climbing up,' answered Will as he began ascending the diagonal wall. With little choice Paul followed and they soon found an opening that appeared to lead well inside the rock.

'Wait will you?'

'I want to have a look inside.'

'You can do – but later on. We're not ready for anything like this. Let's go back to the motel, pack our things and bring them two?'

'No. He's a dick.'

'Come on!'

'If I see him I'll kill him.'

Since Will was still adamant hours after the fracas Paul conceded that he wasn't going to budge: 'Right well I'm going back then. You've got your key. I'll see you later.'

TWELVE

BACK AT THE MOTEL Paul found the other two already packed and having breakfast in the dining room. To his disappointment he found Rob no more willing to reconcile than Will. It was left to Conrad to do the talking: 'Well where is he then?'

'He just went out for a walk to see that mountain out the back. Looks like we'll have to wait for him.'

'Leave him there,' Rob predictably chipped in.

'What?'

'Leave him there. You stay with him,' Rob continued. 'Get the bus and we'll see you in Albuquerque later today. I don't want to be sat in a car with him for hours right now. Give us a ring when you arrive; we'll be in a motel along the road. I might have cooled down a bit by then – if I see him now I tell you I'll put my knuckles through his head.'

They'd certainly got annoyed with one another this past week and a reduction in their numbers might diffuse the situation. Paul took two mouthfuls of scrambled egg from the tray and left in evident disappointment. Conrad was also surprised with Rob's idea that they should pair off but after thinking about it, made the effort to confirm it to Paul who had begun packing back in his room.

'Look it can't be much more than three hours…There's no way those two will stand the sight of each other right now - you know that. You've got our number and the bus fare won't be that much – like he said we'll be in a motel along the road. We'll see you later…?'

Paul knew he would have to play go-between if Rob and Will were to be reunited and that wasn't a responsibility he wanted so eventually agreed that he would get the Greyhound to Albuquerque.

Hours passed after Rob and Conrad left and there was still no sign of Will. It was coming up to midday when Paul stepped out and looked along the road towards the mountain and saw nothing but departing festival goers and felt a concern pass over him. They would shortly have to pay for their room again since without Will it couldn't be vacated. He went back, reluctantly paid for a third night, locked up and walked to the hill to look for him. He reached the slope and saw the opening that he said he'd like to look in. There was no proof that he'd actually gone in but stood there, a natural curiosity urged Paul to at least stick his head inside. It was a square tunnel twenty feet in diameter and thanks to the sun was lit long round a bend. Tiptoeing along carefully Paul soon saw that the end of the natural light didn't mean darkness; the glow was refreshed by an artificial looking glimmer that pulled him closer. He came to an opening into a big dome with a row of totem poles that he had a second to see before being struck across the back. He fell to the ground; the last thing he saw before losing consciousness was a scratching on the interior wall: four symbols.

★

'I TELL YOU, that's well strange that we found Charlie's family. I can still hardly believe it,' said Conrad at the wheel.

'Well, maybe, but not if you really think about it. I mean, at first glance New Mexico's huge, but it's so bare of people and communities that it's in fact quite likely that if some native has the same name as another they may well know of each other...'

'I suppose, and remember we picked him up on the 40 and they live on the 40, so address-wise he'd hardly moved!'

They laughed before Rob's heart momentarily sank: 'Oh shit...'

'What?'

Rob pointed towards the box still sat there deviously flashing on the dashboard.

'Well...?' continued Conrad.

'Well what?'

'...shall we go back and get them?'

'We forgot. It's too late. So he's separated from the car...'

'Might the cops find him, or us?'

'Either I would have thought...'

'Do you not think it's serious?'

'What do you want me to say? He'll be back within a mile of

the car in a couple of hours and anyway he should have remembered himself. I'm not going to apologise for wanting away from that other one if that's what you mean.'

They arrived in Albuquerque and the familiarity of the urban landscape was a welcome relief after the isolation of Tucumcari. The city was colourful and peaceful; clean streets sprang from the main road that contained gift shops selling more rock art and just about anything that could be deemed a souvenir from this the next town on 66. Flags hung from lampposts, cafés advertised lunch discounts while shiny banks and ancient redrock buildings mixed neatly in the shadow of the Sandia Mountains. As agreed they pulled into a Motel along the front that had a sparkling pool just inside the patio. They checked in and went for a swim, after which Conrad went to check the phone expecting at least one missed call. He couldn't find it and naturally assumed Rob had it.

'You've got it,' Rob called back, 'I tell you this water's gorgeous.'

'I haven't – I've just turned my pack inside out and it's not there. You must have it.'

'What?'

'I've checked all my pockets and it's not there. Seriously.'

'Did you not plug it in to charge?'

'No. You must have it.'

Rob got out and dried off. Standing there looking through the fence Conrad saw a Greyhound pulling into the city's bus stop across the road and thought that though it was still early, the other two could very well be on that very vehicle. He was hardly surprised when they didn't step off it but was still quite sure Rob would find their mobile. He went back in and saw him turn out his bags but no phone.

'Well?' said Conrad.

'Well what? I've not got it. You had it!'

'How are they going to find us if they can't phone us?'

'They can't.'

'Not got any ideas?'

'You used it last, in Memphis remember?'

'Well I've not got it now. We'd better look in the car.'

Out they went and aside from all the maps, magazines, chocolate wrappers and pots of Devil's Dust there was still no phone. It was getting serious; they had become separated by a hundred and eighty miles while Paul and his tag were now well out of range.

'Look, Will's laptop,' Rob said, pulling it out of a pouch behind the driver's seat. 'He must have packed it not knowing we would stay a second night. They've got no PC and we've got no phone. This isn't looking good.'

'Do you remember the name of the last place we stayed in? We can phone them and ask to be put through to their room?'

'But they will have set off already?'

'It's worth a try.'

'I think it was called the Microtel Inn.'

Rob headed to reception to ask for the number. The clerk called directory enquiries while Conrad felt some guilt since he knew it was he who had lost the phone - how and where though remained a mystery. Rob returned and from the room phone dialled the Tucumcari Microtel. 'What number room was Will in?'

'Six.'

'Oh here, you talk. He still won't be talking to me.'

Conrad took the receiver as it was ringing. 'Yes that's right, the young Englishmen in room six…Oh really..? Well can you put me through?' He held the phone to his ear though after a moment the receptionist from the Microtel decided that ten rings with no answer was enough: 'Would you like to leave a voicemail after the beep?'

'Okay.'

'Right stand by.'

Overhearing Conrad announce where they were staying Rob gathered that they'd paid for another night.

'For what?'

'How should I know?'

'Oh well.'

Conrad flicked on the TV and had no trouble finding poker highlights. The World Series was well under way only two States away: 'I must admit I think TV poker's quite exciting, especially since the viewer can see the pocket cards thanks to the cameras in the table.'

Rob agreed, lying down and wondering what the players would do next.

'Raise him!' he shouted at the screen, 'raise him!'

The player he was advising was a fat guy sporting a goatee, stetson and shades. They watched him rattle his chips while the commentator talked up the tension. There was a lot in the pot – he was thinking about raising certainly, but they knew he had no chance of winning

THE DEVIL'S DUST

since his smartass opponent, a skinny oriental guy with a thousand yard stare, had recently landed an unbeatable flush. The guy in the hat was clearly thinking 'you can't lose what you don't put in the middle, but then again you can't win anymore either'. He chose to raise and subsequently lost twenty grand, and probably ached somewhat more than they had back in the Chicago hostel, a loss that was still sore a week later.

'What I felt in Chicago was at least on a par with what he's feeling' Rob announced.

'Yeah right. Somehow I doubt it. Anyway, we out tonight?'

'If you want, though I wouldn't mind catching up on some sleep this afternoon.'

★

AT NIGHT THE street lights lit the roads like a Christmas tree. 'That's strange that they still haven't been back in their room..?' wondered Conrad.

'They'll be okay; they're big boys. Look at all these boarded up shops, even the ones that aren't shut have signs saying "everything must go" and "no vacancies". There's a place open. Let's go in?'

It was a salsa club somewhat less macho than shooting ranges or theatrical burial ceremonies. The queue was about ten people long. 'What the hell's this man?' asked Conrad looking through the tinted windows at all the curvy Latina honeys spinning round in heels.

'We need to broaden our horizons once more. Just don't tell the other two okay!'

The music was provided by a Pueblo band with congas, mandolins and dulcimers. The lyrics were Spanish and as the pair stood there sipping their beers, they didn't know where to start. People were dancing in couples; men and women, women and women and even men and men. On the floor moving was an art; beautifully executed and seemingly with the strictest of discipline. It was far from the punk moshing that they could manage in dark clubs at home but rather a formal skill that was either loudly approved or harshly criticized. Under stark lights that exposed even slight errors observers were not slow to give the thumbs down, and those that did put a foot wrong were booed right back to the bar never to be seen again. Expectations for Conrad getting a perfect ten were not high when he was yanked up and twirled round by a blonde girl in ripped jeans and trainers. She would obviously have to play teacher.

'Hello,' shouted the girl in his ear, 'where you from?'

'Albuquerque.'

'No you're not.'

'How do you know?'

'Because you've got skin like milk and you move like a submarine.'

Not a great start. Rob looked on, possibly a little jealous.

'I was kinda hoping to blend in,' replied Conrad, by now feeling almost assaulted by the close grinding of her body coincidently just in time for the tempo of the music to drop and the lights to dim. Stood there turning green Rob had seen enough; he put down his drink, slicked back his hair and strutted towards her friend who on his approach started laughing. Rob was horrified. 'Something wrong?' he asked in puzzled dismay.

'Yeah; your dandruff!' she answered.

'What?'

She reached over and started brushing his shoulders. It was a strange ice breaker he thought but at least it was progress.

'You really need to change your shampoo!'

'What?' again said Rob, finally sensing that he was being belittled. He looked down and to his horror saw that under the disco lights his flaky white skin was illuminated all over his dark shirt. At his supposed moment of strutting cool he nearly died of classic British embarrassment, though in a face-saving effort he simply ignored the shame and dragged her out to show some footwork. It was a bold move but he figured his reputation couldn't be damaged any further and the young lady seemed to accept, obviously out of pure sympathy. Two friends were soon enjoying sultry dancing with two friends and many songs later things were still going well.

'So what do you do?' asked Conrad.

'We're both unemployed,' his dance partner answered without shame. 'There's little work here right now because of those sharks in the banks who lent too much of the town's money to Californian businesses that aren't paying them back, so people are getting laid off all over the place. It don't matter since when I get my office gig back I'm saving up and moving to New York. I want to be around more people and have more to aim for.'

'Do you not think that the jobs might have gone forever?'

'Hey I keep my chin up. Anyway, you know we like a swim to cool off round here?'

'I'm sure you do.'

'Tonight, might you guys like to join us?'

'What…where?'

'Out in the river!'

'The river?'

Sarah and Becky they were called, and both thought a late night dip might be fun. Outside the club, arm in arm Conrad and Rob were not likely to turn down their offer and were fully prepared to indulge if that was the social etiquette. It was certainly warm enough.

'So you guys really swim in a river out here?' asked Conrad, amazed at how approachable these girls appeared, clearly without the shield of brooding aloofness that women back home eternally wore.

'Sure, everyone does it,' answered Sarah, 'come on, this way.'

They were led just out past the majority of the buildings and in near total darkness down a small stoned embankment where they could smell strong natural water.

'What is this place?' asked Rob.

'It's the Rio Grande,' replied Becky.

Glistening under the moon was the urgent flowing water. There was no problem with the air temperature but there certainly could have been with safety. It was hard to believe that two girls would just strip off and jump in, especially with such little reserve and that they would do so in front of men they'd known only a couple of hours, and, what would they be wearing? The answer it turned out was nothing at all, as having put down their towels in they jumped, totally natural. After the shock they surely couldn't back down now.

'You not fancy nicking their purses and pissing off?' asked Rob.

'When in your life are you ever going to be naked outdoors with strange girls again?'

'After you then…'

'Okay, let's go. And don't be looking!'

'Relax, it's too dark, and besides I'd need a magnifying glass.'

'Christ it's cold!' yelped Rob as his skin hit the water. Conrad pulled out his contacts and submerged completely whilst tightfistedly holding his glasses; of course he didn't want to be fumbling around naked unable to see his clothes back on the bank.

No one got arrested and no one had their clothes stolen, just scratched feet and dirty hair. Sarah and Becky were feeling quite pleased with themselves for introducing these foreigners to the delights of skinny dipping and asked them to join them for a coffee at a friend's place only half a mile up the river. Refreshed and freezing Rob and Conrad agreed once more. As they strolled round a bend, they saw more people doing what they'd been doing. There were quite a few people in sight, half of whom were in the river and the others sat wrapped in blankets on the gravel lit from their car headlights and a crackling fire. To Sarah and Becky stripping off with strangers was just standard social behaviour and disappointingly then, for two lonely Englishmen, not quite an engraved invitation to further naked fraternization. Damn it. Further up the bank they attempted to chat pleasantly with small groups of fishermen sporadically standing in and around the water.

'Why you interested?' answered one, clearly in guarded privacy.

'Relax man,' answered Conrad, 'so, you caught much tonight?'

'Nothing. How I'm gonna pay my bills I don't know. Now leave me alone!'

'Bills! Are you working?'

His question was ignored; they were a bunch of illegal Mexicans looking to pull out brown trout for their employer. It was a dangerous operation that far up stream where the pace of the current was rapidly increasing, making it quite hard for some of the smaller guys out there to keep balance in the water. The couples standing safely on the craggy riverbank thought they were either brave or foolish to be that far out, especially in the dark and that far from the town.

'Those guys are pretty crazy,' said Sarah, who for a local was also surprised. 'Please come in – it's dangerous!' she shouted as two of them - young women - were almost up to their necks in the ever more aggressive water. She got no response. They just stood out there, in their macs and hats watching what little they could see of their coloured floats being yanked along by the flow.

'Come on, it's not our problem,' said Becky as they passed a bunch of them standing close by on the safety of the bank, preciously guarding the boxes of fish that they'd all pulled in already. It was very hush hush.

'I hope you young ladies know where we're going,' announced Rob, still hobbling on the gravel that he'd unwittingly put in his shoes. He could see it wasn't too far to the next bridge where they rejoined the concrete and spotted two buses in a nearby yard that were obviously what the fishermen had arrived in. 'Look, that window's been put through...' he noted.

'All the windows have been smashed,' said Sarah 'and the tyres burst, look.'

It seemed it was an attempt from genuine American anglers to disable the illegal fishermen's transport. They were competing for piece work for a local market that didn't care from whom or how their product was coming in.

Becky knocked the door of a small basement building and a tall hippy opened up and gave her a hug. He was topless with shoulder length dirty blonde dreadlocks and several string necklaces decorating his skinny torso. He invited them in where the stench of marijuana hit them. Brad had been a former work colleague of Sarah and Becky at a downtown insurance company before they were all made redundant. 'You guys been out tonight?' he asked.

'We went to Club Heat, we had flyers to get in free before ten thirty and met these cool English guys and then went for a swim. This is Rob and Conrad.'

'Anyone else out there?' asked Brad, shaking hands with his right and taking a drag with his left.

'No one in the club but in the river there were a couple by the bridge but we didn't get close enough to see anyone we might know. What you been up to?'

'Nothin' much,' Brad answered in a rather moping manner.

Everyone sat down as the drinks and smokes were passed around. Rob accepted and inhaled but Conrad did not. The scruffiness of both the place and tenant was familiar to anyone who understood the tedium of unemployment. Brad had left pizza boxes and CD cases across the floor while piles of dirty clothes were left on his tatty furniture.

'So you guys going to the Grand Canyon?' he asked; the obvious question for visitors in the region.

'Maybe. We don't really know where we are. We just met Sarah and Becky and now we're here in a strange guy's place enjoying a smoke. You'll have to excuse us if we seem a little quiet,' Rob explained.

'Relax man you're totally welcome. Enjoying your vacation so far?'

'We are. There are four of us driving across the country, we left the other two back in Tucumcari for a while, you know on the way from Amarillo?'

'Sure.'

'You never told us there were more of you?' said Sarah.

'Well Rob and this other guy we're with got into a fight...' admitted Conrad, much to his mate's annoyance: 'Leave it out will you?'

'...and we agreed to meet up again here in Albuquerque hoping that they'd have time to cool off.'

'Are all four of you going to the Canyon?'

'We've just arranged to spend the weekend in Las Vegas that's all.'

'Las Vegas Nevada, or Las Vegas New Mexico?'

'Huh?'

'The one up the road here?'

'Nevada....'

'The famous one, like most people.'

Brad turned on his gas heater which was a gesture that was much appreciated since everyone's skin was still stinging beneath their thin clothes. He was also kind enough to find a couple of clean towels and even made a small effort to tidy up. It was nearly four in the morning but the girls knew he would still be awake; on the Internet all night playing poker.

'You win any money?' asked Sarah, cracking open another can.

'There's nobody playing for real money at this time of night - which is just as well since my redundancy packet's wearing a bit thin. Christ I gotta get a job soon.'

'Which site do you use?' asked Conrad, 'poker site...?' he spoke up naturally upon hearing that his host was also a bit of a player.

'I'm signed up to eight of them.'

'You play Hold 'Em?'

'Sure do. The Rolls Royce of poker.'

'We sometimes play. Not much online though, how do you find it, compared to face-to-face?'

'There's no money to be won online. I'm not interested in seeing spurts of digital figures on my computer screen anyway, right now I want to feel the steady cash in my hand - to pay the damn rent. There's no face-to-face games going on around town either, especially since all the lay-offs. To get a decent game I get down to El Paso for the time being.'

'Not get to Vegas? Nevada?'

'Not after last time.'

'What happened?'

'Man it was painful.'

'Come on, I can imagine, believe me it's happened to us all at one time or another.'

'I was there for a few days a couple of years back and had to leave a bit soon.'

'Surely in the first rounds the stakes weren't that high?'

'I got too big headed too early.'

'And you got cleaned out?'

'No I won…'

'What?'

'Without knowing who he was I beat this champion guy within three hours. The manager of the casino congratulated me; he gave me a bottle and asked would I pose for the newspaper and do a quick interview. Then next day I'm known all round town and nobody would play me! I tell you I couldn't get a game anywhere. I was stuck in low limit hell!'

Brad sat down and began looking for a new table and soon noted that as usual there were only five and ten dollar limit games going and they weren't even full.

'See this is the most popular site and there's hardly anybody there.'

'Have you got much money in your account?'

'About two hundred and twenty dollars.'

'Try table eight?'

Brad took a seat and when prompted by the curser threw in his blind.

Conrad took a closer look: 'When money's tight I always say try and win only one pot an hour, at least. You'll have to fold a lot, nearly always if the blinds are high and often straight away if your pocket cards don't suggest much…'

'The money's never risky here.'

'Opportunity for us to experiment with different tactics then?'

As Conrad and Brad were glued to the screen Rob was working hard on the girls: 'So you got a boyfriend?' he asked Becky.

'He's down in Las Cruces. He moved there a couple of months back since he got a job in a record store.'

'How far is that?'

'More than two hundred miles.'

'You must be struggling to keep a relationship with that kind of distance?'

'Two hundred miles is nothing! Besides he comes back at weekends.'

'Today's only Thursday?'

'It's Friday morning now.'

'Sorry. I stand corrected.'

Conrad was having more success showing Brad his talent: 'Being passionately in love with your pair of queens and the flop comes anything higher will likely cost you a lot, especially if there are a number of players, since someone else is likely to have something that'll make them a higher pair. Swallow your pride and muck.'

It wasn't just Conrad teaching Brad about poker, the American with too much time on his hands had a few top tips of his own. Not long after sunrise the three Americans were required to go and claim their benefits.

'I didn't love my job but it was better than nothing. At times since getting laid off I've just about learned to manage having no money but the boredom has come close to killing me,' said Sarah as they were out and on their way to claim. 'Being unemployed is the hardest job of all because it's relentless,' she continued, 'like when you're in work you can look forward to relaxing when you've knocked off, when unemployed there's nothing like that; you just float along and time soon comes to mean nothing.'

As they reached Albuquerque's welfare office they were not alone. The queue stretched round the block and there were many, unlike Sarah, Becky and Brad, who were not moping but visibly angry at the Mexicans who made up a large number in the queue.

'It's been nice meeting you guys,' said Conrad implying that it was time for them to part. 'You've got our email address...'

'Stay with us guys, we can cash our cheques when we get through here and hang in the mall?' said Sarah.

'Are you in the queue young man?' asked a security guard, 'if not then please step aside.'

There on the street the queue had got so rowdy that railings had been introduced before the doors and security guards deployed to patrol the numbers. Conrad and Rob stood well back and were able to get a look at the near fighting that was going on further down the line.

'Look give me your number...?' Rob asked Sarah, 'we'll call you tonight, when we've found the other two and got some sleep. We'll hang then?'

Sarah wrote her number on Rob's arm and gave them directions back to their motel where they expected a message.

A message wasn't there. They paid for another night.

THIRTEEN

PAUL AWOKE IN A stone room inside the Tucumcari mountain. He'd been out for almost a day and didn't know where he was. He saw a big Red Indian towering over him. He was heavily tattooed, wore smeared face paint and many thick knotted feathers in his long hair. With miserably wrinkled skin and blackened eye sockets he was an imposing scarecrow like figure.

'Where am I?' coughed Paul from his position on the floor.

'You're in our temple, the rock of Tucumcari.'

'Who're you?'

'My name is Maska, but that's not important.'

Paul was immediately scared. He was both awake and in pain. 'What's going on?' he tried to ask.

'You've got one chance to save your friend.'

'What?'

'Come here.'

Maska grabbed Paul, hauled him up and frog marched him across the room and made him look through a huge glass window at a larger darkened space lit only with weak torch flames. In shock Paul attacked him but it was no use; he was weak, sweating, hungry and easily knocked back to the floor. Almost insulted by his feeble attack Maska momentarily began tapping on a keyboard he had on a nearby desk with some radio and phone scanners.

'Listen boy, I know he's your buddy...'

'Who is?' Paul attempted to shout. He was pulled up again and forced to sit in a chair. There, inside the town's foothill had been carved two spaces, they were in the civilized smaller one; neither were recent work but certainly the neighbouring dome looked as though it provided an environment for some kind of ceremony. Through the glass he saw the three totem poles from when he first wandered in, an aisle in between rows of wooden benches and sets of hammers, anvils and knives lying on the dusty ground. Silhouettes of men suddenly throwing coal onto torches near blinded Paul with the light. He could feel the heat on the glass while clusters of crows jumped and fled in fright. Sitting with his hands now tied the dome looked holy and primeval.

'Look boy,' said Maska.

Paul was slowly able to open his eyes.

'What? What?'

'Look there!'

After a long look Paul could identify Will. Down in the dome off to one side he was sat tied to the floor with long chains underneath one of the torches next to the benches and a bowl of fruit. His head was bobbing up and down. He was alive.

'You have an opportunity to save him…'

Paul was silent; horrified but this was real; he was finally getting his bearings.

'Listen,' said Maska, this time showing Paul his knuckles, giving him a view of the same four symbols that Charlie Wimbush had badly burned into his chest.

'What do you want?'

'It's not about what I want. It's about what you want, and how bad you want it because it is going to cost you, but not too much. You do want to save your boy don't you?'

'You've got the wrong guys. Now what the hell's all this about?'

Maska was studying Paul's passport: 'British huh? I think you can get me the money. You give your daddy a call and have him transfer the money and you make the withdrawal from the town's bank? Say ten thousand dollars ain't too much for your friend's life?'

'Don't have any money man!' Paul snapped, helplessly kicking out in anger. Maska picked up his phone and called in one of his gang. A younger man soon arrived who was equally muscular, had the same grim features and the symbols more neatly on his body. It was the same guy who gave him and Will directions on Tuesday night. It was he who had identified them as victims.

'This is my nephew, Yuma,' said Maska. 'He's going to be watching you outside, just to make sure that you don't go running to any lawman, 'cause if you do, then you can just keep your money because that pal of yours is gonna be tied up, burned, killed and given away.'

'Killed?'

'See my son's getting married here on Sunday and if I can't get the money, I'd like to at least give him one of our *full, traditional* weddings since the family hasn't had one of those in years and one's certainly due. Though I'd rather you save him, any interference from anyone and I tell you he'll be turned off on the spot. I'll be listening to all the radios, CBs and phone lines in the area…'

Maska made this chilling threat during what appeared to be quite a leisurely spot of Internet banking. There he sat, checking his statements while two young men had suddenly been thrown into a situation that he was responsible for. Cool and aloof, he nonchalantly told Paul that he was being charged too much interest on one of his credit cards.

'You're sick,' Paul continued as he looked into the dome. He could see the totem poles; they were clearly now gallows poles. He looked back at Will down there - he was catatonic and shaking violently. Enjoying himself, Yuma nodded along. It was harrowing. Maska was chillingly calm and totally sure of himself. The civilization of the modern world had clearly not been adopted much by these people with regards to their traditions; they were talking and behaving like barbarians with no regard for innocent human life. That their motivation was so little money was as shocking as the equipment there in the lair. There was a stack of screens from security cameras covering the all round exterior next to rows of walkie talkies charging in their cradles. Along with the scanners and computers then whatever was projected to happen in the dome, be it a wedding, a human sacrifice or both, was clearly being planned with military-like precision that would give little chance for any disruption. It was clear that Paul simply had to come up with the money or Will would die.

'This is the bank code and account number that you'll need should you wish to transfer me my money online, I'm fine with that,' Maska explained as he folded a note and shoved it down the front of Paul's pants. 'I'll be watching my balance, you have my word. You've got three days; midnight Sunday. Don't waste time. Here's your key and wallet. Just ten thousand if you please.'

'Phone?'

'Oh sure.' Maska gave him back his phone, though without the battery or sim card. Paul was untied and thrown into the back of a pickup truck. Yuma leapt behind the wheel and drove at speed out of the hill to the centre of town. It was little after six on Friday morning when Paul was thrown out into the road. Yuma watched him stagger his way back to the motel. Paul collapsed on his bed and was asleep in minutes. Yuma turned off the engine and sat tight.

At eleven thirty the motel phone rang waking Paul with a start. It was the front desk telling him that if staying he must soon pay for another night. Had it been a nightmare? It couldn't have been; he was still bruised and through the window he saw Yuma in his truck staring right back at him from over the road. Paul needed time to clear his head; he showered, changed and walked across to the ATM. Yuma left the truck and followed close behind with phone in hand. With more money Paul entered the motel with the intention of telling them to call the police. Before he could get a word out Yuma walked in behind him. With cold feet Paul paid for another night. As he was leaving he overheard Yuma book the room next to his. Though posing no immediate danger he was already a leach.

Back inside Paul saw a light flashing on his phone and played Conrad's voicemail. He knew they were okay and waiting in Albuquerque. The phone was there - all he had to do was ring for help. He knew Maska would be listening in and that on sight of any police Yuma would call in. It was risky, and to deny himself the temptation tore the line from the wall making sure the plug was snapped. Outside Yuma had pulled a seat from where he would be easily able to watch his comings and goings. Paul locked himself in and pulled shut the curtains. Now that it had sunk in, he was worried. He remembered seeing Will sat there chained up by evil Indians looking to carry out their sick religious beliefs unless they got what they wanted and there was nobody to turn to. Tucumcari was in the middle of nowhere and felt ignorant and nepotistic; people just went about their business with little time for outsiders upsetting their peaceful frontage. He figured that none of the town's few police officers would take him seriously anyway. He eventually went back to sleep hoping to wake up back in some kind of normality.

He woke in the early evening strong and fully refreshed. He opened the door, saw Yuma still sat there with his drink, phone and newspaper and slammed it closed again. There was no way he could overpower him, he was far too big. The decision to at least try though was almost made but he finally remembered that with his tag he'd long been out of range of the car and he'd surely be well and truly done for if he got in any more trouble. He opened up and faced him: 'I'm going to get some food. Wanna hold my hand?'

Paul walked to reception and bought virtually the entire vending machine. Like clockwork Yuma followed but without suspicion from anyone since he was also now a legitimate guest. The clerk saw Paul from behind the desk.

'Young sir, at last…' he said.

'Yes?'

'There's been a couple of messages for you….'

'What?'

'Yes, the young men you were staying with on Tuesday and Wednesday have been trying to get in touch. They're now in Albuquerque and want you to ring them on this number. I've been trying to call you but you've had your phone unhooked.'

'The phone's been broken.'

'Really? Unfortunately then it'll be Monday now before we can replace it but you can always use the phones here. Shall I dial right now?'

Paul looked round at Yuma who smartly kept up appearances by also shopping at the machine, though with his ears peeled at anything that might be said. Paul thought he could hand write a note asking the motel to call the police and pass it over but again imagined Maska listening to the line. On a whim he agreed and let the clerk dial.

'Christ at last,' said Conrad who like Rob had just woken after being asleep all day. 'We were about to go to the police…'

'What?' Paul was careful, knowing that if he said anything too revealing it could mean the end for Will.

'Why have you not come to Albuquerque like we agreed?'

'Er, it's Will…'

Yuma peered round.

'…he's still mad at Rob and wants more time out. You know what he's like.'

'Have you been trying to phone us?'

'I can't, my mobile's just broke.'

'That's okay since we've lost ours anyway. So what have you been doing then?'

'We've just been hanging out with Ry again remember? He's a top guy.'

'Okay. So what's happening then, now that we know you're alright?'

Paul stuttered; he needed more time: 'I tell you what, we'll meet up tomorrow in Vegas? We can catch an overnight bus that'll have us there by afternoon.'

'Vegas? Why not here, we're on the way aren't we?'

'The only bus we can get before Monday doesn't stop anywhere else, it goes straight there, Ry told us, and I'm getting a bit bored of these little towns. I'd rather take my last full weekend in a place where I can see some serious nightlife.'

'Are you sure?'

'It'll be alright. Are you guys good for money?' he asked.

'Think so why?'

'I mean for diesel to Vegas, just the two of you?'

'I might have about three thousand dollars left – I don't think Rob's got that much but we'll easily have enough to get us there. Where we meeting then?'

'Do you know the famous hotel on the Strip?'

'I'm sure there are loads of famous hotels on the Strip…Here, Rob wants a word.'

'Paul! How've you been man? We went clubbing and skinny dipping with these babes last night…'

'As if…'

'Honestly. Listen you know you're out of range from the car?'

'I know. I forgot. It's done now. Don't worry I'll take the blame if they come and get me.'

'So Vegas then?'

'Yes. Find the big Circus Circus hotel. We're coming in on the bus: we'll check in tomorrow sometime…?'

'Circus Circus?'

'That's the one.'

'Well we'll see what we can do.'

'Good. Listen how much have you got?'

'Enough I hope?'

'No really…'

'I don't know, maybe fifteen hundred dollars…? I've just been guessing the exchange rate but without my balance I can't exactly tell. I've not even paid for the car yet.'

'No neither have I, it's alright. The hotel won't be that dear. So we'll get staff there to put us in touch tomorrow okay? I've got to go and get Will and get him to pack, he's over playing pool. We don't want to miss this bus tonight.'

'Alright then we'll see you tomorrow at the Circus Circus. Viva Las Vegas!'

With only slight guilt over his fibbing, Paul hung up, and after answering the clerk that Will had merely been back resting this past day carried his armful of snacks back to his room with both his shadows. He now knew that even if they all put their money together it wouldn't be enough to save Will. How would he possibly get ten thousand before midnight Sunday? The consequences of the situation were equally untidy; Maska had made it clear that the money would do but should he not deliver what would happen to himself? As a witness, would his own life also be in danger? If he resigned himself to not finding the money should he run out of the State and inform the authorities? Would they suddenly become best friends if Will was actually saved?

Too many thoughts were speeding through Paul's head; his scruffy motel room was now a container of horror, frustration and aching loneliness. In irritation he flicked on the TV. As usual it was Las Vegas poker. The commentator talked about the amount of prize money that was being banded around and Paul ached that if only he could get his hands on just a fraction of that. On the carpet was Will's video camera but strangely no laptop; he correctly assumed that Rob and Conrad had driven off with it. Things were going from bad to worse but he soon had a brainwave – perhaps it wasn't quite impossible after all. He would think overnight.

'SO WE GONNA give Sarah and Becky a ring?' asked Rob, 'out for a couple of hours on a Friday night before we set off?'

'I'd rather just get going, I can't drink anyway. I've got a big drive staring me in the face.'

'But I'm in there with either of them...!'

'No you're not - they were just being sociable. There are no goodbyes on the road - you know that.'

'But we've paid for tonight here – Paul suddenly gets in touch and tells us that we have to jump and head off? Remember the danger of the last overnight drive?'

'Yeah, but unlike last time we've been asleep for a lot of the day. Come on.'

Conrad and Rob wrote off their bill and left just after evening rush hour and without any delays got into Arizona and Flagstaff before midnight. Stuck behind a bus at an engaged level crossing there was slight reason to believe that Paul and Will might be on it.

'Paul said there's only one bus that goes to Vegas before Monday so they might be on there?' suggested Conrad, 'Then again maybe it's a private bus...'

'By a stretch of the imagination I suppose they could be on there...'

'You're missing them aren't you...? It wasn't that long ago you were trying to knock Will's head off.'

'He did hit me in the face with a tin can? Man this is a long train.'

Rob was right. Cart after cart went by - it was possibly a mile long. It wasn't an Amtrak but a series of freight carriages carrying tonnes of wood and steel. There was plenty of room for the stowaways who weren't even hiding; under the lights many scruffy figures were seen with their belongings clinging to the cabooses. Conrad and Rob could only assume that they were more careful during the day.

'No time for the Grand Canyon then?' said Rob, finally getting a look at the sign to the famous national park - it was a two hour drive north.

'We haven't the time, and it wouldn't be open now anyway. So what? It's just a whole lot of nothing isn't it?'

They finally got off the 40 and turned right at Kingman onto US 93. There was no other traffic by the early hours allowing them to speed on north. Having sat there for several hours they'd become accustomed to the air-conditioning in the car; it was pleasant cruising the desert highways with the radio on but after another fifty or so miles they had to fill up. It was three in the morning and according to the thermometer a shocking one hundred and nine degrees. Conrad, suspecting a malfunction, jumped out and put it to the test. There was no malfunction; he was bludgeoned by the heat. He staggered into the gas station instantly sweating to the drip and made sunblock a late and desperate addition to the shopping list.

'God only knows what it's like during the day,' he thought back on the road as it soon snaked round the top of the mighty Hoover Dam on the Nevada border. The catseyes were the only lights and soon an uneven cluster of them emerged on the horizon. As they drove closer it got bigger; they quickly realised that it was in fact the shimmering skyline of Sin City, true to its reputation alive and kicking no matter the hour.

The traffic was quite heavy; Conrad had them creeping along while Rob was struggling to read from the book. He found Vegas and the map. 'What's this street called?' he asked in hopelessness.

'I don't know – you may as well just keep an eye out for this hotel through the window – The Circus Circus. Paul says it's a big one on The Strip.'

'Yeah but where's The Strip?'

'I don't know; I can't see any signs. Shall we park up somewhere and get directions?'

Conrad, now having them in a fairly well-lit tunnel underneath a closed theme park, decided to chance it: 'I'll stay here and keep it running. If I get moved on I'll just keep driving up and down this stretch and you'll have to flag me down?'

'Right. I'll be back soon.'

Rob got out and nearly melted. The lights were dazzling, the glitz was overwhelming and as luck would have it a convenience store was open all night where, after picking up some toiletries, he was told that the Circus was on a straight line into the centre of town. Conrad had gathered as much with the book by the time he returned. It was right in the middle of Las Vegas Boulevard and conveniently opposite an all-night branch of Conrad's bank.

Pulling into the car park and looking at the site map it was clearly a small city within a hotel. Casinos, conference halls, the circus and incredibly even the hotel lobby was listed. It was much more expensive than the chain motels in the heartland but since it was where they'd agreed to meet there was no alternative. They drove to the barrier and collected the parking ticket before dragging their bags into reception. Paying even more for an 'unsocial arrival time' they got keys to a twin room and as the sun was coming up hit beautiful silk pillows up on the sixth floor.

FOURTEEN

PAUL WAS CONVINCED IT was the only possibility. It was Saturday morning and the clock was ticking. Again like a robot Yuma followed on his trip to reception. The ever helpful guy on the desk took the money for two more nights and on request dialled the Circus Circus who forwarded him to their room.

'You arrived yet?' said Conrad after being woken by the ringing.

'We're on our way; the bus is at services in Arizona' Paul again lied. 'Listen I suppose you guys will want to play a little cards this weekend?'

'Whatever gives you that idea?'

'Well if I bankroll you with all the money I won't be spending with you lot in California next week would it be a wise investment?'

'I can't say...'

'I need ten grand...'

'Don't we all?' There was a pause. 'Ten thousand quid? Dream on mate!'

'No dollars.'

'What? Why an interest all of a sudden?'

With Yuma pretending to be browsing the leaflets on the desk Paul knew he couldn't reveal much like the truth, not that they would believe him anyway but he figured that the sooner they could get playing the sooner the money would be up. 'It'll be a life saver,' he said – pretty much the only true words coming from his mouth.

'This hotel you've sent us to is reducing our disposable income if you know what I mean. I suppose you just picked it out of a hat?'

'Listen on your best sessions could you come up with ten thousand between the two of you?'

'With a bankroll and at a stretch maybe why?'

Paul needed an explanation. 'Ten grand is my fine,' he said, 'the cops got me and my tag in Tucumcari and told me that's what I must pay.'

'So they got you and read you the riot act?'

'They were quite alright about it actually. It's just that apparently I'll be cleared of a lot of bother if I can pay before I leave on Monday. Any chance of helping me out?'

'I don't know; ten k is quite a lot. I'll tell Rob when he wakes up. Not promising anything though. Who're you supposed to pay?'

'I told them I'm flying out of Vegas so they've gave me these forms of the people to pay there. The address is off The Strip so it won't be far. It's not actually as bad as I thought it would be in Memphis, not if I can pay the fine anyway…'

'How much have you got to put to?'

'A bit – but not much more than a buy in at a decent table. With it you guys could be up ten pretty soon surely?'

'Look we'll talk about it when you arrive. How's Will?'

'I think he's over it now. He's in shopping. He is a bit pissed off though that he left his laptop in the car with you.'

'We noticed.'

'Look I'll see you later alright? And feel free to get started at the tables,' said Paul before hanging up.

He had progressed little. How on Earth would he convince them that the money was needed to save Will's life? He was sick of that damn motel room – it was filthy but for the third morning in a row turned the maid away insisting that it didn't need tidying. He just sat there pondering and peering at the mess. He saw Will's camera and remembering his lesson in Oklahoma picked it up, saw that its battery was fully charged and a tape was loaded. In with the mess was also the note he'd taken of Conrad's bank details and, after seeing a mental lightbulb opened the door and faced Yuma.

'Just going to the bank machine. I suppose you want to come?'

Paul withdrew his daily cash limit of five hundred dollars, went to the convenience store, bought some food and quickly disappeared back into his room. Ten minutes later he again opened up this time holding Will's XL2 and its cable. He made a demand of his watchman:

'Take me to your uncle.'

'You have the money now?'

'Not yet.'

'What's the camera for?'

'Let's just go!'

Walking back into the secret hole inside the Tucumcari Paul was unfazed. Still sat there in his hideaway overlooking the dome Maska was surprised to see him back so soon carrying a video camera.

'Can you save him now?' he asked.

'Midnight Sunday, like you said. Give me some leeway before then...?'

Maska appeared uninterested; bizarrely he appeared to be browsing geology websites: 'You know adobe rock is made from natural sand and clay and accounts for some of the oldest and most amazing buildings on Earth?'

'What the hell you talking about?'

'There's a beautiful big adobe in this town you know? And I can get it! It's been hijacked by those pot squatters for far too long now but finally, with your rescue of that boy before Monday I can make a claim and be well on my way to owning what I believe is my family's by right.'

'Well if you want the money then you gotta let me down there.'

Maska ignorantly continued playing with his computer and shouted directions down to his workers who were preparing the dome for the wedding. It was looking ever more striking with those symbols now carved everywhere though Paul was concerned only about Will – whose condition he saw had worsened - and proposing to record proof of the terrifying situation.

'Look the only way you'll get the money is if I can prove this is real?'

'Nobody films our ceremonies. Too sacred.'

Maska went back to tapping on his computer.

'If I get you the money you'll let him go?'

'You've got my word. You know the deal: that money will get me the most valuable adobe in town. Otherwise that kid is gonna be sent to Lucifer and believe me that'll give me almost as much pleasure as when my boy ties the knot.'

Through their brief words and daunting demeanours, Paul was starting to believe that Maska was a man of principle and wanted his money whereas Yuma wanted Will dead. Looking down at him still in chains his catatonia was clear. His sporadic, zombie-like movements bore no resemblance to that of the healthy young man who he'd always known. Lying on the dusty ground he began repeatedly rolling around and fitting before again dropping back into a near motionless stupor. On sight Paul was losing his cool: 'What did you do to him?' he ranted.

'He's had a little medicine – to keep him quiet, and keep him ripe,' answered Yuma with evident and evil satisfaction. Naturally Paul attacked him but was easily brushed aside.

'You're wasting your time son, he might be dead soon,' said Maska with no patience for another protest.

'I don't want to film the wedding. Just let me film this place now?' Paul pleaded.

'And do what?'

'Show the tape to some guys who'll get you the money…Look you know there's not ten thousand dollars in this town so I gotta show some people in Vegas.'

'How?'

Paul nodded towards Maska's equipment. 'On your computer right there. I'll email them the film and then they'll send you the money…?'

After a moment's pause Maska said, 'you've got ten minutes'.

Yuma was told to escort Paul into the dome where he immediately ran down and embraced Will whose eyes were black, clothes filthy and features slothful.

'How you doing man? Look I'm gonna get you outta here.'

Will didn't reply. He was still shaking, seemingly unable to speak or show any emotion. It was as though he couldn't see Paul even a foot from his face. Paul noticed needle marks in his forearms and was absolutely furious.

'Can I get some light in here?' he shouted.

Maska signalled for coal to be thrown onto the torches. Paul turned on the camera and pressed record.

★

IT WAS FAIRLY safe to say that Las Vegas didn't have much of a purpose during the morning, and especially not in the middle of August; hotel pools and air conditioned amusement arcades were where people mostly hung out and before Rob woke Conrad decided to try his luck downstairs in the Circus where the games rooms were immense. There were card tables with roulette wheels and video games but it was the slot machine room that caught his attention. Having changed a couple of notes he sat next to a man and made no secret of his desire to watch and learn. After a minute or so of having him staring over his shoulder the player naturally broke the ice.

'Okay there son?' he said as he yanked down on the lever.

'Just watching. Hope you don't mind.'

'No not at all. You been to the morning Circus?'

'Here?'

'Sure. The trapeze has just been on in there?'

'Oh no, I'm not into that stuff. I'm just watching here. Are you in luck today?'

'I'm doing fine. I usually put in a couple of dollars after work.'

Since the guy was well into his seventies Conrad was surprised to hear that he was still working: 'So what do you do?'

'I work here; I'm an usher at this casino. I've just finished my shift. I was on since midnight.'

'Right. So you must be pretty good at this?'

'Overall I've probably lost more than I've won of course, but with my salary it's kinda hard right now to get by, so I figured that if I just put in a small amount that I can afford to lose then I may get lucky and win something that'll bring my income up to something that I can live a bit better on…'

Conrad was a little shocked that this old man was essentially gambling for a living. As he now began the repetition of continuously dropping in quarters and watching the fruit bars spin round, he noticed that nearly all the gamers in the room were elderly guys wearing the same uniform: they were off duty employees of the Circus. It was as though their employer was giving them their wages with one hand and taking it back with the other.

'So do you know some of these guys?' asked Conrad, assuming that since they were work colleagues the answer would be affirmative.

'Oh sure; many of us here first worked together on the Dam as kids back in the fifties and then worked here on many buildings as the Strip expanded.'

'Construction work?'

'That's right. I got my fist job when I was twenty and worked mostly right through until I was sixty-one. I retired fifteen years ago.'

'Do you not get a pension then?'

'Yeah but it's not too much. We have to rely on our tips and winnings here more and more these days. Apparently there now aren't enough workers paying tax to give pensioners a whole lot but so what? – I'm getting good on here.' Again he yanked down.

They'd been chatting for twenty minutes and Conrad had won more than him. The whole story was depressing: Imagine working on building sites for your whole life and then still having to work for scraps in a thieving casino when pushing eighty? It was really happening but the more he talked the more the old guy seemed convinced his time had come, especially as he'd finally landed three gold apples in a row. Bingo. 'This'll take care of my electricity bill this week,' he said with obvious satisfaction as his winnings noisily fell out.

'You enjoy playing?' asked Conrad.

'Sure do. One of us won forty thousand just last month on the wheel of fortune. The fella was my brick hod for years.'

'You know it's important for these places to publicize big winners to make you think that everyone's in with a chance?'

'I tell you son I've seen it happen, many times.'

'Have you seen people throw their lives away and wander out to the gutter?'

'Well I choose not to remember all that,' he said putting his electricity money straight back in.

For residents of a town where gambling was virtually the only industry it took thick skin to stay away but when you've still got to pay bills into old age, evil capitalism had a captive punter. Saddened, Conrad said his goodbyes and continued his stroll round the complex where he soon saw many suits.

'Hey what's going on?' he politely asked one of them just aside from a cluster all holding wine glasses and stuffing their faces in front of a conference room.

'It's our annual launch convention – for version four; it's coming out for Christmas.'

'Version four of what?'

'The communication tool, this time they've built motion sensors into it so it has no buttons.'

They guy pulled from his pocket a sleek mobile phone like device that contained no physical controller. He demonstrated the new touch screen 'virtual' keyboard.

'See.'

'And what's on there?'

'Well of course you have the phone, camera, iPod, Internet and any applications you want to download…'

'Alright so this is to announce it to the media?'

'Of course. I don't feel as though I'm working - it's just really a vacation on the shareholders, with no expense spared. Even though the company is receiving federal aid right now, they've given us all penthouse suites and unlimited expense accounts until Tuesday. Our CEO even rented a fleet of limos just to drive us two hundred yards round the block and back to the hotel this morning; all for the cameras.'

'Oh right well enjoy the rest of the day,' said Conrad, not personally blaming him for such a heinous waste of money but the risks companies like that were prepared to take for publicity. He'd been in town less than a day and already believed that many were interested in just keeping up appearances. This man-made gathering in the middle of the desert appeared to have little personality beneath the showy facade. He headed back to find Rob awake and happily counting out what must have been four hundred dollars in cash.

'Where've you been?' Rob asked.

'Just had a look downstairs. You know before you woke this morning Paul phoned from services on the road. They're on their way...'

'And..?'

'The cops got him in Tucumcari; they came to find him and his tag since he was out of range from the car. The satellite doesn't miss a thing.'

Rob looked at Conrad with raised eyebrows.

'No he says it's okay, he just has to pay a fine and he'll be out of a lot of trouble actually.'

'How much?'

'Ten thousand dollars.'

'Well that's him knackered then isn't it?' predicted Rob as he massaged a handful of gel through his scruffy blonde spikes.

'He wondered if we could help him out, you know if we all put to and hand over anything we might win?'

'He's taking the piss. So in two days he wants us to help him hand over ten grand, have a good time and be on a plane out? He's dreaming. Any profit I make I'm keeping.'

'Well you never know, he might have most of it himself?'

'He's an agency lorry driver who's been splashing the cash like crazy since he landed. There's no way he's got anything close to ten grand. I'm not letting him spoil more of my holiday, which really begins today! You coming back down to build some towers?'

'I'm getting a shower. Look I'll see you later okay? Quit while you're ahead remember? Most of that what you're packing there could easily pay for what you owe me! My credit card is probably already guzzling in the interest.'

'I'll sort you out today. Later.'

With Rob gone Conrad ordered himself a BLT and pulled out Will's laptop and began browsing the net. Back in England he learned that it was raining, postal workers were on strike, MPs were charging too much in expenses and another football season was fully hyped and ready to start. Flicking through the history files he saw that Will had naturally spent some time on a home video site and was delighted to discover that he'd uploaded what he'd filmed of the Grant-Lee Phillips concert they saw on their second night. For Conrad, who had nothing of the show but a few tipsy memories, they were excellent souvenirs, especially since Will had luckily captured all the best songs.

Out of curiosity he was tempted to check Will's email. Three mails were incoming; two were newsletters from film clubs and there was another, bigger mail that the software's progress bar indicated would take a while to arrive. He was in no real rush to see it but somewhat disappointed when the signal wasn't strong enough to allow it to arrive smoothly. He opened the balcony doors and carried out the computer where it soon strengthened due to the height. He left it there as he showered and then thought to go and ask down at reception if there was any sign of the other two. The woman said not.

In no time at all Rob had almost doubled his original stake and was well on course to be able to pay the whole lot of the money he owed for the car and the hotel bill for however long he wished to stay. His raising was spot on, his folding was wise and his bluffing hardly failed. Before he knew it he had a tower of chips in front of him so tall he had to tilt his neck to see the board. Though it was a low limit game it was easy money; and the only thing that would stop him from cleaning up was fatigue. Before taking a break he asked the dealer to provide him with a medium dry vodka martini: shaken not stirred and a waiter soon delivered and duly received the biggest tip he'd gotten all day. Rob strutted across to the nearby café area carrying a box of chips that he needed both hands to hold.

'You pick up all that this afternoon?' asked a most impressed young bartender, pleased to see his only customer.

'Sure did.'

'Are you a dropout?'

'A dropout?'

'…obviously not then.'

'That's local slang right? I'm foreign – forgive me.'

'Well with the World Series and the like going on right now a lot of poker players from that type of tournament get beat on purpose once they've done a little more than earn back their buy-in.'

'They lose on purpose?'

'Well see the further they progress in those competitions the tighter the rules. After the first couple of games no matter how good you are you're only guaranteed to win so much in the remaining rounds and then you can't get a game cause everybody knows who you are, so what they do is they drop out deliberately and take what they've got and put it down in the underground matches where there are fewer rules and looser betting structures and I tell you, a good couple of wins in those games and you can easily walk away with more than the guys who do well at the commercial tournaments.'

'You know a lot about those type of games?'

'I've been working here a few years – word soon gets around. These hotel casinos are usually graveyards for losers on the way down, trying to win what they've lost from stupid tourists but occasionally they can be a place to find guys on the way up.'

'I'm on the way up!' Rob nodded, 'tell me more…'

'Well like poker itself, bigger rewards are there for those who take bigger risks. The local mafia set the rules. They can be a bunch of bad guys but I hear they believe in fair game.'

'Get outta here!'

'Honestly. There's a subculture in this town and has been for decades; it just don't get reported on. No licences, no TV, no celebrities or fancy bracelets. Just pure gambling and all you need to get in is the contact, cash and a pair of brass balls.'

'So the guys who play in these games do pretty well?'

'Let's just say if you ever see a guy coming out of a warehouse at six in the morning carrying a black bag you know he's done okay. Excuse me.'

The bartender smiled as he turned to serve a group of customers leaving Rob to ponder what he'd just heard. Conrad then appeared and spotted Rob with his pile of chips.

'Thought I might find you in here. Reception told me there's no sign of them two.'

'Alright mate.'

'You win all that?'

'Easily. This town's easier than I thought.'

'Give me six hundred dollars worth, that's you sorted for the car?'

Rob counted out the chips and slid them over. 'You know there are loads of illegal games going on round town right now for big money?'

'I'm sure there are. Brad told us about that sort of stuff; that's where you can play without an identity remember?'

'I was too busy trying to chat up Sarah and Becky. Anyway you know that barman reckons that with the right money anyone can get in? Let's see what more he knows?'

Conrad rolled his eyes. Same old Rob.

'You know where these games are then?' Rob asked after downing another vodka, figuring that as a stranger in town he had no reputation to lose and a low paid member of the Circus's catering staff could well use another tip. Upon hearing the fairly inevitable question the bartender appeared reluctant, that was until Rob discreetly showed him his palm containing a tightly folded fifty dollar note.

'Look I get off at ten tonight. Meet me here?'

'No problem,' answered Rob, accepting his offer to shake hands and letting him scrape out the paper.

'What the hell you playing at man?' asked Conrad in familiar despair.

'Relax I'm just curious. Let's take a seat at one of the thirty-sixty tables?'

'Thirty-sixty? Confidently showing off your wealth then?'

'Anything less ain't worth the effort. Believe me it's easy money in there, no matter what the structure.'

They wandered back through to the gaming hall and sat opposite each other at a seven man table.

Four hours and dozens of opponents later their balances had not dropped but they hadn't increased that much either. Having underestimated the caution of this late afternoon breed of player Rob was getting impatient and began flicking his thumb. It meant keep raising, Conrad knew that and took him up on his offer and on occasion won a decent sized pot as a result of this illegal communication. Rob was still not satisfied. He began chatting his teeth together and naturally Conrad also knew what that meant: call at the most: don't raise since they'll fold. Sat there with the most chips the pair of them were in the strongest position; they could price out rivals and afford to lose the blinds when they chose not to play for a while.

After four hours their cheating was becoming routine and their stacks getting higher. Rob was getting through vodka almost as fast as he was opponents; though they were all just betting small and that was frustrating. He figured the dealer too dumb to suspect any of their sign language and was getting ever more reckless. Conrad was getting worried and began to fold since by his reckoning it would be getting obvious. It would have been hard not to notice that they were the only two who'd been sat at the same table all day and had been by far the most successful, though without either of them ever actually landing an especially huge pot. He got up and left for some fresh air. Rob followed.

'This is Vegas man. We're supposed to be robbing the damn place! What you getting so pissy for?' he snapped.

'You're drunk again.'

'We've not won that much! They've all been betting peanuts.'

'There are cameras all over the place and you may as well be shouting across the table!'

Walking out onto the grand steps of the Circus their conversation was getting louder and more animated. Within seconds they were approached by doorstaff.

'Evening gentlemen. Everything okay?'

'We're fine,' answered Conrad.

'It's not permitted to take casino property outside,' said the doorman since they were still holding their chips.

'Can we just have a minute?'

'Sirs you must step back inside or leave the property here on the shelf.'

'I said "give us a minute!"'

The doorman stepped forward and attempted to pull the chip box from Conrad's hands. He resisted and, after nearly seven hundred dollars worth of plastic was spilled to the ground, was dragged by two of them into a basement cell. Rob laughed.

Conrad was banned from the Circus's gaming facilities for a period of forty-eight hours. Released he headed back up to the room where Rob was still laughing.

'First Paul and now you!' he smirked, conveniently not mentioning his own little bridge climbing misdemeanour that actually started this increasing trend.

'They knew all about us cheating you know?'

'What?'

'When they pulled me aside from the cell - that was packed with caught cheaters I might add - they showed me the tape and there we were, as clear as day signalling to each other. We couldn't have been more obvious. They can show the tape to all the casinos in town and apparently if I'm caught playing anywhere I'll be arrested.'

'Just playing..?'

'Yep – for the next two days. You just couldn't help it could you?'

'Hey I don't remember twisting your arm to play along.'

'One of the boys in there was in fact a guy who we'd played against.'

'Who?'

'That fat guy at about five o'clock, remember him in the red Mickey Mouse shirt?'

'Him?'

'We thought he was another dumbass. He is in fact an ex mechanic, security advisor and former World Series quarter-finalist - he knew all our tricks.'

'No wonder he bet small! What about the money?'

'I was given a choice: give it all back or face charges. Not much of a choice is it?'

'Suppose not.'

'What about your money?'

'Changed it into cash.'

'Well you're lucky they didn't go after you.'

'We going to find those two now?'

Conrad had forgotten all about the laptop out on the balcony where he left it that afternoon. The large email had arrived.

★

AFTER SENDING THE email and money from Maska's computer Paul was in a daze in Tucumcari. There on the street he coincidently saw the Wimbush pottery store in all its stateliness once again and paused to think. Perhaps he would be able to talk to them about the situation and see what, if any, help they could provide. Would they remember him? Would they believe him? Though Yuma was right behind as always, he decided to step inside and to his surprise noted that he could do so alone. The store was a public place, and assuming that Yuma was as dedicated as ever to watch over him there was no obvious reason why suddenly he had his own space for the first time outside of the motel. It was as though he'd stepped onto holy ground.

Paul saw that the store was just as it was three days ago and, looking out through the window after five minutes browsing saw Yuma still outside. Since he had no money – he'd put all his cash in Maska's hands who then agreeably sent it to Conrad – Paul could not pose as a customer. Anna was on the till and didn't recognize him.

'Hello, could I speak to Ry please?' asked Paul.

'And what's it regarding?'

'Remember I was here the other day with the photo of Charlie, your brother?'

'Oh of course! Just one moment I am sorry. Didn't think you guys would still be in town!'

Anna picked up the phone and told her other brother on the line that he was wanted. Two minutes later Paul was upstairs and had Ry's full attention who was surprised and thrilled to see an Englishman again, even if he was alone and that they hadn't personally spoken much on Wednesday.

'We're in some trouble across town and we can't tell the police…' Paul began.

'What?'

'Look one of us – Will remember? – his life's in danger and we need a bit of money to save him…'

Ry was suspicious. Was their story and photo of his brother just an elaborate set up to coax a couple of bucks? There was no easy way of putting it for Paul but he asked as sincerely as he could for only a little benefit from what he knew was a lot of doubt. Ry said nothing as Paul told him about the dome inside the mountain, but, when he was told that the ten thousand dollar ransom demand would be used to eventually buy an adobe building in town he reacted.

'What are these guys called?'

'Maska, Maska Orenda…'

Ry stood up and closed the door. 'That bastard' he fumed.

'Yeah right,' Paul agreed. 'One of his guys is outside this building right now. He's been watching me since they got us. Yuma – his nephew.'

Ry walked over and flicked the curtain. On the spot he recognized Yuma. He was off down the stairs with Paul close behind.

'Hey get the hell off of the property,' he shouted, 'away you go – right outside the wall!'

Yuma backtracked out onto the street. Ry knew that the Orendas were still after his family's home, and, if they got their deposit down for the old motel round the back before he did the same for the house in its grounds they could very well get it. Yuma didn't say anything after being shooed away; he merely switched his attention to the more immediate object of Maska's desire. He made no secret of the fact that he was noting the number on the real estate sign of when and where to put down the money. Ry remembered that he also needed to get a deposit down for what had been his family's home for over a hundred years. Meanwhile Paul still believed that Yuma would prefer to see Will dead. They left him on the street and stepped back inside.

'Listen man,' Ry began, 'your friend is in real danger. That family will attempt to take his life, like they tried with my brother. They've been kidnapping and killing people in this town for decades and if Maska says you've got an opportunity to save him, then you've got to try and take it.'

'Do I look like I've got ten thousand dollars?'

'When did they tell you about this?'

'When we were caught in the cave two days ago.'

'Have you had any ideas on how to get the money since?'

'Yeah well Conrad and Rob who you met are in Las Vegas now and they play cards. I sent them an email telling them everything and told them to get started.'

'You should call and tell them again. Do you know where they're staying?'

'The Circus Circus hotel.'

Ry picked up the phone and got the number. He handed the receiver to Paul who once put through could only leave a message: 'Guys, we're in some trouble....' he began. When he hung up Ry wanted to know more:

'They usually have an occasion to kill...did he say anything about why they're doing this, I mean apart from to get the money for the deposit?'

'He said something about a wedding in there...'

'A wedding...? My God! Their weddings are witchcraft ceremonies where someone has to die! You're lucky they've even given you the belief that you can save him. It's a religious cult obsessed with loyalty to whoever it is they worship.'

'How the hell do you know all this?'

'The Wimbushes and the Orendas have been business rivals around these parts for centuries. I tell you - while they may appear as normal as the rest of us with their respectable blacksmith shit, they're a satanic family that prey on innocent people, often passers by; they exploit urban people's fear of the open spaces round here and you guys I'm afraid are just the latest in a long line of victims because you were in the wrong place at the wrong time.'

'Well thanks for the good news...'

'Look I'm just telling you how it is.'

'Why not just go to the police?'

'Useless. The lawmen round here have had their hands burned so many times by that family – they always successfully claim that their 'peaceful' tradition and way of life is being violated by Caucasian bigotry – that they simply won't listen anymore. They're pretty untouchable. And like you say if they sensed a cop approaching they'll kill him there and then.'

'Well is there nobody else?'

Ry was honest: 'The blacksmiths are the County mafia, everyone knows but nobody ever talks about it for fear of reprisal. Nobody crosses them, I'm afraid its just the town's dirty secret.'

'Dirty secret? They're having a wedding man! – someone who knows right from wrong must know about what's going to happen?'

'Course they do, but to all those invited death is a good thing. They see it as an inevitable part of life; a passage to be celebrated.'

While Paul didn't doubt Ry's sympathies or that the Wimbushes were a relatively successful business family, he knew that they were definitely not wealthy enough to be able to pay for both Will's release and the house deposit. If they did have any spare money in the next day and a half, Ry would want to put it down to secure their home. Human life was precious but your family's historic home of more than a century couldn't exactly be disregarded either. Ry told Paul that he had less than five thousand dollars available and no idea where he'd find his other five and Paul was even further short. It didn't look good for either of them.

'Have you been thinking about your brother?' Paul sighed, sensing that there was little more they could do.

Ry nodded.

'You know he told us that he fled to protect you guys? He told us that after The Orendas scarred him they gave him a choice: if he left they would leave you alone...'

'Why would he tell four strangers this?'

'He probably thought we'd just disappear thinking that if nothing else we'd remember him as a great storyteller, and I did think it was all bullshit until right now. He told us that he'd been mixing whisky near Knoxville and that he was doing okay until the taxman arrived and he had to run. He said that he was a frequent traveller around the South East; he showed those two a secret code that he uses to communicate with fellow hitchhikers away from the law.'

'I can imagine; we used to do that type of thing all the time when we were kids; jumping on the train to Gallup to work for the week's clay and fabric. Those were the best days of my life.'

'Do you think you'll see him again?'

'You know I've got my doubts. If he really wanted to come home he would have long ago.'

'He did say he was on his way home and from what I could tell he seemed a pretty sincere guy. Remember he's probably saving up in Little Rock?'

'This past few days since you guys showed me that photo to be honest I'd kinda wished it wasn't true. We adjusted to not having him around and it was hard, really hard and if suddenly he walked back into our lives I'm not sure how I'd handle it. My mom was devastated after he disappeared. She still lights candles for him all these years later and you can't just now say that counts for nothing – I think she may not actually want to see him again.'

'That's nonsense. How old must he be? Mid-thirties?'

'About that yeah.'

'He's still a young man; you'll have plenty of time to catch up if he makes it back.'

Ry was silent. Paul had given up: 'Look I'm going back to rest. My motel phone's broken so if you want to get a hold of me come and knock the door. I'm in room six in the Microtel.'

Ry still couldn't say anything as Paul left.

Back on the street Paul headed back to the motel where on the way he passed a bunch of public telephone booths; again the temptation was there. If he didn't like Yuma before he absolutely hated him now – he saw him still yards behind with his cell phone but just one quick call of his own to the police could well legitimately defuse everything. Time was running out and for all he knew Conrad may never even get his message, never mind believe him and then win and send through the money in time. He decided to chance it, and no sooner had he picked up the receiver when he heard the sirens of a police car approaching; Paul immediately considered that Ry may have just signed Will's death warrant or maybe someone really had now come to see why his tag had strayed from the Freestar. His heart was hammering as the sirens got louder but, amazingly, to his relief the car drove right past. Without his nerve Paul went in for the night with more doubts than ever that his friend could be saved.

IT WAS NEARLY ten and reception was heaving. As the sun was setting, Vegas was waking up. Fellow Brits were over to support a slugger on the undercard at the MGM, Wayne Newton was at the Thomas and Mack and Titanic had sold out Caesar's Palace; leaving not just the Circus but hotels, hostels and flophouses everywhere desperately trying to accommodate thousands of last-minute arrivals.

'I can't be doing with all this,' said Conrad still somewhat annoyed as he was forced to step aside and let an apparent conga line of wedding guests rampage past him. 'My head's starting to spin.'

'What can we do? This wouldn't have happened had you not lost the phone. They've probably arrived by now and are round here somewhere. Let's go and see that barman?'

'I'm not in the mood…'

'But he can get us into a real game!'

'But I don't want in!'

'Well how the hell else you going get that money back? Come on.'

'Thanks for the tip today,' said the knocked-off barman true to his word waiting for them after his shift. 'So you guys want to know about these poker games?'

'Naturally…' answered Rob. 'My boy here is no longer allowed to play in places like this while we're in town and has just seen seven hundred dollars slip through his fingers. We need an opportunity and we'd like to think you're the man who can help us..?'

'Well we'd better go then,' he smiled.

The barman was called Lewis and he ushered the two of them out onto the filthy streets on a Saturday night. Catalogues advertising call girls blew in the breeze while every couple of yards flyers were being handed out for that same purpose – women of any age or ethnicity direct to your room paid for strictly by the hour. They could hardly move without learning of spars, escort agencies and sexual health clinics all screaming for customers. This was a side of town that wasn't shown in the films.

Flagging down a taxi was no small task but eventually Lewis jaywalked in front of one and told the driver to take them out to the west side of the city. Looking through the windows at the neon Conrad was disgusted by the evil of the place. How much of the money could he see was the result of bullying and exploitation? How much of it was related to drugs? In just a day he'd seen the high rollers, the fun loving tourists and now out on the streets only blocks from The Strip spotty young women flashing their legs at passing vehicles. He was in a way quite happy when they left the city limits and headed to a neighbourhood of flat buildings spread just off the Los Angeles Interstate. There was little light outside as the driver pulled up and asked for twelve dollars.

'Is this the place?' asked Rob in a puzzled tone as he peered at what he assumed to be a warehouse with three burly security guards watching the door.

'Not just yet,' said Lewis handing over the fare, 'first I need to see a guy to get you guys in. Shouldn't be too long.'

As they approached they were told to step into the short queue and wait for further instructions. It didn't look legal but they weren't expecting anything more, the guards were calm and polite and came with some surprising news: 'There's a forty dollar entry fee and there's no alcohol on sale.'

'No alcohol?' said Rob.

Lewis didn't confirm anything; he proceeded to count out his cash and stepped inside the barrier.

'That's right,' the guard went on, 'management doesn't want any drunks inside. But all soft drinks are provided free of charge.'

'What's the danger?'

'They don't want the girls to be at any risk.'

'The girls?'

Rob took back his passport and realised it was a lapdancing club, and, since Lewis had already paid and gone in, he and Conrad decided to go through with it – they wouldn't do anyone any harm and no one of any reputation need ever know; what happens on the road would stay on the road.

Inside was like a small theatre, with only dim red light and a couple of dozen mainly middle-aged men sat close to the stage upon which a young woman was spinning round a pole. There were also a couple of other girls, including the waitresses, wandering around in garter belts chatting to customers. With their macho soft drinks in hand Lewis suggested they take a seat and wait for his contact who he claimed would be ready by midnight.

'How do you know about this joint?' Conrad asked Lewis, soon actually kind of enjoying the novelty of the place; it was obviously upmarket and in fact had quite a sophisticated ambiance that relaxed his early inhibitions. Rob was yet to say a word – his eyes were glued to the stage.

'One of the owners of this club is connected to a couple of high stakes games back in town. He takes commission from all the players he gets in.'

'How much?'

'I'm not too sure.'

Lewis was looking at the guys down the front throwing fifty dollar bills onto the stage: 'I'm moving into this business you know. I tell you there's some real money to be made. The bar at the Circus is kind of like my cover right now. I see a lot of girls there audition for parts and those that aren't successful I try and help out by sending them here. I'm here to collect my referral fee. If everything goes to plan I'll be moving up to San Francisco next month to start my own agency.'

'Well I wish you well,' said Rob, 'anyway, can I imagine that the commission you mention for these games is high?'

'Yes, you can.'

'Hey if the winnings are worth it, it's no problem at all.'

Conrad wasn't too interested; he wasn't dying to play anymore. His eyes were black having been at the tables all day and as the girl up there was speeding up with the music he was beginning to unwind.

From where they were sat near the back it was difficult to tell if her skin coloured lingerie had been shed by now, which was something that Rob had clearly already been wondering:

'Is this a fully nude club?' he inevitably asked; also not able to tell exactly because of the strobe lighting. As the girl was coming to the climax of her burlesque routine it was hard to believe that her petite frame possessed the strength to get her up and round the pole with such élan and then, following a prolonged flash of gaudy illumination, everything was revealed. And she looked no older than twenty.

'How much do you think she's getting for that?' wondered Conrad, trying to decide who was being exploited; the girl who needed the money or the men who needed the show.

'Don't know. But she deserves more,' answered Rob still looking on as she crawled along the stage scraping up her tips and panties. The man at the mic then introduced the next girl and started another song. 'I want to sit nearer the front...'

Lewis said nothing. He was nervously looking up around the balcony, presumably for his contact. Though he'd been to the club before he was still interested to see how Conrad would react when he was made the inevitable proposition: the girl who'd just been up there, now not quite fully nude, didn't hesitate to approach and sit down on his lap.

'Hi,' she whispered in his ear. He was startled.

'Er hello...'

'Where you from...? Quiet huh?'

Conrad was hardly able to speak. Rob's eyes nearly popped out of his head. She was even more beautiful up close.

'My name's Nautica,' she continued, literally licking Conrad's ear and rubbing his hands all over her thighs that were as smooth as a snooker ball. Outside it would have been sexual harassment. 'I'm half Hawaiian, half Japanese and I love this job but you know it's really tiring...'

'You were great up there,' was just about all Conrad could mutter.

'Oh really,' she smiled, nose to nose with him and gazing right into his eyes. 'You know I'm lonely...?'

'Oh dear...'

Nautica was now straddled on Conrad and tightly holding both his hands. 'I would like you to come and play with me in private...' she continued in a slow, seductive slur.

'Hold on....'

'Come on, it'll be fun?'

'Well I need to know what's available?'

'Well over there on the couch I can dance for you for two songs - twenty dollars a song or, for five hundred dollars I can take you upstairs and treat you in one of the VIP rooms for a couple of hours which is really awesome. There's champagne and lots of contact...'

It wasn't as though Conrad wasn't getting any contact as it was, but for five hundred dollars he would expect nothing but the full fireworks. 'I don't have five hundred on me!' he said with his eyes closed just imaging what would happen if he did have. Nautica smiled and massaged his neck and eventually, purposely, tilted his head to the right. He opened his eyes and saw the club's ATM conveniently only feet away and no doubt fully stocked - there was little stopping him from making the necessary withdrawal. It wasn't called Sin City for nothing.

'Five hundred is still a lot...'

There were now more guys having just come in and Nautica was evidently getting impatient. Since she'd been trying to tempt Conrad two more girls had finished their pole dance and had likewise strutted out onto the floor looking for prey. She gave him one last lick but it wasn't enough; he subtly announced that he may find her later and not the slightest bit hurt by the rejection she cut her losses and approached the guys at the bar.

'Christ man! What was all that about?' blurted Rob just aching for the details.

'She offered me a lap dance – twenty dollars a song or, for five hundred dollars, a couple of hours in a VIP room upstairs!'

Lewis knew they were just a commodity. Had they not been there for another reason and without alcohol they would either hire a girl or simply go home and now Rob was no longer merely thinking about a possible card game or Lewis's payslip since five or six lingerie clad babes were aggressively promoting themselves around the room. With all the hostility of professional athletes it was obviously quite a bitchy competition for them to hook the punters and Rob gathered that he could literally have any he wanted, and in private. He got up and made a move on a nearby brunette. He got a quote, agreeing to two fifty for one hour and claimed her hand. Conrad quickly followed: 'You sure?' he asked.

'It's just a bit of fun, one hour..?'

Thinking ahead Conrad asked Rob to let him look after his debit card; he gathered how the girls worked; two fifty for one hour would no doubt be tantalisingly paced as a mere cliffhanger for another hour at the same price and that he could never afford. Since Rob had the cash from earlier he let him confiscate his plastic and excitedly followed her into a door by the stage. Conrad returned to Lewis.

'Why couldn't he just have had her for a couple of songs over on a couch? He'll be back in an hour. We can wait that long can't we?'

'Dude, I didn't bring you guys here for this,' answered Lewis seeing some movement up on the balcony.

'Did you never think at least one of us would be tempted?'

'Sure. It's okay. Come on let's go.'

Lewis got up and walked towards the bar. Conrad was hesitant but didn't want to be sat alone in a room full of attractive and expensive young business women; he watched Lewis have a word with one of the waitresses who gestured them past her into a staff-only door. Up steps they went and were soon walking along the balcony to another doorway that was guarded by a camera high on the wall. Lewis knocked and looked up to face the lens. He heard a bolt unlock and the pair of them walked in.

'How's it going man?' said Lewis.

The man he was talking to was small, mature, bald and spoke quietly with a European accent. Sat in his chair behind his enormous desk he looked like a librarian and as Conrad could soon tell he wasn't too happy with Lewis. There had clearly been some history between this guy and the young bartender; their conversation was naturally about women – one of the girls Lewis had recommended from the Circus had apparently not been performing to the required standard in the club. The little guy spoke of how he felt betrayed by Lewis's word. Lewis was most apologetic.

'Look Mr Fooshon I'm sorry. What more can I say?'

'I'm afraid that was your last chance.'

'Oh come on!'

A silent Conrad was now not enjoying himself. He gathered that since Lewis, a strapping young man, was obviously quite scared of this little guy he must be someone of authority and the temperature was rising. The three of them were not alone in there; two weightlifters were silently stood across the room completely motionless, as if they'd seen this sort of exchange many times but were no doubt well prepared to step in if the line was crossed. Naturally they were dressed all in black.

'There's one thing you can do,' said Fooshon, offering to do Lewis a favour.

'Anything.'

'Five thousand dollars by lunchtime Monday.'

'What?'

'Bring me five thousand dollars here on Monday. If it helps they're still expecting you at the Full Moon club. Isn't it about time you finally made an appearance down there?'

'I don't want to go to the Full Moon.'

'They're still waiting to meet you – you know where it is!'

Lewis was silent. Conrad wasn't exactly aching to introduce himself and was wishing himself elsewhere. He was in a room full of strangers and the door was bolted. Fooshon was not quite finished.

'The money will cover what I've lost because of that little whore you brought me! Dismissed!'

The door was unlocked and they were both shown off the premises. Lewis's big meeting had lasted ten whole minutes and had not quite been as productive as he told Rob it would be. Outside by the line of taxis that the club reserved for customers Conrad stood like a spare part while Lewis was frantic: 'I don't even play - I can't find that kind of money in less than two days!'

'And what if you don't?'

'He's a German gangster – I don't want to even think about it. In fact I'm hitting the road tomorrow; I'm off to San Fran. Enjoy the rest of your vacation. I'll see you...'

'Wait, what's that Full Moon club he was asking you to go to?'

'Oh it's the poker club I was telling your buddy about. Look if you still want to play you can go in as me. They're expecting me but they've never seen me so they don't know what I look like. Tell the guys on the door you're Lewis from Fooshon's. I was kidding about a commission – it's just a buy-in. Only around two hundred dollars.'

With that Lewis hopped in a taxi leaving both Conrad and probably Las Vegas altogether.

'Where the hell is the Full Moon club?' Conrad shouted in desperation at the disappearing car. What he'd just heard was madness and he was now in no mood to wait out there for Rob and he certainly wasn't going to spend another forty bucks just to get back in. He got in the next taxi and headed back to the Circus.

In and exhausted, he saw a flashing light on the phone and played the message. Finally it was word from Paul:

'Guys, we're in some trouble. We're still in Tucumcari. I've sent you an email to Will's laptop. You've got to hurry and help us. There's no other way. I'll ring again as soon as I can.'

They were still all the way back in Tucumcari? Hadn't Paul phoned earlier from Arizona services asking for help with some kind of fine? He played the message a couple more times and then phoned reception who told him that there had still been no new arrivals under those names. Why hadn't they come to Vegas? When Conrad finally found the computer out on the balcony where he'd left it, he had to plug it in since the battery had long gone. Once connected he opened Will's email to discover that the huge file that he remembered arriving earlier had come from someone called Maska Orenda. There was a short note that came with the attachment:

'This is Paul

Please deposit ten thousand dollars into this account before midnight Sunday…

…Conrad, I've put what money I can into your bank account. Four hundred and sixty dollars today and I'll make another deposit tomorrow. With it and whatever you've got hit the tables and save Will. And don't tell the police.

Attached.'

Conrad thought it was a joke. He clicked on the media icon and once the player had opened he saw someone who looked like Will lying in some dirt. It didn't make any sense. It was filmed pretty amateurishly; all grainy and wobbly but after a few more seconds saw a scratching on the wall behind the forlorn figure: four symbols. Conrad remembered then that that was what Charlie Wimbush had burned into his chest. He looked again at the name of the addresser of the mail and any lingering doubts were dispelled when he remembered the name of Charlie's nemesis: Orenda.

What Charlie and Ry had told them then was all true and now Will had been kidnapped and, unless ten thousand dollars was placed in that account in less than twenty-four hours he would die! Conrad sat there horrified. He tried to phone Paul at the motel in Tucumcari but got no reply and even sent a quick reply mail asking for more information. In a state he took out his debit card and phoned the overseas number on the back. The guy at his bank told him that one M Orenda had indeed made a deposit of four hundred and sixty dollars; most of what Paul could get out of the ATM yesterday. It all chillingly fell into place: there was no fine for Paul for straying from the car – it was what he needed to save Will.

Conrad couldn't be sure it wasn't real and with no sign of Rob to argue he went down to reception, paid for another two nights on his credit card and before retiring asked staff to give him an early wake up call.

★

ROB HAD BEEN his girl's last client of the night. After her shift she saw him stranded out in the car park where Conrad had deserted him an hour earlier and, when he saw her he thought the least she could do was give him a ride back into town, especially since she'd just emptied his pockets.

'Can you not get to the machine?' she retorted after his pleading.

Rob shook his head.

'Come on let's get in this cab,' she eventually agreed before telling the driver to take them to her place. The club's doorstaff saw that she left with a customer, and decided there and then to report her and likely terminate her employment. Girls in her profession they knew were very easily replaced.

'A friend of mine's just looking after my card for me,' said Rob now trying to break the ice socially, away from the mere business of the last hour they'd shared together. Since they almost immediately got stuck in tinted window traffic he figured he may as well try and make conversation.

'You know you were my only private client in a nine hour day?'

'I don't believe you!'

'Really.'

'What about couch dances?'

'I got a couple but it's not enough. The owners of the club keep hiking up the commission. They let me work there for two hundred dollars; a ten hour day.'

'Is that all you get?'

'No silly! I have to pay them two hundred dollars and anything I earn after that I get to keep. I need ten couch dances just to get my money back.'

'Oh I understand. So er, what's your name?'

'My dancing name's Loreena, but my real name's Kate.'

Kate was twenty-nine and lived alone in a complex that was mostly occupied by girls from Fooshon's. Rob saw it was in fact quite a plush pad when she invited him in. She told him that she was seeking independent work away from the controlling brass which he could understand. As she was changing into something more casual Kate told Rob that she loved her jobs and was grateful to her employer, for providing her with the apartment: 'If I wasn't working in their clubs I'd never get this place so cheap.'

'You from Vegas?'

'I came here from Portland last year, been working at both the clubs now for nearly as long.'

'So you've got two dancing jobs?'

'No, I'm a waitress in a card club – The same guys run the dancing I believe just to take the tax burden. The pay's all in cash at the card club.'

'A card club?'

'Sure, it's called the Full Moon, just on the corner of Paradise Road and Convention Center Drive, close to all the big hotels.'

'So do you often invite clients back to your place?'

'Hey you're an ex client! I'm just a little lonely right now. I got the evening shift on Saturdays while all the other girls in this building are out through the night. My Saturday nights are usually spent watching trashy talk shows on cable.'

'But I could be a psycho! This is Vegas after all..?' Rob joked.

'Believe me, I can already tell that this town's just full of shy people who've got worried that time's running out.'

'Do I seem that type?'

'Yes, you do. I think you're here to explode baby!'

'I'm twenty-six, and at home I'm becoming a nobody because I've spent a long time waiting for the future.'

'So you're here to finally live in the present?'

'Exactly!'

'That's what I mean.'

'And what about you, in five years…still dancing?'

'My looks will have gone completely by then. I'm kinda interested in getting into something like photography actually. I like that stuff.'

'And what type of photography?'

'Well since I already know a little about the glamour business I'll try and use what contacts I've got.'

'Go for it. You know since you say that you've got this place cheap what do you do with your extra money, I mean when your bills are paid?'

'Well I'm stretched right now with my sister's medical expenses but when she's okay again I'll get back to my shopping. I just love Gucci and Prada! I'm also gonna save up a do a photography course at college.'

'You know in the UK we have socialised health care?'

'I bet that sucks.'

'It does the job.'

'Do you not get what you pay for?'

'Of course, but at least everyone can afford to be sick.'

'And what's that mean?'

'Like say if you guys feel an illness coming on, do you have to run and get your bank balance to see if you can afford it?'

'Yes, we do.'

'But what about your employer?'

'I don't have enough hours dancing for them to cover me. Since everyone gets paid in cash at the card club I have to pay insurance myself. I have no problem with that.'

'But you would like help?'

'Sure, but I wouldn't pay for anyone else other than my family so I don't complain. If you spend your time and money caring for other people then you're just gonna get nowhere.'

Now sat casually in jeans and a sweater Kate looked like the girl next door, far from the slinky fox from Fooshon's. She looked like the Tuesday night barmaid from Rob's pub and in a way he found that even more attractive.

'What about this card club you work at?' he asked.

'The Full Moon, on the corner of Paradise and Convention. You gonna come and visit me?' she smiled, slowly but surely moving closer and grabbing his hand.

'Well you know I do actually play poker...'

'Great.'

Kate was now sat on Rob's lap. She leaned in and put her tongue in his mouth. 'You know if you were still a client I wouldn't use tongues…'

Rob was suddenly vulnerable, and he knew it.

'Look, Kate, babes you're a lovely girl but I gotta get back to my hotel.'

Rob could immediately see that she was saddened when he pushed her off but he didn't want his emotions threatened. No way. He got up and headed for the door. She followed.

'Please stay for another drink?'

He opened the door and left. Kate was nearly thirty and still single.

FIFTEEN

CONRAD'S 8 AM CALL gave Rob a rude awakening as he'd only just put his head on the pillow:
'What? What?'
'This is your early morning call sir...'
'Huh?'
'That you requested last night?'
'Did I? Oh right thank you. Got it.'

Rob put the phone down. He didn't even open his eyes. Conrad snored through the whole thing.

It was five in the afternoon when he woke naturally. Conrad turned on the TV and checked the email as soon as he got connected but there were no more messages. The video was still there – he again watched Will helplessly held captive and when he realised what time it was he began to panic. He drew the curtains and the insurgent sun roused a still well hungover Rob.

'What's wrong? What's wrong?' he coughed in his bed opposite.
'I told this damn hotel to give me a ring in the morning!'
'Oh they did, at about eight this morning. Why?'
'Well why didn't you wake me then!'
'What the hell's the rush?'
'We need all the time we can get to earn the money we need to save Will's life.'

Rob's head dropped back on his pillow. He wasn't in a mood for jokes.

'Hurry up if you're going out and close the curtains on your way!'

'I put another two nights here on my credit card. You'll go your whole life owing me!'

'Don't worry I'll pay you back. Keep it down will you?'

'Where the hell were you last night?'

Rob leant up; he was feeling both provoked and worried by Conrad's unusual urgency.

'Er, you left me in the titty bar with no money remember? I had to walk it three miles back. You should be grateful I didn't wake you coming in!'

'Since you haven't used your bank card since midnight you can get the full five hundred dollars out right?'

'Think so why?'

'To buy chips. We need time and money to save Will's life.'

'What?'

Rob began to wake up but Conrad was no calmer.

'Half the day's been wasted.'

'What is the problem man?'

'Just play the voicemail message we've got and then watch the video attachment that came with the email we received yesterday. I dare you. I'm going out to buy us some food. Where's my credit card?'

Conrad found his wallet and went across to his bank and with his ID was successfully able to withdraw $2900 in cash; it was everything he had, overdraft and all; there would be no money at all for next week but that was the last thing on his mind.

When he returned Rob was as frantic as him; he'd done as he was told: played the message; watched the clip and again unable to contact Paul had thought to ring the Wimbush store and Ry duly confirmed the lot. He told him that Paul had been round yesterday but was at that moment back in his motel resting up with his phone broken. Rob too now knew they were Will's only chance.

'What happened to Charlie is about to happen to Will! We'd better get playing!'

'You're a smart boy! The tiny little problem is I'm not allowed to play anywhere in town remember?'

'What?'

'I got banned because of you cheating yesterday!'

'But we don't have a choice!'

'You'll just have to play on your own.'

'But I've got no chance alone. I may as well play the lottery!'

'Look I've just been over to my bank and got nearly three grand, is your bank not in town?'

'Won't be, I'm only with a British building society.'

'Okay right well with my three and the half you can get out and my loose change we've got about thirty six hundred dollars and we only need ten before midnight. You can do it…'

'If we play somewhere across town no one there will know about you yesterday…?'

'That's not that what I'm worried about. If we sit at the same table it's inevitable you're gonna be sharking again and we just can't take the risk. It's either you or me. You up for it? All you have to do is just triple your stake. You've done it loads of times at home…?'

'Oh don't put me under any pressure! Come on we'll play straight I promise?'

'Never. You're just not capable.'

'But where can I play with stakes high enough to triple up in just a few hours?'

'When you were with that girl last night Lewis mentioned some club called the Full Moon where you wanted to play, remember? But he didn't say where it was. We should go and see if he's on now and get him to tell us?'

'The Full Moon club?'

'That's what he said.'

'It's on the corner of Paradise Road and Convention Centre Drive.'

'How do you know?'

'The girl I was with last night told me.'

'During your private dance she told you that?'

'Er no, I kinda went back to her place afterwards…'

Conrad's mouth was open.

'…she told me that she also works as a waitress at a card club called the Full Moon; apparently the dancing's the legal business as a tax cover but the card club is where the real money is…'

'You never cease to amaze me. So there's a high stakes club called the Full Moon on where…?'

'Paradise and Convention.'

'Well it's our only chance - you'll win the cash and transfer it from my bank across the street; it's open all night. Ready?'

Rob was hesitant to accept the responsibility of literally playing to save Will's life. He could hardly face Conrad and appeared to stare right past him at the TV; the weatherman was throwing sunshine across the map. All over the States he told viewers that there was nothing but spectacular conditions: 'Eastern Time – sun, Central Time – sun, Mountain Time – sun and Pacific Time more sun!' Looking at the screen Rob noticed that New Mexico was a different colour to Nevada.

'Look, look' he said with a start.

'What?'

'The time zones are different!'

'Huh?'

'The time in New Mexico might be ahead of us…!'

Conrad caught on: 'Well how much ahead?'

'I don't know!'

'They want the money midnight New Mexico time…'

Conrad called reception that told him that as the sun moves west each time zone is an hour behind the last one. They had to make the transfer by eleven pm, not midnight. He handed Rob the cash: 'Ready now? Let's go.'

They ran down and impatiently waited in line to get directions. It wasn't far and once skipping through the streets Rob was unsure. Las Vegas had broken many over the years and as they saw families and children leisurely strolling along in the muggy evening air he was wishing he hadn't left his mates back in Tucumcari. He believed it was all his fault – this trip across America had been his idea and would likely be their last experience of mobility and hedonistic youth, free from the oncoming onslaught of adult responsibility. The fact that absolutely everything could end in tragedy in the next few hours would do nothing but cripple him with guilt if he couldn't do his bit to save his long time friend.

'All I have to do is triple up,' he kept telling himself as he also got everything he could out of a machine on the way.

'Corner of Paradise and Convention? Looks like we're here…' said Conrad.

For guys looking for an underground card club not attracting attention they were disappointed: the building looked like a shopping mall swarming with customers.

'…Are you sure she told you Paradise and Convention?'

'Yes.'

'Well?'

'Just give me a minute will you?'

'You don't have a minute! Time is money! Have you forgotten one of us is about to be tortured to death by a family of evil Indians..?'

Rob was now angry with Conrad, who since making it clear that he wouldn't be playing was yet to provide any words of encouragement. Conrad was a guy who Will had introduced him to from his college after he returned from the army and in the years since had undoubtedly become his more hip wingman but now seemed something of a coward, throwing him in the deep end and stepping aside. He watched him survey the site wondering where this place was.

'Maybe we should just go back and play in one of the hotel casinos?' suggested Rob, still hoping for an alternative.

'Look, perhaps that's the way in?'

Conrad pointed to a door that looked like a fire exit to one of the stores.

'There's only one way to find out' he said before skipping over under the camera and gesturing Rob to follow. He knocked on and it opened. They stepped into another room and the door behind them sprang closed. They were trapped in a near totally lightless brick room about twelve square feet with another door locked opposite.

'Any ideas?' said Conrad.

'I'm like you.'

Suddenly a laundry hatch rolled up low on their right.

'You here to play?' said a foreign male voice.

'We are.'

'Both of you?'

'No just me,' said Rob squinting down to try and get a look. All he could see was silhouette.

'How much have you brought?'

Rob leaned in and placed down the cash. They gathered they'd found the Full Moon club since he saw what was a small man sit back and begin counting out the money. He took more than three and a half grand away.

'Who are you?'

'Someone who wants to play,' replied Rob. His sarcasm cut no ice and the hatch suddenly came down. After a minute they were starting to feel cheated and well ready to react.

'What the hell's going on?' snapped Conrad back in the dark.

'You little shit!' shouted Rob punching the hatch. He opened the door they stepped in and headed out, off looking for another entry to the premises and likely something to smash. There was simply no way he'd write off thirty six hundred dollars. Though the claustrophobia of the bricks was soon grating Conrad remained, but as he too was about to storm out, the hatch opened once again.

'Who are you?' said the guy.

'What does it matter? Where's the money?' he half shouted.

'For the last time, who are you?'

Should he tell them his real name? Conrad was confused. He couldn't be sure there was no danger but when he saw that the guy had converted what was likely their cash into chips he remembered Lewis from the strip joint learning that he was expected but since he'd never shown they didn't know what he looked like. If he said he was Lewis he'd get the chips and get in? Since Rob was off outside somewhere and with the clock ticking he decided to try it.

'I'm Lewis...' he began. The box of chips was placed on the counter and the second door opened. He stepped in and it slammed closed behind him.

It would be Conrad and not Rob who would play.

★

IT WAS GETTING dark in Tucumcari and the wedding guests had started to arrive. Dressed in masks and extravagant rag like costumes, unlike the joyful experience of The Day Of The Dead this seemed to be their Halloween and they were the only people out. More than twenty of them were scurrying along the road and off onto the dirt towards the rock. They passed the Microtel Inn in which a young Englishman sat anxiously. There was little fight left in him when there was a knock at his door. It was Ry: 'Your guy Rob has just called me. They know and they're on it. He asked me to do what I could. We're going in there. Let's go.'

'Why are you carrying that pumpkin and that hat?'

'Quickly, dress in what dark clothes you've got.'

Outside they saw that Yuma had finally disappeared and like shadows they followed the guests towards the mountain. Many feet behind, Ry suggested that they simply walk right into the dome and hope no one said anything to raise the alarm.

'You been in here before?' asked Paul.

'Me and my brother used to hang in there. It's actually an old fall out shelter that the government once had people hide in when they were testing nuclear weapons a few miles south of here. I knew that the Orendas claimed it more than twenty years ago but I didn't think they were still there...'

'Are you worried about them putting deposits down tomorrow?'

'One of our neighbours just told us that someone else was checking out the sign today. There may be more than just them after the motel now. She said that some man got out of an orange jeep and started checking out the sign - writing down the time of where to put down the money. All of a sudden our home is at risk and yes, since you ask, I'm very worried.'

If they weren't about to attend the likely execution of his friend, Paul would have thought it funny talking to a grinning pumpkin head. At least he didn't look quite as bad in the sombrero, not even with the war paint that Ry insisted he wear.

The preparations were complete. The shelter-cum-wedding venue looked set for the ceremony. The torches were lit, the masked young groom was waiting at the altar and the guests in their Carnival Of Venice like garbs were patiently sat excited about what they believed lay ahead; they were going to witness both the matching of a young Orenda and, as a special bonus the sacrifice of someone his father had kidnapped. When Paul and Ry arrived, unmolested, it was difficult for them to sit still and behave. Seeing all the masks and elaborate face paint Ry's emotional scars were starting to burst. There he was in the den of a family that had tormented his own for years and Paul, an innocent victim of bad luck was at once doing his best to spot Will who he noted had been removed from his chains down near the alter. There was a fire crackling away by an anvil, sets of hammers and knives and above them all were the three totem poles all now freshly scratched again with those symbols.

Paul looked up, saw what he now knew was in fact the old control room of the shelter and as always Maska looking down as the Master of Ceremonies.

'Let's go up there?' he whispered in Ry's ear, 'Let's try and talk to him?'

It was a pretty dumb idea but Ry could think of nothing less dumb. Slipping away Paul led him up to Maska's nest. They pushed open the door and once they'd removed their disguises the pair of them were instantly recognized.

'Young Ryland,' said Maska with an almost pleasant surprise. 'So you've come to help us celebrate my boy's wedding?'

'Look you gotta let that kid go. You know he's innocent.'

'Oh I will let him go - if I get my money. You have my money son?'

Paul said nothing both in truth and a natural disgust.

'And why do you want the money?' asked Ry.

'You know full well that that house you guys have been living in rightfully belongs to us and as I'm sure you're now aware I finally have my chance to get it.'

'Could you not think of another way? Did you have to threaten the life of an innocent boy?'

'No, I don't, but did that brother of yours have to kill my son?'

'It was an accident I've told you! Charlie was protecting our mother when your sons tried to burn us down remember..?'

'You should be grateful we didn't kill him...'

'Yeah well you may as well have done! We've never seen him since.'

'We gave him a chance to save your lives so be grateful for that!'

Hearing all this Paul felt like the unluckiest man in the world. What were the chances of him and his travelling mates accidentally stumbling into the middle of a murderously bitter feud between two Native American families, one of whom thought that taking someone's life was worth rejoicing the same as a family wedding? He was getting anxious as beneath them the bride and her father were walking down the aisle.

'Where's Will!'

'Oh he's ready to say goodbye,' sounded the familiar and evil voice of Yuma, stood behind them slamming the door and like Maska in no special dress. Maska was evidently less than pleased with his nephew speaking up and implying that the money wouldn't be secured, something that Paul was even still trying to contest: 'Look my guys in Vegas will get you the money...'

'They haven't got long left...'

'I've got five hundred dollars on me. Let me make another transfer? I need to stake them a little more.'

Maska linked himself over to his bank's website and since he still had Conrad's details from yesterday's transaction amicably took Paul's cash once more and transferred over the same amount.

THE DEVIL'S DUST

'How's the blacksmithing?' asked Ry, curious for an update on their professional status; he was still as competitive as ever – aside from accommodation, the Wimbush pots and the Orenda metals had long been the town's money makers and that rivalry had been the beginning of their dislike of each other.

'Oh we've left the business,' said Yuma, 'but you know we feel it would be a shame to throw away all the equipment. You know the tools: the pokers, torches and hammers. After all those years it's difficult for us to let go and we think that on occasions like tonight we can still find a good use for them...' He nodded, and everyone knew exactly what he was implying.

'That's enough!' said Maska in an unusual snap at his unruly nephew. He told him to be quiet as the female vicar, dressed as Medusa, began her address:

'We are gathered here today, in the presence of these witnesses to join these people in matrimony, which is commended to be honourable among all men...'

Behind her a new hammer was being welded by someone in a clown mask. On its staff the symbols were being carefully forged and looked well capable of mauling someone's body. The fire was white hot while the guests sat sharply focused on the splendour of the occasion.

★

THE FULL MOON Club was busy with players from all over the country who'd got as far as they wanted in the World Series since pesky celebrity was creeping up on them. Some however had been knocked out legitimately and were there in a desperate attempt to claw back their losses. There were guys playing to save their girlfriends from Fooshon's, guys from New York wanting to test themselves against the best in the West and even the odd amateur like Conrad who'd fluked in and believed they would do pretty well just to make a profit. Walking up to the eight Hold 'Em tables all in full swing he counted what he'd got: the door had taken five hundred off him. He now needed to do more than triple up and was met with the dilemma; it wasn't whether he could win but rather how to win.

He had 3k: he could certainly sit at the hundred two hundred dollar tables but couldn't afford a comfortable number of bets. The alternative, aside from no limit, was the fifty hundred structure. The big limit game would fatten him up sooner but the risk, he eventually decided, was too high. Conrad took a seat at one of the lower structured tables but as he feared his first hour or so was not productive. There in the smoke he was playing mostly against Europeans who'd sat there all day and could barely count what they'd got, never mind notice if they'd just landed a royal flush. While never feeling daunted by this competition or the fact that he hadn't dropped much, he soon figured that there simply wasn't enough to be won there in the time he had, time that he could almost see slipping like sand through an hour glass. The tactics of the guys reflected where they were: it was the beginner's game where few were brave enough to fill the pot. Most were seemingly happy to play Texas Fold 'Em all night so inevitably, with not much more than he came in with, Conrad got up and took a seat at one of the higher structured tables. He was one of six players at this hundred two hundred dollar game.

'Anyone know what time is it?' he asked.

'It's eight forty' said a woman immediately to his right, who despite being the only female there was by a distance the chip leader.

'Looks like I'll be asking you the time tonight - see I'm trying to save someone's life, you know how it is...'

'Oh I know the feeling' she giggled. 'Time really drags when you're playing this game.'

'Oh no it doesn't,' thought Conrad who had just two hours to do a bit more than double up, get to his bank and make the transfer. Though in no mood for charades he was introduced to everyone: to his left was Bob, then Chad, Ashley, Dwaine and Emma with the time. Playing tight for the first hour Conrad folded mostly but had to make a move soon, time was slipping away and he was also being slowly raped by his mandatory blind bets. When it was his turn to deal he decided to go for it since he would be the last to act and therefore have more information about his opponents' styles.

Bob was the small blind – fifty dollars - and Chad the big blind – a hundred dollars. Conrad dealt everyone their two pocket cards. Bob landed the king and six of hearts, Chad the nine of spades and eight of diamonds, Ashley two jacks - clubs and spades, Dwaine the queen of diamonds and six of hearts and Emma the king of spades and four of hearts. Conrad provided himself with the ace of clubs and king of diamonds and immediately thought of Anna Kournikova, the tennis player with the same initials: she looked beautiful but rarely won.

Since Ashley was to the left of the big blind he was the first to act.

With his pair of jacks he was never going to fold though only cautiously put in the minimum hundred dollars. Dwaine folded without betting a cent. Emma called with her king. Conrad decided to raise and put in two hundred. Bob with his king and six suited sensed a flush. As the small blind he'd already put in fifty and only had to call a hundred and fifty. Chad had an eight and nine and sensed a straight and also a blind, the big, was only required to call a hundred. Ashley and Emma each topped up to Conrad's raise with a hundred to see the flop.

There was a thousand dollars in the pot. Conrad turned over the ace of spades, the jack of hearts and the ten of hearts. Bob was thrilled, especially since two hearts appeared; he now had four and had two more chances to make his flush, though as the first to act he decided to check – make no bet - hoping that everyone else would do the same and he'd get the turn card for free. Chad was also happy; he now had an eight, nine, ten, jack and now needed either a seven or queen for a straight. Since now, on the flop, no one had to be the first to bet he also checked. Ashley now had three jacks and spoiled their party and raised a hundred. The going was too tough for Emma who folded. Conrad, Bob and Chad all called.

Fourteen hundred was in the middle before the turn card that was the seven of clubs which did nothing for Bob who again checked. Players could now only bet by two hundred and raise to four and Chad had made his straight: seven to jack but only modestly threw in two hundred. Ashley, still with his three of a kind, called it. Conrad was getting worried by this confidence; what Chad and Ashley had was too good to muck; he was thinking about folding but had already put in far too much to write off now, so he called it. Weak for two rounds Bob finally dropped out. Conrad turned over the last card: the queen of spades. Chad threw in two hundred still with his straight. Ashley with his jacks called and Conrad, now with his own ace high straight, knew he couldn't be beaten and to flood the pot put in four hundred which the other two topped up to match right away.

The final pot was thirty two hundred dollars and Conrad knew that for Will he was most of the way there. He'd won on the last card, one of only four that could have saved him. He pulled in his winnings, racked them up, got up and asked the guy in the hatch to look after them while he went for some air. It was ten o'clock and he had seven thousand dollars.

Locked outside Rob, who didn't want the responsibility, had

been feeling like a spare part. While Conrad had been in playing he'd wandered on a guilt trip around town thinking about what was happening to Will; flashing through his head the memories of the friend he'd known for fifteen years; they started high school together, played truant together and smoked their first joints together. They grew apart somewhat when he was posted overseas and Will went off to college but they remained close. Though he was in the most famous twenty-four hour city in the world, he didn't have a lot of company there on the streets on a Sunday night and found himself round the block back at the hotel. Strolling across the parking lot he saw their Freestar and with the keys in his pocket clicked the button and slid open the door. Surveying the mess he picked up one of the jars of Devil's Dust that Ry had given them. He remembered him telling him something about it being lucky for card players. On a whim he grabbed two handfuls, wrapped them in tissue, stuffed them in his pockets and ran back to the club just as Conrad stepped out.

'You been waiting here all this time?' he asked.

'How's it going?'

'I've got seven, and an hour left. I told them I was Lewis and they let me in.'

'Excellent! Be careful – tight but aggressive...'

'I got it. I just need a minute out here.'

They looked at the traffic, the lights and thought about all the times people had thrown away their lives in that town, but, sometimes they both knew, just sometimes, people did actually win, and now with a healthy bankroll they too could both win and save someone's life, regardless of what was happening in the World Series across town.

Although time was money Conrad was entitled to a breather; he yawned and stretched but was nothing less than confident going back in to get what he needed.

'Here' said Rob, handing him a wrap of Devil's Dust.

'What's this?'

'When you go back in there drop some of it under the table.'

'What?'

'Just do it. Throw some under the table. It's for luck.'

'Hey this is a skill game; I'm not leaving anything to chance.'

'Just take it...'

Conrad kept him happy. He knocked and went back in. 'Won't be long.'

THE DEVIL'S DUST

★

THE GROOM HAD kissed the bride and Will, still alive, was now tied to the middle pole with his torso laid bare. It was eleven-forty and if Conrad was going to put the money in Maska's account he was cutting it close. There was a deafening drum being struck and the noise was rapidly echoing round the dome and suddenly everyone was up dancing around like it was some kind of sickening heavy metal concert. All the masks and capes were spinning across the floor as the tension built to fever pitch. There was ticker tape flying through the air and the fatal hammer was now forged to completion. Maska and Yuma still had Paul and Ry locked in with them up in the control room.

'Why not just move out of the house?' offered Maska.

Ry didn't reply. Forty-four years old and he was shaking.

'No, you stay in the house,' said Yuma, 'you've been there your whole life and we'd hate to see you have to leave…'

'That's enough!' Maska again barked at Yuma who was getting tired of forever being overruled. 'You're just like your father. Ryland, tell me you guys are going to move out right now and I'll cut him loose…'

'Let me down there!' shouted Paul but to no avail. He picked up a nearby stool and in an attempt to mobilize himself threw it at the glass which cracked but didn't shatter - Maska knocked him to the ground before he could put it through completely.

'We've been holding these ceremonies for hundreds of years you know? And as far as I know we've completed everyone we've started. Since our business folded last month we got a bit of money and we thought that with a little more we would now finally be able to buy the adobe that a Wimbush stole from us back in nineteen hundred. It's a beautiful building but it looks like we still won't be getting it just yet.'

On the floor now with his face covered in blood Paul screamed: 'Just keep checking your bank!' He hadn't given up.

Maska, perhaps out of respect for such fight saw no problem with that; after all it wasn't midnight just yet. For Will's blood Yuma couldn't wait any longer and quickly went for the monitor and hurled it to the ground. Maska was furious and punched him like he had Paul. Ry grabbed the monitor and put it back on the desk. No one was sure what difference it would make but Maska did indeed check and see that there was no deposit. Down in the dome the clown lifted the hammer and identified the symbols that were forged onto its staff.

'Sacrifice', 'honour', 'worship' and 'eclipse' he called out in front of a helpless Will tied up for the slaughter. Paul again pleaded with Maska to refresh his statement.

★

CONRAD KNEW THE consequences, his own more than anyone, but it was simply time to finish off. Holding his chips he saw two guys who were sat alone playing face to face – and no limit. There was no betting structure; each man was free to risk every chip in front of him should he so desire. The winning of just one pot may well be all that he required but it was reckless; should he drop money he'd likely have to stick his neck right out to get it back and or return to the kiddies' table, but, he had his faith, and, for what it was worth, a pocket full of apparently useful sand. He took a seat and asked to be dealt in next hand.

'What are the blinds?'

'Hundred and two hundred.'

With just three at the table there was a two out of three chance that he'd have to cough up.

'Sure,' he answered as if he was still in his comfort zone. He'd asked to play, time was running out and he still needed the money but now it was also a bit of pride talking. The player to his left was Oriental while the guy to his right was black. Ethnically it was an even spread but even at that early stage what really mattered was that Conrad could afford a bit of aggression. All cutting the deck revealed that with the lowest card the Asian would be the dealer and clockwise Conrad the big blind. Two hundred dollars gone already. The pocket cards were dealt. Conrad landed the eight of hearts and the ten of diamonds. The black guy to his right the two of clubs and the seven of hearts while the dealer got two threes; hearts and spades. With this pair he decided that fifteen hundred was a nice round bet to begin with which was something that the black guy decided was too high. He got out leaving Conrad going one on one with this sleek foreign hustler. Conrad had six thousand eight hundred dollars in front of him and figured that he could afford a bully raise; he put in fifteen hundred which added to his blind meant that that was seventeen hundred in from him. To call the dealer would have to top up with another two. Which he did. Three thousand five hundred was in the middle before the flop. Jesus Christ. Conrad knew these were big swings and immediately wondered what he'd got himself into. He could fold but then he would have wasted seventeen hundred dollars in five minutes. He was suddenly thinking about Will again; his concentration was slipping and perhaps his opponent could tell; he noted Conrad doing something under the table but considered it a body language bluff and proceeded to turn over the first three community cards: a nine, a jack and a queen. Maybe the Devil's Dust had done it: Conrad had flopped a straight – queen high.

'I came to this country from Hong Kong,' suddenly announced his opponent, 'came to make money....' Was this a bit of friendly banter across the table? Did he need to unsettle Conrad? After all he still had a bank roll and a promising pair of threes. Conrad checked; hoping to get fourth street without paying '...and now I suppose it's time to put my money where my mouth is...' continued the dealer as he looked at Conrad's chips. He saw that he had little more than five thousand dollars and put five in – of course challenging him to virtually go all in. In minutes the swings had gone through the roof but Conrad didn't mind, since considering all that was on the board - a nine, jack and queen unsuited - at the moment he couldn't be beat. If the dealer had a pair, and the forthcoming turn and possibly river card were both the same number then he'd have four of a kind, or, if one presented him with three of a kind then another nine jack or queen appeared that would give him a full house but he knew either were very unlikely.

Conrad called the five thousand leaving him with only three hundred dollars. Over turned the four of hearts and after Conrad threw in his every last cent - the final card did nothing and his new friend knew his game was up. With job done Conrad was up and out.

'That sand was the charm man!' he yelped back on the street. 'I went no limit and doubled up.' In his brown paper bag was more than fourteen thousand dollars in cash as he and Rob dashed to the bank.

'What the hell was it, that sand?'

'Ry told me that putting Devil's Dust under the table is lucky for card players.'

'Oh was that what he put in those pots for us?'

'It was.'

'Well he was right – I flopped a queen high straight against this Chinese guy who folded on fifth street when I was all in. He was smart.'

'You were all in…?!'

'Hey high risk, high reward.'

'You've got balls, man.'

It was almost ten-fifty but when they got there, to their horror, they found a queue - two people long. There was only one cash desk open and no matter how urgent their need the big ass security guards would never let them jump. While waiting they thought to count it out.

'I'll get the paying in slip' said Rob as Conrad emptied the bag in a booth. 'What's the code and number?'

Conrad looked up in more horror: 'Shit! I didn't write it down!'

'What? It's five to eleven!'

'We can make it back to the room, let's go?'

'I'll go. You fill out as much of the slip as you can.'

Rob sprinted across the road and into the Circus's reception. Unable to wait for the lift he hit the stairs and had his key card out ready. Slicing it though the lock the damn thing as usual took six swipes to open. As the laptop was powering up he grabbed the notepad by the phone. He opened the mail and clearly and quickly copied down the six figure sort code and eight figure account number. He was back in the bank in minutes and without a breath remaining gave Conrad, now at the desk, the note as the woman had the machine counting out the amount.

'What's the subject line?' she asked; she obviously had more time than they did.

'Anything!'

'I'm sorry?'

'Anything!'

The clock over her shoulder said ten fifty-eight: it was two minutes to midnight in Tucumcari. Conrad copied the numbers onto the slip.

'Poker money' was all Rob could say. 'Poker money!'

The woman took the slip and began typing away: 'You guys do well at the tables tonight? I bet you did!'

'Is there anyway you can speed this up?' asked Conrad as politely as he could, which wasn't very.

'It's done,' she answered with a final keystroke. And they were done. Conrad got the receipt on which the computer had printed: 23:00.

According to that they were too late.

THE DEVIL'S DUST

★

YUMA HADN'T BEEN knocked unconscious. In a last ditch effort to stop his uncle from getting his balance he leapt up and attacked him but it was too late; Maska saw the arrival of a ten k deposit and agreed to let Will go but there were only seconds to spare.

'You can stop him,' he told Paul as he grappled on the floor with his treacherous nephew. Sidestepping them both Ry threw the stool through the glass and Paul jumped, falling sixty feet and dislocating his shoulder in the process. Throwing aside the newlyweds his body check on the clown was in time. Just. The hammer fell to the floor and Will was untied. The drum continued to pound and the guests continued their wicked pow-wow dance as Ry ushered them both outside. They had escaped, but Maska, left fighting with Yuma, now had the money to get both the motel and the Wimbushes' endangered home.

They carried Will back there and lay him down on one of the two spare camp beds in the basement. He was still shaking but his vital signs were quite good; he recognised Paul and managed to announce that he was sorry for everything. Paul thought of his own condition: 'My shoulder came out when I fell.'

'Want me to take you to the surgery in the morning?' asked Ry.

'Will they look at him?'

'Maybe not. Albuquerque is the nearest hospital. It's only a three hour drive. Shall we go?'

'I'd rather not. I'm taking him back to the motel.'

'Don't be silly. You both rest here until morning. Honestly, you okay?'

With a sigh Paul nodded and with Will seemingly quite healthy having fallen asleep Ry had to face up to the fact that he was now likely to lose the house.

'I suppose we'd better say goodbye to this place then…'

'And they tell you that even though your family has been here for more than a hundred years? Doesn't it mean you can argue about the ownership of the land it's on?'

'The law says that since the house is in the motel's grounds whoever gets that can get this building unless it's being bought or is owned by somebody else.'

'Why have your family not bought it before this happened?'

'Well until my father died only six months ago I always thought we owned it. My father and his father were in fact only ever renting.

It was such a shock when I found out. What am I going to tell my mom?'

'Maybe they won't be queuing up tomorrow?'

'He's probably waiting outside the building right now. Hey what's that on your leg?'

'Huh?'

'That thing there?'

'Oh it's my electronic tag; police gave me a tracking device – I'm under a type of car arrest.'

'What?'

'So police know where we are, I was supposed to stay within a mile of our car after I got into some trouble last week. I was arrested for protesting a politician in Memphis the day before we found your brother.'

'And your car's now been hundreds of miles away for three days and nothing's happened?'

'I let them drive off – I forgot. I was told that national security will come and get me, and they expect me to be out of the country by the fourteenth, which is today.'

'You have to be out of the country by today?'

'That's right. Security at an airport expects to take it off when I'm to get on a plane.'

'You'd better get to the airport then…? We'll get in the car in the morning, pick up your things and take him to the Albuquerque hospital and you the airport?'

'I can't just leave him here, and anyway I can't afford to buy another flight; I can only fly with my airline and Las Vegas is the only airport in the South West that it uses.'

'If you're going to Vegas you'll have to get the bus there tomorrow then?'

'He was kidnapped for three days – you think he'll make it?'

'I don't know. Let's wait till morning and see how he is. You want to take the other spare bed…?'

At that moment Anna entered the room in her pyjamas and saw the state of them.

'What the hell's happened?'

'More trouble with those blacksmiths but we'll be alright,' answered Ry.

Anna immediately rushed and provided them with what medical

care she could. She had Paul assure her that he was okay and that there was really no need to call out a doctor. Will was fast asleep.

'Look you stay in the other spare bed there,' said Ry. 'If you guys are going to Vegas tomorrow then I'll see that you get checked out and get on the right bus…?'

'If you don't mind. Hey can I ask a favour?'

'Anything.'

'Can I give Rob and Conrad a ring and let them know we made it?'

'The phone's there – take as long as you like. I'll see you in the morning.'

Anna and Ry left them for the night. Anna was disturbed as they went up to the living room.

'I can't believe that. How did those guys get involved with the Orendas?'

'They were just unlucky.'

'Listen I saw some guy outside today checking out the real estate sign. What are we going to do if he puts down for both the motel and the house tomorrow?'

'You saw who?'

'Some guy with a big mark across his chest.'

Ry wasn't surprised. It sounded like Yuma again: 'Well what did he look like?'

'I don't know. I was across the yard and couldn't see his face; his hair was blowing all over. I just saw him copying from the sign and then driving off in an orange jeep.'

'An orange jeep?'

One of their neighbours had also told Ry about a man with an orange jeep but as far as he knew Yuma had no such vehicle. It was concerning, but he sent Anna back to bed while he sat up thinking about tomorrow. Will and Paul needed medical care, Paul was expected to leave the country and it was likely that someone else would be legitimately allowed to claim the only home he'd ever known.

Back at the Circus, Conrad picked up and Paul told him that the transaction went through in time and Will was saved. He told them that they really did expect to see them at the Circus later that day before he hopped on a plane out. With nearly every human emotion surging round their bodies Conrad and Rob collapsed with relief. They'd pulled it off and a celebration was in order.

'What you got in mind?' wondered Rob.
'So that private dance you had at Fooshon's last night…'
Rob grinned.
'…by a stretch might you ever recommend one to someone in need of a bit of relaxation?'
'You know they're expensive?'
'Hey I won more than we needed. Let's go?'
'Don't tease me…'
'I said, "Let's go"!'

SIXTEEN

UNLIKE WILL, PAUL didn't really sleep. The night was as short as ever and he welcomed Ry's knock at a little after six.

'We going to get your things?'

They left Will sleeping and at the Microtel gathered up everything. Paul was finally saying goodbye to that little room and as Ry was putting their belongings in his car he made a special effort to thank staff when giving in the keys. Paul had a root round his bag and found his insurance forms that he'd paid fifty English pounds for; it covered him for up to a million dollars of American healthcare and Ry duly drove him the short distance to the local surgery.

'Let's go back and get Will?' said Paul sat in the waiting room.

'I'll go. Won't be long.'

It was almost an hour later when Ry returned with Will who looked as might be expected but his vital signs were in fact quite good.

'I'm sorry man...' he said with an ache.

'Don't be...' replied Paul.

'Where's Rob and Conrad?'

'They're in Las Vegas - where we're going today.'

When they were called, Paul insisted that they see the doctor together. He let out a small squeal as the doc clicked his shoulder back into place but Will, who was glassy eyed and told to eat something, was diagnosed as not having any serious problems. They said that they'd been mountain biking and had a fall; a story that seemed to be successful enough since they were both given only minor medication. Outside Ry was talking with the receptionists when the door of another doc's room opened and out walked Maska Orenda; he'd been in getting treatment first thing. He may have been covered in bandages but as he hobbled away Ry knew it was definitely him. The altercation with his nephew had obviously left him in more urgent need of medical care than his need to be at the town's real estate office that had been listening to offers for the properties for more than an hour now.

'Thanks for everything you've done for us this past few days…' said Paul, arm now resting in a sling as they were back at the house finishing the fine breakfast that Anna had prepared.

'Don't mention it. Let's get you guys onto that bus.'

★

WHEN HE RETURNED Ry finally saw for himself the orange jeep pull up outside the window. He knew this was likely the moment that a town official and someone – he of course had his suspicions but didn't exactly know who – came to explain that his family's beautiful home would soon be taken. In the two hours since the house had been officially on the market he couldn't stop anyone from making a claim and as two men walked into the yard he prepared himself for the news. His mother was still in bed while James and Nikki were tidying the store for the day's trade. When he opened the door the surprise was *un-be-lieve-able*; his brother Charlie, missing for fifteen years had, true to his word, come home and apparently with money he was owed from a whisky dealing friend in Little Rock had secured the down payment for the house. Charlie was thrilled to be introduced to his nephew and niece but when his mother came down after hearing the noise she received the biggest hug of all. It was a perfect circle. And their hold on the house was now secure.

Maska had conceded that he was too old to continue the town's civil war. All his hate had been the result of brainwashing from his father and was never his personal emotion. That's what he told them that evening when he visited to apologise for last night's trouble. Seeing him there wrapped in bandages, Ry believed that he had personally always been sincere and never directly responsible for any of the provocation, something that even Charlie confirmed when thinking back about his own experience when he was spared. He did say that he would be forever jealous of their home and always intended to release Will if and when the money came, but since he'd now missed out and that his blacksmithing days were over it was time to move on.

'Move on?' asked Charlie.

'I'm leaving town. All I've ever known is Tucumcari and my eyes are bored. Now that my remaining son's married off I'm hitting the road and it's unlikely you'll see me again. If you get chance tell those kids I'm sorry.'

'What about Yuma?' said Ry.

Yuma, he explained, had fallen into the dome like Paul but hadn't been as lucky; he'd impaled himself on glass shrapnel and bled profusely. There were many unsuccessful attempts to save him. He had been the last of the Orendas passionate about the traditions and now he was no more.

THE BUS RIDE from Tucumcari to Las Vegas took until early evening. Paul finally got some sleep and in a one-armed way was just about able to get into a taxi to the Circus. Will, looking remarkably good considering what he'd been through, was able to give Conrad and Rob the kind of embrace not normally performed by men on men in busy hotel receptions. He took the opportunity to book himself a room whereas Paul saw no point. His airline's last flight to England was departing from McCarran shortly and just like before they were off, back in the trusty Freestar with Rob taking the wheel.

'Thought you weren't allowed to drive?' said Will.

'I'm only banned from driving in a country that's thousands of miles away. What the hell! I didn't know she handled so smoothly…'

With his new ticket organised, passport scanned and bags down the conveyer Paul voluntarily identified himself to security. They took him in a private room and amicably removed his tag and followed him out to the car and likewise took the box from the dashboard. There was no riot act, nothing. Paul was surprised by the polite and efficient manner of the officials: 'You guys must be pretty experienced at doing this kind of thing…' he wondered, 'you know, the security tags and the like..?'

'We sure are. You're the twentieth guy today. And the sixteenth from England.'

'Guys I'll see you back in the rain next week,' he said to the others with one last bear hug and off he went to the departure lounge, handing over his heavy tin of change to his snack waitress before boarding. 'Here's your tip' he smiled.

EPILOGUE

'SO WHAT DID YOU guys get up to in Vegas and California that last week?' asked Paul as they sat looking out at the rain back in Manchester.

'We took the week off,' answered Conrad, 'I think we were entitled to a holiday sometime... In LA we accidentally ended up in this seaside town called Santa Monica which is where a lot of British people live. No one told us to go there; it was as though our nationality just pulled us in like the magnetic west. I tell you it was like we'd flown to America but our nationalities finally arrived by boat. It was great - we could finally get brown sauce, cups of tea and a full English.'

'You know I put another five hundred dollars in your account the last night we were in Tucumcari?'

'Well you never did formally pay me for your contribution to the car bill!'

'Did you return the old Freestar to the rental offices in one piece then?'

'Just about,' said Rob, finally enjoying a real pint, 'we more or less had to push it the last mile since we ran out of diesel – there was no way we were going to put some in just as we were leaving.'

'Three weeks was long enough,' agreed Will, as healthy as ever. 'After a while it's good to get back where you belong.'

'You know I can't believe that Charlie made it home,' said Conrad. 'I wish I could have been there. Will, you should post your pics on the net so we can all take a look. All I've got of those guys right now is my pot – it's on my mantle piece.'

'Will do. So what are your favourite memories?'

'Er, skyscrapers in Chicago, grits in Memphis, Gunsmoke shooting contest, The Day Of The Dead...?'

'So anyway,' began Rob, 'does anyone fancy coming to Asia next year?'

'What?'

'Maybe Hong Kong or Tokyo?'

'Man I'll never be able to afford another holiday in my life,' said Conrad. 'I can't even guess how much I spent in America. Another foreign trip may be a bit beyond me.'

'Come on man. We saved up all year for that and it was hard, but don't tell me it wasn't worth it; just think you've done it and quite literally got the tan.'

'What's in Tokyo anyway?'

'I have no idea – which is why we should go.'

Paul was interested, 'How much would it cost?'

'Oh there you go again! Forget the cost. Before we know it we'll all be really, really old and not able to go anywhere without wheelchairs and hearing aids. Zoom! That was your life! It was fast and you can't have another one. The fountain of youth is soon going to run dry.'

'Alright we get your point; I'll consider it as soon as I can,' said Will. 'Anyway you know we went to Graceland that Sunday..?'

'Was it good then, that guy's house?'

'Oh yeah. He's out the back you know…?'

'Who is?'

'The King. He's buried in the back garden with his relatives, honestly. Me and Conrad got pictures next to the grave. I even tried to dig him up but security wouldn't let me.'

BROKEN YOUTH

A novel by Karen Woods

"Sex, violence and fractured relationships, a kitchen sink drama that needs to be told and a fresh voice to tell it."

TERRY CHRISTIAN

ORDER THIS BOOK NOW FOR JUST £6 - WWW.EMPIRE-UK.COM

When rebellious teenager Misty Sullivan falls pregnant to a local wannabe gangster, she soon becomes a prisoner in her own home. Despite the betrayal of her best friend, she eventually recovers her self-belief and plots revenge on her abusive boyfriend with spectacular consequences.

This gripping tale sees the impressive debut of Karen Woods in the first of a series of novels based on characters living on a Manchester council estate. Themes of social deprivation, self-empowerment, lust, greed and envy come to the fore in this authentic tale of modern life.

Other novels from Empire

THE CARPET KING OF TEXAS

PAUL KENNEDY

"TRAINSPOTTING FOR THE VIAGRA GENERATION"
SUNDAY MIRROR
"DRUG-TAKING, SEXUAL DEPRAVITY... NOT FOR THE FAINT HEARTED."
NEWS OF THE WORLD

ORDER THIS BOOK NOW FOR JUST £6 - WWW.EMPIRE-UK.COM

This shocking debut novel from award-winning journalist Paul Kennedy tells the twisted tales of three lives a million miles apart as they come crashing together with disastrous consequences.

Away on business, Dirk McVee is the self proclaimed "Carpet King of Texas" – but work is the last thing on his mind as he prowls Liverpool's underbelly to quench his thirst for sexual kicks.

Teenager Jade Thompson is far too trusting for her own good. In search of a guiding light and influential figure, she slips away from her loving family and into a life where no one emerges unscathed.

And John Jones Junior is the small boy with the grown-up face. With a drug addicted father, no motherly love, no hope, and no future, he has no chance at all.

The Carpet King of Texas is a gritty and gruesome, humorous and harrowing story of a world we all live in but rarely see.

COMPLETIST'S DELIGHT - THE FULL EMPIRE BACK LIST

ISBN	TITLE	AUTHOR	PRICE	STATUS†
1901746003	SF Barnes: His Life and Times	A Searle	£14.95	IP
1901746011	Chasing Glory	R Grillo	£7.95	IP
190174602X	Three Curries and a Shish Kebab	R Bott	£7.99	IP
1901746038	Seasons to Remember	D Kirkley	£6.95	IP
1901746046	Cups For Cock-Ups+	A Shaw	£8.99	OOP
1901746054	Glory Denied	R Grillo	£8.95	IP
1901746062	Standing the Test of Time	B Alley	£16.95	IP
1901746070	The Encyclopaedia of Scottish Cricket	D Potter	£9.99	IP
1901746089	The Silent Cry	J MacPhee	£7.99	OOP
1901746097	The Amazing Sports Quiz Book	F Brockett	£6.99	IP
1901746100	I'm Not God, I'm Just a Referee	R Entwistle	£7.99	OOP
1901746119	The League Cricket Annual Review 2000	ed. S. Fish	£6.99	IP
1901746143	Roger Byrne - Captain of the Busby Babes	I McCartney	£16.95	OOP
1901746151	The IT Manager's Handbook	D Miller	£24.99	IP
190174616X	Blue Tomorrow	M Meehan	£9.99	IP
1901746178	Atkinson for England	G James	£5.99	IP
1901746186	Think Cricket	C Bazalgette	£6.00	IP
1901746194	The League Cricket Annual Review 2001	ed. S. Fish	£7.99	IP
1901746208	Jock McAvoy - Fighting Legend *	B Hughes	£9.95	IP
1901746216	The Tommy Taylor Story*	B Hughes	£8.99	OOP
1901746224	Willie Pep*+	B Hughes	£9.95	OOP
1901746232	For King & Country*+	B Hughes	£8.95	OOP
1901746240	Three In A Row	P Windridge	£7.99	IP
1901746259	Viollet - Life of a legendary goalscorer+PB	R Cavanagh	£16.95	OOP
1901746267	Starmaker	B Hughes	£16.95	IP
1901746283	Morrissey's Manchester	P Gatenby	£5.99	IP
1901746313	Sir Alex, United & Me	A Pacino	£8.99	IP
1901746321	Bobby Murdoch, Different Class	D Potter	£10.99	OOP
190174633X	Goodison Maestros	D Hayes	£5.99	OOP
1901746348	Anfield Maestros	D Hayes	£5.99	OOP
1901746364	Out of the Void	B Yates	£9.99	IP
1901746356	The King - Denis Law, hero of the...	B Hughes	£17.95	OOP
1901746372	The Two Faces of Lee Harvey Oswald	G B Fleming	£8.99	IP
1901746380	My Blue Heaven	D Friend	£10.99	IP
1901746399	Viollet - life of a legendary goalscorer	B Hughes	£11.99	IP
1901746402	Quiz Setting Made Easy	J Dawson	£7.99	IP
1901746410	The Insider's Guide to Manchester United	J Doherty	£20	IP
1901746437	Catch a Falling Star	N Young	£17.95	IP
1901746453	Birth of the Babes	T Whelan	£12.95	OOP
190174647X	Back from the Brink	J Blundell	£10.95	IP
1901746488	The Real Jason Robinson	D Swanton	£17.95	IP
1901746496	This Simple Game	K Barnes	£14.95	IP
1901746518	The Complete George Best	D Phillips	£10.95	IP
1901746526	From Goalline to Touch line	J Crompton	£16.95	IP
1901746534	Sully	A Sullivan	£8.95	IP
1901746542	Memories...	P Hince	£10.95	IP
1901746550	Reminiscences of Manchester	L Hayes	£12.95	IP
1901746569	Morrissey's Manchester - 2nd Ed.	P Gatenby	£8.95	IP
1901746577	The Story of the Green & Gold	C Boujaoude	£10.95	IP
1901746585	The Complete Eric Cantona	D Phillips	£10.95	IP
1901746593	18 Times	J Blundell	£9.95	IP
1901746 607	Old Trafford - 100 Years	I McCartney	£12.95	IP
1901746615	Remember Me	K C Kanjilal	£7.95	IP
1901746623	The Villa Premier Years	S Brookes	£8.95	IP
1901746631	Broken Youth	K Woods	£8.95	IP

* Originally published by Collyhurst & Moston Lads Club + Out of print PB Superceded by Paperback edition

† In Print/Out Of Print/To Be Published (date)